AARON'S PATIENCE

TIFFANY PATTERSON

Copyright © 2018 by TMP Publishing LLC/Tiffany Patterson

All rights reserved.

This is a work of fiction. Names, characters, businesses, places, events and incidents are either the products of the author's imagination or used in a fictitious manner. Any resemblance to actual persons, living or dead, or actual events is purely coincidental.

A special thank you to Melissa at There For You Editing (thereforyou.melissa@gmail.com) for editing.

AUTHOR'S NOTE

Dear reader,

Thank you for picking up Aaron's Patience. Please be aware that this story contains aggressive language, intense love scenes, and some violence. If these topics are sensitive for you at this time, please take care of yourself and return to the book later.

If you are read to proceed, enjoy Aaron's Patience.

PROLOGUE

P atience

"Why does he want me at this dinner? He never wants me to be around when he hosts one of these." I frowned, looking down at the dress my nanny, Ms. Ryan, held out to me.

"You know I don't question your daddy. I just follow his orders." Ms. Ryan's dark chocolate cheeks creased as she smiled.

I eyed the dress with the flower print. "I don't like flowers."

"Then which one would you prefer?"

"The plain black one." I motioned to the dress hanging in my closet.

"There are going to be some important people at dinner tonight. You can't wear that dress. It's too tight on you now."

I rolled my eyes, hating the reminder that over the past summer, right before I started high school, my body betrayed me. My hips had widened, my breasts have grown past the training bra I first got the previous summer to a C-cup, and my ass now filled out my jeans. I'd even caught one of the male teachers checking out my backside. I may've been fourteen, but at heart I was still the nerdy girl that loved nothing more than to curl up with a good book. I hated the increased attention.

"Your father would not like that," Ms. Ryan continued.

"Like he'll notice," I snarked.

"Don't say that. Your daddy is just an incredibly busy man. He loves you very much."

I let out a long-suffering sigh before taking the floral dress from my nanny. "If you say so. I'll wear the dress." I moved to the bathroom across the hall to change into the dress and stockings Ms. Ryan had laid out.

"I'm leaving the braid in," I insisted, returning to my room.

"That's fine. It looks–"

"Patience!"

My stomach jumped as my father's voice reverberated up the staircase, reaching into my room to my ears.

"Yes, Dad?"

"Patience, don't yell! Go to your father."

Pushing out a heavy breath, I stomped off to reach the top of the wooden banister that led to our two-story home's staircase.

"Yes, Dad?" I looked down at my father's dark brown eyes, and for a moment I thought I saw a glimmer in them as he peered up at me. However, a blink later and it was gone. Pretty sure it was just my imagination.

"Are you ready? Our guests will be here shortly."

I held back the sigh that wanted to escape. "I–"

"She's ready, Mr. Thiers. Doesn't she look lovely? Our little girl is all grown up," Ms. Ryan gushed, wrapping her arms around my shoulders from behind. Ms. Ryan was the closest thing I'd ever had to a mother, and I had to admit hearing the pride in her voice as she talked about me made me smile a bit.

My father clearing his throat caught my attention. "Well, then come down so we can meet our guests."

"Okay, I just have to grab–"

"No books!" both Ms. Ryan and my father yelled at the same time.

"You will be social tonight, Patience. Not have your head stuck in a book. Go on." Ms. Ryan nudged my shoulders in the direction of the stairs.

"Don't most caretakers do their best to encourage reading in children under their watch?" I grumbled.

"Yes, but most teens aren't spending their time avoiding social interactions with their heads stuck in books all day long like someone I know," she sing-songed the last part.

I shrugged. "Not my fault books are more interesting than most people."

"I swear," she tutted, shaking her head. "You're fourteen, Patience. You need to be more social by making more friends and actually interact with the world around you."

"Whatever," I mumbled as I took the stairs.

"Come, Patience." My father didn't bother waiting. He pivoted on his heels and left me to follow as he moved to the kitchen to ensure the caterers were setting up properly.

I pouted as I followed him down the hallway, watching while the caterers set the long table. This was another one of my father's business dinners. However, he usually never hosted at our home, and I never accompanied him. I wondered what's the big deal about tonight's dinner that my father actually took an interest in me enough to ensure that Ms. Ryan got me dressed and ready to attend.

"Don't sit yet, Patience. We have to greet our guests," my father insisted just as I began to sit at one of the high-back wooden chairs. I lowered my head as I bit back a retort. A heartbeat later, the doorbell rang and my father beckoned me to follow him with a motion of his head. I did so, just wishing we could hurry this along to end this night so I could get back to the latest *Harry Potter* book I was reading, and then move on to Mitch Albom's *The Five People You Meet in Heaven.* The book may've been a little advanced for my age range but I couldn't wait to devour it. Just thinking about it made me wonder about my own mother and if I'd really ever get to meet her once I made it to heaven. *If* there was a heaven.

"Robert! On time as usual!" My father chuckled as he pulled the door open.

I took a step back, giving my father some room to move aside and let the man he referred to as Robert pass. I squinted, studying the familiar face of a man I'd seen on one of the news and business channels.

"Thiers, good to see you," he responded, referring to my father by his last name. Most people did. "This is my son, Aaron."

"Pleasure."

A chill moved through my body at the male voice. Out of curiosity, I peeked around my father's shoulder to see Robert's son. My mouth went dry at the sight of the tall, handsome man. No, not handsome, gorgeous–jet black hair, hazel eyes, and freckles that lined his masculine cheeks. He had to be a little over six-feet tall. Even the hard frown he wore on his face made him look appealing, though it scared the hell out of me. When he turned his eyes on me, my stomach dropped and I turned my head to my father, who was now introducing me to Robert.

"Patience, this is my dear friend, Robert Townsend, and his son, Aaron. Say hello."

I pasted a small smile on and nodded. "Pleasure to meet you Mr. Townsend." I tried not to look toward Aaron but something tugged at me and I found my eyes landing on him.

His gaze lingered for a moment before he nodded sharply. "Patience."

More butterflies…hell, an earthquake felt like it erupted in my belly.

Thankfully the men began engaging in business talk and proceeded down the hall, leaving me to follow. Over the course of the next fifteen minutes or so more guests arrived, but the Townsends were the only ones my father actually greeted at the door. The butler he'd hired for the night answered the rest and escorted them to the kitchen. I rolled my eyes when Wallace McCloud showed up with his jerk of a son, Wallace Jr. The McClouds were a huge real estate family in the city of Williamsport, and like me, their son attended Excelor Academy. He was a junior while I was in the middle of my freshman year, and he was a grade A asshole.

I barely spoke three words throughout the dinner. As I chewed my shrimp risotto, quietly staring into my plate, I felt eyes on me. I knew it wasn't my father who was busy talking with Robert Townsend and his other guests. I dared to peek up from my plate, looking around the table. My attention got stuck on Aaron Townsend again, though he wasn't looking in my direction at all. I took that opportunity to stare at his profile as he talked with a man sitting next to him. Even while speaking, the scowl he'd worn earlier remained in place. This guy wasn't friendly and didn't even try to be. But there was something about him...

I pulled my attention from Aaron, not wanting to be caught staring when my eyes then landed on Wallace. The stupid, lopsided smirk his face held told me he'd caught me staring. I planted my gaze back on my plate and didn't move it until it was empty. As discreetly as I could I leaned over and told my father I was heading to the bathroom. I doubted he even acknowledged my words but I didn't pause to find out. I placed the cloth napkin that was in my lap on the table and hightailed it out of the dining area to the downstairs bathroom, down the hall.

Once alone, I exhaled and pulled out the *Harry Potter* book I'd conveniently tucked underneath the sink cabinet. I peeked out of the bathroom door, and when I didn't see anyone, I made my way to the den that was off to the left. I figured my father wouldn't even notice my absence and I could get some reading done in peace. Unfortunately, that wasn't to be.

"What're you doing in here?" I questioned, startling Wallace Jr. whose back was to me.

He turned in my direction with that same stupid smirk on his face. "Waiting for you."

I sneered. "Why?"

"I needed to use the bathroom."

"Oh. Well, I'm out." I moved to the side to give him space to pass me but he just stood there.

"What'cha got there?" he asked, walking up to me.

Before I could hide the book behind my back, he caught my arm and tugged it from me.

"Should've fucking known," he chuckled. *"Harry Potter."*

"Can I have that back, please?"

"Come get it." He held the book over his head.

I rolled my eyes and balled my fists at my sides. Wallace was at least eight inches taller than my five-foot, three inch frame.

"Just give me my book back!" I growled low which only caused him to laugh.

"Someone's getting upset."

My hands squeezed tighter the more he laughed. And finally my anger exploded when he snatched the book away as I lunged for it. I reared back and kicked him in the shin.

"Fuck! You bi—"

Bracing myself, I squeezed my eyes shut as Wallace balled his fist and aimed like he was about to punch me. But the blow never came.

"You've got a real fucking problem."

I gasped and blinked my eyes open to see Aaron Townsend with one hand wrapped around Wallace's throat. His face was beet red and terror filled his brown eyes. Aaron's back was to me and his voice was low but I heard it.

"Your father's a shit businessman and obviously an even worse father. What kind of shithead tries to beat up a little girl?"

My eyes widened and my heart plummeted. Not because it started to look like Wallace was close to losing consciousness but because Aaron had just referred to me as a little girl. Why did that sting so much?

"You're going to go back into that dining room, tell your father you're not feeling well, and take both your sorry asses out of here." Aaron shoved Wallace away from him, then angrily watched as Wallace coughed and rubbed his throat before stumbling off in the direction of the dining area.

Slowly Aaron turned his eyes roving over me. A tingling feeling started in the pit of my stomach again.

"Are you all right?"

I swallowed and then remembered that this guy had just called me a little girl. I don't know why that ticked me off but it did. I put my hand on my hip.

"I could've handled him on my own," I told him sharply.

His eyes widened just a smidge and for a second I worried that he was going to give me a piece of what he'd just given Wallace. Much to my surprise, a small smirk broke through on his full lips. A lump formed in my throat.

"I do believe you could have." He gave me one last look, nodded, and turned to leave.

I was left standing there wondering what had just happened. And why the space between my legs had begun tingling as well.

CHAPTER 1

P atience

"Do you have to go, Mommy?" my five-year-old daughter, Kennedy, whined as she sat on top of my folded clothes in my suitcase.

Stepping out of my small closet, I smiled at the pout on my little girl's caramel-colored face. I moved over to her, getting on my knees and pushing one of her curly ringlets behind her ear.

"I told you this already, sweetheart. Mommy will only be gone for two days."

"I knooow, but who's gonna read with me? Kyle hates reading!"

"Reading sucks!" my other five year old yelled from his position on my bed.

"Kennedy, don't say hate and, Kyle, you stop saying sucks!" I admonished the twins. "Ms. Sheryl will read to you every night I'm gone."

That didn't make Kennedy any happier.

"But she won't do it like you. And who's gonna take us to the library?"

"Baby," I began, plucking Kennedy out of my suitcase and sitting her on my lap, "Mommy will only be gone for two days. That's only two sleeps. We will go to Mommy's job when I get back and check-out all the books you want. Okay?"

Kennedy's little body shook as she sighed but she nodded.

"And what about you, Kyle? Will you come with us to the library once I get back?" I asked my son as if he had a choice.

He jumped off the bed, scaring the hell out of me, and ran to sit opposite his sister on my other leg.

"Libraries are boring. Can we go to Fun Zone?" His hazel eyes lit up, tugging at my heartstrings.

"Sure we can," I agreed because I could rarely deny either one of these two anything. Though it pulled at my heartstrings that Kyle loathed reading so much. Kennedy had inherited my voracious love of all things books while Kyle was the complete opposite. Reading was so difficult for him that it felt like punishment every time I asked him to sit and read for a bit.

"Okay, you two, how about Mommy orders pizza for dinner?"

"Yes!" they shouted in unison. Pizza was a rare occasion in our home. We had it only on nights I didn't feel like cooking, and since I had an early morning flight, this was one of those times.

"Mushrooms and peppers please!" Kyle requested.

What five year old asks for mushrooms and peppers on their pizza? Mine did apparently.

"Yuck!" Kennedy made a face at her brother's request.

As usual, I ordered a half-plain, half-mushroom and green pepper pizza, and then continued to finish my packing. I was headed to a conference hosted by the American Library Association in Chicago. The event was scheduled for three days but I was only staying for two, not wanting to be away from the kids for more than that. The annual conference was the only time I left my children for longer than a night, and that only happened because I trusted their sitter, Ms. Sheryl, with my life. She had saved all three of ours once already, and she loved my kids almost as much as I did.

***

"Judy, what are we doing here?" I questioned behind my friend as we crossed the street to the bar. I had just wanted to spend a relaxing evening in the hotel, after the full day of meetings and discussion groups we had at the conference.

"You need to live a little. You were just going to go back to your hotel room and call your kids." Judy glared at me over her shoulder.

I shrugged. She was absolutely right. That's what I'd planned on doing before she ruined it by banging on my door and insisting I get dressed to go out with her.

"What's wrong with wanting to call my kids after being away from them for a whole day?"

Judy shrugged a thin shoulder. "Nothing's *wrong* per se, but you're a single mom who rarely gets a night off from her kids. It's been years since you even went on a date, hasn't it?"

I frowned. Judy knew damn well how long it'd been since I was on a date. The last guy I'd dated had been over a year and a half ago. We dated a few months, and after the first time we slept together I never heard from him again. After that, I decided to focus on just raising my children. It wasn't a conscious decision. I just didn't think men were worth it.

"I knew you'd turn into a prude the minute I left Oakland," Judy continued.

I rolled my eyes. Judy and I had met while we worked together for the Oakland Public Library, but close to two years earlier, she'd gotten a job in her hometown of Chicago and decided to move back.

"I'm *not* a prude," I insisted.

"Oh yeah? Prove it!" she urged at the same time she shoved me through the doors of a local bar she'd said would be our first stop for the evening.

I shrugged. Whatever. I was only in Chicago for one more night, I might as well live it up.

"Fine!" I told Judy and stepped around her, heading straight to the bar to order us two beers.

"That's what I'm talking about. Live a little. Single moms deserve a night off," my friend yelped, twirling her hand in the air in time to the loud music that blared.

I grabbed my beer and made a beeline for the dance floor, grabbing Judy's arm to accompany me. We danced and laughed as we continued to sip our beers. When Judy caught me nursing mine, she practically forced me to finish it and quickly ordered us a second round, which all too soon was followed by a third round. Never having been a heavy drinker, I was definitely feeling the effects of the alcohol by the third beer. I refused another one, wanting to keep my wits about me and still remembering that we had another full day of the conference left. However, Judy was far from done for the evening. She begged me to let her take me to yet another bar turned nightclub, and I obliged. There we met up with a few friends of hers and danced some more. I stuck to seltzer water for the rest of the evening, doing my best to avoid a hangover. But I will admit it was the most fun I'd had in a long time with anyone over the age of five.

"Admit it, you enjoyed yourself!" Judy pressed as we stumbled into my hotel room. It was late and I didn't want Judy taking the train home alone, so she agreed to stay with me for the night. Her fiancé was out of town anyway.

"I had fun," I admitted a bit stubbornly.

She clapped, giddy with excitement. "If you enjoyed tonight you're going to *love* what I have in store for tomorrow night."

I shook my head. "I'm not doing anything tomorrow night besides—"

"Oh, come on! It's your last night in Chicago. Plus, what you told me earlier deserves a little investigation."

My eyes widened. "Are you crazy?"

Judy giggled at my obvious mortification. While out with her friends, the conversation got a little heated when the subject of sex was brought up. One of her friends brought up a secret fantasy and before I knew it we all were sharing our deepest sexual fantasies. I'd spilled about wanting to be tied up and spanked. As soon as the words were out, I denied them, claiming it was the alcohol. I wouldn't dare tell them the truth was that I'd already done that with someone, but I'd never trust anyone else to be that vulnerable with again.

Judy let out an exasperated sigh, reminding me of Kennedy when she doesn't get her way. "You're taking this whole librarian thing a little too far."

I furrowed my eyebrows. "First of all, *you're* a librarian, too. Have you forgotten that? Second of all, I'm not being a prude or whatever you call me. Just ..."

"Just what?"

My mouth opened but nothing came out. I didn't have the time or energy to explain it to her so I said nothing.

"Exactly. You have no explanation. You're coming out with me tomorrow. And we're going shopping beforehand because you are *not* wearing that outfit again."

Frowning, I looked down at the T-shirt and dark blue slacks, and black two-inch pumps I'd worn for the evening. "What's wrong with my outfit?"

Judy rolled her eyes before plopping down against the king-sized bed, arms wide. "You're *such* a librarian."

"Whatever," I retorted.

CHAPTER 2

𝒜*aron*

"Mr. Townsend, if you look at the quarterly and annual projections on page eighty-three of the annual report we provided, you will see—"

"Bob, is it?" I let my eyes slowly roll up from the documents before me to the man standing at the front of the room. I blinked slowly, waiting for an answer to my question.

"Y-yes," he answered, clearing his throat.

"Oiltec's quarterly net earnings last year were one-point-four million, one-point-three million, two-point-one million, and one-point-nine million, respectively. The document you're telling me to refer to projects your quarterly net earnings will double despite the fact that your expenses have risen dramatically over the last year." I paused, placing my elbows onto the shiny wood of the conference table, and leaned in. "What type of game are you playing, Bob?" My tone was hard, and afterwards you could hear a pin drop despite the fifteen or so people who were in the room.

"Well, uh ..." Bob Lundy looked to his side of the table for answers.

"Mr. Townsend, we assure you that Oiltec is an extremely viable company. In spite of—"

I cut my eyes in the direction of the man who spoke. He sat opposite me. "I asked Bob a question. Not you." I turned back to the President of Oiltec. "Oiltec is viable, yes, the numbers say so, but your projections are extremely overinflated. Your expenses are too high given output, and your marketing and research divisions are woefully inept when it comes to developing alternative energies. It will take Townsend Industries at least six months to get the newly acquired Oiltec's R&D division up to speed, and that's *if* everything goes smoothly. There's no way we're paying asking price for this acquisition. Make a better offer."

I cut to the chase. It has been meeting after meeting to see through this acquisition. It was my duty as CEO of Townsend Industries to ensure we took on the best deal that would enable our company's growth. There was nothing I took more seriously than doing my job right.

Sitting back in my chair, I watched as Bob's eyes darted from one employee to another.

"We've been at this for hours now. How about we break for lunch and then return with clearer heads?" Bob offered.

"We'll order lunch in," I firmly stated. "While we wait, you and your team can come up with a better offer." I watched as Bob went out to tell his assistant to order lunch for the meeting. He then came back and began discussing, in whispered tones, with his team. While that was going on, I conferred with my legal and financial team that I'd brought to this meeting.

We spent the rest of the day and well into the early evening going over price purchase per share until we finally came to an agreement. It was far less than Bob's initial offer, but given his real numbers, it turned out to still be a profitable merger for Oiltec. Before we even exited the building, I was on the phone with my people in Williamsport, informing them of our next moves to get Oiltec up to speed and make sure this merger went as smoothly as possible.

I sat back in the town car as it began pulling off and blew out a steep breath. The weight of the months leading up to this merger were settling around me. The pressure from my job was nothing new

—I thrived on it—but it was starting to feel as if there was something missing. I refused to let myself go there. Instead, I pinched the space between my eyebrows and inhaled while I waited for my cell to ring. Two heartbeats later and the distinct tone I'd set for this caller began to chime in my hand.

"Father."

"Did you get it done?"

"Is my name Aaron Townsend?"

"Goddamn right it is."

"Then it's done."

"My boy."

I cleared my throat.

"When will you be home?"

"My flight leaves tomorrow afternoon. I should be home in time to make Mother's family dinner."

"Good. You know your mother lives for these dinners."

I grunted.

"As do I. All my boys under one roof. Makes a man proud. You bringing anyone?"

I frowned. "Why on earth would I do that?"

"Just asking. Your mother thought it might be time. Since Carter married, she thinks you're next."

I let out a sigh. "And you didn't do anything to thwart her nonsense notions, did you?"

"Why would I do that?"

I laid my head back against the seat.

"I want to see all of my sons happy."

Here it came. Yet another speech by my father on the importance of family.

"A man can't survive this world alone."

"I'm not alone."

It was my father's turn to grunt. "You've got us, but you deserve more. And those one-night stands or dates you keep on standby for work events aren't cutting it."

Rolling my eyes, I pinched the bridge of my nose again. Ever since my older brother, Carter, got married, both of my parents have been talking about relationships more frequently. It was getting redundant but I didn't dare interrupt my father. I just zoned out, making a mental list of everything I needed to do for business that evening.

As I hung up the phone with my father and readied myself to exit the vehicle in front of my hotel, a thought came to mind. My father's talk of relationships had stressed me out more than the day-long negotiations.

"I'll need you back here at seven to pick me up," I informed the driver as I exited the car door he held open.

"Seven this evening?"

I blinked. "Is that a problem?"

"No, no, sir. Just checking to make sure I heard correctly."

I nodded and then sauntered off, breezing through the door held open by the concierge. I deserved a night out and Chicago had just the right spot for such an occasion.

* * *

WHAT THE FUCK *am I doing here?* That was probably the first common sense thing I'd asked myself since stepping out of the back of my town car. I glanced around the underground garage, and undid the button of my Tom Ford suit jacket.

"Would you like me to escort–" The chauffeur's question was cut off by the sharp slicing of my hand through the air.

"I got it from here." I turned toward the metal doors of the elevator. "I'll be back in a couple of hours," I told him, not even looking over my shoulder.

"I'll be right here, Mr. Townsend."

I didn't waste time acknowledging his statement. Of course he'd be there waiting on me. That's what he was paid for while I was in Chicago on business. But as I slid the shiny black keycard into the slot next to the elevator, it was obvious that this little venture was anything but business. I'd spent the entire past seventy-two hours in business meetings and beating any adversary over the head with my strategy. I needed this outlet like I needed my next breath. Not that a quick blow job or a frenzied fuck would ever be enough to ease all of the tension rolling through my body, but it would offer a short respite.

I turned to the opposite side of the elevators upon hearing the dinging of the bell, and the doors spread open, revealing the comforts of The Cage's fourth floor. Just as I stepped off, a long-legged blonde dressed in only a pair of leather shorts and matching pasties, with a leash around her neck, passed. Holding onto the opposite end of the chain, leading her, was another woman, this one with dark chocolate skin, shaved head, and dressed head to toe in a pinstripe black suit. I watched the pair strut down the hall. *The bondage room.* That's where they were headed.

"Welcome back, Mr. Townsend," the petite redhead behind the registration desk offered with a smile.

I returned her graciousness with a curt nod.

"Your table has already been set up for you. As promised, two women will be by shortly. We hope they are to your liking." She smiled, revealing perfect, pearly white teeth.

I moved around the registration booth, past the leather loveseats where groups of twos, threes, and fours were in various stages of undress. Removing my suit jacket, I carefully laid it on the back of the loveseat, and sat down, picking up the glass of cola with three ice cubes that I always requested be waiting for me on my arrival. I took my fill of the club. Another couple made their way down the dark hall into either the bondage room or eating area. The elevator door opened and a pair of women stepped off, dressed in only short bathrobes. *They must've come from the Wet Room on the third floor*, I surmised.

I found myself watching the women as they moved closer, hand in hand, one finally catching my gaze. One was the color of cinnamon while the second had skin the color of sandalwood. Both average height, with small yet curvaceous bodies. They moved to stand in front of me, and I was pleased to see that my preferences had been noted by whoever sent these two.

"Mr. Townsend," one of the women giggled, causing a frown to mar my face.

I glared at the two, over the rim of my glass, taking another sip of my drink.

"How are you tonight?" the cinnamon-toned one spoke up. When I didn't move, she took that as a sign to move in closer, placing a knee on the loveseat and crawling toward me. These women were beautiful, but I'd had plenty of beautiful women. They'd be fine for the night, I guessed...until one slid her hand up my forearm to my elbow, pushing the sleeve of my shirt out of the way. She gasped and jumped, when my other hand slammed down over hers.

"Don't touch me." I tossed her hand away. "I do the touching," I told both women, sternly. "Give me a dance while I finish my drink."

They blinked, looking between one another, before slowly sliding off the loveseat to stand in front of the table. I sat back, arm outstretched with my drink in the other hand. I watched semi-bored as both women began stripping one another.

Movement at the elevators caught my attention. The doors slid open and a thirty-something Asian woman stepped off. She didn't catch my attention, though she was pretty. It was her companion that made me sit all the way up, body going rigid.

* * *

PATIENCE

How on Earth did I end up here? I was in a sex club for God's sake!

"Patience, your I.D.," Judy insisted, looking back at me.

I began shaking my head. "Judy, I don't think I should be here." My eyes bulged when I glanced over Judy's shoulder to see a half-naked woman sitting on one of the leather loveseats, straddling a man who I could only see from the waist down.

"Patience, I told you to leave your prudish side at home," Judy insisted, bringing my attention back to her five-foot-three frame.

"I can't leave my prudish side at home. I *am* a prude. I'm a librarian for goodness' sakes! And a mom." I whispered the last part, ashamed to admit that I was a mother in a place like this.

"You weren't such a prude when you were telling me about that little fantasy of yours. And your kids are all the way in Oakland. You're in Chicago tonight. Live a little. You'll be the same boring librarian and mother when you get back on the plane tomorrow morning. "'Kay?" With that, she snatched my wallet out of my hand, rifling through until she found my license. Then she flipped her long, dark, silky hair over her shoulder and turned to the hostess at the registration table.

I sealed my eyes shut and inhaled a deep breath. Maybe she was right. The kids were at home, in the great care of their nanny, while I was there on a work conference. I could just make myself comfortable at the bar, have a couple of cocktails and let that be that. I wouldn't bother to tell Judy that there was only one person who'd ever brought out the non-prude in me. And that was a long time ago.

I sighed and blinked my eyes open, ridding myself of those memories.

"You're still meeting Kevin here?" I asked Judy when she returned my I.D.

"Yup. He texted me. He's on his way. Isn't this place cool?" she questioned, looping her arm in mine and pulling me toward one of the loveseats that had a card at the center with the name "Russell" on it her fiancé's last name.

"It's cool all right," I murmured. "Look, I know I told you about my fantasy and everything, but that was just all in fun. I'm not doing anything with any of these men...or women." I plopped down on the loveseat, looking around. I'm sure my facial expression mirrored a damn deer in headlights. I still couldn't believe I'd gotten drunk enough to share my fantasy of being tied up and spanked with Judy the night before. Now, here I was, at some place in the West Loop where I was certain most of the people in here had more than just read about rope play, as I had.

"You say that now."

"I mean it!" I hissed at Judy.

She shrugged. "I said the same thing, when I first came. Then I met Kevin, and…" She just smiled and then giggled. "Oh, he's here." She pointed at the elevator and got up to greet her fiancé. I remained seated, still feeling so uncomfortable. When a man passed, throwing a smile in my direction, I returned it in kind but wished he'd keep moving. That wasn't going to happen, apparently. He stopped.

"Hey, beautiful."

"Hello." I shifted in my seat, looking around.

"You're new here, huh?"

"Just visiting." Saying I was *new* gave the insinuation that I was planning to return but that would not be the case. This would be my first and last time at this place. A visit was the more appropriate term for this situation.

"Have you visited the other floors yet?" He leaned his body against the loveseat, inching in just a tad bit closer.

I wanted to squirm away, but I held my ground. "I just arrived."

"I'd love to take you to the Wet Room. A body like yours should never be covered up." His pale green eyes slid down, stopping at the ample cleavage my black dress exposed. They moved farther down, pausing again at the sight of my exposed walnut-colored thigh. The dress had been Judy's idea and I was regretting it. I shifted, pushing my long sister locks over my shoulders to cover as much cleavage as possible.

"Beautiful brown skin like yours…" He paused, moving his hand closer to my arm. Just before I could pull away a voice sounded.

"If you fucking touch her, I will break all two-hundred and six bones in your body."

The deep voice sent shockwaves through my entire body.

It can't be.

As the strange man stood, moving out of the way, I nearly passed out when my greatest fear was confirmed.

It was him.

Aaron.

He looked a little older, and still just as mean as ever. And that was his appeal, part of it, at least. The man was handsome, bordering on beautiful by conventional standards. With his dark hair, hazel eyes, square jaw, and perfect nose with a splattering of freckles across the bridge.

"This one yours?" the strange man asked, looking toward Aaron.

"She's off limits...to you," he snarled. "Leave. Now."

Aaron gave the man a hard look and before I knew it the guy was backing off. Aaron's gaze lingered on his retreating form for all of two seconds and then he pinned me with his gaze.

I felt as if I was being lifted, even though I remained seated. I couldn't avert my eyes as all types of emotions swirled around in my gut, each fighting for dominance over the other.

Don't be so sensitive.

That reminder, of his harsh words, allowed the anger I still held to reign supreme. I'd let my anger at him lead the way.

"What the fuck are you doing here?" he growled, before I could speak. His words knocked all the wind out of my sails.

"I-I," I stammered, but then caught myself. "Having a drink and minding my damn business." I turned my head, to reach for the glass on my table that had been dropped off by the waitress, but my arm was caught in a steel trap. I dared to look down at his creamy hand, encircling my forearm.

"Get up," he demanded, but didn't wait for my compliance. He yanked me up out of my seat with one arm. Once standing, he pulled me tight to his body. With his free hand, he gathered my sister locks at the nape of my neck. His hard eyes moved from mine, down to my lips, face, neck, and stopping at my breasts. Unlike when the other man had done this same thing, my nipples began throbbing painfully against the cotton fabric of the dress.

"You're not wearing a bra."

Why did his simple observation cause a flood in my panties? I should hate this man. No. I *do* hate this man for the way he treated me.

"Let go of me."

His jaw tightened along with his grip around my arm.

"You think you're all grown up now? Think you're ready for a place like this?"

"It's none of your goddamn business what I'm ready for, you son of a—"

His free hand clamped around my lower jaw, and his lips crushed mine, pushing my angry words back down my throat. I didn't want his kiss or his touch. I squirmed to break his grasp, but he was too strong and I was always too weak for him. I gasped in pain and pleasure when he bit my lower lip and pulled back, not trying to soothe the bite like he'd done in the past.

"Watch your fucking mouth. Let's go."

I stumbled over the heels I wore, which weren't my own, when he began pulling me by my arm. I tugged and attempted to yank free. "Let go of me! Where the hell are we going?" I hissed, trying to keep my voice low to not draw attention from the surrounding patrons. Aaron didn't even bother to turn and look back at me, pulling me easily toward a long hall.

We passed one room where tables full of food were set up.

"Aaron, where the hell are we—" My question was cut off when he tried the knob of one of the closed wooden doors. The knob turned and he pushed it open. I felt myself propelled forward, just barely able to keep on my feet when he tossed me inside, slamming the door behind him and then my back against the door.

His dark gaze seethed and a twinge of fear scattered up my spine just before he crushed his lips to mine again. Fear, anger, and all, it still felt good. Too good. I didn't want to feel anything but hatred for him. I squirmed and twisted my head, ultimately breaking free of the hold of his mouth.

"Don't touch me!" I yelled, pushing him away. He barely budged but it was enough distance that I was able to reach up and smack him across the face with all the anger I felt. The loud "pop" echoed around the dark room.

He took a step back, his hazel eyes burning an ominous stare into my eyes as his thumb reached up, swiping at the corner of his mouth.

His eyes lowered and my chest heaved when I registered the drop of blood on the tip of his thumb. My stomach plummeted when he turned even darker eyes on me and a smile crept on his handsome face.

Aaron didn't smile.

Crazy bastard.

That was my last coherent thought, before he invaded my space again, pushing me against the door with his entire body weight, mouth moving over mine, this time even more harsh than before. I tasted the coppery taste of his blood. The blood I'd drawn from him, and instead of turning me off, the way it should have, it caused a tremble in my thighs.

"Ah!" I yelled, when he pulled back and with his two hands ripped the dress I wore down the middle. My breasts spilled out. I went to cover myself, but he was quicker than I was. He grabbed both of my wrists, hoisting them over my head. I was too preoccupied with the feeling of my nipples rubbing against his chest, to realize that he tied something around my wrists, suspending them there. His mouth moved to mine again, and I felt his large hands travel down my body, cupping and massaging my breasts before they moved lower, shredding the rest of my dress. I attempted to push him away again only to find my wrists were bound.

"A-Aaron," I panted. "What the hell? Untie me!" I tugged at the ropes, looking up.

"Don't struggle. You'll hurt yourself," he growled. "It's polypropylene rope." He moved his head lower, to my neck, licking the spot below my left ear.

I shivered.

"The core's been removed," he continued in between biting and licking at my neck. "But pulling too hard can cause rope burn."

I panted, my thoughts becoming hazy. My head fell back against the door. "Aaron," I breathed, trying one last time to get him to release me, but it was my weakest attempt yet. I began to lose my reasoning as to why I shouldn't just give in. Submit to him. I became really undone when he moved lower, his insistent lips blazing a trail from my neck to my chest, savoring and feeding himself at my breasts. His tongue rolled over one nipple while his fingers pinched the other. My hips bucked and he gave a devious chuckle at my obvious agony.

"You still come apart for me." He moved lower, nipping and sucking at my abdomen until he reached the apex of my thighs, coming to his knees. "You thought you were going to give this to someone else tonight?" His angry eyes reached mine at the same time he cupped my sex. "Answer me!"

My eyes narrowed. "Yes! I had plans on giving it to the first man who asked!" I taunted, lying my ass off.

He made a deep, hard sound at the back of his throat just before he tore my panties. The lace fabric stood no chance in the face of his apparent enmity.

"Fucking mine!" he growled just before pushing my thighs apart and thrusting his face into my core.

"Ahh!" I screamed at the intensity at which he sucked and feasted on my sex. He lifted my right thigh over his shoulder and used his fingers to split me open, allowing his tongue full access to the most sensitive part of my body. My hips went wild against his face, my head lolled against the door. My hands tightened into fists, suspended in the air, tugging at the rope, but this time not to get away. It was the natural reaction to the devastation he was causing to my pussy. I screamed and creamed into his mouth and he fed off of it all. My yells and cries causing him to become even more insistent, driving me higher and higher to my climax. Just when I thought I was about to fall over the cliff, he pulled back.

"Fuck you!" I growled and tried to kick at him as he stared at me, amusement glittering in his eyes.

His deep chuckle caused my pussy to clench. My nipples ached painfully and my entire body was primed for an orgasm as he stared at me, rising slowly, flicking on a dim light. I blinked a few times, looking around, seeing a huge bed at the other side of the room, shiny hardwood floors, a walk-in closet to the right covered in huge mirrors. On the left, was a metal stripper pole. I turned back to Aaron to see him reaching up. When I felt his hands at my wrist, I figured he was undoing the restraints. I was going to punch him the first chance I got, though it might turn him on as my smack had done earlier.

Sick bastard, I thought again, even though I was just as sick as him remembering how turned on I'd become from the taste of his blood.

"You're going to pay for your earlier comment." I heard moments before I was yanked from the door. Unfortunately, I was still bound at the wrists, but I fought to free myself from his grasp, even as he tugged me toward the bed. We wrestled, but somehow, I found myself lying flat on my stomach against the bed, my hands stretched out in front of me, tied to the metal, shiny black headboard.

"Tell me, sweetness, what the fuck are you doing here?" His voice was lethally low next to my ear. His hand pushed my hair back out of my face so I could see him fully.

I hated the way my pussy clenched at hearing the term of endearment he'd become accustomed to using for me.

"None of your fucking business!" I yelled and turned my head, avoiding his gaze. It did too much to my insides. Let alone the fact that I was stripped naked on a bed, my entire body still trembling from the release it never got.

"Everything you do is my business."

I tugged at the restraints once more, pissed all over again.

Smack!

I stilled when a sharp slap to my ass reverberated through me until it reached my core.

"Hsss!" I hissed at the intense wave of pleasure that rolled through my sex. My hands and feet clenched. I heard wrestling noises but still refused to look in his direction. When the bed dipped and I felt the heat from his body move behind me, I tried to kick at him, but his hand gripped my ankle, preventing me.

"I'm not yours!" I yelled, my voice choked with tears. It was a lie. He knew it and I knew it. But I fought to hold onto that lie as if it were my lifeline. Even as he spread my legs apart and his thick cock brushed against my aching wetness. I gasped when he roughly pulled my head back by my hair.

"You've always fucking been mine. From the very first time you put your lips on me. Your lips, your pussy, your ass, and anything else I want is *mine*."

I whimpered at the feel of his hard rod at the apex of my sex, ready to breach me. He slid in easily due to the outpouring of my wetness for him. I tried to shake my head no, denying his words.

"Say it," he growled in my ear.

I shook my head as much as I could with his hand still tugging at my hair.

"Say it!"

"I–" I broke off, shaking my head again.

"Say it!"

"I'm yours!" I finally let out, and when I did he made me his over and over again, breaching me. I screamed out, feeling every ridge of his cock when he pushed into me all the way to the hilt. I needed time to adjust. It'd been a long time since this part of my body had been invaded, but Aaron was relentless. Pushing in and pulling out before thrusting in again in rapid succession.

"A-A," I panted, unable to get his name completely out of my mouth. His thrusts stole my words, and replaced all thoughts and memories with nothing but what he was doing to me at that moment. And my body took it all, weeping for more of him. My breasts ached as they bounced against my chest from his relentless pounding. My ass jiggled, high in the air, my hips were sore from the tight hold of his hands on them, and most of all, my pussy throbbed and rippled from the glide of his cock. I twisted my hands in the silk sheets of the bed, moaning loudly until my throat felt hoarse. I was close, oh so close. But again, before I could reach my zenith, Aaron pulled completely out of me.

"Son of a–" My curse was cut off by a hard smack at my ass. I cried out at the ripple of pain that moved down to my pussy, turning into another wave of pleasure I wasn't sure I could handle.

"I told you to watch your fucking mouth!" he roared, undoing my wrists and flipping my body over.

I wanted to strike out at him but I was too undone and he was too fast. He retied my wrists and then pushed my legs at the knees high up, so they were bent and spread wide for him. My knees nearly came to my armpits. Blinking, I looked up at him, to see he was completely nude. My eyes zeroed in on the scars over his chest, but they paused at the ink I saw there. It looked like a Chinese symbol but I didn't know what it meant.

Tattoos are useless.

I remembered his words plain as day. I thought maybe I was imagining things but couldn't orient myself long enough before I was impaled again. My head thrashed against the pillows of the bed. With my hands bound and knees held up by his hands, I could only take what he was giving me. Again, he pounded me into the mattress, ferocious in the way he was taking siege of my body. I gasped, when he pushed my legs even higher and wider, allowing himself to go just another inch deeper. My head rose off the bed, the feeling of being impossibly stuffed. I glanced all around the room, my eyes wide, until my sight finally landed on his face.

He looked so in control. The lonely bead of sweat that moved down the side of his face was the only indication he was exerting himself. That, and his eyes. His eyes were so stormy and acute. He watched me. Took into consideration every reaction I had to his thrusts. He sped up his strokes and I lost my breath, and he still watched me intently—never breaking eye contact, and never allowing me to either. He slowed down his pace, pulling almost completely out of me, staring at me with just the tip of his cock inside of me. He reached down, let his thumb rub my clit at the same time he pushed all the way back in and sent me spiraling.

I finally broke eye contact when my eyes fell shut against the current. Wave after wave of overwhelming pleasure from built-up, unexpressed orgasms came over me. My body shook and I screamed and then gasped when I couldn't scream any longer. I trembled, every muscle in my body tightening up. The orgasm was totally consuming and felt endless. And still, through it all, Aaron rode me, pounding as my pussy muscles clenched around him. His own grunts mixed with my moans and cries. It wasn't until I was totally spent, weakened from my orgasm, that he pulled completely out of me again, and came himself, releasing his hot come all over my belly and breasts. He massaged his thick cock with his hand, squeezing out every last drop, making sure it covered me.

My legs fell limply to the bed. I was spent. I watched wordlessly as the last drops of his semen fell into my belly button.

"Like I fucking said, you've always belonged to me."

* * *

I AWOKE, feeling groggy and disoriented. My mouth felt like it held a ball of cotton in it and every muscle in my body ached when I tried to turn over. The memories of the night before slowly came back to me. I closed my eyes against the shame and guilt I felt. I was never supposed to be in this position. Not with him. Again. I sent up a silent prayer that he wasn't still in the room even though I knew he wasn't there. I didn't feel his presence.

Slowly, I sat up, blinking a couple of times to let my eyes adjust to the dimness and sure enough, he was gone.

"Ugh," I moaned against the soreness between my legs and of my body as I stretched one leg and then the next over the side of the bed. With measured movements, I looked around the room for the clutch I'd brought with me. I found it on the nightstand next to the bed, sitting on top of a pile of folded clothes. I grabbed my purse, pulling out my cell, and gasped at the time. It was just after six o'clock in the morning. I had a nine a.m. flight back home. I needed to go. Just as I was about to rush to look for my clothes from the previous night, I remembered that the dress I wore had been torn to shreds

"Bastard," I mumbled.

I went back to the night stand, remembering the pile of clothes there, and found a pair of jeans, T-shirt, panties, and bra. All were the correct size but they weren't mine. However, he'd obviously left them to replace the clothing he'd destroyed. I briefly wondered how many women he'd done the same. Probably right here in this place. I needed to go.

I quickly dressed and hurried out of the room, down the hall toward the now quiet dining space. Save for a few stragglers who looked as if they, too, had spent the night, I was the only one there. I pressed the elevator and rushed on as soon as it opened. Once I made it into the ground floor of the garage, I opened the app on my phone to retrieve an Uber.

"Ms. Thiers?"

I glanced up and saw a tall, older man waiting by a Lincoln town car.

"Yes?"

He smiled. "My name is Joseph, I will take you wherever you need to go."

I wrinkled my forehead.

"Mr. Townsend insisted I wait for you and see to it that you were delivered back home safely."

"My hotel," I corrected.

He nodded. "As you wish."

"I have a nine a.m. flight."

"We will pick up your belongings and I will get you to the airport on time for your flight."

I didn't have time to think. I just got in the back and allowed this man to take me to my hotel to gather my belongings. Once I was back in the car, I pulled out my cell and opened one of the three messages from Judy. I responded to her, telling her that I was fine and on my way to catch my flight. I left out any details of the previous night. Of course, she insisted that I call her as soon as I got home. I agreed and stuffed my cell back into my pocket just as we were arriving at O'Hare.

I refused to let myself even think as I charged through the elevator, thankful that I'd gone with the early check-in, saving me time. Thirty minutes after making it to my gate, my flight was boarding and soon enough I was on my way home. I tried to sleep but images of the previous night kept replaying in my head. I finally gave up the notion of sleep and instead pulled out my Kindle to get some reading done.

Hours later, I was greeted at my apartment door by my two shrieking children.

"Mommy's home!"

"Yay!"

They both ran up to me, hugging my knees. The tension that I'd been feeling since I'd awakened that morning began to ebb just a little. I sank to my knees after smiling over their shoulders at Ms. Sheryl, their babysitter.

"Did you bring us anything back?" Kyle asked.

"Did you have fun, Mommy? Bring any books?" Kennedy chimed in.

"How about toys?"

"Did you meet anyone nice?"

My heart plummeted at Kennedy's final question. Of course, I wasn't about to tell my five-year-old daughter that I'd ran into the father I'd led them both to believe was up in heaven. Instead, I pulled my babies to me and then showed them the keepsakes I'd brought back for them.

CHAPTER 3

aron
"Is that the case, Mr. Townsend?"

I ran my thumb across my lower lip, absently staring out of my office window, taking in the Williamsport skyline. *I wonder what she's doing right now.*

"Mr. Townsend?"

I blinked.

"Jerry, why don't we give my brother a break. We'll reconvene later this afternoon."

I stuffed my hand into my pants pocket, sighing heavily. I waited until I heard the door to my office shut to finally turn around and glare at my second youngest brother.

"Why the hell did you send them out?"

Joshua didn't even flinch in the face of my harsh tone. He pushed out a full breath and went to sit in one of the chairs across from my large wooden desk, propping one leg over the other.

"You're out of it today."

My ever-present frown deepened a smidgen. "I'm right fucking here."

"You've been out of it for days now, come to think of it. I haven't seen you like this… in quite some time." He angled his head, staring at me as if waiting for an explanation. Well, he damn sure could keep on waiting.

"I don't have time for pow-wows in the middle of the day. We need to complete things with Oiltec and get our team together to go up there again. Then, I need to prepare my R&D guys for their international trip." I moved to my desk to rifle through some papers. Unable to find what I was looking for, I told him, "Since you're just sitting there, go out and ask Darcy or Marcy, whatever the hell her name is, to bring me the Downes report."

"You mean Marsha?"

"Whatever."

"Can't do it."

I lifted my head, pinning Joshua with my gaze.

"You fired Marsha last week."

I wrinkled my brows trying to recall.

"You said she was too slow in prepping the paperwork you needed."

I nodded, remembering. "She was. Now I need a new junior assistant."

"That'll be your third within the last year and a half."

"What's your point?"

"Just making an observation."

"Do me a favor."

Joshua hesitated. "What?"

"Observe how to get me my damn report."

Much to my chagrin Joshua chuckled, before pressing his palms to the arm of the chair and standing.

"How about the report be left right where it is for now and you tell me what has you so wound up? I mean, even more than usual."

"I'm not wound up."

My brother made a disbelieving sound with his mouth. "Something's getting to you and it's not just business. I've seen you get wound up about business. Hell, it's one of the *only* things that actually gets your attention. But you've been distracted and extra irritable ever since you came back from Chicago last week. I know it wasn't the deal. That went smoothly and we came in under budget as far as the acquisition. It's something else."

I twisted my hand in my pants pocket and tightened my jaw, remaining silent.

Joshua watched me, silently observing, but I refused to flinch. Finally, he shrugged. "Whatever it is, you'll either get over it or it'll be revealed."

I sighed. "Now you sound like Mother."

"I am my mother's son." He grinned. "Let's have lunch."

"I need the re–"

Josh held up his hand. "It's after two o'clock and we haven't eaten lunch. The Downes report will be here when we get back. Thirty minutes away won't fucking kill you."

"As long as it's close." I stepped around my desk, pulling my arms into my suit Armani jacket.

"Those pin stripes look good on you, bro."

"Fuck off," I grunted. Before Joshua could respond, the cell in my pocket began ringing. Removing my phone, I glanced at the number and jerked my head back in surprise at the caller. "Thiers?" I answered after the second ring.

"H-hi, is this Aaron Townsend?"

I frowned at the female voice I heard on the other end. It wasn't a familiar one.

"Who is this?" I questioned, sharply.

"M-my name is Wilhelmina."

"And how did you get my personal cell number?"

"It's Thiers. He's had a heart attack."

I paused from following Joshua, right before we stepped into the elevator. "Is he still alive?" In my peripheral, I saw Joshua glance over at me.

"Yes, thank God. He is alive. The doctors say he may need surgery. He asked that I call you. He wanted you to come see him at your earliest convenience."

"What hospital is he in and what is his room number?"

"He's in Williamsport General. Room four-twelve."

"Is his situation dire?"

"Not at the moment. The doctors believe his prognosis is good."

"I will make arrangements to see him as soon as possible." I ended the call without waiting for her response and began texting my senior assistant instructions.

"Thiers?"

"Making arrangements to visit tomorrow."

Josh nodded and proceeded to the elevator.

I explained everything the woman, Wilhelmina, had just told me over the phone to Josh as we got in the awaiting car to head to lunch. Throughout our meal I did my best to keep my mind off Thiers... and who else I might run into at the hospital.

* * *

PATIENCE

"Kyle, stop jumping on the couch please!" I admonished my son who was shrieking and laughing while he watched one of his favorite cartoons.

"Mommy, I'm hungry!" he whined, plopping down on his butt on the couch.

"I'm making breakfast now. Do me a favor and go wake your sister, and the both of you go brush your teeth."

He blew out a breath. "Okay."

It was a busy Thursday morning, and as usual Kennedy was the last in the house to wake up. Kennedy was like me when it came to sleep. Until I had kids, I hated getting up early in the morning. Now, the only time I could get a little quiet time was early mornings, so I made due.

I whipped the pancake mixture some more before dumping a packet of fresh blueberries into the batter and folding them in. Next, I ladled a couple of spoonfuls of the batter onto the griddle, and waited for the bubbles to appear before flipping them. By the time the children came running up the hall after brushing their teeth, I had two pancakes for each of them on their plates.

"Kyle, slow down. The food isn't going to run away."

That caused Kennedy to giggle.

"Thank you, Mommy!" Kyle said through a mouthful of pancakes.

"You're welcome, baby." I pressed a kiss to his forehead.

"How'd you sleep, baby girl?" I asked Kennedy while sitting down with my own plate. I tried to make it a point to slow down and eat with the kids whenever possible. Mornings could be busy but I wanted to savor the time I had with them first and foremost.

"Good!" Kennedy nodded in response to my inquiry.

"Sweet dreams?"

"I dreamt of ponies. Can I have one, Mommy?"

I began shaking my head, ready to let her down gently, when my phone rang. My eyes darted to the clock on the wall. It was barely seven-thirty in the morning. I wondered who was calling so early.

"Hello?"

"Is this Patience?"

"Yes. Who is this?"

"Hi. My name is Wilhelmina. I'm a...friend of your father's."

I frowned. What the heck was this woman calling me about?

"I'm sorry to be the one to tell you, but your father had a heart attack."

I pressed my hand to my chest, gasping. I glanced up and saw Kyle shoot me a concerned look. I turned my back.

"Is... is he..."

"No. No. He's actually doing well. The doctors may have to perform surgery later this week. But he's asked to see you." That shouldn't have been a surprise to hear, but it was. My father requesting anything of me came as a shock.

"Wh-what hospital is he in?" I grabbed a pen and pad from one of my kitchen drawers and wrote down the information Wilhelmina gave me.

"All done!" Kennedy yelled from the table, holding up her plate to show me.

I gave her a small smile. "Good job. Put your plate in the sink and go wash your hands to get ready to get dressed," I told both her and Kyle, who was staring at me worriedly. I bent down and pressed a kiss to his forehead. "Go on." Kyle was definitely the most intuitive of my two children.

"Hi, Ms. Sheryl, I'm sorry to call so early but I have a family emergency." I explained to her what happened and we came up with a plan for her to watch the kids while I saw to my father. Next, I had to call my job and request at least a week off, before moving on to make flight and hotel reservations. This morning certainly had not turned out how I'd expected it to.

CHAPTER 4

Patience

I had an eerie feeling as I proceeded down the hall to my father's hospital room. I'd arrived the night before and only had a few minutes with my father before visiting hours were over. At his insistence, I agreed to return early the next morning. I rounded the last corner of the hallway where his and only one other room resided. It was just after nine a.m. and the nurse at the desk had already informed me that the doctors had done their rounds and my father had been checked. I figured he would be alone, since Wilhelmina had informed me she wouldn't be in until ten or eleven that morning. I lightly tapped on the door and opened without waiting for a response. As soon as I stepped in, all the air rushed from my lungs. My eyes locked with a pair of hazel orbs that were very much *not* my father's.

All rational thought fled my brain and I just stood there, staring at Aaron. He did the same until my father spoke up, breaking into my thoughts.

"Patience, you came back. Come in."

I finally looked from Aaron to my father, whose perfectly white teeth appeared as he greeted me with a smile. I can't remember a time, if any, in which my father had greeted me with such enthusiasm.

"I-I can come back if you're busy." I cleared my throat, hoping to remove the tremble from it.

"Nonsense. Aaron is an old family friend."

I began to feel queasy. Then the anger began to start. *Old family friend*. I bet.

"How're you feeling?" I asked my father, choosing to ignore the other man in the room. That was the only alternative I had. But I felt him watching me.

"I've definitely been better, but for an old man who just had a heart attack, I'm not doing so bad."

I gave my father a tight smile. It was the best I could do at his attempted humor.

"I was just telling Aaron that the doctors have scheduled my surgery for this Friday."

I blinked. "Already? Don't they need to run more tests?"

"Nope. It's all set."

A sense of dread filled my abdomen. Open heart surgery was a huge deal. And though I shouldn't be this emotional over a man I barely kept in contact with, I was.

"Well, if they think it's for the best." I swallowed the lump in my throat.

"It is. I'll be up and around in no time."

"The world still needs you around."

I bit my bottom lip, refusing to acknowledge Aaron or the first words he'd spoken since I entered the room.

"The world will be fine with or without me. Anyway, Patience, I was telling Aaron about you living in Oakland."

I raised my eyebrows.

"You've been there what five, six years now?"

"Almost six." I cleared my throat again. "I'll let you two catch up and then come b–"

"Nonsense." My father waved his hand, dismissively. "We were talking about some of the changes Oakland has seen in the last decade. You know Aaron's company, Townsend Industries, does a lot of donating to literary charities here in Williamsport. I bet you could convince him to extend that to Oakland. She works at a library in Oakland," my father informed Aaron.

I bit the inside of my cheek, both anger and embarrassment rising up in the pit of my stomach. I will most assuredly not be doing any convincing where Aaron Townsend is concerned. I mostly remained silent while my father continued talking about God knows what. Aaron chimed in a couple of times here and there but I did my best to ignore him, never once looking in his direction. But just as if they were his hands, I felt it every time he looked my way.

I don't know how many minutes went by, but finally Wilhelmina entered the room. I decided that would be my time to escape and I could make an appearance later in the day once Aaron was gone. I told my father I would be back and didn't give anyone a second glance as I made a beeline for the door.

I pushed out the air from my lungs as soon as I shut the door behind me, while I rubbed my forehead with my fingertips, attempting to quiet my nerves. Two seconds later, I jumped as my father's hospital room door was forcefully thrust open again and the man who was the cause of all the stress that just barely begun to unravel in my body emerged. I finally gave him a once over, taking in his immaculately tailored suit. Probably something Italian because Aaron only wore the best. He towered over me by ten inches. I let my eyes travel up his body but I refused to let my gaze settle on his eyes.

"Patience."

A ringing in my ears sounded. Why did my name sound both like a command and a plea from his lips? I was not going there. I quickly side-stepped him, thanking God that my balance remained intact while I wasn't so sure about my sanity.

Refusing to acknowledge him, I moved toward the opposite end of the hall, toward the nurse's station, to get to the elevators. He didn't call my name again, but I felt him. He was still there, following me. I wanted to either break out in a run or pick up the nearest pair of scissors and stab him with them. I couldn't decide which to do so I kept walking. Within ten steps of the elevator, the door chimed and opened up.

"Mommy! Kyle keeps teasing me!" Kennedy ran to me, circling her little arms around my legs. "Make him stop."

"Mommy, Kennedy's a liar! I just told her the truth," came Kyle's petulant reply. He also ran up but stopped a few inches from me, cocking his head to the side as he stared behind me.

I squeezed my eyes shut. This could not be happening.

"I'm sorry, Patience. They got restless and wanted to come see you," Ms. Ryan came rushing around the nurse's station to inform me.

I gave her a tight smile. "Th-that's okay."

"Mommy, I'm hungry!" Kennedy whined, arms still around my legs.

"We're leaving now, baby."

"No. Why don't you stay?" a deep, booming voice sounded behind me and I wanted the floor to open up and swallow me where I stood.

* * *

AARON

I had to be losing my fucking mind. I absolutely had to be. Maybe the late nights and early mornings in the office were finally catching up to me. Because I refused to fucking believe what I just saw. It *had* to be a figment of my imagination. Of course, I doubted I even had a fucking imagination. I didn't indulge in bullshit fantasies, so whatever I was seeing in front of me had to be reality.

"Are they mine?" I asked Patience, seething, as soon as I slammed the door behind us. I'd practically dragged her into one of the private waiting rooms.

She forcefully pulled her arm away from me, giving me the same deadly glare I was giving her.

"Don't touch me!"

I flexed my jaw, trying to clamp down on the rage inside. "Are. They. Mine?" It was a bullshit question. I knew the answer before I even asked. The boy. Kyle. He looked just like ... me.

"No."

My head shot back. She was lying.

"They're mine! Now, if you'll excuse m–"

"Do not fucking play with me, Patience." I pressed her back against the door, gripping her arm. Again she snatched it away from me, pushing me back, only because I allowed her to.

"I'm not playing, you jackass," she hissed. "What the hell are you upset about? I wasn't going to abort my children. And never, not once, in the last five years have I ever disturbed you after you made it abundantly clear you wanted nothing to do with us!"

I took a step back as if she'd smacked me or pushed me away. What in the hell was she talking about?

"Have you lost your damn mind?"

"Have you?" she shrieked. "Pulling me away from my children like a damn lunatic. You probably frightened them."

"*Your* children?"

"Yes, *mine*. I'm done with this conversation." She tried to brush past me but my firm hand on the door stopped her.

"What type of game are you playing?"

Her face collapsed into one of confusion. "What game am *I* playing? Why don't you ask that of yourself."

"I don't need to ask myself anything. How the hell could you have my children and not tell me?"

"What are you talking about?! I told you!" she shouted. "And very unceremoniously, I was informed by your *fiancée* that I was to never contact you again. Right after she tossed an envelope stuffed with five hundred dollars for an abortion in my face."

My throat squeezed, stomach clenching. She tried to hide it behind her anger but the pain in those sepia-colored eyes was apparent.

"What?" I managed to get out.

"Don't act like you don't know what I'm talking about."

She attempted to pull the door open, but once again my hand stopped her efforts. She turned back to me, staring. I pressed my lips together, my free hand clenched tightly at my side. I was doing everything in my power to rein in the outrage I felt. Without removing my eyes from her, I lowered my hand to the doorknob and pulled it open. I took a step back, allowing her to exit.

She frowned, taking one last glance at me, as if asking without words if this was me letting her leave.

Not by a long shot was that what this was. But I silently watched as she exited the door and went over to the shorter, older woman who stood supervising the children while we were in the room. I glared as Patience took both of the children by their hands and walked swiftly down the hall to the elevators, not bothering to look back as the door closed behind them.

I pulled out my phone and began dialing. My whole life had just been turned upside down.

CHAPTER 5

Aaron

I heard the clacking of her heels against the concrete as soon as she exited the elevator.

"Do you know I was almost married to your boss? That means I was almost your boss. How dare you treat me with such aggression!" her shrill voice demanded.

The anger I'd thought I'd done a good job of suppressing came roaring back and I snatched the door open.

She gasped, obviously not expecting me so abruptly.

"Aaron," Alicia stated, "this man has been extremely rude."

I looked from Alicia to the man next to her, Brutus, my head of security. I nodded. He returned it with a nod of his own before turning and walking away.

"Aaron, what is all of this about? And why aren't we meeting in your office?" Alicia batted those long, false eyelashes at me, forming her red-tinted lips in a pouted moue. I took in her outfit—a form fitting black dress that clung to her lithe body. Her long, brunette hair sat in a bun high atop her head. Her makeup flawless, per usual. It all disgusted me.

"Alicia, have I not let you lead a good life?" My tone was low and I could tell it was menacing by the way she took a step back. "Have I not let you live in peace? In Paris, no less?"

Her forehead wrinkled. "Aaron, what is this about? Why are you asking me this? Why did you have me brought here to you? Why are we not in your office?"

"This," I extended my arm wide, "is my office for visitors like you. Come in." I stood to the side, letting her move through the doors unabated, mostly because I didn't want to touch her. She jumped when I slammed the door behind her.

"You knew," I seethed, turning to her slowly.

Another confused expression befell her face.

"Answer me!"

She startled. "Knew what?"

"Patience! She was pregnant, and you fucking knew."

The answer was written all over her face. Her eyes glossed over, and her eyelids drooped in response to my demand.

"I thought she was lying," she confessed. "You know how some women are. Lying to keep a man."

"You mean women like you."

Her mouth dropped as if I'd hit her. "Women like me? She was the whore who was sleeping with my fiancé! That bitch tried to call your cell two months after I found you at her apartment. I answered and she said she was pregnant. I knew she was lying. The skank!"

I took a threatening step toward her until I was in her face. "Don't ever form your lips to call her that again. Because of you, I've missed five years with my children."

"Children?"

"Twins. She was pregnant with twins. Twins you fucking gave her five hundred dollars to abort!"

Alicia's mouth opened and closed a few times. "H-how do you even know they're yours? How do you know you're the only man she was sleeping with?"

I raised my hand, but stopped just two inches from clamping it around Alicia's throat. "Don't ever...You're making me seriously consider my rule of never putting my hands on a woman." Taking a step back, I thrust my hands into my pockets. "You've cost me time I can never get back. And for that, our deal is off."

She gasped, but I kept going.

"Forget living in that comfortable little villa in Paris. Good-bye to the nice multi-million dollar bank account. You are on your own from here on out." I turned to walk away, but she wrapped her hands around my arm. I yanked it away so forcefully she lost her footing, nearly falling. I just stood there, staring.

"What am I supposed to do?"

"Go to hell," I answered before pulling the door open and nodding again at my security. They had their instructions on how to handle her from here on out. I had much bigger matters to take care of.

* * *

P*atience*

"Ms. Sheryl, I appreciate your willingness to stay here in Williamsport with me for the rest of the week," I told my friend as we finished cleaning up after dinner. It'd been three days since I arrived back in Williamsport, and two days since my run-in with Aaron at the hospital. I was looking forward to ensuring my father's surgery went well and he was on the road to recovery before getting back to Oakland and my life. Ms. Sheryl's presence had not only been helpful with the kids, but for me as well.

"Don't think anything of it. I've been waiting to visit the city you grew up. The kids seem to like it."

I nodded. "They like anywhere there's a park for Kyle and a library or bookstore for Kennedy." I laughed along with Ms. Sheryl.

We continued talking a little more about what there was to do in the city with young children. She was going to take them on another venture the next day while I visited my father in the hospital. Just as we cleared out the last of our room service dinners, a knock sounded at my door.

"You order something?" I asked.

"Not me." She shook her head.

I went to the door, hoping the person wouldn't knock again. I didn't want them to disturb the kids who were just settling down for bed. I looked through the peephole to see a man dressed in a brown suit standing.

"Can I help you?" I asked, pulling the door open.

"Patience Theirs?"

I nodded. "That's me."

"You've been served." He thrust a large envelope in my hands before quickly walking away.

Confused, I watched him leave, and make his way to the elevator, practically leaping on once it opened. I closed the door, wondering what the hell was going on. Opening the envelope, I pulled out the stack of papers, and began reading over the letter. It was addressed from a Michael Cavalleri, Esq. My heart rate sped up the more I read.

"What?" I whispered, reading the words over and over again.

"Everything all right?"

I looked up to stare at Ms. Sheryl. "He's suing me for full custody."

Her eyes bulged. "He who?"

I blinked remembering that Ms. Sheryl still didn't know the full truth. I hadn't told her that the man from the hospital the other day was actually Kennedy and Kyle's father. I'd never told anyone the full story about Aaron and I.

Before I could answer her question, my cell phone began ringing from the table. Absentmindedly, I walked over to the table to see who was calling. I frowned, not recognizing the number.

"Hello?"

"You've received the papers." It wasn't a question. He knew I had.

My shoulders sank. "Aaron."

"I'll assume that's a yes."

"What are you doing?"

"It says it right there on the form."

"You want full custody of children you've never met? Of children you didn't want to begin with?"

There was a moment of silence on the other end.

"Come to my office at nine a.m. tomorrow morning."

Click.

I pulled the phone from my ear to see the call had been disconnected.

"So that's him?"

I blinked, realizing Ms. Sheryl was still in the room.

"Kyle and Kennedy's father. *The* Aaron Townsend."

I remained silent. The answer was obvious.

Ms. Sheryl whistled. "Always knew there was a story behind those twins." She patted me on the shoulder. "I'll go put them to bed," she informed me before heading into the bedroom that had been designated for the children. I simply continued to stare at the papers in my hand, completely dumbfounded.

* * *

I HAD a knot in my stomach as I watched the huge man who'd greeted me at my car, punch in a code for the elevator.

"This will take you directly to the top floor to Mr. Townsend's office."

I nodded and stepped on the elevator. The papers I'd been served with were in my left hand. I wondered if I should've spoken with a lawyer before showing up here. Aaron hadn't given me much more than twelve hours between the time I was served and the time I was supposed to meet him in his office. I hadn't had time to even contact a lawyer, not that I knew of any family law attorneys in Williamsport. I rubbed my forehead again, refusing to allow myself to feel overwhelmed by everything.

"Ms. Thiers. Mr. Townsend's office is right this way," another man welcomed me as soon as I stepped off the elevator.

I followed him through the glass doors and down a hallway to the only corner office that rested on the right side. The sign on the door announcing where we were, *Aaron Townsend, CEO,* the shiny placard read. The man knocked.

"Enter."

He pushed the door open and stepped to the side to allow me to walk in. I did so, but jumped when the door slammed behind me. I turned from the door and glared at Aaron who stood in front of his huge office window, arms folded over his chest. He looked like the definition of a power broker, a man on top of the world, in his spacious office. He said nothing. Out of the corner of my eye, I saw movement and turned to see another man. He was inches shorter than Aaron, and a little more stocky.

"Ms. Thiers," the man said, "Michael Cavalleri." He held out his hand for me to shake.

I narrowed my eyes, gaze trained on his hand then back up to his face. "You're the lawyer." He was the attorney who was listed on the custody forms.

He withdrew his hand. "I am."

I turned to Aaron who still hadn't spoken. "What is this about?"

"Ms. Thiers, let me explain."

"Why can't he explain?" I asked sharply, still staring at Aaron who remained silent.

"Mr. Townsend has instructed me to do the talking on his behalf."

"So, you're his puppet?"

Michael Cavalleri's face tightened, lips forming into a thin line. "No need to throw insults, Ms. Thiers."

"I shouldn't be too surprised. Your client has a habit of letting other people speak for him where I'm concerned." I shot Aaron another look, and although he remained silent, his eyes flickered, frown deepening as he glared at me.

"Ms. Thiers, please. There is no need for the hostility."

"No need?" I snapped my neck back to the lawyer. "You're trying to steal my children!"

"Legal custody is not stealing. As the father of the children, Mr. Townsend is due his parental rights."

"I've read every word in this envelope." I held up the envelope in question. "Three times. He's not petitioning for sharing of parental rights. He wants *full* custody."

"Ms. Theirs, Mr. Townsend has considerable wealth and resources, and as such, he believes the children should be raised with the full advantages of their birthright."

"Birthri–" I laughed a humorless laugh. "You're kidding me, right?"

Michael Cavalleri turned his gaze toward Aaron, who hadn't moved from his spot by the window. I let my eyes roll over to Aaron as well. He nodded at Michael.

"Mr. Townsend is willing to come to a compromise."

"Oh, how generous of him," I scoffed, folding my arms.

Michael hesitated for a moment and then shot another look in Aaron's direction. "My client is more than willing to drop this custody lawsuit under one condition."

A feeling of foreboding ran through my entire body. I knew I wasn't going to like this condition. But I had to ask. "And what condition is that?"

"You marry him."

A laugh burst from my lips. "No, really, what does *your client* want in exchange for dropping this ridiculous lawsuit?"

I waited.

And waited.

Michael's face remained placid.

A lump formed in my throat. Slowly, I pivoted my head in Aaron's direction. His face was set in his usual scowl, jaw rigid.

I took a step backwards.

"You're serious."

"Very much so, Ms. Thiers." Michael moved to the large, shiny wooden table that sat to the far end of the office. "We have two sets of forms here. One is an application for a marriage license and the other is the same custody forms you were served with last night. You can either go with the marriage signature or we will proceed with the custody hearing. And I assure you, my client will win."

"I've raised them on my own for five years. No judge will separate children from their mother needlessly."

Michael pulled at the sides of his suit jacket. "That's where you're wrong, Ms. Theirs. Go check the stats on fathers with considerable wealth who fight for custody. They always win. My job is to see to it that my client wins and I'm *very* good at my job. Not to mention you may not be the dedicated mother you pretend to be."

Tilting my head, I narrowed my gaze at Michael.

"No judge would like to hear about a single mother who attends sex clubs in her spare time."

I gasped. "I don't–"

"No?" he asked, eyebrow lifted. "Were you not in attendance at a club named The Cage in Chicago just a few weeks ago?"

My eyes ballooned and I shot Aaron the harshest look I could muster. "It was one time. He was there, too!"

I turned back to a frowning Michael. "There're no records of my client ever being there. Besides, even if he were there, he was not aware he was a father at the time. Thus, it cannot be held against him. You, on the other hand–"

"Enough. She understands," Aaron finally spoke up.

I swallowed the lump that had risen in my throat and blinked, trying to remove the tears that'd gathered in my eyes. I wouldn't look at him. I couldn't.

"Step out," he ordered.

Michael turned to leave, and I stared out of the window of the office. I heard movement and felt him nearing me but I refused to look at him.

"I'll give you five minutes to decide," Aaron stated firmly in my ear, causing goosebumps to rise along my skin. "Choose wisely." With that, he turned and a heartbeat later the door to his office slammed shut.

I was left alone to make my decision. Slowly, I walked over to the table, looking at both sets of forms. A pen rested in between the middle. I could pick it up and sign the marriage license, agreeing to marry Aaron, or walk out of here and take my chances at a custody battle. I squeezed my eyes shut before blinking them open. I'd made my decision.

CHAPTER 6

Patience

"How'd it go?" Ms. Sheryl questioned as soon as she and the kids entered the hotel suite.

I'd been back from Aaron's office for a few hours, but Ms. Sheryl and the kids had been out and about in the city. I was thankful for that. It'd given me some time to come to grips with my decision.

"Mommy, look! I got a new book!" Kennedy stated proudly, holding up her new book for me to see.

"That's great, honey."

"Kyle didn't want a new book, so Ms. Sheryl got him a new toy."

I glanced over at Kyle who was already playing with his new action figure on the circle coffee table in the middle of the living room.

"Did they have lunch yet?" I asked Ms. Sheryl.

"Yes, they did."

I blew out a breath. "Good. So, I have to tell–" I was cut off by a knock at the door. "What now?" I mumbled. I went to the door again and saw a middle-aged woman through the peephole.

"Ms. Thiers? Or should I say, Mrs. Townsend? Good to get used to your new name before the big day, right?"

The woman pushed her way through the door and to my surprise she was followed by two more people—a young woman and a male who looked somewhere in between the two women, age wise.

"Who are you?"

The first woman turned and smiled. "I'm Janet Johnson, your wedding planner. These two are my assistants, Jacob and Stephanie. And they," she turned dramatically to the living room, "must be Kyle and Kennedy. We have some lovely children's suits and dresses that these two will look adorable in for their parents' wedding."

My stomach plummeted.

"Wedding?"

"Will I get to dress up?" Kennedy asked, eyes wide, jumping up and down.

"You sure will, doll." Janet smiled at a laughing Kennedy.

I turned to Ms. Sheryl who looked to be in shock.

"So, about that custody thing..." I began.

* * *

AARON

"You're getting married?" my brother, Carter, shrieked, causing me to glower deeper than usual. "What unlucky woman agreed to holy matrimony with you?"

Snickers came from my other two nitwit brothers, while my mother and father simply looked on in stunned silence. I'd just announced at the family dinner at Townsend Manor that I was getting married.

"Carter, don't be rude," his wife, Michelle, admonished.

"We're going to a wedding?" my new nephew, Diego, questioned.

"Looks like it, buddy," my youngest brother, Tyler, answered. "So, who's the lucky lady?"

"You mean unlucky," Carter chimed in.

I snarled at my brother across the table. "You talk too damn much."

He grinned. "And obviously you don't talk enough since you're getting married and we didn't even know you were seeing someone seriously."

"What's her name?" Joshua asked, next to me.

I picked up my glass of seltzer water with lime and took a sip before answering.

"Patience Thiers."

I sighed against the audible gasps around the table.

"Thiers' daughter?" my father, at the head of the table, questioned.

I took a sip then took a bite of the lobster tail that'd been served for dinner.

"Care to share how this came about?" Joshua asked.

"No." I took another bite.

"I just visited Thiers in the hospital and he never made mention of this," my father queried.

I said nothing.

There was silence at the table until Carter finally spoke up again. "Patience is the daughter of one of my father's business companions. But she's been out of Williamsport for quite a few years now, last I heard."

I glanced up to see Carter explaining all of this to Michelle.

"How long ago did she move from Williamsport? Five, six years?" Tyler asked.

Sixty-seven months. Exactly five years and seven months.

But I wasn't revealing that.

"Anyone know why she left?"

My stomach muscles tightened.

"She's a librarian, right?"

I looked up, realizing the table was waiting for my response.

"Mother, dinner was delicious."

"Come on, Aaron. Give us something," Tyler insisted.

Just then my phone buzzed. I pulled it out.

"Aaron, you know we do not allow work at the table."

I stood. "My apologies, Mother. I need to take this." I stood and moved from the table, opening the email I'd just received. It was nothing too pressing but I used the excuse to have a moment to myself to regroup. I didn't intend to explain my relationship with

Patience, even to my family but their probing questions were getting to me. After a few minutes, I went back to sit at the table

"When's the big day?" My father lifted a eyebrow at me.

"Two weeks."

I rolled my eyes at the shocked noises that went around the table.

"Two weeks? That isn't a little fast, Aaron?"

I shook my head. "No, Mother."

"Why so abruptly, son?"

I inhaled, bracing myself for the onslaught that was on the way due to what I was about to reveal. "Because I want my children raised in a home with their mother and father."

"Children?" Michelle blurted, then clamped a hand over her mouth.

I looked from her to my mother who'd gasped in surprise as well.

"Twins, a boy and girl. Kyle and Kennedy. They're five. And no," I looked to my three brothers and finally my father, "I will not be going into more detail about it," I stated with finality.

After a moment or two, I watched as Carter picked up his fork and continued eating. Everyone else soon followed, knowing that once I made up my mind about something that was it. If I said I wasn't going to discuss it, then it wasn't up for discussion. End of story.

But in truth, I knew that wasn't the end. It was just the beginning.

CHAPTER 7

Patience

What happened to my simple, quiet life? Three weeks earlier I was living in Oakland in a three-bedroom apartment with my two kids. Now, I was surrounded by a picky wedding planner and her assistants, as they plucked and prodded me, ensuring the long, off-white dress I wore looked perfect.

"Where're the kids? Are they dressed? They need to be at the front with Ms. Sheryl," Janet stated into a walkie-talkie she had. The woman actually carried a walkie-talkie for these events.

"Is all of this really necessary?" I mumbled.

"Of course it is!" Janet insisted. "I'm surprised this wedding isn't more over the top. You're marrying one of the wealthiest men in the country."

I pinched my lips. "Don't remind me."

Janet paused, gaping at me as if I'd lost my mind. I would've told her that, *yes,* I had indeed lost my mind, but I didn't want to hold us up anymore than was necessary. The past two weeks had been a flurry of motion. The same day I agreed to marry Aaron, not only had wedding planners shown up at our hotel to begin organizing the event, movers had shown up that night, insisting on moving our luggage and items into Aaron's home. I was ready to ream Aaron out as soon as we got to the house but he wasn't there. For his part, he'd moved out, insisting that he wouldn't move back in until we were married because he wanted to give the children time to adjust.

The following evening, he showed up, expecting me to introduce him to the children. It was awkward to say the least. I'd had to explain to Kennedy at least twice that no, her daddy wasn't in heaven as she'd previously thought. After a few moments of hesitation, the children were completely taken with Aaron. It didn't surprise me as much as it should've. Despite his less than friendly demeanor, children always seemed to take to him. Children and animals...and me.

"Okay, I think we're ready." Janet clapped with excitement.

I wanted to ask for a drink but bit my tongue. We were marrying in a small ceremony held at Townsend Manor. Save for Aaron's immediate family, Ms. Sheryl, and the children there were no guests. I hadn't even told my father about the wedding. He was home recovering from surgery and I figured I could let him know when everything died down. I knew that was silly, but me and my father's relationship was...strained, to say the least.

"Are you sure you don't want anyone to escort you down the aisle? I can have Jacob do it." Janet asked for a third time.

"That's not necessary. Let's get this over with." I pushed out a breath as we emerged on the back patio. There was a white trail covered in red rose petals that led down a path overlooking the lake out back of Townsend Manor. It wasn't the beach wedding I'd dreamed of in my early twenties, but as far as views went, it could've been a lot worse.

I let my eyes scan the couple of rows of chairs, seeing Aaron's family on the right and only Ms. Sheryl, Kennedy, and Kyle on my side. I looked toward the front and saw a flower arch that'd been created by Janet and her crew. Under it stood the officiant and next to him stood my husband-to-be. My breath caught at the sight of Aaron in an all black tuxedo, tailored to fit his frame perfectly. He'd trimmed his dark hair, and for a second a memory of me running my hand through that silky mane when it was longer, sprang to mind.

I lowered my head, and raised my hand to pat the chignon that my locs had been formed into. The music started.

"That's your cue," Janet said at the same time everyone rose to their feet.

Inhaling, I proceeded down the aisle on shaky legs. I glanced to the left, looking at a smiling Kennedy and Kyle as I put one foot in front of the other until I made it to my destination. Not until I reached him did I look up to see Aaron's stern gaze staring me down. I chose to ignore the butterflies in my stomach. Too many emotions whirling around to pick just one.

"Please be seated," the officiant began.

I heard the rustling in the background as the guests took their seats.

"We are gathered here today to join this man and this woman in holy matrimony."

My grip tightened around the stem of the bouquet of white lilies I held.

"Has the couple written their own vows they'd like to say to each other."

"No," Aaron impatiently answered, looking toward the man.

My eyelids drooped and I stared off into the distance for a moment before giving the preacher an apologetic smile.

He cleared his throat. "That's fine. I am a fan of tradition myself," he tried to joke but Aaron's placid expression held. He continued on, reciting lines I'd heard numerous times in movies, television shows, and even in real life at the handful of weddings I'd attended. But they rang hollow at my own wedding.

"Aaron Richard Townsend, do you take this woman, Patience Marie Thiers, to be your lawfully wedded wife? Forsaking all others?"

I could barely look at Aaron as he held my hand, moving the white gold wedding band down the ring finger of my left hand.

"I do."

I fiddled with his matching but larger wedding band in my hand.

"And Patience Marie Thiers, do you take Aaron Richard Townsend to be your lawfully wedded husband, forsaking all others?"

A chill ran through my entire body. I glanced up at Aaron who was frowning, waiting impatiently for my response. I turned my head, peering toward my children who were on the edge of their seats, smiling. Kennedy had told me over and over how much I looked like a princess in my dress. I turned back to Aaron and watched a flicker of emotion appear in those hazel eyes but half a second later it was gone.

"I-I do," I finally answered. I slid the ring down his ring finger and went to pull my hand back but found it locked in his grip. Our eyes connected again and I couldn't turn away.

"You may now kiss your bride."

I'd forgotten about the kiss. It was expected of a new husband and wife. I froze but my new husband didn't. He caught my chin in between his thumb and forefinger, lifting my face, and just before he pressed his lips to mine, he paused. An expression of possession mixed with anger and…something else was in that look. Next thing I remember was the feel of his soft lips on mine. Such a contrast to his demeanor. I didn't want to like this kiss, but my body wasn't my own when it came to Aaron Townsend.

"Congratulations, Mrs. Townsend," he stated as he pulled back. He didn't wait for my reply before taking me by the hand and turning us toward our clapping guests, mainly his family.

As we moved down the aisle with my hand in his, I wondered what the hell I'd just gotten myself into.

* * *

"Ouch!" I tripped due to my stubbed toe. "You still can't dance worth a damn," I mumbled. It was our first dance as husband and wife and he'd just stepped on my foot for the second time.

"My talents lie elsewhere. You should know that more than anyone," he retorted.

I stiffened my body against the shiver that attempted to move through me, refusing to remember exactly how talented he was off the dance floor.

"Whatever," I grumbled. I peered over Aaron's shoulder to see

Kennedy and Kyle running around a table with their new cousin, Diego.

"You didn't invite your father."

I pulled back slightly to stare up at Aaron. "You didn't invite him either."

"He's not my father."

I shrugged. "You're closer to him than I am." I peeled my gaze away from his again, glancing around at the scenery. This wasn't my first time at Townsend Manor, but it'd been years since I'd been there as a teenager.

"I want more children."

My dancing steps faltered, this time not because of Aaron's lack of dance skills. I stared at him, trying to figure out if he'd said what I thought he'd just stated.

"Three more, to be exact."

"And you expect *me* to provide you with these children."

His lips pinched. "You *are* my wife."

I didn't respond.

"You can have more children, correct?"

I swallowed. "What?"

"Medically? There's nothing preventing you from having more children, is there?"

"N-no."

"Then it's settled. Of course, adoption is always an option as well."

I wrinkled my forehead. "It's not sett–" My words were cut off by sudden loud tapping sounds. I looked around to see Aaron's parents and brothers tapping their champagne flutes with their knives.

"They expect us to kiss."

I frowned. "I know what that means."

I tried to pull my head back but he caught my chin again between his two fingers. My breathing hitched as he lowered his face closer to mine.

"It'd serve you well to remember I *always* get what I want."

This time I couldn't prevent the shiver that moved through my body at the same time our lips connected with his insistent and assessing kiss. His grip tightened around my waist for a half of second but an instant later he loosened it and took a step back.

"Pardon me, dear. Do you mind?"

I turned to see a smiling Deborah Townsend staring at me, questioning. She looked gorgeous with her sparkling blue eyes, dark hair that was pulled off of her lightly made up face, in her long off-the-shoulder powder blue gown.

"How about I take this handful of a man off your hands just for a little while?"

I looked between Aaron and his mother, realizing it was time for the groom's dance with his mother.

"Please." I nodded just before pivoting to leave the dance floor. I felt Aaron's eyes on my back the entire time.

I went straight to the bride and groom's table, picking up a glass of champagne that had been left for us. I thought about swiping the glass that had been left for Aaron knowing that he wasn't going to touch it but I nixed that idea. I went to look for Kyle and Kennedy, but stopped when I saw them running around Aaron and his mother as they danced. A second later they were taken by the hand by Joshua and Tyler and began playing. A tug in my heart started.

"It's strange, right?"

I turned, a little startled. I squinted at the woman who'd come up on my side without my noticing.

"Michelle, right?"

She nodded, smiling, her caramel skin shining due to the light makeup she wore. She was Carter's, Aaron's older brother, wife.

"What's strange?" I questioned.

"That." She nodded in the direction of Kyle, Kennedy, and now Diego playing with Aaron's three brothers and his father. 'I was a single parent for six years before Carter. You get used to them being totally dependent on you. Then once you get married, they've suddenly got this big family they can rely on."

I glanced over at the children and then back at Michelle, giving her a half smile. She was right.

"You'd think I was happy about it, right?"

She laughed. "Being a single parent is hard work. It's tough. But they're your babies so you don't question it. Then overnight you become a family and suddenly they're not as reliant on you. It's an adjustment, but you get used to it."

I nodded.

"I just wanted to give my congratulations." She looked out at Aaron and his mother who were finishing their dance.

"Thanks," I murmured.

"I, uh…" She paused. "Well, you've certainly…um, Aaron seems like quite a catch."

I gave her a genuine grin. "No, he doesn't. He's scary as hell."

Michelle's eyes bulged and she gaped at me, startled.

I giggled. "It's okay. I said it so you wouldn't have to."

Her shoulders slumped as she blew out a breath, relieved. "I don't know him that well."

I nodded. "Not many people do." For a short period in time, I thought I was one of the lucky ones who had gotten to know him—the *real* Aaron Townsend—but I was wrong.

Michelle asked me about the children's schooling and we moved from the topic of my husband to safer territory. I was grateful to talk about something other than my new marriage, especially since I was still trying to wrap my own head around it all.

* * *

*A*ARON

"She looks beautiful."

Warm jealousy rose in the pit of my stomach at my brother's words. I turned to face Joshua, whose eyes were still trained on Patience and Michelle as they talked near the bride and groom's table at the head of the dance floor.

"Take your eyes off my wife."

Joshua turned his hazel-green eyes from the women to me, a serious look filling his gaze. "You sure you know what you're doing?"

I squinted.

Josh shrugged. "Far be it from me to question your private life–"

"Then why are you?"

"I'm just concerned. You two seemed…distant. Far from a loving, newlywed couple. You opted not to have a prenup involved. And with the children–"

"What about my children?" My face tightened.

Joshua raised an eyebrow. "Have you actually had a DNA test done? How do–"

"Joshua, if you value your life, you will not finish that sentence."

Joshua tilted his head, giving me a look. "You're Aaron Townsend, CEO of Townsend Industries, and you've opted to marry a woman without a prenuptial agreement, no DNA tests to without a doubt determine the children are yours–"

"He looks just like me!" I roared, causing a few of our family members to look over at us.

Joshua nodded, unperturbed by my outburst. "That he does, which is why I'm sure they are yours. Plus, Patience doesn't seem like the type to lie about something like that. I'm just pointing out that you are behaving uncharacteristically. My usually precise, micromanaging brother who plans everything down to the last detail seems to be…off."

"I know what I'm doing."

Joshua stared at me for a long time before giving me a curt nod. "Be sure that you do."

I watched as he turned and walked away. I was about to head back to the table when Kennedy came running over to me. She barely reached my knees but something moved deep inside of my chest when her honey-toned cheeks bunched up as she smiled, staring up at me.

"Daddy, will you dance with me?"

My knees almost buckled.

Daddy.

I felt my face soften. Only one other woman has had the ability to cause this much emotion in me. I glanced up, my eyes locking with my daughter's mother. That tug began happening again.

"Absolutely," I told Kennedy, turning my attention back to her. I lifted her so her feet were on top of mine. I didn't want to squash her feet the same way I'd done her mother's earlier while we danced. I knew my limitations. My heart rate quickened as Kennedy giggled when I spun her around.

"I see the fairies," she whispered as we danced.

I lifted an eyebrow. "Fairies?"

She nodded. "They're all around you."

I swallowed and spun her again, not wanting to delve into that conversation. Children and animals. They were always a nuisance to me, hanging around me, though I did my best to avoid them. But I couldn't avoid these children. They were mine. Mine and…I glanced up to see Patience, this time she was on the dance floor with Kyle. Mine and my wife's.

CHAPTER 8

Aaron

"Are you going to say good-bye to your family?"

I paused, turning to a frowning Patience. I hoisted a sleeping Kennedy a little higher up on my shoulder. Patience was holding Kyle in the same position, because he'd fallen asleep as well. It was close to ten at night and we were readying to leave Townsend Manor to head to our home for the night.

"No," I answered curtly.

Patience rolled her eyes, pushing out a heavy breath. "No manners."

I watched as she turned her back on me and moved farther from the door.

"Um," she began, getting everyone's attention. "I'd like to thank you for attending today. I'm sure all of…this," she gestured to herself in the wedding gown and the children, "came as a bit of a surprise to you all." She glanced back at me before returning her attention to the family. "I also wanted to thank you for welcoming Kyle and Kennedy into your fold. They're, um, lucky and blessed to have you as their family. Enjoy the rest of your evening." With that, she turned and didn't bother giving me a second glance as she passed through the glass doors into the house toward the front entrance, leaving me to follow.

I looked back at my family, most of whom were smirking at me. Frowning, I turned to follow Patience to the awaiting car.

The fifteen minute car ride from Townsend Manor to our home in Cedarwoods—just outside of the city of Williamsport—was quiet, save for the light snoring of the children.

"I'll put them to bed," Patience insisted, attempting to take Kennedy from my arms once the short ride was over.

"You can't carry both of them."

She looked at me sharply. "I've been doing it for the last five years."

"And now you're not," I explained just as sharply.

She glared at me before turning and going up the stairs to the children's room. The home I'd had built almost a year ago was close to eight thousand square feet with five bedrooms, four full bathrooms and two half baths, plus additional spaces for a TV room or den, three car garage, and office space. The master bedroom, as well as the children's separate rooms, were located on the second floor. The same day I found out about Kyle and Kennedy I had interior decorators over here, fixing up their bedrooms.

I passed by Patience as she took Kyle into his room, while I carried Kennedy to her room. I laid her on the Barbie bed the interior designer insisted every little girl would love, and then rifled through one of the dressers until I found a nightgown to put her in. I marveled at the way Kennedy barely stirred as I changed her clothing. Once I tucked her in, she rolled over and her snores grew in volume. I stood and was at the door, shutting out the light, when she turned over and kicked one leg out from underneath the blanket, but remained contently asleep.

"She sleeps like her mother," I commented under my breath before turning the light out. I moved farther down the carpeted hall to the master bedroom and began removing my tuxedo jacket. I tossed it on the edge of the huge sleigh bed that had obviously been remade this morning, before retrieving a few items of clothing from one of the grey-stained wooden dressers. I glanced over my shoulder as Patience entered the room, pausing as if she wasn't expecting me to be there. I stared as she moved to the far side of the room, going into her walk-in closet. I didn't wait for her to emerge. Instead, I moved into the attached bathroom, taking a shower and then changing into a pair of plaid pajama bottom pants and a white T-shirt.

When I emerged from the bathroom, Patience was propped up in the bed, her back against the headboard. I let my eyes skim over the smooth, walnut brown skin of her bared shoulders. She wore a sleeveless silk top and matching shorts, which I saw peeking out from underneath the blanket she had tucked up to her waist. She didn't even look up at me from her Kindle. A stirring in my groin began and I knew I needed to leave.

After gathering my cell phone and tablet that I placed on my dresser, I headed to the door.

"I'll be downstairs if you need anything." I didn't need to say it but it'd come out. Hearing her rustle in the bed, I turned to look over my shoulder.

She gave me a perplexing look. "Y-you're not sleeping in here?"

"No." I went to turn the doorknob.

"Why not?" Confusion laced her voice.

"Did you want me to?" I gave her a stern look.

She shook her head. "No."

"Well then."

"You can't blame me," she defended. "You didn't want my children five years ago, and now you force me to decide between marrying you or losing custody of th–" Her statement was cut off by my slamming of the door.

"I never denied my children."

A wrinkle appeared between her wide eyes. "Yes, you did. I–"

"I never knew you were pregnant." My voice sliced through her argument.

Her face crumpled. "What?"

"She lied. I never knew," I insisted.

"Then how... She said–"

"She was a fucking liar. And you believed her." My voice was low, full of the betrayal I felt.

"*I* believed her? Of course I believed her. I wouldn't have known *she* even existed if it weren't for her."

My jaw tightened and I gritted my teeth.

"It wasn't like you told me you had a fiancée. Not until she showed up–" She cut herself off, turning her head away from me.

I directed my gaze down at the floor, my hand still resting on the doorknob. "I never would've denied my children. Ever. And the fact that you believed I would says everything I need to know about what you thought of me." My voice dripped in an icy coldness that chilled the entire room. I gave Patience one last look. The frozen block in the center of my chest lurched against my ribcage at the expression of hurt that passed over her face. I turned, opening the door and shutting it behind me, moving down the hall to the stairs to get to the den that I used as a home office.

* * *

By the time I reached the den, my chest was heaving with anger, resentment, and a deep sadness I hadn't allowed myself to feel in nearly six years. I flicked on the light and went to my large desk, plopping down in the leather chair. My gaze was pulled to the large sofa that was long enough for me to sleep on. I knew because I'd spent plenty of nights sleeping in this very room, even before Patience and the children moved in. Rising, I walked over to the opposite side of the room to the small refrigerator I kept in here, pulling out a bottle of water. I went to the window, opening the bottle and staring at the night sky.

"I told you she would be your wife someday."

My lips pursed, the bottle stopped just inches from my lips. I remained silent and continued drinking, choosing to ignore the female voice in the background.

"You're going to sleep down here while your wife and children are two floors up?"

I grunted, still gazing out the window. "You're not real."

The voice sighed. "You've been trying to play that game since you were eight years old. I'm very real and you know it."

"Ghosts aren't real," I persisted.

"We've been through this. I'm not a ghost. I'm a spirit."

I angrily turned from the window, to see the woman standing in the middle of my office. She wore a long white nightgown, same as always. Her dark brown hair hung around her shoulders.

"You're not real," I stated it again, more trying to convince myself.

"We both know the truth, Aaron. And despite what your real daddy tried to drill into that thick head of yours, you know I'm real."

"Stop it!"

"You know it. The children around you see it. You have a gift and you choose to ignore it, making your life more difficult."

I gave the woman, Emma, a deadpan expression. "My life would be a hell of a lot more difficult if I went around declaring to the world that I saw ghosts or spirits, whatever the fuck the difference is."

"You don't see spirits. You just see me. Your *real* gift is in your keen intuition. The insight you've been blessed with that no one else can see. It's what makes you so great at your job. It's a gift passed down from generation to generation on your mother's side of the family."

I snorted. "My mother, right."

"It's true. You have greatness on both sides of your family. The Townsends and your mother. There were a number of important businessmen, entrepreneurs, and politicians. It's why your father chose her to marry."

I gave her an incredulous look. "If she was so blessed with such keen insight, why the hell would she choose to marry *him* of all people?"

"She failed to listen to caution. Much like her son."

I peered at Emma through narrowed eyes.

She shrugged. "It's your distrust of others that gets in your way."

I rolled my eyes, grunting. "Great. I get the *spirit* that loves to psychoanalyze me."

She had the audacity to laugh. "I'm only calling it like I see it. Just like I told you nearly six years ago that Patience Thiers was going to be your wife. And now look where we are."

I flexed my jaw again, remaining silent, but turning once more to stare out of the window, remembering that time six years ago, when Emma had indeed informed me that Patience was my destiny.

* * *

THEN ...

"You're dining with Thiers tonight?"

"Yes, Father," I responded into my cell, as I exited the door the driver held open.

"At his home?"

I glanced up. "No, at *Buona Sera*."

"Okay, don't forget to remind him of the agreement. You know our stock prices have dropped…"

I sighed. As if I would've forgotten such a thing. Thiers wasn't even a big time power dealer in the world of energy, but he was a close family friend…well, as close as business associates could get. My father and Thiers went back years to their childhood, having grown up on different sides of the tracks but attending the same school.

"You need to be on top of things while I'm in Japan," my father continued.

"You think I don't take my position at Townsend seriously?"

My father grumbled, "I did not say that, Aaron. I know more than anyone how hard you work. You want the CEO position, and as far as I'm concerned, once I retire, it's yours. But I'm not the only one who has a say on the matter."

"I understand."

"I know you do. Go have dinner with Thiers. Give him my apologies for missing this outing and get back to work tomorrow morning."

"Will do." Hanging up the phone with my father, I entered the restaurant door that was held open by the door attendant.

"Welcome, sir. Your name?" the hostess asked.

"Reservation is under Thiers, first name, Gary."

She smiled, beckoning me to follow. "Right this way."

I did so, scanning the dining space as we moved through it. I caught Thiers' eye a moment before the hostess stopped at the table that sat next to one of the restaurants' windows.

"Aaron." He stood, extending his arms for an embrace.

I frowned.

"I forgot," he chuckled, then reached out for a handshake.

I obliged. My father was more of the hugger, at least with Thiers he was.

"How're you doing these days?"

"I'm well."

"I bet you are. Next in line to be CEO of Townsend and not even thirty years old."

"I'll be thirty in a few months," I reminded.

"Nonetheless, you're on track to surpass even your father's expectations, I'm sure."

I nodded. "And yourself? How are you?" Unfolding the cloth napkin in my lap, I leaned back against the wooden chair, awaiting his reply.

"I'm very well." He smiled. "Ju-Oh, Patience."

I looked over my shoulder to see the same hostess approaching our table, this time a woman behind her. I squinted, noting the walnut skin, and sepia, wide-set eyes. I let my eyes trail down her frame which couldn't be more than five-foot-four. She wasn't overweight but her body was incredibly curvy. Our eyes locked as soon as she arrived at the table. Hers widened in surprise and the muscles in my stomach clenched.

"Patience," Thiers stated.

She pulled her gaze from me. "Dad." She smiled and moved to place a kiss on his cheek.

"Patience, you remember, Aaron, Robert Townsend's son."

She turned to me again, nodded. "Hello."

I had an urge to crowd her space, to pull her close to me, but I clamped down on that compulsion, instead, taking her proffered hand into mine. Something sharp moved through me at the contact. I stared at our joined hands for a moment, trying to figure something out before she pulled hers away. She moved around the table and for a second I let my eyes drop to watch the sway of her hips as she walked.

"I hope I'm not late," Patience stated, sitting next to her father.

"Not at all. I was just preparing to get Aaron up to speed on what I've been up to since I got back into town two weeks ago."

Out of the corner of my eye, I saw Patience's body stiffen. I turned to see her doe eyes wide, lips turned downward.

"Two weeks ago?"

"Yes," Thiers responded. "You knew I was out of town on business."

"Yes, I thought you returned today. You've been back in town two weeks?"

I heard something in her voice that made me want to comfort her, which was completely opposed to my normal interactions with women, or most people for that matter. I turned accusing eyes on Thiers.

"Yes, well, I had business matters to tend to. You're a busy graduate student. I figured you wouldn't want to be bothered by your old man." He waved off her obvious disappointment as if it were no big deal.

I glanced at Patience who lowered her eyes before reaching for the glass of water in front of her and taking a sip. No more questions came from her regarding her father's whereabouts.

"Aaron, tell me about the Collins' deal you and your father are working on," Thiers continued.

I gave Patience one last look and then turned my attention on her father, answering his question about Townsend's newest venture. We talked for a few more minutes before our waitress arrived, taking our orders. Thiers then talked a little about his business that had taken him to Canada. The entire time I kept an eye on Patience who silently listened, as if she'd had years of experience being in the room being neglected.

Once our food arrived, the conversation shifted a bit, but that was because Thiers received a call. I looked again to Patience whose eyes skirted away from me.

"You're in graduate school?"

She nodded. "Yes."

"For what?"

She cleared her throat, sitting up a taller.

I bit the inside of my bottom lip at the way her movement made her breasts stand out against the blue V-neck she wore.

"Library sciences." Her voice was soft, yet strong and steady. Welcoming.

"A librarian."

She gave me a half-smile and again something in my chest shifted.

"Sorry about that. That was my Canadian contact," Thiers informed, picking up the conversation where we'd left off, once again leaving his daughter out of it.

Upon finishing our meals, Patience stood. "I need to go to the restroom."

"Okay." Her father nodded.

I watched her as she walked away, willing myself not to completely turn my back on Thiers just to watch the effort of the jeans she wore to contain all those curves.

"Tell Robert he owes me a round of golf for skipping out on our monthly dinner."

I nodded, standing along with Thiers. "He sends his apologies for missing it." I glanced down at my watch.

"You know what? I hate to eat and run but I just remembered I had a late evening appointment."

I picked my head up, a wrinkle in my forehead due to his abruptness.

"Do me a favor," he began, tossing a few bills on the table, "tell Patience I will give her a call in the next day or two."

I leaned back, surprised, but Thiers came over, tapped me on the shoulder as a way of saying good-bye, and was headed toward the door in less than a few seconds. I glowered at the back of his head as he crossed the street, wondering why he couldn't even say good-bye to his only child.

Instead of dwelling on Thiers, I headed in the direction of the restroom, not totally understanding why I felt the need to be there when Patience emerged.

*　*　*

PATIENCE

I exited the bathroom and got the surprise of my life to see a scowling Aaron standing there. I glanced over my shoulder just to make sure I hadn't accidently entered the men's room instead of the women's bathroom. Nope. That wasn't the case.

"E-excuse me." I went to step around him but he didn't budge in the tiny hallway space.

"Your father left," he said.

I paused, easing back to stare up at his face. I tilted my head to the side. "He left and is coming right back or left for the night?"

"He's not coming back."

I swallowed down the sadness that overcame me. I barely had a chance to even speak with my father. I had thought this was a dinner just between us. Instead it was a business dinner where I find out he'd been in town for two weeks and hadn't bothered to call or stop by my place. Now, he'd run out while I was in the restroom without so much as a good-bye. Whatever. That was my father's style when it came to his relationship with me. No use dwelling on it.

I stood, squaring my shoulders, and figured I had other things to do anyway. I looked up into Aaron's hazel eyes, a heated feeling overcoming me as I realized he'd been silently watching me. "Thank you for sticking around to tell me he'd left. Um, enjoy your evening."

Again, I went to step around Aaron and again he didn't move. In fact, he seemed to have moved closer, as there was barely more than a few inches separating our bodies. I felt my body growing warm all over.

"Did you drive here?"

I shook my head. "I took the subway."

"I will give you a ride home."

I swallowed. "That won't be necessary. I wasn't going home."

"I will give you a ride wherever you were going."

Somehow I knew he wasn't asking, nor was it negotiable. Wherever I was going, Aaron Townsend was giving me a ride.

He stepped to the side, allowing me to pass. Once I did, he followed closely, placing his hand on my lower back and holding the door to the restaurant open for me to pass through.

I turned to him once we were out on the sidewalk. "I understand if you have somewhere else you need to be. I wasn't going directly home."

He stared down at me, not saying anything. The look he gave me should've intimidated the hell out of me. And on some level, it did, but something inside of me also wanted to reach up and pull his face to mine. And that scared me more than anything. Even at twenty-three, I hadn't had a lot of experience with the opposite sex, but I knew men like Aaron Townsend were one of a kind. And dangerous.

"Where are you headed?"

"Right down the street," I answered, nodding in the direction of where I was headed.

"I'll walk you." He turned and made a motion with his head. Out of nowhere, two burly men stepped forward.

I gave Aaron a confused look.

"My security. They will follow us," he responded to my silent question as if it was no big deal.

"You travel everywhere with security?" I had to ask.

"Just about." He was short on words, but strangely I didn't mind that at all.

I felt his firm hand at my lower back and a shiver ran through my body. I silently prayed he hadn't felt it.

The walk was mostly silent, but it was short—only about a block down from the restaurant.

"A bookstore," he commented.

"Not just any bookstore. They sell vintage books," I defended.

He snorted but used his free hand to pull the door open, his other hand still at my back.

Entering the bookstore, I inhaled the scent of old and used books, loving it. "Hi, Sam," I greeted the clerk who seemed to always be here at the store.

He lifted his head, his wire-framed glasses sliding down the bridge of his nose as he did. A smile blossomed on his handsome face, but it quickly disappeared when his eyes moved from me to the man standing closely behind me.

For some odd reason, I felt the need to make introductions. "Sam this is, uh, Aaron Townsend. He's a friend of my father's."

Sam's pale face seemed to grow even paler, his lips clamping together before parting. "Aaron, nice to–"

"Mr. Townsend," Aaron corrected.

I looked back at Aaron who was staring at Sam, relaying something silently with his eyes. I had no idea what was going on. I turned back to Sam, whose eyes had narrowed, but he quickly looked away from Aaron.

"Sam, did you get the books in?" I asked.

He nodded and went to move from behind the counter but stopped when he took a quick glance behind me. "They're on the shelf in the back row. You know where we keep them."

I wrinkled my forehead but nodded and proceeded down the two stairs to enter the main part of the store. Aaron followed me all the way to the back of the bookstore. I smiled widely when I saw the newly stocked books on the shelf. Stooping low, I took out a copy of Toni Morrison's *The Bluest Eye*, followed by *Home*. I stood with the books in my hand, and that giddy feeling I always felt when I wrapped my fingers around new books overcame me.

"They just got these in," I stated, smiling, my eyes still trained on the books. "This one was published this year." I held up the copy of *Home*. "I've read this one but this is a vintage copy. One of the first published. I've been waiting weeks for the bookstore to get it in." I went on to talk more about the books, but paused when I saw Aaron simply staring at me, his usual scowl set in place. "I'm sure you have better things to do than to watch a librarian geek out over books."

He lowered his chin, eyes boring into mine. "I'll let you know when I have other matters to tend to."

I swallowed, feeling uneasy and oddly comforted under his penetrating gaze. How was that even possible?

I turned back to the bookshelf, realizing Aaron wasn't going anywhere unless he wanted to, and for now, he didn't. I didn't want him to leave either, but I'd never say as much out loud. Browsing some more, I picked up two more books I hadn't intended to get right then but just couldn't turn away. I headed to the register, placing the books down on the counter. Sam gave me the same smile he always gave whenever I was in the store, until, again, he ventured to look behind me.

"That'll be two-hundred–" Sam was cut off when Aaron thrust a credit card in his face.

I turned. "You don–" My refusal stopped short on my lips when Aaron turned stern eyes on me, telling me without words that his paying wasn't up for debate.

Sam silently took the card and rang up my items.

With Aaron's hand again at the small of my back, we exited the bookstore.

"Do you like ice cream?" I questioned without thinking.

Aaron lifted an eyebrow and I dipped my head on a smile. He looked perplexed, as if he was trying to figure out what he was still doing with me.

"There's a shop right across the street. I was going to stop by to get my favorite praline ice cream before heading home for the night."

He turned his head in the direction of the ice cream shop I'd just gestured toward and then nodded.

I took that as a yes, especially when he placed his hand at my back again, urging me forward. We got our ice cream—my vanilla and praline while he ordered regular chocolate—before he offered me a ride home. After telling him that I opted to walk, he took that as an opportunity to walk me all the way back to my third floor walk-up apartment.

"Your father allows you to live here?" he questioned once we reached my door.

I squinted. "He doesn't allow anything. I'm twenty-three. He doesn't really have a say in the matter."

That frown deepened.

I angled my head. "The neighborhood isn't that bad."

He didn't respond but the expression on his face revealed he didn't think too highly of my neighborhood.

I went to thank him for purchasing my books and walking me back home, but what came out instead was, "Would you like to come in?" I had no idea where that came from. A part of me wanted to get away from this man as fast as I could. He both intrigued and intimidated me.

He stared down at me for a few heartbeats. His face remained set but I could feel an internal debate happening. "You live alone?"

Fidgeting with the bags in my hands, I nodded.

He gestured toward the door with his head and I moved to unlock it. He followed me inside, after saying something briefly to his guards who'd followed us up the stairs, then shut the door, locking us in.

CHAPTER 9

Patience

I awoke the morning after our wedding feeling groggy. Probably due to the three glasses of champagne I'd had. I also blamed the champagne on my dreaming about the first night Aaron and I had ever spent together. That night after he walked me to the bookstore and then back home was the beginning of all of this. We talked...rather, *I* talked while Aaron listened about the books I'd bought, along with other authors I adored. How he didn't get bored I'll never understand, but he listened intently, all while scowling. By the second hour I came to realize that scowl was his natural face, save for certain moments. Like, when at close to one in the morning, he fell asleep on my couch. Just before I fell asleep against his chest, I noticed the softening of his eyebrows and lips. He truly was beautiful.

"Long time ago," I reminded myself as I pushed the blanket off of me and got out of bed. I stood, stretching, and went to pick out a pair of yoga pants and a T-shirt to do a few minutes of early morning yoga before the kids woke up. After about thirty minutes on my mat, which I'd brought with me when we moved into the house, I pulled out a sundress to wear for the day. It was moving toward the middle of summer in Williamsport and that meant sunny skies and possible humidity.

I showered, moisturized, and styled my hair in a french braid, then proceeded to get dressed. On the way out, I stopped by the children's bedrooms, unsurprised to see Kyle's bed empty. I knew he'd likely already gone downstairs. I went to Kennedy's room to rouse her out of her sleep, which could be an ordeal.

"Wake up, baby," I cooed, tickling her under her chin. It took a little while, but eventually Kennedy began giggling. "Let's go, time for breakfast. Your brother's probably eaten all the waffles by now," I teased, especially since I hadn't even made anything yet.

I led a still groggy Kennedy down the stairs by the hand, and made a right behind the stairs toward the kitchen. My nose was immediately hit by the aroma of something delicious. I stopped abruptly when I was confronted with a wide, sculpted bare back at the kitchen counter. My heartbeat quickened and I swallowed.

"Mommy, I have to go potty," Kennedy whined, peeling my attention from her father.

"Go ahead. You know where it is," I told her, pushing her toward the half-bathroom that was just off the kitchen. "And don't forget to wash your hands!" I called.

That grabbed Aaron's attention who glanced over his shoulder at me. We stared at one another for a long moment, but Kyle burst into the kitchen, breaking the hold his gaze had over me.

"I'm hungry!" he called before passing between us and making his way to the dining room table just beyond the kitchen. "Mommy, Daddy made pancakes!" Kyle informed me.

I'd already surmised as much.

Aaron remained speechless as he carried two plates over to the dining table, setting one down in front of Kyle before taking a seat at the head of the table.

"Kennedy's and your plates are on the counter. We didn't know when you'd awake."

Glancing at the counter, I saw two covered plates, and stood there, dumbfounded. I didn't know what to say while Aaron sat at the head of the table staring me down, and our son ate his pancakes as if this was an everyday occurrence for him.

"What's that?" Kyle's question broke our stare down.

I glanced down to see Kyle was staring at Aaron's bare chest. I followed his gaze and saw it, too. The scars that lined his broad chest and upper torso. My eyes also flickered over the tattoo that had me perplexed since the first time I saw it. I pushed that image out of my head—the memory of him that night at The Cage. I looked over to Aaron to see his eyes locked on me and I realized he was remembering that night, too. My pussy muscles began to vibrate and I had to shake myself loose of his hold. I turned my eyes over to Kyle who was still staring at the scars on Aaron's chest.

"Kyle, don't be rude. We don't ask people questions like that," I admonished.

Kyle frowned my way.

"My *son*," Aaron's booming voice disrupted the ensuing silence, "can ask me anything he wants."

Our eyes latched onto one another's again. Aaron effectively stared me down. My eyes narrowed, but I remained silent as he began to explain to Kyle.

"I was in a very bad accident as a child. These scars are a result of it."

I shoved the memory of him explaining his accident to me to the back of my mind. It was much more than that, but he's minimized the explanation for our five-year-old son.

"Oh, and what's that?" Kyle inquired some more, this time pointing to the tattoo.

I bit my tongue.

Aaron ran a hand over the tattoo resting just over his heart. "This I'll explain another time," he stated, his eyes flicking over to me before moving back to Kyle.

"All done!" Kennedy came out of the bathroom running.

I went over to the counter to retrieve her breakfast and my stomach tightened upon seeing the chocolate chip pancakes he'd made. Inhaling a deep breath, I swallowed down the memories threatening to flood my brain. I carried the plate and placed it in front of Kennedy.

"You aren't eating?"

I turned to Aaron. "No appetite. Kyle and Kennedy, when you're finished with your plates, place them in the sink and then come upstairs to get dressed."

I didn't give the dining area a second glance as I hustled out of there and back up the stairs. I figured I could spend the day getting in contact with a number of contacts in Oakland to finish closing accounts I had there. Aaron didn't leave me much time to settle my business in Oakland between moving here and planning for the wedding. I wrote out a few numbers I needed to call in my planner, and a few minutes later the door to our bedroom opened.

Aaron barged in, going over to his walk-in closet and pulling out a suit, and then laying out a watch and cufflinks. I watched him silently for a moment before I realized what he was doing.

"You're going into the office today?"

He paused at the dresser before looking over at me, perplexed. "Why wouldn't I?"

Reminding him that we just got married the day before seemed foolish but it was my only reasoning.

"I told my employees I'd be in a little late today. You and the children have a busy day. My assistant has made an appointment at Excelor for their registration. You will need to contact their former school to have their records sent over. There is also a camp that I've signed them up for that begins next week, and continues for the next three weeks. After that, they will have a week off before school begins."

My mouth fell open. "You've already signed them up at Excelor? Without consulting me about it?"

A dark eyebrow lifted. "Excelor is a great school. I attended, as did you."

"I know what school I went to."

"Then what is the problem?" he asked, agitated.

"The problem is you took it upon yourself to do all of this without asking me."

"I was supposed to *ask* you?"

I rolled my eyes up to the ceiling. "I *am* their mother. You don't think it makes sense to at least have a conversation with me on where they'll go to school, or what camp they'll attend?"

"I am their father."

I blew out a breath. "We've established that."

"A father who's lost five years of their life already," he stated accusingly.

"A choice I thought *you* made," I explained, defending myself.

"A choice you should've *known* I'd never make!" he seethed.

My instinct was to shrink back in the face of his anger, but I refused. I was not in the wrong in this. If he'd have never lied, we wouldn't have been in this mess.

"Jackass," I uttered, because I couldn't think of anything else to retort.

"I've been called worse."

"I bet you have," I mumbled, and then climbed off the bed to head into the bathroom.

Just before I stepped over the threshold of the bathroom, he asked, "I assume you'll be taking the children to visit your father at some point today or tomorrow."

I froze.

"They were not allowed into his hospital room while he was recuperating and the children have not spoken of visiting him."

I glanced back at Aaron, who was now staring at his wrist while he fiddled with the cufflink he was fixing. I hadn't even realized he was getting dressed, having done my best not to glance in his direction.

"He doesn't know about them," I stated just above a whisper, but Aaron heard me loud and clear.

All movement of his halted. His stormy eyes moved over to me.

"Thiers does not know about his grandchildren?"

"No." I looked around the room, avoiding the scrutiny of his gaze.

"Why not?" His voice was low.

"I have my reasons."

"That is not an answer."

"It's the only one I've got."

"You've not only kept my children from me and my family, but from Thiers as well."

I thrust my hands on my hip. "Goddammit, I did not keep your children away from you," I hissed in anger. "And my relationship with my father is none of your damn business."

He angled his head, eyes narrowing. "Sweetness, I've already told you, *everything* you do is my business. Especially now. Don't forget it."

I shook off the shiver that ran through me at the term of endearment. I particularly hated the way it alone made my lower lips flutter.

"You will tell him. Today."

I eyed him harshly. "Are you ordering me?"

"Yes."

"I don't take orders."

He moved around the bed to stand in front of me so quickly, I barely registered his movements until one of his firm hands rested against my waist while the other gripped my chin. He tilted my head to look up at him. His warm breath caressed my face and my body felt like someone just flicked on a light switch.

"You of all people know I don't repeat myself." He released me, taking a step backwards before turning to grab his wallet and cell phone and then moved to the door.

"I didn't want him to treat them the same way he treated me," I stated.

Aaron's hand paused on the doorknob, just barely opening it. His back remained to me but he stilled, listening.

"I never wanted them to know what it was like to be treated as if they were an option in someone's life, instead of a necessity. From the day they were born, I promised them they would be surrounded by people who loved them unconditionally and would move Heaven and Earth to be there for them. *That's* why I never told him about them or them about him. I wanted to spare them what I felt growing up," I confessed, blinking away the tears that had gathered in my eyes. I wanted to continue telling him that it was also why I never pursued his involvement with the twins after his fiancée told me he wanted nothing to do with me or my children.

I heard the door close. Aaron turned toward me, his lips set in a firm line. He stared for a few moments, letting the silence engulf us both.

"You will tell him. Today." And with that, he turned and left the room, slamming the door behind him.

Pushing out a breath, I let my shoulders sag. I could feel the little bit of control I thought I had over my own life slipping away from me.

CHAPTER 10

Patience

"I-I can't believe it," my father stated yet again.

We'd been at his home, the home I'd grown up in, for the last thirty minutes, and he was still in shock. I couldn't look him in his eyes as he kept staring at Kyle and Kennedy.

"She looks just like you...and your mama." His voice was solemn on the last half of his statement. "And Kyle, he's the spitting image of Aaron. I never knew...you two were..." He trailed off, waiting for me to explain.

"It's a long story," I informed. "We can discuss it later. But Aaron figured it was time you get to know your grandchildren." I flinched after clamping my mouth shut. I had meant to say that I thought it was time but the actual truth spilled from my lips instead. If it weren't for Aaron's insistence, I probably wouldn't have brought Kyle and Kennedy over to see him. At least, not then.

"When is their birthday?"

"April first."

He let out a laugh. "You're kidding. April Fool's Day?"

I gave him a nod. "Seriously." Most people got a kick out of the twins' birthday date but the day doesn't hold much pleasure for me.

Their actual due date was May first. They were born a month early for reasons that still keep me awake some nights.

I stood from the rocking chair that was a few feet from my father's king-sized bed that he was still resting in. He was coming along well after his surgery but still needed to take it easy. Kyle and Kennedy were sitting at the edge of his bed, watching an episode of *Doc McStuffins*. I frowned, hating that they've been watching so much television lately. I made a note to make a list of outdoor activities and parks we could play at until their camp begins. Since Ms. Sheryl had gone back to Oakland, it was up to me to make sure they were occupied during the day now. Which was fine by me since I didn't have to go to work during the day at the moment. Though, it did make me sad to not have a job.

"I understand why you didn't tell me about them."

My father's words grabbed my attention, pulling me from my thoughts. I turned to see a glum expression on his chestnut-toned face, as he stared on at the back of the twins' heads.

"I understand," he stated again but didn't go into any further explanation.

Nor did I ask him to. Some things are better left unsaid.

Once the episode of *Doc McStuffins* ended, I insisted the children turn off the TV. Kyle grumbled a bit but Kennedy offered to read her grandfather one of the books she brought with her. She always had me carry at least two books whenever we went out in case we have time to stop and read.

"She's just like you."

I smiled at my father's comment.

"You know your mama loved to read at your age, too."

Kennedy nodded as if that were old news. "Mommy's a librarian. Her job has books all over," she stated in awe.

"Not anymore," I mumbled to myself, remembering that I no longer had a job.

After a little while longer, Wilhelmina arrived at my father's and I took the opportunity to make our departure. It was late afternoon and I still had to get the kids to Excelor for their registration, since the school was closed in the morning. At Aaron's insistence, we were chauffeured around in a dark SUV by a driver. I hated not being able to drive, but like much of my belongings, my car was still in Oakland.

After registering the children for school, we headed home so I could make some phone calls to get their school records sent over. Since Williamsport was two hours ahead of Oakland time, I had plenty of time in the day to get that task done. By the end of the day I'd accomplished the list of items that my husband had ordered me to get done. Again that night, after laying the children down in their beds, he retrieved a few items and went to sleep downstairs. And so it continued for the next three weeks.

* * *

"I'm starting to feel like their nanny instead of their mother," I complained to Michelle. She and I had just dropped our children off at camp. Turned out, Diego was attending the same camp. He and the children got along great. I was happy to see Kyle and Kennedy have another family member around their age.

"How so?" Michelle asked.

I shrugged as we head out of the double doors of the huge school building where the camp was being housed.

"Aaron makes all of the decisions, which trust me, there were times in the last five years I wished I had someone to make all of the major decisions and take some of the responsibility from me. But not like this." I sighed.

"Want to stop and get donuts?" Michelle asked.

"You don't have to work?"

She shook her head. "Wasn't feeling well this morning so I took the day off."

"Sure."

We walked to a specialty donut shop that was a few blocks from the school. Michelle and I had grown closer in the last few weeks since the wedding.

"Have you talked to him about it? I mean, telling him that you think he's taking over?"

I snorted. "Have you met my husband?"

She turned honey-toned eyes on me, giving me a sympathetic look.

"Besides, he's been out of town the last few days on business." Add to that, we weren't even sleeping in the same bedroom, but I didn't tell Michelle that part. Some things are best kept between a husband and wife, even if it was a forced, fake marriage.

"I'm sure he's just trying to be helpful."

I didn't say anything. Aaron was being his controlling self. I decided to change the topic and we discussed the upcoming school year that started in the next two weeks. Michelle and I walked around the neighborhood for a few blocks until we came upon the Williamsport City Park.

"Carter doesn't work too far from here, right?" I questioned.

Michelle nodded. "He just got off, though," she stated, peering at the time on her cell phone.

"How'd you two meet?" I asked.

A wistful smile crossed Michelle's face and she began telling me of how she met Carter after getting in a pretty scary car accident. He was a Williamsport Firefighter and his station received the call for the rescue.

"After that, I was pretty much his," she giggled.

"They seem to have that type of appeal."

"They?"

"All the Townsends."

"Yours in particular?"

I sighed. "Aaron and I are..."

"Complicated?"

"Very." I nodded.

Thankfully, Michelle didn't ask too many more questions about Aaron and I. We parted early that afternoon after Carter called Michelle once he arrived home after his shift. I grinned at the smile on her face as she hung up and made up some excuse about needing to go. Luckily, I wasn't too disappointed when Michelle pulled off. I realized that only two blocks from Excelor Academy was the newest branch of the Williamsport City Library. Never one to turn down a trip to the library, I ventured inside and to my delight one of the first things I saw was a flyer advertising a position for a librarian at that branch. A job there would be perfect since it was so close to the kids' school, and of course, I'd get to do what I loved.

I headed straight to the front desk and struck up a friendly conversation with the head librarian. She informed me of the qualifications for the job and after briefly going over my experience she granted me a warm smile. I still had to submit the application online and go through an interview but this opportunity was looking up.

"Tell me your name again?"

"Patience To-Theirs. Patience Thiers," I informed, giving my maiden name.

"Great. Submit your application as soon as you can and we should be able to schedule an interview by the end of the week."

"Great." Smiling, I went to do a walk through of the rest of the library. By the time I left a couple of hours later, I was feeling a little more like myself.

I passed through the doors of the library, preparing to walk the few blocks to the school to pick up the children, but stopped short when a prickle of fear ran down my spine. I turned my head to the right and then the left, looking up and down the street. Other than the normal passersby that frequented the city streets during the summer there was nothing out of the ordinary. Still, that familiar feeling of being watched fell over me. I pivoted in the direction of the children's school, walking swiftly, and for the first time feeling relief upon seeing our normal driver waiting at the sidewalk. Even as I loaded the children into the car, I peered over my shoulder, looking for what or whom I didn't know, but the feeling of unease lasted with me all the way until we arrived home.

* * *

"I'LL BE in my office downstairs if you or the children need me," Aaron informed me. He said the same thing every night right before leaving our bedroom and going down to sleep in the office.

For the first time, I wanted to beg him not to go. To stay with me for the night because that uneasy feeling from earlier was not yet a distant memory. But instead of telling him this, I simply nodded and flipped to the next page of the book I was reading on my Kindle. I felt his gaze linger on me, but he didn't say a word. The next thing I heard was the door closing as he left. I sighed and continued reading for the next hour until my eyes couldn't stay open any longer. Placing my Kindle on the nightstand, I turned off the light. A few minutes later I drifted off into a restless sleep.

"You whored yourself out for him! While I was right here!"

"No! No! No!" I yelled, waking myself out of my sleep. I arose, panting and looking around the darkened room. I scrambled to get out of bed, stumbling as my foot got caught up in the sheet. I didn't even think as I moved to the bedroom door, pulling it open and going first to Kennedy's room. She was sound asleep in her bed. Next, I moved to Kyle's room and found him in the same state as his sister. Safe and sound asleep.

I made it back to the master bedroom and pressed my back against the door, doing my best to take deep inhales. Placing my hand over my pounding chest, I pushed away the memories that so often found their way into my dreams.

"It was just a dream," I whispered to myself. "They're okay. You're okay," I repeated over and over until my heart rate slowed to its normal rhythm. It was my usual routine after one of my nightmares. I hadn't had one in months, but I knew that uneasy feeling from earlier was what brought it on. That was how it usually went. Every now and then, I'd find myself looking around a crowd, feeling as if I'm being watched, yet finding nothing out of the ordinary. Later that same night a nightmare would make its appearance of that night five years ago.

I shook my head, forcing myself not to think about it. Climbing in bed, I willed myself to go back to sleep.

The next afternoon, I received a phone call from Moira, the head librarian at the Williamsport Library branch I'd applied to. I had an interview scheduled for the following Monday. Smiling, as I hung up the phone, I shook off the remnants of the previous night's nightmare and went to pick the kids up from camp. I knew one thing: I was going to ace that interview and get that job. At least then I'd have something to do during the day.

CHAPTER 11

Aaron

"Mr. Townsend, can you read the Daly report and sign off on it?"

I stiffened at the question that fell from this woman's lips. Slowly, I turned from the window in my office to my new junior assistant who stood at the door. Suddenly, her face turned to a deer-in-headlights expression, and it became all too obvious that she'd realized she'd overstepped.

"Janice, you don't ask Mr. Townsend to read over and sign anything without speaking to me first," my executive assistant, Mark, informed. He pulled back from the conference table in my office and rolled over to her in his wheelchair, saying something in hushed tones. I merely watched as the new assistant grew paler and paler. A few moments later, she gave me a chagrined look and nodded before disappearing from my doorway.

"My apologies, Mr. Townsend. She's still learning how the office works," Mark stated.

"Not a problem," I answered. Mark had been hired over a year ago, and his first week on the job, there had been a major office fire in which he sustained minor injuries. Thankfully, Carter's squad was able to rescue him and managed to save the entire office from being engulfed in flames. After a short stint at the hospital and some time off to recuperate, Mark was ready to come back. He has been an asset ever since, having been bumped up to my executive assistant role.

"What report was Janet referencing?" I questioned.

"Janice," he corrected.

I grunted.

"The Daly report. Daly is the top accountant at Oiltec."

I nodded, being very familiar with the name.

"Send a copy to my email and I will read it over this evening."

"I'll do so as soon as I get back to my desk."

We continued to discuss tasks that needed to be completed for the week and a series of meetings that I needed to prepare for over the next thirty minutes.

"I'll be in tomorrow at eight," I informed Mark before heading out.

I decided to leave the office a little early to get home. It was just after three in the afternoon and I figured the children and Patience would be home since it was their last week before school started. I was mistaken.

My driver held the door open for me to exit the car, and before opening my front door I knew the house was empty. Unaware of any activities or outings for the day, I called the driver that'd been assigned to Patience and the children.

"Where are you?" I questioned without any greeting.

"In front of the Williamsport Library, southeastern branch, Mr. Townsend," he responded quickly.

The library, of course. Where else would Patience be? But then, the driver said something that surprised me. I hated surprises.

"Mrs. Townsend had a job interview this afternoon. I think it went well since she's been there for close to two hours."

I wrinkled my forehead. "And where are the children?"

"They were dropped off with their cousin, Diego, and his grandmother."

I grunted.

"Here comes Mrs. Townsend now. Would you like to speak with her?"

"No," I answered abruptly, "do not tell her you've spoken with me." I hung up the phone and pressed my hand to the scanner that unlocked the front door. Charging through the walkway, I headed straight for my downstairs office, dialing numbers as I went. By the time my wife arrived home, an hour later with the children in tow, I had all the information I needed regarding her supposed new job.

* * *

PATIENCE

I woke up early the following Monday morning. Not only was it the children's first day at their new school but it was my first day at work.

"Morning."

I stumbled a little, surprised by the voice behind me. I shouldn't have been, I knew he was there, but for the last month, we'd been like ships passing in the night. Save for the occasional family dinner—which, of course, included the children—I barely saw Aaron.

I turned to see him standing in the hallway, in only a pair of workout shorts, his broad chest glistening from a thin layer of sweat. My mouth went instantly dry.

"Morning," I responded.

"Waking the children?" He eyed me suspiciously.

I shook my head. "It's a little too early for them. I was just checking on them before doing a little bit of yoga," I explained my usual morning routine.

"You don't sleep in any longer," he commented.

I lowered my lashes before raising them to him again. "Hard to sleep in anymore with two kids."

He continued watching me, eyes moving down my body, which was covered in a light T-shirt and a pair of spandex shorts. It was my usual morning yoga outfit.

"Still waking up at five a.m?" I questioned, awkwardly. We'd been living together for over a month and still were unfamiliar with each other's morning habits. Mainly due to the fact that Aaron slept in his office every night. I couldn't say whether I was disappointed or relieved.

"Four-thirty," he finally answered.

I swallowed. It was obvious his morning workouts were well received by his body. I did my best not to gawk.

"I will accompany you and the children to their first day of school this morning."

"Oh."

He raised a dark eyebrow. "Is that a problem?"

I hated the tone of voice he used with me. As if I were one of his employees and was just supposed to go along with whatever he said.

I shrugged. "Whatever. They're your children, too."

"Yes, they are." He nodded before brushing past me to head downstairs.

I inhaled, counting backwards from ten to calm my body down from the brief touch as he passed.

The rest of the morning felt odd, whenever I was in Aaron's presence. I could tell he was watching me, but he remained mostly silent, save for when he was talking with the children. It was as if he was expecting me to say something.

Even as we dropped the children off at school, introducing ourselves to their respective teachers, it felt like Aaron was waiting for some type of explanation from me. Well, he wasn't about to get one. I needed to drop the children off and then get to my own job for the day. We'd arrived in separate cars when taking the children to school. Aaron hated driving and had always insisted on having a driver, and now that extended to myself and the children. We were chauffeured around everywhere. Once Aaron's car pulled out of the school parking lot, I told my driver I'd be fine walking since my destination was only a few blocks away. However, he insisted on driving me. I didn't argue, knowing he probably had specific orders from my husband.

I arrived at the library a little after nine in the morning, ready to start my first day of orientation. As soon as I stepped foot into the library and saw the expression on Moira's face as she looked up from the counter, my heart dropped. I knew instantly something wasn't right.

"Is everything okay?" I questioned, going over to Moira. My stomach plummeted when her lips pinched and she avoided looking directly at me.

"I'm sorry, Pa-Mrs. Townsend, but the position has been filled," she stated formally.

My back went erect. I'd never shared with Moira my married name. In fact, I'd made sure to give Moira my maiden name, in person and on the job application.

"The position has been filled," I repeated. "But just Friday I was told, *by you,* that I was chosen as the new librarian. What's changed?"

Moira's eyes bulged slightly. "Well, it seems as though there was a bit of a mix up."

"Really?"

"Yes, the candidate we interviewed last week just prior to your interview had been selected but I hadn't been informed."

"You're the head librarian. Don't you make the decisions as to who fills the job openings?"

"I-I do but this time the decision was over my head."

"Over your head," I repeated again, rolling the words around in my mouth.

"Yes. Look, Mrs. Townsend, I'm sure this will be just a minor setback for you. With your education and experience, any library branch would be happy to have you. If you'll excuse me, I have a meeting to attend."

I stepped back from the counter and watched as Moira scurried around the counter and darted toward the back of the library. My eyes narrowed at the obvious anxiety she displayed while talking to me. Not very many people could put that type of fear and worry in others. I knew of one man who had the ability to do that. *In fact, I'm married to him.*

With that last thought, I turned and charged through the front doors of the library.

"Heading home so soon?" my driver, Daniel, questioned.

"No. We're headed to Townsend Industries." I firmly answered, pulling the back door to the SUV shut, slamming it as I got in.

CHAPTER 12

Aaron

"Mr. Townsend, Daniel has informed me that he is headed to Townsend Industries on instructions from your wife."

"Have her set up in the lounge room to wait until I am finished with this meeting."

"Yes, sir," Mark answered.

I grunted, signaling to Mark that I was ending our call, before pressing the end button.

"Little early for lunch isn't it?"

I picked my head up from my phone's intercom to see Joshua peering at the Rolex on his wrist. It was close to nine-thirty. Any moron could've deciphered that Patience wasn't arriving for lunch.

I merely stared at my brother for a heartbeat and then turned my attention on the other three men in the room, sitting at the conference table.

"So it seems that the golf course is trying to play hardball," I stated, pushing my hands into my pants pockets.

The three men looked between one another.

"Seems that way." Joshua came up on my right side, standing over the table as well. He was the head of the real estate division of

Townsend Industries. He'd been in negotiations to purchase a recently shut down golf course to turn it into a luxury home complex. The location was about three hours from Williamsport.

"What is the hold up, gentlemen?" I inquired.

"Mr. Townsend, I'm sure your brother has shared with you—"

"Joshua."

He blanched. "Excuse me?"

"In this office, his name is not *my brother*. It's Joshua. Or Mr. Townsend."

"*Joshua,*" he emphasized, "is asking a much lower selling price than what was originally offered."

"So, you decided to set up a meeting with me in hopes that I'd convince Joshua to raise the price."

Another round of looks between the three men. "Not quite—"

"Yes, quite," Joshua began. "You all hoped that somehow bringing a meeting to the CEO of Townsend would convince me to raise the asking price for your failed golf course."

I lowered my head, not wanting to reveal the pride I felt hearing Joshua ream out these supposed businessmen.

"Unfortunately, you failed to do your due diligence. Something I *never* forget," Josh continued. He went on to explain precisely why the golf course would not be getting their asking price, in addition to telling them why they would still be selling to Townsend. Because if they didn't Joshua was fully prepared to file a lawsuit against their company for any number of reasons which would hold up any future sales, costing them more money.

"It appears that *my brother* has spoken." I looked sharply at the man who earlier had try to downplay Joshua's importance by labeling him earlier. "Now that that's set—"

"What the *hell* is wrong with you?"

I turned abruptly from the table to my office door where my very pissed off wife stood.

"Get out." I turned to peer over my shoulder at the men. "Now!" I seethed.

I eyed them as the three men scurried out of the room.

Patience wasted no time brushing past them. At the same time I saw one of my security guards enter behind her, a concerned expression on his face.

"You son of a bitch!" Patience continued. "It's not enough you had to ruin my damn life, you couldn't even let me work in peace!"

I was instantly pissed. "I *ruined* your life? You kept my children from me for five years!" I retorted angrily.

She gave a derisive laugh. "Are you *seriously* back to that?" She moved forward, hands flailing.

"Back to it? We never fucking left!"

"Obviously. Why don't you go talk to your goddamn fiancée about that? You pompous bastard. And while you're at it, why don't you just leave me the hell alone! My life was going just fine without you!" She lunged as if she was about to attack me, but was held back when the huge security guard grabbed her by the waist.

I saw nothing else. Just his burly hand wrapped around my wife's body.

"Take. Your. Goddamn. Hands. Off. My. Fucking. Wife!" I flared, fists clenching at my sides. "Now!" I yelled, stepping forward. A second later, my security guard stood half a foot from my wife. "Get the fuck out!"

"You're a goddamned bully!" Patience yelled in my face.

"And you're a deceitful liar!" I retorted.

Her head snapped back. "*I'm* the liar in this non-relationship?"

"You went behind my back. Used your maiden name to apply for the job. And never once told me about it."

"When?" She threw up her hands. "When was I supposed to tell you about it? During the day when you're totally consumed by your job, or at night when you go down to your office to work some more?"

"You had plenty of opportunity to tell me."

"And because I didn't, you acted like a petulant child and went behind my back to get the library to not hire me. But *I'm* the deceitful liar here?" She pushed me by the shoulders.

I barely budged.

"I fucking hate you!" she shouted.

My fists balled again and I crowded her space, lowering my face to hers. "That's too damn bad, sweetheart." I held up my hand, bringing the finger that wore my wedding band in between our two faces. "You're mine!" I gritted out between my teeth.

Her walnut-toned face screwed up, sepia eyes narrowing. "Not for long," she retorted, low, but firmly. A second later, she turned sharply, her locs nearly grazing my face, and rushed out of my office, slamming the door.

Lifting the globe paperweight that sat on my desk, I threw it against the window just next to my door. The glass cracked but didn't completely shatter, as it was bulletproof. I moved around my desk, picking up my phone to call Daniel.

He answered on the first ring.

"Do not take her anywhere except back to the house!" I hung up, not waiting for his reply.

I needed to leave but I also had to get a grip. I pinched the bridge of my nose and that's when I heard it. I blinked open my eyes, lifting my head to see Joshua standing by the conference table, laughing.

"Care to explain what the hell is so funny?"

"You. The both of you. And me, but mostly, you two."

"I don't do riddles."

His laughing reduced to a smirk and he nodded, moving closer to my desk. "I didn't get it at first." He shook his head. "She seemed like the sweet, quiet librarian. Not what I imagined your speed to be at all. But that," he nodded in the direction of the office door my wife had just stormed out of, "was a whole side I didn't know was there."

I wrinkled my forehead at him, wondering what the hell he was talking about.

Stepping back from my desk, Joshua nodded. "Yeah, I think you two have a chance."

I didn't have time to question Joshua any further. I had more important matters to tend to, one being my wife, who'd better be at home or all hell would break loose.

* * *

I BURST through the front door, tossing my briefcase to the side, and looked around. The only evidence of Patience were the black pumps she'd had on earlier, that now laid at the foot of the steps. I knew she was there since Daniel still remained outside, having only dropped her off a few minutes prior.

I charged up the staircase, taking two at a time. I knew where I'd find her, and sure enough, as I entered our bedroom, I found her in a flurry of motion. On our bed was a pile of clothes, haphazardly thrown in a suitcase. A few heartbeats later Patience came charging out of her walk-in closet, more balled up clothes in her arms. She barely glanced at me as she moved to the bed, tossing the clothes in the suitcase.

"What are you doing?" I asked, my voice low, and tight with anger.

"The hell does it look like I'm doing? As soon as I'm done packing my things, I'll pack the children's." She turned her back to me as if going to the closet again, only to stop short at the loud crashing sound of the suitcase hitting the wooden dresser.

My chest heaved, not due to the physical activity of tossing a large suitcase halfway across the room but the idea of her thinking she was going to leave me.

"You're insane."

"You've known that for a very long time."

"I'm leaving, Aaron," she affirmed again, but more cautiously that time around.

"I wouldn't say that again if I were you."

She took a step back, folding her arms over her chest. "You just want to control everything. I'm not you–"

"You do remember what happened the last time you said those exact words, right?" The stirring in my cock, which had started when she angrily burst in my office, began to build.

Her mouth clamped shut and her eyelids fluttered.

Yeah, she remembered.

"You don't want me here. You want to be a father to Kyle and

Kennedy? Fine. We can still work out a custody agreement. I won't keep them from you–"

"Because I would never let you."

She sighed. "But there's no need for us to be married to co-parent. W-we haven't even consummated our marriage. It's a sham."

I glowered at my wife, not saying a word. I let my gaze glide over her smooth brown skin, pinched, heart-shaped lips, down to the vein in her neck that had begun beating wildly since I reminded her of where her words would get her. My cock began to throb painfully in my pants. I took a handful of steps backwards to the door, closing and locking it, all without taking my eyes off of her.

I loosened my tie, completely removing it.

"Don't," she warned.

CHAPTER 13

Patience

There're sayings about poking the bear, or awakening the sleeping giant, that perfectly encompassed what I felt in that moment. It wasn't the way he imposed himself in the doorway, or locked it, making it impossible for anyone to enter, or rather for me to escape. And, it wasn't even the oh-so-obvious bulge in his pants—the same one that made my nipples ache with need.

It was the way his hazel eyes darkened to an almost forest green. And the way he held his tie between his two hands, threateningly. I was all too familiar with that tie hold. He'd used it before on me. And why did that sudden memory begin to surface as he took a second and then a third step in my direction?

"Don't," I warned again, backing up.

No words. He didn't speak, just kept advancing on me, until my back hit a wall.

I ignored the weeping of my nether lips in my panties. Instead, I attempted to push at Aaron's broad chest for the second time that day as he moved closer. The only change in his body was the flaring of his nostrils.

"It's time to consummate our marriage," he stated just before crushing his lips to mine.

A moan broke free from my lips, escaping into his mouth. That spurred him on, his tongue and lips taking possession...no...ownership of mine. The kiss was meant as his response to my attempted declaration just a few minutes earlier. I was his. He knew it and he made damn sure I knew it.

My head was lifted a few inches as his hand moved up, covering my throat. My nipples hardened even more, panties now flooding with need for him. For this. He leaned his body into me, his erection pressing into my abdomen. My entire body felt on fire. My clothes were suddenly an unnecessary barrier to what I needed. Aaron must've felt the same way because he tore his lips from mine, giving me just enough room to grab the white sheer top I wore out of the pants I'd tucked them in, pulling it over my head.

His lips captured mine again as soon as the shirt hit the floor but I felt his hands at the buckle of my belt, pulling it open, and unbuttoning my pants. Soon enough, my pants pooled around my ankles.

"Ahh!" I gasped out, tearing my mouth from Aaron's, when his thumb grazed across my distended clit. I heard a tearing sound in the distance, only to realize that Aaron had just decimated yet another pair of my panties.

There weren't any verbal announcements of me being his. My husband's body was doing all the talking for him, and before I knew it, I found myself completely nude, laid out on the bed from which he'd just tossed my suitcase. He stared at me, with those darkened, stormy eyes, jaw rigid with emotion. His hands went to the buttons of his shirt, tearing it away quickly. Next went the undershirt he wore, exposing his entire upper half. My mouth went dry when he reached for his own belt buckle, rapidly lowering his pants until he was only dressed in a pair of black boxer briefs, the massive bulge pointing directly at me.

"Aaron." His name fell from my mouth on a plea.

His eyes darkened impossibly more right in front of me. But he just kept staring down at my body. Slowly his hand went out, covering the pooch in my belly left after pregnancy. The tip of his index finger outlined the stretch marks that'd been with me since my thirtieth week of pregnancy. I remembered then that the last time we'd been in this position it was in a darker room. He hadn't been able to fully see all the changes carrying twins had done to my body.

"Don't," he growled when I went to cover my belly and breasts, feeling a little insecure under the scrutiny of his gaze. "My children," he said, low, his body moving over me. Finally, his eyes rose to meet mine. I didn't have time to blink before he attacked me with his mouth again, using his knee to spread mine apart. He moved his hips lower so that his covered cock lined up with my pussy, pressing into me.

"Aaron!" I gasped.

His response was to hook his arm under my left knee, exposing me even more, and pressing into me again.

I let out a loud moan, still unsatisfied. He continued to pump his hips against mine, pressing his hardened cock against my clit, sending my mind and body at a dizzying pace. Yet it wasn't enough, and he knew it. He raised my leg even higher, damn near splitting me in two, still pumping wildly, giving me just a taste of what he knew I needed.

"Please," I begged, lifting my arms to his shoulders, digging my fingernails into them.

Lowering, he caught my bottom lip in between his teeth, biting it and then sucking to soothe the burn. He pressed at my core again with this hips and my back arched as the orgasm ripped through my body. My pussy lips fluttered, clutching at nothing. I squeezed Aaron's shoulders, still needing more.

"Please," I beseeched again.

This time he responded, pushing back to lower his briefs before surging forward, filling me all the way up with his member. I yelled, my screams filling the room. Aaron wrapped his hand around a handful of my locs, pulling my head back against the bed, and then running his teeth along my exposed neck. I shivered in his arms, feeling weak and strong at the same time. He plundered my body, taking what belonged him with each stroke.

Save for that one night at The Cage, my body felt fully alive for the first time in years. It knew where it belonged. I chanted his name, moaning it over and over as he glided in and out of me. Just before I could come again, he rolled us over so that I was on top, while he laid on his back.

"Ride it," he ordered.

I felt too weak to even move but I pressed my hands against his chest, sitting up. I opened my eyes fully to see him watching me. His eyes were telling me that he didn't like waiting. I felt my pussy cream even more at the unstated admonishment.

I lifted my hips before lowering myself onto his shaft again.

"Harder!" he growled.

I raised and lowered again, more forcefully this time. I squeezed my inner-walls, clutching around him. His fingers dug into the sides of my waist tightly, gripping me to him, assisting in raising and lowering my hips. I bounced on his cock, swiveling my hips on the way down.

"Just like I taught you," he grunted, urging me on, reminding me of who my first lover was. Who had taught me all about making my body feel alive.

He lifted his knees, planting his feet, and then pressed at my belly for me to lie back against him. He would only let me take control for so long. His hold on my waist tightened even more, and he lifted and lowered his hips, riding me from below.

Wrapping my hands around his wrists, I held on as the building pressure in my pussy began again. I panted and moaned loudly, my entire body tightening up as the orgasm crested, flooding every inch of me. I squeezed my eyes shut, blocking out everything but the sensations coursing through my body, leaving me feeling as if I was floating.

By the time I came back to myself, I was on my back again, Aaron over me, the veins in his neck straining as he came inside of me. We'd never used protection. He completely flooded me, the reverberations of my own orgasm still milking him of everything he had to give.

He pulled out just as one last spurt of his semen fell, landing onto my belly. He wiped it up with his thumb and then raised it to my lips.

"Open."

My mouth went wide, receiving his come as if it were food for my very soul.

Slowly he withdrew his thumb, watching me as I swallowed what he'd just fed me. I don't remember much after that, having slipped into a deep slumber not too long afterwards.

CHAPTER 14

Aaron

"You're pushing her away."

My hold tightened around the glass of seltzer water I held, while staring off into the distance. The voice had come from behind me, as I stood inside my home's office. I'd just left a sleeping Patience up in our bedroom while I came down and locked myself in here to get some work done. I wasn't going back to Townsend offices that day.

I turned to see the woman who called herself Emma standing by the door. She was dressed as always in a long, flowing white nightgown, her dark brown hair—which was greying at the temples—falling around her shoulders. She'd looked this way ever since I first saw her as a child.

"You're achieving the opposite of what you want."

I slowly brought the glass to my lips, taking a sip and swallowing before speaking. "And what is it that you think I want?"

"Your wife."

"I have her."

"No, you don't. Not the way you want." She smirked, moving closer. Though she had legs, she didn't walk, she floated.

"You didn't deny my existence just now. Know what that tells me?"

I grunted.

"You want my help. You're just as confused about how to proceed with her as you've always been. Six years ago you were confused but went with your gut. You pursued her despite being out of your element. You still want her, even more now than before, but the history between you two stops you."

"I'm not afraid," I defended.

Emma nodded. "You are." She smiled and my chest squeezed. She reminded me so much of my mother sometimes. My biological mother. "The man who's not afraid of anything is afraid of his wife."

I scoffed. "This is how I know you're a figment of a child's imagination. Why on Earth would I be afraid of my wife?"

"Because she has the ability to do what no one else on this planet can do."

I narrowed my eyes. "What would that be?"

"Reject you."

"She's tried and has been unsuccessful thus far," I reminded her.

"Oh, you can keep her close with your threats…at least until the children are eighteen. You can use your power and influence to make sure no man ever touches her again. But her heart? You're going to have to win that all over again." She smirked.

I paused, my top lip moving upwards on a snarl. "What the hell do you mean I can make sure another man never touches her *again*? I'm the only man that's touched–" My statement cut off at the expression on Emma's face. It was a look of amusement that pissed me off.

"Six years is a long time," she sing-songed, "and Patience is a beautiful woman."

I threw the glass across the room, liquid splashing all over my leather couch.

"Don't get violent," Emma tutted, folding her arms across her chest. "Listen to me, and you listen good. That high-handed nonsense works in business, and maybe in every other area of your life, but with her it won't work. You want to win Patience and your children over, you've got to do more than bully them into loving you. Your father tried that, remember? See how that turned out?"

"Don't mention him!" I boiled.

"I'm not mentioning him. I'm just reminding you of where throwing your weight around and bullying those who are weaker than you gets you. Your father tried it and he made you hate him. Not just him, but most other people also. Thank God for Robert and Deborah, they showed you what real love looks like. Anyway," she waved her hands in the air, "we have time to sort all that out later. For now, you want to rebuild what you had with your wife, start with sleeping next to her at night. She needs it."

I furrowed my eyebrows. There was something implied in Emma's statement.

"What do you mean she *needs* it?"

"Just what I said. But don't fret, more will be revealed. You just need to layoff the bullying and act like an actual husband instead of CEO and taskmaster of this house. Leave that at the office."

And in the blink of an eye, Emma was gone. I was left staring at an empty office save for the furniture and work equipment. I went over to the cabinets that were pressed along the far wall, opening them to reveal the multiple screens. I hit the power button, turning the monitors on. Each monitor showed a different room in the house. I pressed the touchscreen monitor, zooming in on the screen that focused on our bedroom. I ran my finger lightly over the outline of Patience as she laid asleep in our bed. Each morning, I'd done the same thing. First checking on the children to see if they were asleep or not, savoring the idea of just having them under the same roof as me. Next, I let my spying linger on the master bedroom, watching Patience as she rose each morning and went about her morning routine of yoga followed by some journaling before going to check on the children. In the month they'd been there, I'd lost count of the number of times I'd jerked off to the sight of her first thing in the morning.

I hit the power button again, turning the cameras off and shutting the cabinet doors. I needed to get some work done. I went over to my desk, sitting down and preparing to work the rest of the afternoon, well into the evening.

* * *

Patience

"Mommy, let's do ring around the rosie!" Kennedy giggled as we played in her bedroom. It was close to eight-thirty at night and I was playing with the kids for a little while before I put them down to bed. Aaron still hadn't emerged from his downstairs office, even at six for dinner. I forced myself not to think about what that meant, though the twinge of rejection I felt from him still hurt, especially after what happened that morning between us.

"Join us Kyle," I insisted, grabbing him by the hand as he sat on Kennedy's bed. Though the two had separate bedrooms, they were always in one another's rooms. They may have had very different personalities and likes but their closeness couldn't be denied.

"I'll start," Kennedy began. "Riiing around the rooosie," she sang and all three of us began moving in a circle, our hands clasped.

"We all fall down!" we all shouted in unison, falling to the floor and giggling. It was such a silly little game but Kennedy couldn't get enough of it and seeing her joy always made me laugh.

"Daddy!" Kyle shouted, getting off the floor and running in the direction of the door.

"Daddy!" Kennedy squealed, following behind her brother.

I slowly turned to watch them as they ran up to their father, hugging his long legs, as they couldn't reach his waist just yet. My heart caught in my throat when he stooped lower, enfolding his arms around both children and coming to stand with them at his sides. The scowl on his face softened as he stared at his children. I had to avert my eyes, hating the way it made my heart rate quicken, and the yearn in my body it caused to grow. Not just for his physical touch but for that look. There was a time I saw that same softening cross his face when he gazed upon me. I remembered the first time it happened.

***

Then

I hurried into my favorite bookstore, shaking off the snow that had accumulated on my hood, and stomping my feet. "Hi, Sam!" I greeted the ever-present bookstore clerk.

He lifted his head and smiled. "Hey, Patience."

"Have you got it?"

"Your signed copy of a first edition *Harry Potter*?" His face slowly morphed into a grin. "You betcha!"

I laughed out loud, going over to the check-out counter. Sam lifted the book from the shelf behind him. The book had been earmarked especially for me. I'd ordered it weeks prior and was all too giddy when I got the phone call from Sam that it'd finally arrived.

I opened the front cover and smiled wide when I saw author's signature.

"You're going to enjoy reading that."

I lifted my head, having half-forgotten all about Sam. "It's not for me."

His face contorted into one of confusion and surprise.

"It's for the kids at the library where I tutor. One of the kids, actually. He had so many problems reading, that I promised him when he finished his first book, I'd get him an autographed copy. A little bribery never hurt anyone," I laughed, as did Sam.

He stared at me for a few seconds.

I shifted from one foot to the other. "What's the total on that?"

"Oh." He jumped as if remembering he was at work. "That'll be fifty-five even."

"Really? An autographed copy of a first edition of Harry Potter, I would've thought it'd be more expensive than that. I'm not arguing though," I laughed again. I dug out my bank card to pay for the book and just as Sam took it my cell phone vibrated in my pocket. Pulling out my phone, the widening of my smile and the fluttering in my chest at the name of the caller couldn't be helped. "Hey," I answered breathlessly, walking away from the register for a little privacy.

"Where are you?"

My neck snapped back at the curtness in Aaron's tone. "I'm at the bookstore. I sent you a text."

"I didn't receive anything."

I sighed. "I was letting you know I had to stop by here after my last class."

"The bookstore on Sherman?"

"Yes."

"I'll be there in two minutes."

I pulled the phone from my ear. He'd hung up. I frowned, never having had him be so short with me. It'd been a month since the first time Aaron slept over my apartment after that dinner with my father. Just about every night since he'd been at my place. And though, we'd never so much as kissed, there was an intimacy there I'd never shared with anyone else. I sometimes wondered what he saw in me, or even what we were doing. Were we just friends? Were we dating? Was he falling for me? I didn't need to ask that last question in reverse, I already knew the answer. I had already fallen for him, even with all his brooding and scowling. We spent many late nights just hanging out and talking. He let me tell him all about my day, my hopes for the future, anything and everything. On occasion, he'd even let me read to him whatever book I was reading for fun at the time. My latest read had been *The Shack* which I'd finished just the night before, reading out loud as he listened.

"Everything okay?"

I turned to see Sam looking concerned. "Everything's fine." I went back to the register, retrieving my card along with the bag that held the book in it. "Thank you. Stay warm in this weather," I told Sam before waving and turning to leave.

I stepped out of the door, into the frigid air. It was the middle of March but Mother Nature had chosen to give us one last snow dump before spring, I guessed, tightening my hood around my face and head. Barely thirty seconds after I stepped out of the bookstore, a Lincoln Town Car pulled up directly in front, cutting off my path to cross the street. Aaron didn't wait for his driver to get out and open his door for him. Instead, he got out, staring at me from the space between his door and the car, scowling.

I wasn't perturbed by the expression on his face. "You're not wearing a coat," I chided, going over to him.

He looked up as if just realizing that it was even snowing, then back down at me. The same tingly feeling I got whenever his eyes fell on me occurred.

"Get in." He stepped aside, wrapping a hand around my lower back and assisting me into the backseat of his car. He got in behind me, slamming the door shut and then knocking on the glass partition, signaling the driver to pull off.

"We could've met at the restaurant. I was only a few minutes at the bookstore," I began.

He turned to me, staring. "You took the subway all the way over here, in the snow?"

I squinted, confused. "Yeah, so." I shrugged.

"So?" His voice raised slightly.

I sighed. "What's the big deal?"

"The *big deal* is that I had to leave work early to make it over here to the bookstore to pick you up."

"You didn't have to pick me up. That's what I'm saying."

"So, I was supposed to let you walk around in the snow?"

I rolled my eyes. "I've done it plenty of times before."

"Not when I'm around."

I frowned, not understanding what that even meant.

"I left a big meeting just to be able to pick you up."

I furrowed my brows. "You only called me a few minutes ago."

"And?"

"And your office is across town. How'd you get here so quickly?"

His jaw tightened. "Your text."

My eyes widened. "You said you didn't receive my text."

He slowly blinked. "I lied."

My mouth opened and closed, trying to figure out the words to express my bemusement. "You lied and then got mad at me because you *chose* to leave a work meeting only because you didn't want me taking the subway in this weather?" I waited for an answer to my question, but it never came. Instead, the stopping of the car, followed by Aaron getting out and holding the door open for me, ensued. I took his hand and exited the car, to see we were in front of my apartment complex. "I thought we had dinner plans?"

"I changed them," he informed me.

With my hand in his, I followed as he guided us to the door's entrance and punched in the newly installed code for the front door. I'd given him the code weeks ago. We made it up the three flights to my apartment door in silence.

"Food will be here in fifteen minutes," Aaron stated as he shut my apartment door behind us.

Angrily, I placed my hand on my hip. "What if I wanted to eat out?"

"You don't."

"How do you know?"

His scowl deepened. "Because I said so."

"What the hell are you so angry about? I didn't do anything to you. I told you where I was going and that I'd meet you at the restaurant. You chose to leave your meeting needlessly!"

"I did!" he roared, shocking me.

I took a step back.

"I left a *very* important meeting that my company has been preparing for, for weeks! My father has been away for a month and all of this going well rested on me to pull off, successfully. And it did, but I still left early. For you! Because I didn't want you walking in the damn snow by yourself!" He breathed harshly, chest rising and falling quickly, nostrils flaring.

I wanted to lash out at him. Wanted to kick him out of my apartment and tell him to go to hell. But I couldn't do it. I could see what he so obviously didn't want to reveal. Behind the scowl and the harsh glare in his eyes, I could see it. I saw *him*.

Foolishly, instead of turning away, I walked up to him, closing the space between us. I curled my fingers around his forearm. He glanced from my hand on his arm to my face, the anger ebbing just a little bit.

"You want to talk about it?" I questioned.

His brows deepened.

"Work? The deal you're working on? You don't have to give me the details you can't share but it might help to talk to a non-employee about the pressure."

His eyes went back to where my hand rested on his arm. He examined it slowly, before covering it with his free hand. He looked back at me, his scowl released and my heart nearly stopped. He was so damn gorgeous. I'd never seen anyone's eyes shine as they looked at me until then.

He led me to the couch and instead of letting me sit next to him, he brought me to his lap. A new level of intimacy in our relationship. I laid my head on his shoulder as he began talking about Townsend Industries' merger with a natural gas company that would grow their company's marketplace by a third. It was a risky venture, and one his father had let him take lead on. Success in this merger would guarantee Aaron a shot as CEO once Robert Townsend retired.

Even after the food arrived, Aaron continued talking and I kept on listening, hearing the range of emotions in his voice. They were all there —the excitement, anticipation, thrill, and yes, doubt and fear, though he did his best to mask those two. Well after midnight, we sat on the couch talking. He wrapped his arm around my waist tightly, and I couldn't take it anymore. I sat up, peering down at him. I let my eyes fall to his lips and I licked my own. Lowering my head, I readied myself to feel his lips, but I was stopped. My chin was caught between his thumb and forefinger.

I looked him in the eyes. His had darkened to an unrecognizable shade. He shook his head slightly. It was a cautioning, of what, I didn't know, but I heeded it...that night. I moved off of his lap and positioned myself at his side, laying my head into his chest, letting our breathing slow until we both fell asleep right there.

* * *

Patience

I came back from my memory to find Aaron's eyes on me. I

ducked my head, hoping my facial expression hadn't revealed the memories I had been reliving. When I dared to raise my eyes again, I found his still stuck on me, even as Kennedy talked his ear off, as he tucked her into bed.

"G'night, Daddy. I love you."

My heart squeezed at the same time Aaron turned to Kennedy, face in shock. I didn't wait for his reply. I hurried out of the room, wiping the tear that tried to escape from my eye as I went into Kyle's room. Aaron had already tucked Kyle in, and now it was my turn to say goodnight to our son.

"Hey, baby," I cooed, going to Kyle's side at his Spiderman decorated bed.

He grinned at me. "Mommy, did you know, my cousin, Diego, has the same video game as me?"

I lifted an eyebrow. "No, I didn't."

"Yeah, and even though he's in third grade and I'm in kindergarten, he still says hi in the hallway at school."

I smiled. "That's sweet. Your cousin loves you."

"And Kennedy, too. He's real nice to her."

I nodded. "Good. You three are family now."

Kyle's smile grew even wider. "And Daddy's our family, too, right?"

I swallowed. "Yes."

Kyle's smile faded and he looked around the room, the way he does right before he prepares to tell a secret. "Mommy, did you know daddy has fairies around him?"

My face balled into confusion. "Fairies?"

Kyle nodded vigorously. "Yeah, Diego's seen them, too. They're like little lights all around him. Not always but sometimes."

"That's interesting," I stated because I didn't know what else to say to that. I knew children had always acted…oddly with Aaron, not put off the way most adults were, but strangely attracted to him. It was why I wasn't surprised when Kennedy and Kyle kind of just took to him from the beginning. "Okay, sweetie. You go ahead and get some sleep, and we'll talk more about this another time."

"'Kay. Nite, Mommy!"

"Nite, baby."

I rose and went over to turn out the light before moving farther down the hall to the master bedroom. I'd long since picked up the clothes and the suitcase that had been strewn about earlier. Now the bed was made up neatly, hiding the events of earlier that day. I moved to the connecting bathroom, doing my nightly routine and putting on the silk shorts and strapless top I'd chosen to wear to bed that night.

Just as I was settling into bed, Aaron entered the bedroom, surprising me. Wordlessly, he went into the bathroom. I heard the faint sounds of water running and a few minutes later he re-emerged dressed in only a pair of plaid pajama bottoms. My heart started beating rapidly when he moved to the bed, climbing in. I stared silently as he settled into his side.

"You're sleeping here tonight?" It was an odd question for a wife to ask her husband but an appropriate one given the circumstances.

He turned to me. "Is that a problem?"

I cleared my throat. "Not if you don't make it one," I retorted, trying to sound angry.

The left side of his mouth kicked up into what on a normal person might be considered a smile.

"Then I'm sleeping in my bed, with my wife tonight."

I blinked, hoping the way my nipples hardened at his possessive tone didn't show through my silk top. When I looked up at Aaron, I knew he'd seen it. His eyes were locked on my nipples, and I didn't need to look down to know they were protruding through my shirt.

"Goodnight."

The deep bravado of what I knew was his bedroom voice sent a shiver through me. It was going to be a long night.

*　*　*

AARON

It was a long damn night. I woke up four-thirty the next morning, my usual time, but with a hand over my face and a soft, hairless leg stretched over my lower half. I turned my head to see Patience's eyelids closed, mouth slightly opened as soft snores poured from it. She was still as reckless a sleeper as ever. Carefully, I removed her arm from my face and moved to exit the bed to do my regular morning workout in the downstairs gym. But after getting up I had to pause and stare down at the sleeping woman in my bed. I refused to think about the many nights, over the previous five and a half years, I pictured this very image. No woman has ever made me long like that before or since. Quite the opposite. Once I was done with a woman I was done, but Patience…there was no being done.

I let my eyes trail over her five-foot-four, curvy frame. Her body had changed since the pregnancy. I could see that but it only enhanced her beauty. The little pooch she'd obviously been self-conscious about, I found one of the most attractive parts of her body now. That pooch had housed my children, and will go on to house my future children. Before even consciously thinking about it, I bent down, slowly lifting her top, and pressed a light kiss to her belly. Stepping back, I took one last look before going over to my dresser and pulling out a T-shirt and shorts to work out.

I headed to the hallway to my next stop, which was to Kennedy's bedroom, which was almost directly across the hall from ours. I opened her door quietly and something akin to a grin crossed my face when I saw her splayed across her Barbie bed in almost the exact same position as her mother. A few of her curly ringlets, fanned across her face and forehead. I couldn't stop myself from moving closer to her bed to brush her hair out of her face. Next, I went to Kyle's room, barely making it fully inside before noticing the hazel eyes that mirrored my own staring back at me.

"Morning, Daddy," he groaned, wiping his eyes.

"What are you doing awake?" I whispered.

"I don't know." He shrugged, sitting up in his bed.

"Go back to sleep. I'll wake you when it's time for breakfast."

"But I don't want to."

My eyebrows dipped. "You don't want to sleep?"

He shook his head.

I sighed. "Come with me," I responded, plucking him from the bed.

"Where're we going?"

"Shh," I admonished. "Your mom and sister are still sleeping."

"Where're we going?" he questioned again, this time whispering.

"To the gym."

He grinned as I took him by the hand and led him down the stairs to the main floor of the house and then down the second set of stairs that led to my home office, den, and the basement I'd turned into a home gym.

"Wow!" he whispered, loudly.

"You can use your regular voice here. Mom and Kennedy won't hear you." I'd soundproofed this part of the house when it was built.

"Are you a superhero?"

I squinted. "No. Why would you ask that?"

He shrugged. "Because of the fairies."

I sighed and frowned. *Kids.*

"I don't have fairies. In fact–" I stopped just short of blurting out that they didn't exist, when those eyes so full of awe looked up into mine. I briefly wondered if I'd ever given my father that same look when I was Kyle's age. I shook that thought loose. "I'm not a superhero, but I can teach you a few tricks."

Kyle's face exploded around the smile he gave me.

I led him over to the punching bag I had set up, showing him the small gloves I'd had laying around. Though they were still a little too big for his hands, he got the hang of it and had me teaching him the different types of punches—jabs, hooks, uppercuts, and more. I'd lost track of time, doing my own workout and having Kyle assist me by laying on my back while I did push ups, or sitting on my shoulders while I did squats. By the time we emerged from the basement, we both were sweaty and had worked up a good appetite.

As soon as I opened the door, my stomach growled at the smell of freshly cooked food.

"Pancakes!" Kyle yelled, running down the hall toward the kitchen. "Yay!" he squealed.

I met him to find Patience standing in the middle of the huge open-air kitchen, moving a pancake from the stove to a plate that had a stack of pancakes.

"Kyle, go wash up and get dressed in the clothes I laid out on your bed before breakfast."

"'Kay. Thanks for the workout, Daddy!" he exclaimed as he ran past me to go up the stairs.

I leaned against the entrance wall of the kitchen, staring. Patience wore a pair of yoga pants and a T-shirt that stopped just at the curve of her ass. When she turned to place another pancake on the stack, I took my fill, feeling myself expand in the workout shorts I wore.

"Did you two have fun working out?"

I lifted my eyes to see her turn around, staring up at me.

"We did." I nodded.

"Kennedy?"

She was back to staring at the stove, but her lips split into a grin. "Still sleeping. That girl–"

"Is just like her mama."

She glanced my way, eyelids fluttering, before turning back to the stove.

"I'll wake her up as soon as I'm done cooking."

"I'll do it."

She paused.

I cleared my throat. "You start your job today."

Her eyes widened, then a deep V settled between her eyebrows. "What job?"

"At the library. I called them again."

"Really?" Her expression turned hopeful.

My hand moved to my chest, covering the tattoo that rested just above my heart, rubbing it. "The position's still yours if you want it."

Her hopeful look turned to one of apprehension. "What's the catch?"

I nodded. "I deserved that."

"So what is it?"

I gave a one shoulder shrug. "You just need to use your married name, Mrs. Townsend."

She eyed me. "That's it?"

"That's a lot considering you neglected to use it on your application."

"You know why I did."

I stood erect. "No, I don't, actually."

Her shoulders sank. "Because the name Townsend opens doors everywhere in this city. I wanted the job on my own merit. Something of my own again." She sighed. "You wouldn't get it." She waved the hand holding the spatula in the air, turning back to the stove.

"*I* wouldn't get it? You don't think I, of all people, understand the weight of my last name."

She stiffened. "I didn't mean that, Aaron."

"Then what did you mean?"

She pushed out a gush of air. "Just that my entire life was flipped upside down within a few weeks. Everything changed and I wanted some sense of normalcy, of *me*."

I moved fully into the kitchen, going to stand over her. "Let me take you to dinner. Tonight."

She looked up at me, confused. "Where?"

"Buona Sera."

She grinned as her head dipped. "Not fair. I can't say no to Italian."

I lifted her chin with my forefinger. "I know."

"The kids?"

"Carter and Michelle will watch them. He's off tonight." My older brother and his wife lived right next door, so it wouldn't be too difficult at all to get them to watch the twins.

"Okay," she agreed.

I swallowed, and resisted the urge to bend her over the counter right then and there. I had to fight to remind myself there were children in the house. Thankfully, they made that chore a little easier when both Kyle and Kennedy came barreling down the stairs.

I took a step back and spun around at the exact moment Kennedy greeted me, wrapping her arms around my thighs.

"Morning, Daddy." She giggled when I tickled her under her chin.

After helping the kids settle down into their breakfast chairs, I ran upstairs to take a shower, and then sent a text to my assistant letting him know I wouldn't make it into the office until nine that morning—well after my usual seven-thirty arrival time. I was looking forward to breakfast with my family, and then dinner with my wife that evening.

CHAPTER 15

Patience

The place where it all started. Buona Sera. The Italian restaurant where I'd met my father that night, six years ago, not knowing Aaron would be there.

"Ready?"

A chill ran down my spine when he put his hand at the small of my back, bringing me closer to him.

I nodded and let him guide us to the front door where the hostess didn't even bother to ask whether there was a reservation or not. She simply greeted us with a smile, pulled out two menus, and led us to one of the best seats in the dining space.

"This is D'Angelo. He will be your waiter tonight. Please let him know if you need anything." She nodded and went to return to her post at the front.

"Would you like to start off with something to drink?"

"Seltzer with lime and a Ducale Gold for my wife."

"Right away."

Watching the waiter hurry off to bring us our drinks, I bit the inside of my cheek to prevent the smile that threatened to break free. He'd remembered my favorite red wine from this place.

"Do you come here often anymore?" I questioned after unfolding my napkin onto my lap.

He turned those intense hazel eyes on me, gaze boring into mine. "This is the first time I've been back in over five years."

I dipped my head, unsure of how to respond to that. So many feelings were being stirred up. My logical mind told me that I should hate him. Common sense would dictate that I hate him. Yet, common sense always failed me when it came to Aaron Townsend.

"How was your first day?"

I lifted my head, thankful for the relatively safe question.

"It was great. Moira was a little overly friendly at first this morning. It was a bit awkward but she eventually calmed down once I told her she didn't need to cater to me. I was there to do my job. I got to learn the layout of the library. I mean, most libraries are the same. The Dewey Decimal system doesn't change from one library to the next, but I needed to familiarize myself with the digital archives. I'll be doing that the rest of the week."

I glanced up as D'Angelo returned with our drinks.

"Thank you." I smiled at our waiter, picking up my glass and swirling the wine around a little before taking a small sip. It was delicious, just as I'd remembered. It'd been a while since I'd had a glass of red wine to savor like that. When I opened my eyes, mine caught with Aaron's who was staring intently at me, his breathing obviously increased. My own body began to respond to the apparent sexual tension.

"Stop it," I muttered across the table.

He raised an eyebrow.

"We're in public."

"So?"

I pushed out a breath. "Aaron."

"Saying my name like that isn't helping your case."

I shifted in my chair, uncrossing and recrossing my legs. "Is that all this is to you? Sex?" I whispered, leaning into the table. I wanted to ask if that was all I ever was to him, but I cut myself off.

His eyelids lowered, covering his eyes and not for the first time I admired his long lashes. I could stare at him for hours, memorizing every minute aspect of his body. In fact, I had. Unfortunately, my memory never failed to conjure up images of his perfect body—scars and all—on those long, lonely nights throughout the past half decade.

"It was never just about sex," he finally answered.

I swallowed the lump that formed in my throat. I shook my head, as I stared down at the table. I didn't know if that answer helped or hurt. If it had just been about sex, I might've been able to understand. It might have made hating him a little easier.

"If you say so," I mumbled, taking another sip of my wine.

"She wasn't my—"

"Your what? Your fiancée? Pretty sure she was."

"She wasn't you." He leaned into the table, glaring.

Again, I bit the inside of my cheek. I rolled my eyes, looking away from him because I hated the feeling that overcame me when I stared for too long.

"Let's just get through this dinner. I'm sure you have some work you need to get back to."

Any response he had was cut off when D'Angelo returned to take our dinner orders. We ate mostly in silence at first, until Aaron prodded me about my former job back in Oakland. I decided to play along and answer his questions. I enjoyed talking about my job, and then even went so far as to ask about his work.

"How's the deal with Oiltec working out?"

He looked up, stunned, as he wiped his mouth. "You've been following Townsend?"

I gave a one shoulder shrug. "After Chicago, I saw an article about the merger and couldn't stop myself from reading it." I'd tried to avoid all news involving Townsend Industries, but after our encounter in The Windy City, my curiosity got the best of me.

Aaron went on to breakdown the news about the merger with Oiltec and how he'd hoped it would grow Townsend's market, especially overseas. We both got lost talking about our jobs. That was safe territory for us, which was good. By eight o'clock that night, we were exiting the restaurant, bellies full. I stepped out of the restaurant, looking around the street, seeing the bustling people, but noting the empty space down the street.

"The bookstore closed," I said out loud.

"More than four years ago. Few businesses have tried to buy the space but the owner has been holding out."

I wrinkled my forehead. "That's odd. It's just losing money, owning it and not doing anything with it."

Aaron nodded. "It is. Get in," he ordered, holding the door open for me.

I climbed in the backseat and moved over to make room for him. As soon as he closed the door, we pulled off. I felt a strong hand take hold of my hand, which rested in between us. I looked down to see his much larger one covering mine. He didn't say anything, just kept ahold of my hand the entire thirty minute drive back to our Cedarwoods neighborhood.

I looked out the window, and not for the first time, made note of the Townsend Industries signs.

"Joshua started this endeavor?" I asked, still staring out the windows at the already built homes and the ones still being constructed.

"Almost four years ago."

"All four of you decided to build here?" Carter and Michelle lived right next to Aaron and I. I remember the day we moved in, one of the movers pointed out that Joshua was having his home built there along with their youngest brother, Tyler.

Aaron eased closer to me, his leg leaning into mine. He pointed in the direction of a house that was under construction. "That's Joshua's. He'll be three doors away from us. On the far right side of our home is Tyler's lot. He hasn't begun building yet. Carter was the first to build his home, then me."

I cleared my throat, pushing my locs back over my shoulder. "Just like your age ranges." I turned to smile at him and his lips were less than an inch from mine. The air caught in my airway. Just when I thought he would lower his lips to mine, the car stopped.

"We're here," he informed me just before leaning over me to push the car door open. He climbed over me to get out first and then held his hand for me to exit. We made our way to Carter and Michelle's front door to pick up our children. The outing was officially over but something was just beginning.

* * *

"Have lunch with me?"

I smiled at the card in my hands and then lifted the bouquet of white roses to my nose.

"I think someone's trying to woo you," Moira giggled behind me.

I turned, frowning. "It might actually be working too."

She gave me a confused look.

"We *are* closing early today," she stated, rushing past the awkward moment.

I nodded, knowing that I'd be out of the library by noon that Friday. Aaron knew, too, which was why he'd had this bouquet delivered, requesting I join him for lunch.

"Do you need me to stay late to help with anything?" I asked.

"No. As soon as that clock strikes noon, I'm out of here. Long weekend."

I nodded, remembering Moira was going away with her husband for the weekend. "Okay." Pulling out my phone, I sent a text to Aaron's personal cell letting him know I'd be joining him for lunch at his office.

By the time I stepped out of the library, Daniel was already there waiting, a smile on his face as he held the door open.

"To Townsend Industries," he confirmed.

I nodded and ducked inside the car. We made it to Townsend's headquarters in just over twenty minutes. We pulled into the garage, directly in front of the elevator that went all the way to the top floor. It was Aaron's private elevator.

"The code is 391989."

I stilled as the security guard informed me of the elevator's code. "Are you sure?" I asked dumbly.

He gave me a funny look before straightening his face. "Yes, ma'am. Is there something the matter?"

I shook my head. "No, of course not." I wasn't going to tell this security guard that code was my birthdate. I stepped on, punching in the code, and was carried up the thirty flights to Aaron's floor. I nearly ducked my head as I passed by the administrative employees who were outside in the main office. I hadn't exactly put my best foot forward the last time I'd shown up at this place, less than a week prior.

"Mr. Townsend is expecting you. You can go right in," his executive assistant, Mark, stated from behind his large desk.

I didn't even get the chance to turn the knob before the door was opened from the inside. My breath hitched a little at the imposing sight of Aaron standing there, greeting me with a stern yet welcoming expression on his face. Well, it was welcoming to me. Most people would've seen the usual scowl but I saw the way his eyes lit up slightly, and the gentle softening of his mouth.

"Come in. Mark, hold my calls for the next hour and a half."

My eyes widened as I stepped inside. "An hour and a half?"

"That's a normal lunch time, right?" He gave me a serious look.

I giggled. "You're so unfamiliar with taking a lunch you don't know how long one should be."

He shrugged, moving closer to me, wrapping an arm around my waist. He leaned down close to my ear. "We can always find something more to do than eat." His hand moved lower until it covered my ass, squeezing it.

"Aa—" His name was cut off by his lips covering mine. Too soon, he pulled back and took me by the hand, leading us to the conference table that already had our lunch set up.

"Tuna salad for you. Although it's reeking up my office," he grunted.

I grinned, sitting down in the chair he'd pulled out for me and grabbing my tuna salad sandwich.

"How was work?" he questioned, as he dug into his own chicken salad.

"Great," I beamed. "We're starting a drive for toys for kids in need next week. It's close to the end of September and the holidays will be here before we know it. I convinced Moira it was better to get the drive started early rather than later."

He nodded. "You've always given back."

I grinned. "Not always. I went through a selfish phase."

He grunted. "When?"

"As a teen. I think we all do."

"Most never grow out of it." He frowned.

"Ever the pessimist."

"I'll leave the optimism to you."

We talked a little more about the drive and my idea to get Kyle and Kennedy involved.

When the discussion lulled, I stood to stretch and went to gaze out the window. "You can see all of Williamsport from this view."

I felt him move behind me.

"You said the same thing the first time I brought you to this very office."

My eyelids slowly closed, the memory of those days and his presence at my back too much to bear.

"Said this would be my office one day instead of my father's. And it was my responsibility to do right by it. That was our first night together."

I abruptly turned, anger rising in my belly for some reason. I didn't want those memories forced on me. I was too raw. "Aaron, don't!" I hissed.

"Don't what?" He continued, "Remind you of us? Our first time together?"

I clamped my mouth shut, doing my best to ward off the inevitable. He wasn't about to let me forget it all. No matter how much I tried to.

* * *

THEN

"Let's go, Mr. *CEO*. We're going to be late for our reservation," I giggled, pulling him by his arm from his desk. Aaron had brought me to Townsend Industries on our way to dinner just to pick up a file he needed to review for the next morning. Since he'd taken that day off, and we'd spent the entire day together, he hadn't had any other opportunity to pick it up.

"I'm coming," he gritted out, causing me to laugh even more.

I loved his impatient, arrogant, stern side, which was close to just about every side of him. On the way in, we'd paused at his father's office. He showed me into the large corner office that showed just about every angle of the city through the long floor to ceiling windows.

"Got it. Let's go." He tugged me by the arm and I followed him out.

"I'm starving," I said as we piled into the back of the car, pulling off for the dinner reservations we had at my favorite Italian restaurant—the same one we'd met my father at for dinner more than a two months prior.

We arrived at the restaurant and the hostess seated us at the exact same spot we had dined before.

"What was so important about this file that you just *had* to have it tonight?" I teased Aaron at the same time I swiped a piece of garlic bread from the basket.

"It has the financial report for the tech company in Japan we're looking to buyout."

I nodded. "And it couldn't wait 'til morning?"

"Meetings first thing tomorrow morning. I'll need to review tonight." He began opening the file as if he was going to start reviewing right there.

"Oh no!" I stated, slapping my hand over the folder, closing it. "I just finished my finals. You just completed a different merger deal. We promised today was a day off for the both of us. You can at least give me until after dinner." I gave him a look and that softening of his eyes happened, making my own heart skip a beat.

He inclined his head, placing the folder to the side, appeasing me. We talked more about our plans for the rest of the evening and I surprised myself by asking Aaron if he would attend my graduation. It was in two weeks. I was done with graduate school and ready to start my career.

"I'll be there," he agreed, and I had to stop myself from jumping over the table into his lap. I'm sure I would've kissed him had I done that, despite us never having even done that, still. For some reason he always held back. I couldn't figure out why, save for the notion that maybe this thing really was just some type of friendship for him. But then there were times I caught him staring at me and my entire body felt like a raw, exposed nerve. Maybe it was just me.

"I'll be right back," I stated, placing my napkin on the table.

He stood and pulled out my chair, and I smiled at him over my shoulder before heading in the direction of the restroom. Unfortunately, there was a line for the bathroom so I had to wait. Once inside it only took about five minutes to relieve myself, wash my hands, and head back to the table. Just as I was on my way back, I was stopped by a classmate of mine.

"Hey, Gary," I greeted as he stopped me by the arm. "Out celebrating?" I questioned after seeing a family full of people behind him.

Gary turned to look over his shoulder and then back at me, grinning. "It's my birthday and the end of finals. My family wanted to come and celebrate."

"That nice of them."

We chit chatted for a few minutes about how excited we were to be done with our degrees and our prospects for the future. I hadn't even realized Gary's hand still covered my arm until I heard...

"What the hell are you doing?" The hardness in Aaron's voice literally caused me to jump, even though he hadn't yelled them.

"Aaron," I stated, startled, "this is–"

"Why the fuck is he touching you?" His laser sharp gaze was on my arm where Gary's hand rested. Gary snatched his hand away as if he'd been burned.

"Why are you... Aaron, calm down," I urged as he took a threatening step toward Gary.

I gasped when he grabbed my former classmate by the collar of his shirt, right in the middle of the restaurant.

"Don't ever fucking touch her again," he seethed.

I pushed my hand into his chest. "Aaron, stop. Let him go!"

Aaron stared at Gary as if he was contemplating whether or not to kill him right there or listen to me. Thankfully, in the end, he let him go, pushing him a few feet back. I was just about to light into Aaron when he grabbed me by the arm, tugging me toward the door. We made it to the awaiting car where he damn near shoved me inside. As soon as he closed the door, I whirled on him.

"What the hell is your problem?"

"You fucked him?" he asked me as if that was the appropriate response.

"What the hell? Why would you even ask me something like that?"

"Why was he so comfortable touching you?"

"It was just a friendly gesture. He wasn't trying to screw me in the middle of a restaurant for God's sake!"

"Men don't do *friendly gestures*."

"Whatever," I muttered, grateful we'd arrived at my apartment. I didn't wait for the car door to be opened before I pushed it open and stormed up to my front door, entering the code. I was ready to shut Aaron out of the building, but a strong hand gripped the door above my head, forcing it open behind me. I ignored him as I rifled through my bag while jogging up the stairs to my apartment. I arrived again, ready to lock him out, but he charged in after me, slamming it behind us and locking it.

"I want you to leave!" I demanded.

"Why? So you can call him?"

"Are you serious right now? Why the hell do you care anyway?" I yelled. "It's not like you and I are anything, are we?"

He remained silent, watching me, chest heaving up and down. But his eyes had darkened to a color I'd never seen before.

"That's what I thought!" I continued, angered anew by his non-response. He'd spent the last two months sleeping over my apartment. Taking me on dates, coming down to the library with me as I volunteered, but not once had he touched me in the way a man who wants a woman does. I laid up too many nights wishing he would give me a sign beyond what he already gave to indicate what was happening between us. But even then, he just stood there, half looking like a raging bull ready to charge, while the other part of him look conflicted.

Fuck it.

I made the decision for both of us.

In two steps, I moved to Aaron, lifting myself on my tiptoes and pulling his face to mine, connecting our lips. I ran my tongue along the seam of his mouth, trying to urge them apart. I attempted to move in closer for more, but was abruptly pushed away from his body. Breathless, I stood two feet from him, staring at him as he watched me, the only thing heard in the room was the panting coming from the both of us. My eyes dropped and the huge bulge in his jeans told me what his mouth wouldn't. I moved in again, kissing him. This time his lips parted, granting me a little bit more of a taste of him, before I was pushed away again. I stared some more, watching as his eyes narrowed, his eyes darkening even more.

I charged him again, this time bringing his mouth to mine and tearing at his shirt, revealing his chest. I let my fingers run along his chest but pulled back when I felt rigid lines instead of smooth skin. I lowered my eyes to his chest to find it marred with scars. They were obviously years' old but they were there. I glanced back up at Aaron who was still eyeing me, but this time his jaw was tightly closed as he watched me. I let my eyes fall again to his chest, moving in closer as I pressed a kiss to one scar, then another, and another. I ran my tongue over the longest one that ran diagonally across his chest.

"Ah!" I yelped when my arms were gripped tightly and my back was forced against my front door. Aaron's lips crashed over mine in a way that stole every ounce of air from my body. His tongue invaded my mouth and I felt his rock hardness pressing into my stomach. This wasn't gentle or soft. I knew it wouldn't be. I didn't think Aaron knew how to be gentle. But I didn't need it. I just needed him.

I moaned into his mouth when I felt his hands go to the button of my jeans, undoing them and ripping them and my panties down my legs. He completely removed my pants before undoing his own belt buckle and jeans, freeing himself. All the while, his kisses kept me dizzy with need and anticipation. I wanted to warn him but his kisses felt too good to break free to tell him what I needed to say.

"This is what you wanted, right?" He grunted at the same time he raised my legs to wrap around his waist.

"Y-yes!" I stuttered, teeth chattering as the anticipation ran through my body. I felt him line himself up with my pussy just before he surged completely in, filling me. My vision blurred with tears as pain ripped through my entire body.

"Ahhhhh!" I screamed, fingernails digging into Aaron's shoulders.

He went completely rigid.

"Fuck!" he grunted while pounding his fist against the door behind me. He lowered his head to my shoulder, sighing heavily. "You're a fucking virgin," he stated, more to himself than to me.

"N-not any m-more," I stammered.

Aaron grunted and began pulling out.

"No, don't! The p-pain will go away."

"How do you know?"

"I read it in a book."

He pulled back to stare at me. "A book?" He frowned.

I grinned, which probably came across as a grimace, then lowered my head to his shoulder, squeezing him to me even more.

"Where are we going?" I questioned, lifting my head to see us moving away from the door.

"Your first time won't be up against the goddamned door."

I heard a banging sound as he kicked open my bedroom door, carrying me over to my bed and laying me down.

"Don't!" I said again as he began pulling out.

He pressed a kiss to my lips. "Trust me."

I moaned as he pulled completely out of me.

He moved back, kneeling over me, his hands going to the off-the-shoulder, white top I'd worn just because he said he liked seeing my shoulders. He tossed my shirt and then my strapless bra over the side of the bed. He removed his own shirt and then his pants. That was when I got to see all of him for the first time. Fear seized me when I saw exactly how long and thick he was. I'd felt his bulge before, times when I'd sat on his lap, but seeing it out in the open, I couldn't take my eyes off of it.

"Give me your hands," he ordered.

I held up my hands for him. He took both of my wrists into one of his hands, forcing them back over my head, pushing my legs apart with his knee. His other hand went to my left breast, squeezing it before he covered the nipple with his mouth. I moaned and wiggled my hips against him. He released my breast from his mouth and stared down at me.

"I'll try to be as gentle as possible but I can't promise anything," he warned at the same time I felt the tip of his cock touch my pussy lips.

"I don't want gentle. I want you."

His nostrils flared and he surged forward, pushing all the way inside of me again. It hurt less the second time around but it was still uncomfortable. But I'd meant what I'd said. I just needed Aaron. I didn't want him to hold back.

With his free hand, he lifted my left leg, curling it around his waist, before pulling out and pressing back into me again.

"Breathe, Patience," he ordered. "Breathe!"

I pushed out a gush of air before inhaling again, realizing I'd forgotten my body's basic functioning. I wanted to cling to him, to pull him to me, for our lips to touch. But he continued to hold my wrists down with his one hand, while holding my leg in place with the other. He peered down at me, watching me with dark eyes.

I pushed my head back against the pillow, hips rising to meet his. The pain and uncomfortable feeling began to recede, and it was followed by a blossoming of something much less painful.

"Aaron!" I yelled when he suddenly pulled out of me and flipped me onto my stomach. My hands were again held down to the bed by his much stronger ones and he entered me from behind. I screamed into the bedsheets, biting them, as his hips surged in and out, filling me over and over with his rod. He took my hands in his one hand again and then used his knee to spread my legs. His free hand moved down my waist, over my hip, to that bundle of nerves above the opening he was now pounding, massaging it. I screamed again as the most euphoric feeling flooded every cell in my body. It felt like fireworks went off in my pussy and sent its aftershocks throughout the rest of my body. I panted, calling out his name over and over again, but he wasn't done.

Aaron pulled out, turning me on my back again, lifting both of my knees high and backwards. He pressed into me so much deeper that I thought I might actually gag on his dick.

"Aaron," I panted his name, lifting my head, needing to feel his lips.

He lowered to me, letting me capture his lips with mine. I don't know if it was the kiss or the pressure of he was applying to my clit yet again, but a second orgasm shot off in me. My toes curled at the same time Aaron bit my bottom lip as I came, yelling out his name.

Soon after I felt him grow inside of me just before his own orgasm caused him to spill his seed in me. He fell into me, again taking my lips and kissing me with a possessiveness I had never known. He pulled back, eventually, and removed himself from me. We both groaned as he did. I was spent, but watched as he left my bedroom to go to the bathroom across the hall. The last thing I remembered feeling was him wipe something warm and wet between my legs, before I fell asleep.

* * *

I AWOKE a few hours later to an empty bed. My heart sank at first until I looked toward my bedroom window to see Aaron, completely nude, while he stared out the window. I swallowed deeply as my eyes trailed down his muscular back. I could make out a few scars there, too, down to his well-sculpted ass. I shifted in the bed and my breath was completely stolen by the soreness between my legs.

Aaron turned to look at me over his shoulder, coming over to the bed. He stood over me, completely exposed and bare, and unashamed. He surprised me by ripping the sheets away from me, exposing me as well. His left hand moved down my belly to cup my pussy. I licked my lips, anticipating his next move. I felt too sore to do anything remotely close to what we'd done earlier but I wasn't sure I could turn him down either.

"Are you sore?" he questioned low, his hand still covering my sex.

"No." I shook my head.

Aaron frowned, eyes narrowing. He leaned down closer, face hovering over mine. "Don't ever lie to me."

I shrank back a little into the pillow. "A little," I answered just above a whisper.

"Let me help you with that." He stood, climbing onto the bed between my legs, using his body to spread them. He hooked his forearms under my knees and with his eyes still trained on me, he lowered his face, licking my sex.

I gasped at the pleasure that coursed through me. Aaron took his gaze off me and placed it on the body part he was so intently focused on. He sucked and tongue fucked me. I was pretty sure at one point, he literally spelled his name on my pussy with his mouth. I came quickly from his tongue's ministrations. I thought he would stop after the first orgasm he'd give me with is mouth, but that wasn't so. By the third time he'd made me come, I was trying to push him off me, but that earned me a smack against my ass, right before he gripped it and pressed me even farther onto his mouth. It wasn't until the fourth orgasm that he finally rose from between my legs, licking his lips before hovering over me to kiss me. I tasted myself on him, feeling more wanton than I ever thought possible.

When he finally let me up for air, from the kiss we were both panting. He rolled over to his back, breathing heavily. I moved in closer, letting my hand cover his beating heart.

"You're too tender for me to take you again tonight but I can't promise I won't if you keep touching me."

Grinning at his warning, I moved in closer. I felt his arm come around my backside, squeezing my ass. I let my hand run over the scars of his chest.

"How'd it happen?" I questioned.

I felt him raise his head to look down at me. I continued to keep my eyes on the scars, feeling them.

He lowered his head to the pillow. "Car accident."

"How old were you?"

"Eight."

"Who was driving?"

"My father."

I lifted my head to stare at him. "Robert?"

His lips pinched. "My birth father, Jason Townsend. Robert's younger brother. Robert is my uncle."

"But you call him your dad."

"After my parents were killed, Robert and Deborah adopted me. They're my parents, just not biologically."

I nodded, understanding. I pressed a kiss to his largest scar before laying my head on his chest.

"What caused the accident?"

There was a long pause. "He was drunk, had just gotten into a fight with his brother and then began fighting with my mother in the car. Turns out, drinking and beating your wife while driving is a surefire way to kill yourself."

I rubbed my hand down Aaron's abdomen. It would only be later that I found out that wasn't the entire story.

"Why were you a virgin?"

My hand stilled. I felt his hand run through the shoulder-length locs I had been wearing for a little over a year.

"I just never found someone I wanted to give myself to."

He grunted but didn't question me further on the lie. The truth was since I was fourteen years old there'd only been one person I wanted enough to give my virginity. But I kept that to myself. Instead, I rose up, and straddled Aaron, sitting on his hips.

"What are you doing?"

"Show me."

He looked perplexed. "Show you what?"

"How to ride you."

I smirked when I felt his cock smack against my ass beneath the sheet.

"No," he stated flatly.

"You don't want me?"

His hands went to my hips. "Does it feel like I don't want you." He moved his hips a little, letting me feel his girth.

"Then why not?"

"You're too tender."

I yelped when he rolled us so that I was on my back.

"Next time."

I sighed. "Fine." I moved back into the position with my head laying on his chest. "Tell me more about your family."

His hand stilled while he debated. I opted to wait him out, and in the end he began talking. I listened intently as he shared about his biological parents. And the more I listened the angrier I grew.

CHAPTER 16

Patience

My eyes sprang open to the Williamsport skyline in front of me, through the window. And as breathtaking as the view was it didn't compare to the feeling of Aaron's warm breath against the column of my neck, as he leaned over me. His large hand found its way into the black dress pants I'd worn to work that day. My head fell back against his shoulder when the pad of his finger brushed over my distended clit.

"You remember that first time?" he said low in my ear. "I'd put it off. I was trying to save you from this. From me. But I couldn't stay away from you."

I couldn't comprehend his words due to my brain being fogged up by the sensations he was causing in my body. I pressed my hand firmly against the glass of the window, my hips moving closer, trying to get some sort of reprieve.

"You were mine from the very first night."

I moaned when he pinched my clit between his thumb and forefinger. "W-we can't," I managed to get out. "This is y-your office."

"You think there're any limitations on where I take you? Or *how?*" His hand moved from my pussy lips, over my hip to grab the flesh of my ass. A tingle moved through my core at the remembrance of my first, and only, anal sexual experience.

Somehow I managed to find the strength to get a grip on reality. I grabbed his hand by the wrist, freeing it from my pants and turning to him. A sensation of fear mixed with anticipation moved through me when I turned to see his downcast eyes, staring at my hand covering his wrist.

"You're going to pay fo–" His reprimand was cut off by his ringing phone.

Saved by the bell, I thought, sighing. A minute later and there was a very good chance I would've found myself bent over his desk, ass exposed, being paddled. I wouldn't put it past him to have a paddle in his office.

"This better be fucking important!" he barked into the phone.

I shook my head. He was such an ass. *An ass you've never stopped loving.* I closed my eyes to the truth of that statement.

"Put her through," he demanded, removing the phone from his ear and pressing the button to put the call on speaker.

Sensing he wanted me to hear the conversation as well, I went over to his desk, peering down at the phone.

"Mr. Townsend, it's Mrs. Jamison from Excelor Academy."

My heart rate quickened. *The children.*

"I've left a message on Mrs. Townsend's cell."

"What happened?"

"What's wrong?"

Aaron and I blurted out at the same time.

"Kyle and Kennedy and their cousin, Diego. They're fine but they got into a fight."

"With each other?" I questioned. That didn't make any sense. The twins loved Diego and he them.

"Not quite. The three of them got into a fight with another student."

My eyes ballooned as I looked toward Aaron, whose usual scowl was back in place.

"We'll be there in ten minutes," he stated before pressing the button to end the call.

"You could've given her more time to explain what happened," I chided.

"She can explain once I'm standing in her office." He picked up the phone and called Daniel to have the car ready to take us to Excelor, right before informing Mark that he needed to leave for the next hour. Ten minutes later we were in the car, on our way to the school. I knew as soon as we arrived my husband would be like a raging bull. I just prayed no one ended up on the wrong end of his horns.

* * *

"What happened?!" Aaron demanded as soon as we passed through the door's of the main office.

"Daddy! Mommy!" Kennedy yelled, running up to us in her usual effusive manner.

"Are you okay? Where's your brother?' I questioned, placing her back down, after picking her up to hug.

"Right there." She turned and pointed to the far wall where a sullen looking Kyle and Diego sat next to one another.

"Kyle, Diego, are you guys hurt?"

"No," they both answered in unison, shaking their heads.

"You were fighting?" Aaron asked, coming up behind me.

I watched as the boys' eyes grew big.

"Yes, but–"

"Yes, *but?*" Aaron asked, interrupting Kyle.

"Mr. and Mrs. Townsend."

I turned to see an average height, middle-aged woman walking toward us.

"Mrs. Jamison, what happened?" I asked.

"Please, step into my office. Mrs. Townsend, Diego's mother," she amended, realizing there was more than one Mrs. Townsend in this scenario, "is on her way. She should be here shortly, along with the other little boy's father."

"Kennedy, go sit by your brother," I urged her toward the open chair next to Kyle, while Aaron and I followed Mrs. Jamison to her office.

"Why don't you explain what happened while we wait for everyone else." Aaron started in on Mrs. Jamison before she even had a chance to close her door fully. He planted his feet, folding his arms over his chest, staring the principal down.

"You said they got into a fight?" I questioned, drawing her fearful eyes from my husband to myself.

"They jumped on another little boy."

"My children aren't violent," Aaron insisted.

I looked from him to the principal. "He means, they have never been in a fight before. I find it difficult to wrap my head around Kyle and Kennedy, let alone Diego, just ganging up on another child."

A knock sounded at the door and a second later, Michelle opened it, entering.

"Hey," she acknowledged Aaron and I. "Mrs. Jamison, what happened? I got a call saying the kids fought someone?"

"Mrs. Jamison was just about to explain how that's even possible," Aaron urged.

I watched as Michelle gave Aaron that same wary look most people did.

"Yes." The principal nodded. "I wanted to wait until the other little boy's parents were here, but since you three are already here, I will explain. It seems Kyle got into a disagreement with a boy from another class and Diego stepped in to defend Kyle. It got heated just as the kindergarteners were leaving from recess and the second and third graders were coming in. Kyle, Diego, and the boy began fighting, and one of the teachers stated she saw Kennedy run into the fight to kick the other boy."

I had to tamp down on the pride I felt hearing Kennedy went to defend her brother in a fight. I was a parent and shouldn't be encouraging that type of behavior.

"Was this boy in Kyle's class?" Aaron asked.

"No. He was one of the third graders."

"He's in Diego's class?" Michelle questioned.

"Same grade but different class."

"And they got into a *disagreement?*" I could hear Aaron's anger growing as he pieced the story together.

I reached out, wrapping my arm around his elbow.

"Mrs. Jamison, you're saying that a third grader was *picking* on Kyle, a kindergartener, and none of the teachers bothered to stop it, so his older cousin had to step in? And when it escalated into a physical altercation my son's sister also intervened? Do I have that right?" My own anger was rising.

"Well, I w-wouldn't put it like that?" she stuttered as she looked between the three of us.

"Then how would you put it?" Michelle questioned.

"And who is this other little boy? What was he saying to Kyle? Where are his parents?" I shot the questions rapid fire.

As if in response to my questions, another man came charging through the door. I turned and squinted, realizing this man looked awfully familiar.

"Mr. McCloud," Mrs. Jamison commented.

"McCloud?" Aaron questioned. "As in Wallace McCloud of McCloud renovations?"

I blinked remembering Wallace Jr. from my high school days.

"I was just explaining to the Townsends–"

"How their damn kids beat up my boy?" Wallace seethed. "He has a black eye and busted lip from those damn mongrels!"

"Oh God!" I yelped when in less than two steps, Aaron was in Wallace's face, hand wrapped around his throat. This scene was eerily familiar.

"Two things," Aaron stated through gritted teeth. "Don't *ever* in your pitiful life refer to my children or my nephew in such terms. And two, if we weren't in this office right now I'd show you *exactly* how much of a mongrel their father is."

"Aaron, please," I whispered, going up to tug at his arm. "Our children are right outside."

Slowly Aaron loosened his grip and stepped back from Wallace. I took his hand in mine, pulling him closer to me, and farther away from Wallace.

"And what exactly did his child say that caused Kyle to respond so negatively?" Aaron turned to Mrs. Jamison to ask.

Her eyes shifted from Aaron to myself and then over to Wallace, who was now standing in the far corner of the room.

"To my understanding, there were some derisive comments made about Kyle's reading ability."

Aaron's hand tightened around mine. I bit the inside of my cheek as my heart plummeted.

"Was this the first incident?"

"No, I don't think so, Mrs. Townsend."

"You don't think so?" Aaron repeated condescendingly.

She swallowed and shook her head. "According to Diego and Kyle, this has been an ongoing issue since the first week of school."

"Un-fucking-believable," Aaron blurted. "The school year is a month old. So, this has been going on for weeks then?"

"Mr. Townsend, I understand—"

"You understand what? That you allowed my son to be bullied. Didn't tell either one of his parents and only waited until a physical altercation occurred, which by the way, you framed as our children jumping another boy. When the truth was my son was defending himself against a child who is three years older than himself?" Aaron's voice rose with each question he asked. He stepped forward, planting his fists onto the principal's desk. "Let me explain something to you, Mrs. Jamison. I went to this school. My wife went to this school. We put our children here because Excelor has the reputation of being one of the highest ranking academies in the state. But I promise you if anything like this ever happens again, I will shut this all down!"

He stepped back, pulled me by the hand to the door, holding it open for both Michelle and I, giving Wallace—who'd remained silent—one last glare before slamming it shut.

"Are we in trouble, Mommy?" Kyle asked, using the most pitiful face he could. My entire heart caught in my throat. I always feared a day like this was inevitable.

AARON'S PATIENCE

"Hey, what happened?"

I turned to see Carter, dressed in his firefighter overalls, running toward us as we stepped into the hallway.

"We were on a call. Diego, are you okay?" He bent low, checking over the little boy who was obviously so much more than just his stepson. Technically, Diego was Carter's son, since he'd adopted him.

"He's fine." Michelle went on to explain everything to Carter. He became just as pissed as his brother.

"These two." Michelle grinned looking at me and gesturing toward our husbands.

I rolled my eyes. "Right? Who the hell wants to deal with not one but two angry Townsends?"

"Not me," she laughed.

"Mama, can we get ice cream with my cousin?"

"Yes, Mommy, please!" Kyle and Kennedy shouted, backing up Diego's request.

"No!" Michelle and I both answered.

"Why not?" Carter asked, looking confused.

"They just got into a fight," I explained.

"And?"

My mouth fell open as I looked at Aaron.

"It was self-defense," Carter added.

Michelle and I glanced at one another, shaking our heads. These men were impossible. We put the kids in the car.

"You all right?" I asked Michelle, noticing she was holding her stomach.

"Yeah, just a stomach bug, I think. I was taking half a day at work anyway today to rest."

"You want us to take Diego so you can rest?"

She shook her head. "Carter's taking the rest of the day off, so I'll be good. Those two are like peas in a pod."

"All right. Talk to you later." I went over to the awaiting car and climbed in the door that Aaron held open.

On the way back home, I had to explain to not only the children but their father as well that we would not be stopping for ice cream.

Even though what happened was a form of self-defense on Kyle's behalf, there were still better ways to have handled the situation. I was adamant about only promoting physical violence when and where necessary. I didn't know who wore the biggest pout—Kennedy, Kyle, or Aaron.

CHAPTER 17

Aaron

I watched from the doorway as Patience finished up the night's reading with Kennedy. I'd just put Kyle down to bed after we finished up a round of video games and some drawing. I could hardly believe that this is what my nights had become. Playing video games and drawing before watching my wife complete up her nightly routine with the children. I was also beginning to realize that there was absolutely no place I'd rather be. I was starting to loathe the idea that I had a business trip the following week, even though it was only for two nights.

Patience's lips turned upward as she shut off Kennedy's light and passed me, closing the door. I barely moved, instead forcing her body to brush up against mine. I grinned inwardly when I saw the vein in her neck kick up in its beating rate. I followed her into our bedroom, shutting the door behind us. As she went to wash her face and brush her teeth for the evening, I changed into my pair of pajama bottoms and remained shirtless, per usual. I'd gotten in the habit of sleeping without a shirt, even though the idea had always made me cringe as a child and young man. The thought of someone seeing my scars and daring to ask about them always made me agitated. But ever since our very first time together, when she kissed my scars, that agitation went away. It was why I had no problem when Kyle asked about them. The tattoo, on the other hand...

"What are you thinking about?"

I lifted my gaze to see sepia eyes staring at me.

"Kyle."

"What about him?"

I folded my arms across my chest, tilting my head but remained silent.

Patience sighed, moving to sit on the bed, cross legged. "Ask me."

"Does he–"

"I think so."

Everything in my body clenched. My hands tightened into fists and my lips balled up.

"Aaron."

I shook my head, unable to answer her.

"Aaron!"

I turned my back.

Patience came to stand in front of me, hands at my sides.

"I did this."

"Stop it! Kyle being teased by another little boy is not your fault. It's that boy's parents for not raising him better."

"But his dyslexia *is* my fault."

There it was. My dirty little secret. One of them at least.

"It's no one's fault."

"It's why he hates reading."

She shrugged. "I don't know for sure. He's never been diagnosed because he's still so young. Most of the professionals say to wait until at least the second half of first grade to actually diagnose dyslexia."

"Meanwhile he remains picked on by shithead kids at school."

"Meanwhile, his father can help him."

"How?" I demanded, feeling hopeless.

"Aaron, Kyle's not broken. And neither were you," she affirmed, her grip tightening around my sides. "Y-your father was a jackass, and made you feel ashamed of being a poor reader. You weren't even diagnosed until after his death. You were a child. He was the adult. It was his responsibility to take care of you. Do that for your son. Show him how you learned to read." She got on her tiptoes and pulled my face between her hands. I stared down at her. "You run one of the most successful businesses in this country. And you didn't learn to read until you were eight years old. You don't think that's something to be proud of? Show our son what he's capable of because you've already done it. He'll listen to you."

I lowered my forehead to hers, wrapping my arm around her waist, pulling her to me.

"How do you always do that?" I asked, nuzzling her neck and pressing a kiss there.

She shivered. "Do what?"

"Make me feel like I'm ten feet tall."

"You *are* ten feet tall. To me."

I groaned and spun us both, moving us to the bed, while tearing at the short, silk gown she wore. I loved the way the silk laid against her walnut skin. I made a mental note to order some silk scarves the following day.

"Ah!" she yelped as I pushed her down onto the bed. "You're so damn rough!"

A devious smile spread over my lips. "Just the way you like it."

"Hmph!" came her response. "You know," she began, breathless as I ran my teeth along the column of her neck, "it's not nice to call eight year olds, shitheads."

I paused, then remembered calling the boy who'd picked on Kyle those words. "He is a shithead. And so is his father," I answered in between kisses to her breasts and belly.

Patience snickered. "You called him that the first time we ever met."

I stopped, moving over her to peer down into her face.

"You don't remember. Dinner at my father's. Wallace stole my *Harry Potter* book and when I kicked him you grabbed him by the throat much like you did today. You'd think he would've learned back then."

"He's not particularly smart. His company has shrunk in value by nearly half since he took over. And he is a shithead, just like his father and just like his son is destined to be. And *you* got saucy with me after I kicked Wallace out."

Her eyelids sprang wide.

"I remember."

"You called me a little girl! That pissed me off."

"I've pissed you off a lot more since then," I retorted at the same time I eased my pajamas down and slipped inside of her. I covered her mouth with mine. That was enough talking for one night.

* * *

"Kyle, wake up," I whispered, lightly shaking him by the shoulder.

It was four-thirty in the morning, and I had barely gotten an hour of sleep. But it was worth it for what I had planned. Ever since that first day, Kyle came down with me for my early morning workouts. Most times he would fall back asleep while in the basement, but others he stayed up with me throughout the entire workout.

"Morning, Daddy," he said groggily.

"Morning, son. Let's go." I picked him up out of bed and led him by the hand down the stairs, reminding him to keep his voice down so his mother and sister could still sleep. The lights in the den sprang on once we entered the room.

"Whoa!" Kyle exclaimed.

I looked around at the walls.

"What happened?" he questioned, confused.

"I made some changes." During the night, I'd done some work in my office, researching techniques on helping young children with dyslexia. I printed out tons of charts and graphs that had phonetic alphabet on them, basic words, and more. After laminating the charts, I did some rearranging of the gym equipment, clearing a space to hang the charts on the wall, creating a small reading nook, complete with a child-sized table and chair.

"This is for you," I explained.

Kyle's face scrunched up. "I don't like reading, Daddy."

I squatted low next to him and turned him to face me. "I know. I hated reading when I was your age."

"Really?"

I nodded. "It was hard. I got made fun of a lot so I stopped even trying for a long time. Got into lots of trouble at school, beating up kids, yelling at teachers."

"You yelled at your teacher?" His eyebrows rose high.

"I did. All because I didn't want them to make fun of me."

"You still don't know how to read?"

"I know how to read today. When I was eight, I came to live with your grandma and grandpa Townsend. They took me to some special people who told me the problem wasn't that I was stupid but I had a learning disability. They promised me that if I worked really hard, I could learn to read like everybody else."

"Did you do it?"

"Yup. I still have trouble sometimes but I'm a much better reader." I sighed, feeling a relief having explained all of this to my son. I never wanted him to feel like I had as a child. To that day, only a handful of people in the world knew about my dyslexia. I'd thought I'd moved past the shame my father had drilled into me as a kid but not until Patience told me about Kyle's condition did I understand that I still carried some of it with me.

"You think I can learn to read, Daddy?" Kyle looked from the wall to me, turning those hazel eyes that were the spitting image of my own on me. "Like Kennedy and Mommy?"

"Not only can you, but you will because I'm going to help you. You're a Townsend. We don't give up…on anything." I held his chin in my hand to keep his gaze on me. "Understood?"

He nodded.

"Good. Let's start with a workout." I had Kyle assist me in a series of exercises. Some of them were designed to help stabilize and strengthen the core. Those I had him do along side of me. I'd learned years prior that strange as it may sound, a strong core was great for balance and coordination, which aided eye muscles to work in sync.

That was important for tracking, or reading in a much more fluid manner. I'd never shared that one of the reasons I was so rigorous about my daily workouts was to assist in my overall reading ability, among other things.

After the workout, Kyle and I moved to the area that I'd set up for him. We began with the basics, starting at the alphabet and identifying each letter and their sounds. I lost track of time until Patience came down stairs and saw us in the middle of me reading out loud to Kyle. The expression on her face alone was worth every lost minute of sleep the previous night.

CHAPTER 18

Patience

If it's not one thing, it's another. Those were my exact thoughts as I rushed out of the park where I'd gone for a stroll during lunch. Unfortunately, I was already on edge, having had that creepy feeling that I was being watched. As I was scouring my surroundings, but finding no one even paying me any attention, my phone rang. It was my father, I thought. But nope. It was his friend, Wilhelmina, again. My father had had another heart attack.

"Daniel, I need to get to Williamsport General," I told my driver over the phone, again hating that I didn't have my own car for times like this. While waiting for Daniel, I went in and told Moira of the issue with my father and that I needed to leave. She insisted that I go. On the way to the hospital, I checked the time and realized I had a few hours before the kids were out of school. Maybe I would know what was going on by then.

I raced through the hospital doors, grabbing the first nurse I could find to tell me about my father's condition. She wasn't much help but she did lead me to where Wilhemina was.

"Wilhelmina," I stated, getting her attention. I stopped short when I saw the tears in her eyes.

"Oh, Patience." She lunged at me, pulling me in for a hug. "He's not doing well."

I pulled back, shaking my head, confused. "How can that be? I just saw him this weekend. He was doing well, laughing and playing with the kids."

She shrugged. "I don't know. The doctors aren't saying anything except that it happens sometimes. But go in, he's been asking for you." She pushed me toward the closed, wooden door of the hospital room.

I glanced back over my shoulder before turning the knob and entering. My stomach dropped when I saw my father lying in the bed, appearing so lifeless. He had tubes coming from his arms, chest, and nose. His chestnut skin looked almost ashen in color.

"Dad," I called lightly.

His eyelids fluttered open. "Patience." His voice sounded so weak.

"How're you feeling?" I asked, taking his hand in mine.

"I've been better," he chuckled lightly but stopped short needing to take a breath before continuing.

"Don't try to speak. You need to save your strength so you can get out of here. The twins are looking forward to their next visit."

A smile touched his lips. "They're so precious. Thank you for letting me spend time with them."

I lowered my gaze from his to the floor. I suddenly regretted my decision to not tell him about Kyle and Kennedy before recently.

"Don't make that face. Everything happens as it should. You did what was right by your children. A mother protects her children. That's all yours ever wanted for you."

I lifted my head, surprised. My father never spoke of my mother to me. Save for a few stories here and there and some pictures of her when I was younger, it was as if she didn't exist. As if I'd appeared out of thin air instead of being born on the same day my mother died.

"She loved you so much. I can't wait to tell her how lovely you turned out when I get up there to see her."

I frowned. He was talking crazily.

"Shh." I leaned in and pressed a kiss to his forehead. "You need to rest now. The doctors should be in soon and tell us what's going on.

We'll figure out how to get you well again." I smiled at him. "I'll sit with you until they do."

"I'd like that."

I pulled up the low sitting chair that was in the corner of the room to his bed and sat, wrapping his hand in mine. My father floated off to sleep. I hadn't realized I, too, had dozed off until Wilhelmina shook me by the shoulder.

"Patience, why don't you go get some coffee while I wait for the doctors?"

I sat up, looking at the clock on the wall. It was close to three o'clock. I'd already texted Michelle to see if she could have her mother pick the kids up with Diego.

"Okay," I whispered, before heading out the door. I started in the direction of the cafeteria but just opted for a walk outside. Though it was fall and the weather was getting cooler, there was still plenty of sunlight and warmth outside. I pulled out my phone to send another text to Aaron. He'd called, telling me he'd be at the hospital as soon as he was out of his meetings for the day. I tried to tell him not to bother but he was insistent.

By the time I'd made it back up to my father's hospital room, I was glad Aaron would be showing up at the hospital. I'd need his strength.

"I'm so sorry, Patience," Wilhelmina cried as soon as the elevator doors opened and she saw me come off. "There was nothing the doctors could do," she got out in between tears, before falling into my arms. "He's gone."

* * *

Nobody likes attending funerals, but if you live this life long enough, you can bank on attending at least a few. As the reverend prayed while lowering my father's casket into the ground, I mentally counted the number of funerals I'd been to. There was a friend of mine who'd died in a car accident in college. A cousin of mine when I was a teenager. My father's funeral now made three that I'd attended. I wondered if he'd taken me to my mother's funeral. That would make four but I doubted it. Then I wondered why I was thinking about it at all. Shouldn't I be crying or something? I glanced around and saw Wilhelmina's shoulders shaking as she sobbed. My own mother-in-law had tears in her eyes. Robert's expression gave away his grief. But me? I felt…numb. How do you mourn someone you barely even knew?

"Come on," Aaron urged, taking me by the waist once it was time to toss the dirt onto the casket and leave for the repast. It was held at Townsend Manor.

The entire ride over, I was silent. Feeling only Aaron's hold around my hand. I listened but didn't respond when Deborah commented on how beautiful the ceremony was. Robert had indeed spoke quite eloquently of his and my father's school days together. I moved through the rest of the afternoon in that state, seeing but not really seeing, eating but not really tasting.

"How're you holding up?"

I stared at my mother-in-law, not for the first time noting how beautiful she was.

"I'm okay. How's Robert doing? I know he and my father were good friends."

Deborah looked to the other side of the living room where they were. Robert was speaking with Aaron. I caught Aaron's eye and gave him a small smile before turning back to his mother.

"Robert's holding up. He'll miss their annual fishing trips."

I nodded and cleared my throat.

"The twins?" she asked.

"Michelle's mother was kind enough to watch them along with Diego for the day. I thought they were too young to be here."

She nodded. "I agree."

"They're always welcome to spend the night here so you and Aaron can have some private time."

"Thank you. I appreciate that."

"Don't thank me, it's more my own selfishness. I love them and the house is so quiet now that all the boys are grown up."

I laughed a little with her. We continued to talk some more until a few of the guests began to leave. Each one coming over and giving me their condolences. I grinned and beared it as best I could.

"We need to pick the kids up," I told Aaron as he held the door open for me.

He frowned. "Michelle said they could stay the night with them."

"I know, but I changed my mind. We need to get them."

He shook his head. "No, you need ti–"

"I don't!" I looked around to see a few stares my way, realizing I was yelling. "I don't need time to rest or whatever you were going to suggest. I just need our kids. Under the same roof as us tonight."

Aaron gave me the stare he often does when trying to decipher the meaning behind my words. He finally nodded. "Okay."

I sighed my relief, grateful that I wouldn't have to fight him on this. I didn't have the energy.

CHAPTER 19

Aaron

"Daddy, will you read to me?" Kennedy asked, jumping up and down on her bed, her curls and long nightgown flailing about as she did.

"Only if you stop jumping."

She plopped down on the bed, grinning up at me. My entire chest warmed with just that look. She was so much her mother's daughter. I was sure both had me wrapped around their pinky fingers.

"Which book is it tonight?"

"*Where the Wild Things Are!*" she shouted.

I plucked the book from her white wooden bookshelf and brought it with me to her bed, climbing in. She cozied up to me and I began reading, only for her to take over halfway through the story. She read for as long as she could, but eventually fell asleep against my chest. I waited until she was deep in sleep to ease out of the bed and pull the sheets and blanket up to cover her. I knew there was a good chance that somehow throughout the night that blanket would end up on the floor and the sheets would become all twisted up due to my little girl's sleeping style.

I gave her one last look, before turning off the light and shutting the door. Checking on Kyle, I found him fast asleep in his bed. I started to make my way down to the kitchen but got the urge to head to the bedroom. When I opened the door, I found Patience staring at a piece of paper. She looked up at me and my heart squeezed. The tears in her eyes ripped at my soul.

"Kyle made this." She turned the paper to me.

I could see his drawn images of Thiers, Kennedy, and himself, playing in a park. It had been a week since the funeral and Patience had barely mentioned her father. I hadn't brought it up much either, not out of fear but something else stopped me.

"Did you know my father and yours went on annual fishing trips?"

I squinted, easing fully into the room and shutting the door behind me. "Yes."

She gave a humorless laugh. "I didn't. He wanted to be an astronaut all the way up through high school. Did you know that?"

"No, I didn't."

"Me either. Not until the funeral, at least. He and Wilhelmina really were just friends. She's actually married. I didn't know that either."

"Patience—"

"I didn't know him." She pushed out a frustrated breath and slammed Kyle's picture on the dresser. "How could I be this upset over someone I didn't even know?" Her voice broke on a sob.

My legs carried me to her before my mind even registered the movement. "Patience," I consoled, going to wrap my arms around her.

"No," she stated, moving back and away from me. "I'm fine. I'm fine," she reiterated, heading toward the bathroom door and shutting it behind her.

I watched, wanting to go to her, but my anger kept me rooted in place.

"You're angry."

My jaw tightened. Against my better judgment I turned to see Emma standing in the middle of our bedroom, same long white nightgown and all.

"I'm not."

"Don't lie to me. You're pissed at Thiers."

"Not for dying."

"No, not for dying," she agreed, moving closer. "You're angry for her." She nodded to the bathroom door. "She's hurt. And you're pissed for her."

"He should've been a better father."

"Who says he wasn't a great father?"

"I do."

"Maybe you don't see the whole picture."

"What whole picture?"

"Let me show you." She moved closer, placing her hand in the middle of my forehead.

Everything went dark.

* * *

When I opened my eyes, I found myself standing in a hospital hallway.

"Is she going to be okay?"

I turned and got the surprise of my life when I saw a frantic looking Thiers pressed up against a doctor, begging for answers. I squinted. It was Thiers but he looked around thirty years younger.

"Is she going to be okay, Doctor? The baby?" he demanded.

"What is this?" I asked out loud.

"This is the day your wife was born," Emma responded, coming up next to me. Without touching me, I felt pushed to follow Emma as Theirs moved down the hall, following the doctor.

He entered a room and there I saw a woman who looked like she could pass for Patience, lying on the bed, belly swollen with child.

"You have to protect her, Daryl." Daryl was Thiers' actual name. "You're all she's going to have."

"Jeanette, stop talking like that. You were meant to be this little girl's mother." His voice was panic-stricken.

"Name her Patience," Jeanette continued. "That's the name I decided on."

"No. No. No. No," Thiers kept repeating over and over again, denying the inevitable.

"She died. Poor thing."

I looked to Emma. "I knew she died in childbirth. Why're you showing this to me."

"There's more." Another touch to my forehead and we were now in what I recognized as Thiers' home. The same one he'd raised Patience in. We were at the doorway of a nursery.

"I'm so sorry," Thiers cried, standing over a crib.

I glanced down and my heart stopped. Stepping closer, I saw a baby girl in the crib. She couldn't have been more than a few days old.

"Don't get too close," Emma warned, grabbing me by the arm. "Observe from a distance."

I stepped back just as an older black woman entered the nursery.

"Ms. Ryan, thank you for coming." Thiers stood, wiping his eyes.

"You're so welcome. When Jeanette contacted me a few weeks ago to help her nanny I had no idea it would end like this." The woman shook her head just as cries from the crib began. She picked the baby up. "This little one is hungry." She patted her back and bounced a little with the baby in her arms. "You want to feed her bottle to her?" Ms. Ryan asked Thiers.

He looked at the bottle in her free hand and started to reach for it but then hesitated. "No, you go on ahead. I-I've got some work to do." He rushed out of the room.

My eyes trailed him as he hurried down the stairs.

"He loved her so much, but the pain of losing his wife..."

My jaw flexed. "That's why he treated her as he did." It was a pitiful reason. Patience lost a mother the same day he'd lost a wife.

"Not the only reason."

Again a palm to my forehead and we were standing in a new location within the blink of an eye. I looked around.

"Buona Sera," I uttered. We were in the middle of the dining area of the restaurant. "This feels familiar."

"It should," Emma spoke over my shoulder, pointing me toward the door as Patience walked in. She was wearing the exact outfit she had on that first night I spent with her. I followed her steps and sure enough, she stopped at the table that held her father and myself. The whole scene played out as I remembered it. I couldn't take my eyes off her from the moment she arrived. Something happened the first time our eyes clashed. A warning. A signal. Love. I don't know but it was there from the first instant.

"You two were so cute," Emma gushed. "Oh, pay attention. Not to Patience," she insisted as I watched Patience as she headed in the direction of the restroom. "To Thiers." Emma turned my head back to the table.

Thiers and I had both risen. The younger version of me looked down at the wallet I'd dug out of my pocket. But from my present angle I watched as Thiers' eyes grew wide as he stared out the window. I pivoted my gaze out the window and saw a man standing in front of a dark Lincoln. It looked similar to my town car but wasn't mine. The man shifted, putting his hand in his pocket, moving his jacket aside just enough that I could make out the butt of a nine millimeter. Abruptly, Thiers turned to my younger self, asking if I could tell Patience that he had to leave. He didn't wait for my response. Instead, he threw a couple of bills on the table and made a beeline for the door.

"What was that?" I asked Emma.

"*That* was Thiers keeping his daughter away from the ugly part of his life."

I turned to her.

"Thiers had secrets. He wasn't successful in business on good merit alone. He dabbled in the underworld. More than dabbled, honestly. But he never wanted Patience to be a part of it. He did his best to keep them separated. So, what to you looked like neglect was his form of protection."

By the time Emma finished, we were in front of Thiers' gravesite. His headstone hadn't been put in yet but it had been marked.

"What was he into?" I questioned, my gaze fixed on the grave.

"All types of things. Gambling, money laundering, weapons sales here and there. As you'd imagine, that involved some pretty unsavory people. People who had no qualms about going after someone's child if they were crossed."

"My father—"

"No. Robert had nothing to do with that part of Thiers' life. Though he knew about it."

"He kept her away from his business, but that night my father and I went to his home for dinner…"

"That was my doing," Emma stated with pride.

I looked up from the gravesite to her.

"Thiers' never had business dealings in his home. But I just so happen to have worked a little bit of my magic and put the idea in his head to have Patience there."

"Why?"

"For you, silly. You two were always destined. I made sure to get the ball rolling."

"She was only fourteen."

Emma rolled her dark brown eyes. "Duh! I wasn't trying to set you two up that night. I wanted you to meet. You couldn't help yourself from noticing her even then."

"I wasn't lusting over a teenager."

Emma made a clicking sound through her teeth. "Not quite, but your eyes kept traveling to her throughout the dinner. You were intrigued."

"She looked like she wanted to escape," I stated, remembering how uncomfortable she appeared at that table. Uncomfortable and alone while everyone chatted around her.

"She would've preferred reading alone in her room…except when she laid eyes on you. Her soul knew even before she could understand it. Yours too. The soul always knows. So, nine years later I put the idea in Thiers' head again and let nature take its course."

"It took its course all right."

"And if you would've just gotten out of your own way, this could've been wrapped up sooner."

"What's that supposed to mean?"

"You two could've been happy together a long time ago if it wasn't for your fears. In that way, you're similar to Patience's father." She nodded to the gravesite. "His fear kept him from having a relationship with his own daughter. And yours...well, it kept you from being happy for the last six years."

I turned from her, not admitting anything. Fear wasn't something I readily conceded.

"We're here now," I said.

"Yeah, but there's still more in store for you two to get to where you need to be."

I peered over at Emma, her mouth clamped shut. I knew she wasn't going to spill anymore so I chose not to ask. Again, I turned my attention back to the grave.

"I'm ready."

"Ready for what?" Emma prodded.

"To love my wife the way she deserves."

* * *

I BLINKED my eyes open to find myself standing in the middle of my bedroom. Emma was gone. I headed to the closed bathroom door where I heard the shower running. Turning the knob, I opened it, entering the room. Through the warm steam from the shower I made out the silhouette of my wife's naked body as she stood under the pelting spray of the overhead shower. A deep, overriding urge to protect her moved through my center when I saw her shoulders shaking as her hands covered her face.

My hands moved to unbutton my shirt before ripping it off me. Next, I pulled down the suit pants I still had on from the day, stripping all the way down to my briefs. I moved to the shower, pushing the sliding glass door open and stepping inside. Patience's head remained low, shoulders sagging under the weight of her grief. I reached for them, turning her to me, pulling her into my arms. She came willingly, sagging against my chest, continuing to release her tears and cries for the father that loved her deeply, but she never got to know.

My anger at Thiers had dissolved and all that remained was the desire…no, the *need* to get right what he'd failed.

I pulled Patience tightly into my embrace, wrapping my arms around her soaking wet body and let her let go. I dug my fingers into her long strands as they ran down her back, now dripping with water, holding her face to me. Time dissolved. The need to be anywhere but right where I was fell away. As much as I hated her tears, I hated the mere thought of anyone but myself being there to witness them. So, I let her release the weight of her mourning onto my chest and held my wife until the tears stopped. Then, I dried her off, carried her to bed, and pulled her on top of me to sleep, my arms shielding her from anymore pain.

CHAPTER 20

Patience

"Are you sure you need to go to work today?"

I turned from the sink to see a frowning Aaron hovering over me. He'd been like this for the last three days, since he found me crying in the shower.

"I'm fine," I repeated for the umpteenth time that morning. After taking a few days off work, I was ready to get back to it. Sure, I was still saddened by the loss of my father, mostly the loss of what could've been, of the relationship we'd only just begun building, but that was life. I had children to take care of, a job to get back to, and an extremely demanding and busy husband.

"You said you were fine four days ago."

I pushed out a deep breath. "Aaron."

His eyes squinted. "You know there's a whole story behind the way you say my name." His voice deepened. He moved in closer, our bodies just barely touching.

I shuddered at the way his eyes darkened just slightly.

"When you say it with a little hilt at the end, I can tell you're preparing to ask me a question you know I won't like. When you say it on a sigh as air escapes your lungs, you want me to make you come until you can't see straight. And when you call my name in the middle of the night while sleeping–"

"I don't call out your name while I'm asleep."

"You do…just as you did last night." He ran his pointer finger over my cheek and moving down to outline my jaw. "When you say my name with panic, as you did last night, you want me to protect you."

I lowered my gaze to the floor, needing to avoid his eye contact. I'd had one of those dreams the night before. The one of me being chased but I refused to tell him that. I needed to leave the past where it belonged.

He lifted my face with his hand. "What're you running from, sweetness?" Though he used the term of endearment, gone was the sensual Aaron, replaced by the dark, brooding Aaron that would rip anyone or anything apart that got in his way. The expression on his face was enough to scare a man ten times his size.

"Nothing," I lied.

His eyes darkened, not in that sexy way, but in a way that warned of danger.

I had to turn away when he silently observed me too long. Thankfully, I was spared anymore of his inquisition when the children came stampeding back into the kitchen after having retrieved their book bags from their rooms.

Aaron took a step back, but just barely. I turned my attention on Kyle and Kennedy, ensuring their school uniforms were on neatly. I could still feel his attention on me.

"Daddy, we're getting our Halloween costumes today!" Kennedy cheered.

Aaron finally moved his gaze from me to our daughter. "I remember," he affirmed.

"Yeah, I'm gonna be Spiderman!" Kyle shouted, right before he started his imitation of Spiderman, shooting imaginary webbing from his wrists. "Diego's going to be Aquaman," Kyle continued, obviously excited.

We had plans to go Halloween shopping with Michelle and Diego after work that day.

"That sounds fun," Aaron commented. "And what about you, munchkin?" he asked, picking Kennedy up.

She giggled as she always did when he used that nickname. "I don't know yet," she stated, tapping her chin.

"You'll have to send Daddy a picture so I can approve of your choice."

"Mommy will do it," she agreed for me.

I rolled my eyes. As if I didn't have a say in the matter. I'd only been picking out their Halloween attire since their first Halloween at nine months old.

After a round of kisses and getting the kids settled into the car, Aaron pulled me by the arm, giving me a stern look.

"Our conversation isn't over."

I went to reply by telling him it was most definitely over but he already had my lips surrendered to his by the time the retort formed in my head.

He watched and waited to get in his own vehicle until the children and I were pulling off.

It was a busy day at work. We'd gotten a ton of new books that needed to be catalogued and then put away on the shelves. I also busied myself in making preparation for the library's Halloween celebration that was to be hosted there. It was only the beginning of October but the sooner we planned these things out the better.

By the time I looked up, it was three o'clock and time for me to head over to the school to pick up the twins and Diego. I was picking up all three since we were waiting until five when Michelle got off to go shopping. I was grateful to have the hours that I could work while the children were at school and be there to pick them up afterwards. Since it was still pretty warm out, I opted to take the children to the Williamsport City Park to burn off some extra energy while we waited.

I watched as Kyle and Kennedy laughed and ran after the bubbles being blown by their older cousin. I stopped and bought them two soft pretzels to split between the four of us, since those things were huge. About an hour and a half into our waiting, I really needed to use the restroom. Glancing around, I spotted the women's bathroom. Not wanting to leave the children unsupervised, I waved for Daniel to come over and asked if he could keep an eye on them while I went to relieve myself. He agreed and I went.

Once I pushed the heavy door open, I was surprised yet extremely grateful of how clean the park's overseers kept the bathroom. Though, there was only one stall to use at a time. I entered the stall and covered the seat with one of the toilet seat covers. Just as I squatted to do my business, I heard a knocking on the door.

"Occupied!" I called out, just as the sound of the door being pushed open sounded.

I waited a heartbeat but didn't hear anything else.

"I'm sorry, there's only one stall in here. I'll be right out!" I stated loudly. Again, there was no response. Pinching my lips, I felt a shiver of fear run through my veins. I stopped breathing when I heard heavy footsteps, sounding much heavier and more firm than the steps of any woman.

"H-hello? Who's there? This is the women's restroom," I informed, hoping the person was just confused.

This time I wasn't surprised when no response came, but the fear began to nearly choke me. I stood, pulling my pants up and then grabbing for the tube of pepper spray I kept in the bag I always carried with me.

"Hello!" I called again, this time much more firm.

Just as it sounded as if the person was on the other side of the door, the footsteps began moving farther away. I heard the door open and close again.

Trembling, I stood there with the pepper spray in my hands, but then I remembered ... "The kids!" I whispered out loud right before pushing through the stall door and moving to the exit as quickly as possible. I needed to get to Kyle and Kennedy, to make sure they were all right.

I ran over to where I'd left Daniel with the children, and to my relief the three of them were playing a round of duck-duck-goose as Daniel dutifully watched over them. I turned, hand on my head, looking around for anyone that seemed to be standing too close or out of the ordinary. I tried to remember the self-defense tactics my instructor from years ago said about how to keep aware of your surroundings. No one nearby sent off any alarm bells. Most looked to be college students or retired individuals just taking in a fall walk in the park. I sighed, closing my eyes, willing my heart to slow down.

"Patience. Everything all right?"

I turned my eyes on a concerned looking Daniel.

"Everything's fine. Just fine," I muttered the last part.

Everything was definitely *not* fine.

*　*　*

"Thanks for waiting and for picking up Diego," Michelle said as she pulled me in for a one-arm hug.

I waved a hand, dismissing her thanks. "It was nothing. Those three can't get enough of one another."

Michelle laughed. "That's true. I hate that I'm late though. I had to stay late for a client and then I wasn't feeling well." She shrugged. "Anyway, where are the superhero costumes? Those should be the easiest to pick out for the boys."

I nodded, looking around the high-end department store we'd entered to do the children's costume shopping.

"Come on, Mama!" Diego urged Michelle, taking her by the hand.

"I guess they're over there," she laughed, looking toward me but then pressing her hand to her stomach.

I narrowed my gaze.

"You all go on ahead, I just need to grab something real quick." Michelle gave little argument and the three children walked with her to the far end of the store where the costumes were held. I moved to the cooler that sat up front by the registers, grabbing a can of ginger ale and a small box of Saltine crackers. I quickly paid for my items and proceeded to open one of the packs of crackers while moving in the direction of the costumes.

"I want this one, Mama," I heard Diego shout as I rounded the aisle.

I came to see him holding up an Aquaman costume.

"Kyle, you should get this one." He pointed to a Spiderman costume.

"What about me?" Kennedy asked, frowning.

I moved closer to Michelle, as the three children debated, and talked amongst themselves. "These are for you," I whispered in her ear.

She looked down at the food and beverage in my hand, her wide eyes then returning to me.

"That first trimester is a bitch, isn't it?"

Her eyes ballooned even more. "Is it *that* obvious?"

I giggled. "Not to anyone who isn't familiar with it."

"Thank you," she sighed, taking one of the crackers and biting into it.

"Those were the only things I could keep down during my first tri with those two." I nodded in the direction of Kyle and Kennedy.

"I had such a smooth pregnancy with Diego. Hardly any symptoms beyond some mild queasiness. But this one…" She trailed off, shaking her head.

"It's a Townsend. They come into this world making their presence felt from the very beginning."

She giggled. "If this baby is anything like their father."

I tutted. "Don't I know it."

We both laughed.

"How far along are you?"

"I'll be twelve weeks next week. We wanted to wait until I passed the first trimester to tell anyone."

I made a zipping motion across my mouth. "Your secret is safe with me."

"I appreciate it. And these," she stated, holding up the crackers. "I never really thought they worked but my nausea is so much better than when I walked in here."

I winked at her. "Old tricks of the trade."

We finished our shopping. I was happy Kennedy decided to stick with the superhero theme the boys had chosen and opted to be Wonder Woman. Unfortunately, my husband wasn't going to be so thrilled about her choice in costume.

* * *

A*aron*

"I told you to send me a picture of her costume," I growled, arms folded over my chest as Patience and I stood in my downstairs office.

She poked out her hip, placing a hand on it, exposing just a tiny bit of the flesh of her abdomen in the sleeveless silk top she wore. "No. You told *Kennedy* to send you a picture but she doesn't have a phone, so …" She shrugged.

"And her mother neglected to follow through on my request because?"

"Because I'm not your secretary. What's the big deal anyway?" she asked, holding up her hands. "It's just a Halloween costume."

"What's the big…Have you *seen* the costume? Have you seen that movie of a woman running around in some skimpy outfit? No," I barked. "Take it back!"

"No!" Patience folded her arms over her breasts.

My chest tightened.

"Kennedy wants to be a superhero like her brother and cousin. That's the costume she chose."

"She's five! She doesn't get a choice!"

Patience sucked her teeth. "That seems to be your theme song. Not giving anyone a choice."

I narrowed my gaze.

"Don't look at me like I'm talking nonsense. You did it with me and this marriage. And you're doing it to Kennedy. At least trying to."

I took a threatening step in her direction.

"I'm not backing down, Aaron." She dropped her hands as I took another step her way. "Kennedy wants this. You had no problem with Kyle's costume."

"Kyle's costume covers him. My five year old daughter will not be out trick-or-treating in a costume that was designed by nerdy, middle-aged men to ogle a woman's body!" I seethed.

"She'll be wearing tights and we can get her to wear a cape, like in the movie." Her voice was still full of resolve but it had softened just a little bit.

I ground my teeth, mulling over her words. I hated compromising. On anything. It was a sign of weakness.

"Please."

"You're still angry I forced your hand into this marriage?"

Her eyes blinked, a V deepening on her forehead. "Where'd that come from?"

"You just said it."

"I didn't–"

"You said I didn't give you a choice in this marriage."

She sighed, looking down and away from me. "You *didn't* give me a choice. It was either marry you or lose my children."

"*Our* children," I corrected.

I should've felt some type of guilt or remorse but I didn't. "You don't enjoy your life here...with me?"

Another force of air from her lips. She shook her head. "Aaron, don't do that."

"Ask for your honesty?"

"Yes, you always ask for *my* honesty, *my* truth but never tell me yours."

"I never tell you the truth?"

"When it suits you. You've never given me the full story–" She held up her hands. "No, we're not doing this right now. This is about Kennedy being able to wear the costume she wants."

"She'll wear it with tights *and* a cape. A very long cape."

"Fine."

She waited, hesitated, to turn from me. I knew she wanted me to shed light on the events of our past. I knew that's what Emma had meant when she said Patience and I had so much further to go to get to the place we deserved. Patience wanted me to explain Alicia, my ex-fiancée. The one who'd shown up on her doorstep as we'd slept in her bed, after yet another night of pleasuring one another into the wee hours of the morning. But I had no explanation. Not yet.

"I'm going to bed," Patience informed, giving me one last look before turning and heading out of my office.

I watched her back until the door closed behind her. Picking out a bottle of water from the fridge, I opened the cabinet doors that held the TV monitors connected to the security cameras. I turned them on just in time to see Patience moving up the stairs then down the hall to our bedroom. I surveilled the monitors while she climbed into bed and pulled her Kindle out from the nightstand next to her side and began reading. I stared intently for some time, the contentment of just knowing she was mine was all I needed for the night.

Shutting the monitors off, I turned to the computer on my desk to finish up some work before I headed upstairs to bed myself.

CHAPTER 21

Aaron

"No! Stop! Please!"

I roused out of my sleep, anxious, every muscle in my body tensing, ready to fight.

"Stop! Stop!" came more shrieks from the woman lying beside me.

I reached up, turning on the bed's overhead light. I glanced down to see Patience squirming in bed, her eyes tightly shut, but cries and pleas still pouring from her mouth. I relaxed but only a little at realizing she was just having a bad dream. Slowly, I turned to her, pressing a hand to her shoulder.

"Patience, wake up," I said low in her ear. "It's just a dream. Wake up, sweetness." My voice was more soothing than I ever remembered. "Pati–" I was cut off when I had to duck from a fist that flew in my direction. I stopped a second fist, just an inch from my face. "Patience! Wake up," I called more firmly, seeing she had turned from scared to violent. I wasn't concerned for me, but I didn't want her to harm herself.

Slowly her eyes opened, showing her sepia irises, but they still looked foggy. She looked around, confused. "The children!" she screeched before leaping off the bed and running to the door. I pushed the blanket from over me and made it through the door of our bedroom in three steps, only to see Patience darting into Kennedy's room. A few seconds later she attempted to dart past me to get to Kyle's room.

"Hey," I called, wrapping my arm around her waist.

"I need to check on them!" she insisted, squirming, but my grip tightened.

"The children are fine. No one's getting into this house."

She blinked, looking up at me, her eyes cleared a bit but her breathing remained heavy.

I waited for her breathing to steady. "Come here." Grabbing her by the hand, I pulled her behind me as I walked down the hallway and then down the stairs. When we arrived in the kitchen, I took out a bottle of water, handing it to her. "Drink," I ordered.

She hesitated, but eventually took the bottle from my hand, taking a large gulp.

I stared at her hard, arms folded across my chest. I saw as she avoided eye contact, eyes flittering about the kitchen, everywhere except on me.

"I'm sorry for interrupting your sleep."

"I don't give a damn about my sleep."

She finally looked up at me, clearing her throat. "I'm fine now. We can go back to bed." She attempted to exit the kitchen only to be blocked by my body.

"Tell me," I insisted. I'd known there was something wrong. Something off. She often had dreams that seemed to make her restless, past her usual wild sleeping behavior. I heard it in her voice that night before the way she'd called out my name.

"It was just a nightmare."

"You don't have nightmares."

Her gaze sharpened on me. "You don't know everything about me."

I moved on her. "Tell me what I don't know."

She bit her lower lip.

"You can tell me now or I'll find out my way." I pulled her chin between my thumb and forefinger, turning her head up to me. "You won't be able to sit for a week if I have to find out *my* way."

"Bully," she grumbled, pushing my hand away but not backing away from me. She cleared her throat. "I was attacked," she stated just above a whisper.

I can't even begin to describe the feeling that moved through my very bones. Rage was much too calm to describe it. "When? How?" My voice was filled with something indescribable.

She waffled a little, licking her lips before finally telling the entire story. "I was eight months pregnant, moved to Oakland just five and a half months earlier. I was living in an apartment complex in what I thought was a safe neighborhood. One night, in the middle of the night, I woke up to a man dressed in all black and a ski mask in my bedroom." Her voice faltered. "I-I was terrified. As soon as he saw I was awake, he lunged to the bed, trapping me with one arm around my waist and another held a knife to my throat." She wiped away a stray tear. "I begged him to not hurt me. But he said, I deserved it. Said that I was a lying whore who pretended to be innocent–" She stopped abruptly, and took a deep breath. "God, I remember every word he said. *I should kill these babies right now*, he repeated over and over. Kept calling me a liar. Then," she swallowed, "he, uh, he began undoing his pants, saying he was going to force himself down my throat before he took me. I began to fight then. I punched him as hard as I could and tried to scramble off the bed to get away. He caught me by my ankle and dragged me back across the bed, punching me in the face first and then my stomach. I didn't even feel the pain. I was so scared for the twins. I kicked and tried to claw at his face but he was all covered up. Finally, I landed a kick to his groin, which was still exposed. It gave me enough time to get away. I ran out of the bedroom, to my front door and into the hallway. I banged and knocked on three doors before a woman answered." She peered up at me through a sheen of tears.

"Ms. Sheryl. She took me in, locked the door, and called the police. I hadn't even realized I was bleeding until I saw her hands covered in it. I had a busted lip, cuts all over, and my stomach...the pain was horrific. By the time the paramedics arrived, they determined I was in full on labor, caused by the trauma. I gave birth at five in the morning, three hours after being attacked." She wiped tears from her face, swallowing deeply.

"D–" I stopped, trying to rein in my feelings to not scare her even more. "Was he ever caught?"

She nodded. "Not that night but months later the police contacted me. By then I'd moved. Apparently, there was a serial rapist in the city. They connected him with a number of break-ins and assaults on single women in the area. There was no DNA left at the scene of my crime, except for mine, so they couldn't connect him to my attack, but the police assured me they had the right guy. But ..."

"But what?"

"I don't know. I just, I can't be a hundred percent sure. I never saw his face, no DNA." She shook her head. "But the police were certain so I didn't press it. I did my best to forget. I was just grateful Kennedy and Kyle were okay. They were born more than a month earlier than expected but there was no permanent damage from the attack."

"You're still having nightmares," I commented.

"It happens every so often. Just a side-effect, I guess."

She was trying to downplay it. For my sake, not hers. She knew I wasn't taking this well, though I hadn't even said anything beyond a few questions.

"Aaron." She came to me, tugging on my clenched fists. They were sealed so tightly my own fingernails had begun to dig into the palms of my hands.

Animalistic.

That was the only way to describe what I was feeling. My family had been in danger and I was nowhere around to protect them.

"Aaron, it was just a night–"

"Don't." It came out on a whisper but it still echoed around the kitchen. "Don't downplay this."

"I'm not," she defended. "I-I'm just saying don't feel whatever it is you're feeling right now. I can see it in your eyes. You're blaming yourself. It wasn't your fault."

"Who's fault was it then? I should've—" I stopped, my fist going into wooden overhead cabinet. I heard Patience gasp. I pulled my fist back, seeing the blood from the impact and then the dent in the cabinet but not feeling the pain.

"No!" she yelped, grabbing my arm as I went to punch the cabinet again.

"You need to go to bed."

She shook her head. "No."

"Patience—"

"No! Come with me." She pulled at my arm.

"I'm not going to do anything rash."

"Then come to bed with me. Please...I need you."

I grunted, but bent low to pick her up in my arms.

"I can walk."

"So?"

She folded her arms around my neck and laid her head on my shoulder as we ascended the stairs. I carried her into our bedroom and laid her on her side of the bed.

"We need to clean your hand and put some ice on it."

"In the morning." I knew my hand would be throbbing by the morning but I had no intention of worrying about it until then. Patience snuggled into my side, resting her head on my chest. She moved, wrapping my arm around her, until I squeezed her waist into me. Even being in this position that always seemed to calm the jarred edges of my emotions, wasn't enough that night. By the time I heard my wife's soft snores I had already formed a plan in my head on how I was going to handle this. I knew the first person I needed to see. She assuredly would be liking this visit with me even less than our last one.

* * *

"A<small>RRGGHHH</small>!" I grunted as I threw the wooden chair Alicia had just been strapped to against the concrete wall, shattering it into large pieces. I was so fucking tempted to pick one of those boards up and end her life with it.

"Aaron, stop! Please!"

Her cries had zero effect on me, unlike my wife when she spoke the same words the night before.

"Why are you doing this?" she begged to know.

I came to stand before her as she slouched on the floor, dressed in a pair of dark sweatpants and an old Williamsport University T-shirt. It was a far cry from her much more glamorous days, growing up as the daughter of a supposed oil tycoon. But her outfit was overshadowed by the large purple bruise and busted lip that marred her face. The marks hadn't been courtesy of me but I'd called in some favors.

"Why have you brought me here?"

"You couldn't leave well enough the fuck alone, could you, Alicia? Answer me!" I yelled when she didn't speak.

"I-I don't know what you're talking about."

"Patience! My children. It's one thing to send her away and not tell me about it. It's a whole different animal when you have my family attacked!" I snatched her up by her shoulders, shaking her. I was fighting hard to keep a grip on reality but the part of me that wanted to end her and be done with it was close to winning out.

"No! No! I never–"

"Don't fucking lie to me!"

"I swear! I don't know what you're talking about."

Releasing her, I took a step back and stared at her intently. She shook like a leaf.

"Who'd you have do it? Who'd you send to Oakland to attack her?" That fucker was going to die a slow, painful death. I prayed to whatever God there was to grant me that ability to kill someone twice.

"N-no one! I didn't even know she was in California!" Alicia ducked when I advanced on her again.

"She's telling the truth, Aaron!"

I peered up, toward the corner of the empty basement of a supposed abandoned house. Townsend Industries owned the home via dummy corporations on our real estate side. It was untraceable back to me but useful for situations such as this one. It wasn't the first time I'd found myself down in this dank basement but this was the most meaningful.

Emma.

She stood at the corner, worried eyes on me. "Don't do this. Alicia's telling the truth. She didn't have Patience attacked."

My chest heaved up and down as I let her words sink in. I stepped back, turning my gaze from Emma to Alicia who eyed me warily.

"Please, Aaron. I-I didn't do it."

Again, her pleas barely stirred up any emotion in me besides rage but I took another step back. I'd never trust my ex, but Emma...she was a different story.

"You're still partly to blame for what happened," I seethed. "If you wouldn't have sent her away, she would've never been in that fucking city. Alone." I was nearly choking on my anger and helplessness. "That, I won't forgive." I shook my head at the impossibility.

"Wh-what does that m-mean?" she stuttered.

"I'm calling the Razzioli family."

"No!"

"Aaron, don't!" both Alicia and Emma shouted.

"Your protection by the Townsends has ended. Our debts to your father have been paid in full. We're done!"

The Razziolis were one of the most notable crime families in the country. Alicia and her father had screwed the family over nearly ten years prior. She was only granted the opportunity to live this long because of my family. That had just ended.

"Aaron, pl–"

"Don't say my fucking name! Ever again!" I stormed over to the wall where I'd tossed my suit jacket and Patek Philippe, not giving a fuck that it alone was worth more than the entire house, picking them up.

I moved to the door, yanking it open to see my head of security standing there. Even I had to look up to meet his eyes. His stern look went from me to over my shoulder, and narrowed when he saw Alicia.

"Call the Razziolis," I instructed before brushing past him, not giving a solitary fuck about Alicia's cries and yells for me not to do this. I had sacrificed myself for my family and the business once before and it nearly cost Patience and my children their lives. If she had been with me, she never would've been attacked. I was due into the office but there was no way I could hold it together in the state I was in.

Instead of having my driver take me into the office, I had him take me home. There I let off the anger that continued to radiate through my body by going nine rounds with my punching bag. When my arms felt too heavy to lift any longer, I opted for a five mile run. Not until I reached the house did I begin to feel the anger lifting ever so slightly. It also helped that at the same time I received a text from my head of security that the package had been delivered. Meaning, Alicia had been taken care of.

"She didn't deserve that you know."

I slammed the refrigerator door shut in the kitchen and angrily pointed the bottle of water I held in my hand at Emma. "Trust me, that's not half of what I wanted to do to her. And if you were more than just a figment of my goddamn imagination, I would've done more to you, too!" I growled.

Emma sighed, shaking her head. "After all these years, that's all I am to you? A figment of your imagination? Aaron, you know that isn't true."

I grunted, slamming the bottle onto the kitchen counter, and brushed past Emma, heading to the front of the house toward the stairs, to take my second shower of the day.

"Aaron, listen to me!"

"Fuck you!" I shouted, reaching my bedroom. "You knew! This whole time she's been back you fucking knew she was attacked! And you never said a word. You begged me to spare Alicia's life though." I turned on Emma with angry eyes.

"Yes," she nodded, "I did. Because she was not responsible for what happened to Patience that night."

"So who is?" I yelled.

Emma gave me a sorrowful look, her lips sealed into a thin line, remaining shut.

That pissed me off anew and I ran my arm across the top of my dresser, knocking everything over.

"Aaron, please!" she yelped, looking almost as frightened as Alicia had that morning.

"Please, what? Spare your life? You're lucky you're already dead."

Her eyes widened in shock and then horror. Hurt.

"You're not real." I shook my head. "Just a figment of a child's imagination. A lonely, scared child that needed someone to save him. Instead, I got you. A fucking ghost that holds secrets and lies to my face."

"I *never* lied to you."

"But you damn sure never told me the entire truth. Even now, you know who attacked my wife and my children and you haven't said shit!"

"I can't! There are things I can't tell you. It would alter too much. But I can help you–"

"Yeah, help me by leaving me the fuck alone. Forever!"

"Aaron, you don't mean that."

"I do. Leave. Me. The. Fuck. Alone. Forever! Keep your snide, *I told you so's* and your fucking hidden truths and take them back wherever the hell you're from."

Emma made a move in my direction, but the snarl on my face caused her to stop. All I saw was red.

"Is this how you truly want it?"

"Have you not been listening?"

"Okay," she stated, nodding solemnly. "I will abide by your wishes. I will only return upon your request."

"A request I wouldn't hold my breath for if I were you."

Her enlarged brown, watery eyes peered up at me. "We will see each other again. At your request."

I snorted and stormed off for the bathroom, slamming the door behind me. Twenty minutes later when I emerged from the shower, the room was empty. I glanced at my dresser, expecting to find the mess that I'd left, but it wasn't there. Everything had been placed on the dresser where it had been. Even the mirror that had been knocked off and cracked, was restored and placed on top of the dresser.

I stood in front of the mirror, looking myself in the eye. I saw the anger boiling behind my hazel irises. I blinked my eyes closed, inhaling deeply, attempting to pull myself together. I needed to get to the office, but most importantly, I couldn't let my wife and children see how upset I was. I would never want my children raised in the type of home I lived in the first eight years of my life. And to do that, I needed to tamp down on my aggression while at home.

That was a feat easier said than done, in the state I was in. But I'd done impossible feats before.

I finished buttoning my suit and removed my cell phone from my pocket as I raced down the stairs to the front door. As I got in the backseat of my town car that was held open by my driver, I pressed the button for my head of security. I told him to meet me in my head office later that afternoon. We needed to go over increased security for my family. The Oakland police may have believed Patience's attacker was caught but she hadn't seemed convinced. And neither was I.

CHAPTER 22

Patience

"Mmmm," I moaned as the delicious sensations rolled through my body. I felt as if I was being elevated into the highest, brightest light possible. My muscles clenched and I wiggled my hips, seeking more and more of that ecstasy I was experiencing. Slowly, my eyes opened and I realized I was flat on my back in my bed. When my vision cleared, I peered lower down my body and felt another gush of moisture release from my body, when I saw Aaron's dark head between my thighs. His arms wrapped around my legs, holding them in place, as his mouth worked its devastation on my pussy.

I let out another deep moan, slamming my head back against the pillows. I went to reach for his head, to push it away. I'd already had one orgasm—the one that woke me up in the first place, and he was obviously trying to wring another one free from my body. I couldn't... we didn't have time for that. But when I moved my hands, I could only lift them a few inches off the bed. They were handcuffed and tied around one of the posts of the headboard, restricting my range of movement.

"A-Aaron," I panted, my voice caught between confusion, anger, and lust. "A-Aaron, untie me n–" I was cut off on a gasp when he ran the tip of his tongue across my swollen clit. I felt his thick fingers as they invaded my pussy. I gushed again when he curled them, brushing my inner walls. Another orgasm was coming and I couldn't do anything to stop it, or him. He rose to his knees, bringing the entire bottom half of my body with him, pushing my upper body deeper into the bed. Finally, his eyes opened and caught mine. They were almost black with need. He still hadn't said a word, past the moaning he did against my nether lips, as if my body had been the only thing he had ever hungered for. I came again, that thought pushing me over, with his intent eyes still on mine. I shook and convulsed and he continued to lap up all the cream that spilled from my body.

I was still trembling but completely spent by the time he lowered my legs to the bed. I watched through half-closed eyes as he moved over me, the bulge in his pajama bottoms bumping against my aching need. He moved over me, staring down at me, the scowl on his face another one of my turn-ons. I ached to feel his lips, to lick the wetness from his mouth that I'd left there. I lifted my head to meet his lips, but his hand to my throat stopped me.

"Have you been with anyone else?" he gritted out, as if the words were nearly incomprehensible to him.

My eyes widened a smidgen, not certain I'd heard him correctly. "Wh-what?" I was still breathless from the two orgasms he'd ripped from my body. Certainly, he wasn't asking whether or not I'd had sex with another man.

"You heard the question."

"You *cannot* be serious."

He gave me a hard glare.

"You're asking if I cheated on you since we've been married?"

He shook his head. "While we were apart. Were you with anyone else?"

"Aaron, what does that ma–"

His hand around my throat tightened. "I'll take that as a yes." His jaw was so rigid.

"You had a fian–"

"She wasn't you."

I blinked and shook my head, swallowing. "This is ridiculous. Uncuff me, the children are probably already awake."

"They're in the den, watching TV."

I looked at the clock, noting it was almost eight o'clock. "Aaron, I need to make them breakfast. We ha–"

"No. I will make them breakfast and get them ready to spend the day and night with their aunt and uncle. We will see them again at Mother and Father's for the family dinner."

"What?"

"You're spending the entire day in bed. Just like this." He moved from the bed, leaving me there, as if his word was final.

I yanked my hands, still in the handcuffs. "Aaron, uncie me!" I hissed.

He didn't even look my way as he threw a T-shirt over his head and ran a hand through his mussed hair.

I called his name again, yanking at the cuffs, and kicking at the bed. Surely, he was not going to leave me like this. Again, he ignored me. Just as I was about to yell and curse him out, a knock sounded at the door.

"Mommy, I'm hungry," Kyle's little voice came through the door.

Before I could answer him, Aaron moved to the door, cracking it, but using his body to block Kyle's sight of me. "Shh, Mommy's still sleeping. She's not feeling well today. Daddy will get you and Kennedy some breakfast."

"I want cereal," Kyle announced.

"Cereal it is," Aaron responded, not sounding at all like the jealous lover of a few moments ago.

I hated the way my anger faded slightly at hearing the tone of voice he used with Kyle. But it returned when I caught him give me one last look over his shoulder as he moved through the door, shutting it behind him and our son.

"I'm going to kill him!" I grumbled, pulling at the cuffs one last time to no avail. All I could do now was wait for him to return.

* * *

IT TOOK THIRTY MINUTES. Thirty minutes for my asshole husband to return to our bedroom. When he did, he just stared at me, his back pressed against our closed bedroom door, arms folded across his chest. His face held a scowl but there was a gleam in his eyes. I guessed it was from seeing the annoyance written all over my face.

"Untie me," I seethed.

He moved from the door, slowly. "Carter picked the children up."

I eyed him as he carefully walked around the bed, inching closer to my side.

"Untie me."

"Are you arms sore?" he questioned, running his hand along my arms, assessing, stopping to peer at my wrists.

"I'm going to kick your ass as soon as the handcuffs are taken off."

He turned, staring down at my face. "Is that so?"

My eyes narrowed.

"I asked you a question earlier…" He trailed off, staring at me. He took a step back from the bed and then moved to circle to his side of the bedroom, going to open the top drawer of his dresser.

"I'm not answering that. Untie me!" I demanded.

"You keep tugging like that and you're going to hurt yourself. Better to just relax."

I sucked my teeth. "You're such an ass," I declared. He was silent while his back was to me, but when he moved I gasped at what he held in his hands. "A-Aaron," I warned, but I could feel my body growing warmer as I stared at the contents he held.

"Now," he began, moving back to the nightstand beside me. He placed the items on the nightstand. "I'll ask you again."

My gaze remained on the tube of lube, the gold plated vibrator, and the crystal butt plug my husband had just arranged on the nightstand.

"Have you been with anyone else?"

"I-I—" I struggled to pull my eyes away from the sex toys to him as he glowered down at me. "I'm not answering th-that," I stated through trembling lips.

He picked up the vibrator, turning it on. The only way I could tell it was on was because I saw him flip on the small switch, but the actual vibrator was completely silent.

"I'm not spending all day in this bed either," I argued against his earlier comment.

"You will. On both accounts," he countered, lowering the vibrator between my legs.

I gritted my teeth against the first sensations that rushed through my body at the initial contact. But I bit down on my lip, refusing to give him what he wanted. He pried my thighs apart when I tried to clamp them shut, in an attempt to shut out the feelings brought on by the vibrator.

"Ah!" I yelled when he tugged my head back by my hair with one hand and turned the speed of the vibrator up with the thumb of his other. "A-Aarooon!" I yelled when the orgasm took me completely off-guard. I squirmed and wiggled my hips, trying to get free from his onslaught, but he continued to stare down at me, and turned the vibrator up yet again. "D-don't!" I demanded through clattering teeth.

"Don't what?" He tugged my head back farther, tightening his hold in my hair. "Answer the question, Patience. I will do this all day."

I squeezed my eyes shut. I felt his warm tongue on my neck as he licked and bit me. A shudder ran through my body, making its way to my core. That, along with the contact of the vibrator, stirred the beginnings of yet another orgasm. That one started in the soles of my feet, running up my legs.

"A-Aaron, please!" I panted at the same time more core exploded, lifting my hips off the bed. Everything in me strained, painfully. "Yes! Okay, yes!" I yelled. "I've been with someone else!"

The most thunderous grunt I'd ever heard from Aaron spilled from his mouth. His hands were at my wrists, removing the cuffs, but pinning my hands to the mattress with my own. He moved over top of me, using his hips to force my thighs apart even more. Before I could release another breath, he was impaling me with his erection. I yelled out his name, but it was cut off when he covered my mouth with his, possessively. I wanted to hate him. But it all felt too good to hate. So, I did the only thing I could in my position. I bit down on his lower lip, hard. That spurred him on and he pounded into my wet pussy with a vengeance, shaking the entire bed as it bumped the wall. His hands tightened around my wrists and his kiss became even more insistent.

I wrapped my legs around his waist, holding on for dear life. I turned my head from his kiss, needing to pull in oxygen. He moved to my neck again, licking, sucking and biting at my exposed flesh. I called his name over and over. I'd admitted to being with someone else, and he was doing his damned best to erase that memory. I would've told him he needn't have worried about that. Would've confessed that I'd only had sex with another man, but this…what was between Aaron and I could only be experienced with him. I would've said all of that, but I was coming again, on a silent scream. My lips parted, back arched, pussy continuing to be beaten into submission by the only man to ever bring this out of me. I was coming.

I came to just enough to glance up at Aaron as he peered down at me, neck still straining as he poured himself into me.

"We're making another baby today."

His words barely registered due to everything around me fading to black as I passed out.

* * *

I CAME to a few hours later, my arrogant, mean ass husband laying on his side, head propped up by his hand, staring at me. My treacherous body began to warm up at the picture he made, lying in our bed, naked from the waist up. My mouth watered with the urge to lick and kiss his chest, his scars. It was my favorite way of turning him on.

"Stop."

I rose my gaze to meet his.

"We'll get back to that soon but you need to eat."

I narrowed my eyes, finally remembering my anger. I checked to see if my hands were bound. They weren't. I raised my hand up, ready to smack the hell out of Aaron, but it was caught in his stronger hand. I found myself flipped over onto my back, arm raised above my head, him over me.

"We've played this game before." His voice was full of warning. "You already know how it ends."

I breathed heavily, chest heaving up and down.

"With you calling my name, your pussy walls milking my cock for all I'm worth. We'll get to that, but first you need to eat," he growled, moving from over me back to his side of the bed.

"I'm not hungry," I spat out but in the ensuing silence my stomach betrayed me, growling loudly. I didn't say anything and avoided his eye contact. "I don't know what possessed you to think you could keep me in bed all day like I was some kind of prisoner but I'm not!" I rose out of the bed, coming to stand beside it, staring down at Aaron. I had to hold on to the edge of the nightstand when my legs wobbled. "I'm going to shower and pick up the kids from Michelle and Carter and take them to the zoo like I promised!" I hissed. Before he could retort, I grabbed my robe off the floor, using it to cover my nude body, and made a beeline for the bathroom.

Once inside I ripped off my robe and stepped into the shower, hoping it would help cool me off. But that was a total failure. The warm water streaming down my already sensitized flesh caused goosebumps to cover my arms. I glanced up toward the bathroom entrance and standing there, legs crossed, chest bared in his usual plaid pajama bottoms was the man who left me feeling like an exposed nerve. Our eyes caught and the memory of him coming into the shower just to hold me as I cried over my father, a few weeks prior, assaulted me. My knees began to tremble when he strolled to the shower door, slowly sliding it open.

I gave little protest, as he lowered his pajama bottoms, his semi-hard cock springing out, and he kicked them aside to enter the shower with me.

"I won't take you in here. Shower sex has never been my favorite." His voice was so low and deep. "I just needed to be near you."

Everything in me squeezed tightly. My heart blossomed at the vulnerability in his voice at his admission.

"Why?" I whispered, not looking up at him.

"Because I love you."

I slumped back against the shower wall, needing something to hold my body upright. That was the first time I ever heard him utter those three words. I just knew I was imagining it, but he said it again.

"I love you."

And again.

"I love you." He pressed a kiss to my forehead, then the tip of my nose, and then my lips before moving backwards, granting me space. He stared down at me.

In another time and another place I would've said those three words back to him. But not then. I couldn't. Not after last time.

"You don't have to say it." He lifted the loofah that rested next to my favorite body wash and used it to wash me from head to toe. I did the same for him with his own washcloth. By the time we got out of the shower the entire bathroom was steamed up. He dried my body before ordering me to hold out my arms for him to place my robe on.

Once back in the bedroom the smell of food permeated, tearing another round of growling from my stomach. At the center of our bed, stood a Rosewood tea tray, holding a box of pizza and seltzer water. I grinned as I climbed onto the bed. Surprising me, instead of going to his side of the bed, Aaron climbed in behind me, pressing our bodies together. He pressed his semi-hard cock against the curve of my ass. I gasped.

"Later," he growled in my ear, before reaching over me to hand me a paper plate. He placed a slice of plain pizza—my favorite—on top. I smiled when I saw the other half of the pizza covered in green peppers and mushrooms. Both his and Kyle's favorite.

We ate in silence for a little while but something kept nagging at me. It kept my anger in place, though I wanted to let it go.

"What is it?" he questioned.

"What's what?" I replied, narrowing my gaze at him.

"Something's on your mind."

I tutted, shaking my head. "I hate it when you do that."

He raised an eyebrow.

"Watching me to read my thoughts. You always di–" I paused, not wanting to dredge up the past.

"What I always did," he finished for me. "I watch everything that belongs to me."

My stomach knotted.

"In business and in my personal life. I keep an eye on what's mine." His hand moved to my waist. "Since that first night at Buona Sera, you've been mine."

I shuddered when his hand moved to the sash of my robe, loosening the bow that held it closed.

I stopped his hand with my own. "I wasn't yours. You had someone else. And now, six years later you question me about who else I've been with in that time." I sat up, tossing my plate onto the tray and staring at him in his narrowed eyes. "I don't get to ask you about the women you've been with but I was supposed to what? Have waited for you while I raised our children alone?" I went to push his hand away but he held firm.

"She's not a factor."

I snorted and gave a humorless laugh. "She sure as hell was back then." I cut my eyes at him, seeking to move away from his hold, but he tightened his arm around me.

"She's not anymore, nor will she ever be again."

Something final was in his voice. I lowered my brows, half torn between asking what he meant by that and being afraid to ask.

Lowering his head so that our faces were nearly touching, he took my chin between his fingers. "She was business. You are something entirely different."

I frowned, scoffing. "Yeah? And what's that?"

"My life. You and our children."

He released my chin and moved to get off the bed, taking the tray with him. He carried it to the other side of the room, placing it on the leather chair that sat in the corner before returning to me. Again, he stood at the side of the bed, looking down at the items on the nightstand that still remained.

"We're done talking about her," he said as if all my questions were answered. "We've got more important matters to discuss." He lifted the lube, uncapping it.

My eyes widened. "Such as?" My voice was breathless.

"When are you giving me more children?" he answered in a nonchalant manner, squeezing lube onto his fingers.

I swallowed, my body growing hot, nipples hardening at the sight of his actions.

"W-we just got married."

"Three months ago," he muttered, moving to the bed.

I nodded and began crawling backwards.

"You know what happens when you try to run," he warned, angling his head menacingly.

I could hardly believe how my body was already responding to his taunting considering he wasn't even touching me. But it was always like this with him.

He caught me around one leg, pulling me to him at the edge of the bed. "You've never let another man touch you here." He lowered the fingers with the lube on them to the opening of my backside.

I inhaled sharply when he began probing my hole. It hadn't been a question but I still felt the need to answer. "N-no," I moaned as his fingers sunk in deeper to my anal cavity. The idea alone of anyone but Aaron touching me in that way was unfathomable.

"Good. I would kill any man that has." He kept his eyes on me, pulling his fingers in and out, ensuring I was well coated. "The knowledge that another man has seen you naked is taking all of my restraint to not have my security find him and bring him to me, as it stands now. You don't want to know what I'd do to the man who's had your ass as well." His fingers picked up pace and his other hand moved to my clit, rubbing it.

I tightened my hands into the bedsheets, lifting my hips.

"You're tight. Not ready for my cock yet but the plug will help." He withdrew his fingers, pulling a whimper of need from my lips. He lifted the butt plug from the nightstand, lowering it to my anus. "Don't tense up. Exhale," he ordered.

I did as instructed and he slipped the plug into me at the same time I released the breath. I watched, my eyes halfway closed, as he lowered his briefs, freeing himself. He positioned himself on the bed, placing the tip of himself right at my vaginal opening. For once, he left my hands free, allowing me to wrap them around his waist. He peered down at me, eyes and face intent as he pushed into me with one forceful thrust.

A gush of air expelled from my body and I let out a silent scream, mouth ajar. I felt completely stuffed. Aaron wasn't small by any account. Without the plug he was almost too much for me but with it, I felt impossibly tight, almost like a virgin again. But unlike that first night, Aaron didn't give me time to adjust to his girth. He rammed in and out of me, in an obvious way of claiming me.

He growled, and pulled at my hair, exposing my neck again for him to taste as he saw fit. I dug my nails into his muscled ass, which only spurred him on. He was dogged in his strokes, giving me deep plunges that were on the borderline between pain and pleasure. I didn't need to hear the words to know he was telling me, once again, that I was his. He took my mouth, claiming it savagely, the same way he was doing to my pussy.

I knew from the first night we'd been together, until then, why he'd waited so long to get physically intimate with me. Why he'd stopped me from kissing him those times. It was because of this. Because he knew he'd lose all restraint. He thought I was too sensitive to take the beast that laid inside of him. But as I came for probably the hundredth time that day, I pulled him to me, urging him to go deeper, to give me more. He wasn't too much for me. He was exactly what I needed—who I needed.

When he lowered his head and bit my bottom lip before sucking it into his mouth and moaning as he came inside of me, I knew too, that we had indeed made another baby that day.

CHAPTER 23

Aaron

Holding the car door open, I took my wife's hand and helped her out. I heard my parents' front door open.

"Mommy! Daddy!"

An excited thrill moved through me as the children ran to us screaming. Kennedy caught Patience around her legs first, nuzzling her face against her stocking-clad legs. Kyle was in my arms before I even realized it.

"Did you guys have fun?" Patience asked.

"I'm a girl, not a guy, Mommy!" Kennedy informed, causing Patience to giggle.

"I'm sorry, baby. Did you guy and *girl* have fun?"

"Yeah! I read grandmother a story. She never heard of *Where the Wild Things Are*." Kennedy sounded truly amazed that her grandmother had never heard of her favorite book. My mother was lying, of course, having read the book to me as a child many times while I recuperated in the hospital.

"How about you, son?" I asked Kyle, placing him down on his feet.

"Grandfather took me fishing." He told us all about their fishing trip, which was really just a walk out to the lake that rested out behind Townsend Manor.

My mother waited patiently at the door for our arrival. She greeted Patience with a kiss on the cheek and a cheerful grin.

"I truly wish the children could join us for the rest of the evening," my mother stated, frowning. Our family dinner had turned into more of a business dinner with a few of my father's associates showing up. The children would be kept with a nanny in a separate part of the house while the adults mingled.

Once inside, I helped remove Patience's light jacket. My mouth watered at the sight of her brown, bare shoulders due to the sleeveless dress she wore. It cinched at her waist, flared a little at the hips that had grown deliciously from bearing my children, and stopped an inch above the knee. I ran my eyes up her body and my frown deepened at the sight of the Burberry scarf she wore to hide the marks I'd left behind after the previous day's events.

"Stop it," she hissed in a whisper.

I raised an eyebrow.

"Looking at me like that. You're insatiable."

The left side of my mouth kicked up and I pulled her to me, laying my hand firmly against her abdomen, bending down low so only she could hear me. "Only for you, and don't you fucking forget it," I growled, nipping at her earlobe. She gasped and pulled away from me, throwing daggers my way with those sepia eyes. My grin grew.

"I'll be damned. I think that might be a genuine smile."

If it was, it surely morphed into a frown at the sound of Tyler's voice as he approached. Reluctantly, I pulled my gaze from my wife to my youngest brother.

"Tyler," Patience greeted. "How're you doing?"

"I'm doi–" His movement toward her along with his words were cut off by my hand to his chest.

"Don't get too close."

Tyler blinked his hazel-green eyes my way.

"Uncle Ty! Uncle Ty!" the children returned from the living room shouting.

Despite the fact that he was wearing a suit, Tyler bent low, scooping both Kyle and Kennedy in his arms. They shrieked with laughter. He placed the children down just as Diego entered, to which he greeted his oldest nephew with a secret handshake just between them.

"He's so good with them. Maybe we should let him babysit more often."

I cut my eyes to my wife. "That's because he's a child himself. And we're not leaving my children alone with him."

"*Our* children," Patience reminded as if I could ever forget.

"You should listen to your wife. I've found when I listen to mine, life goes much smoother."

I pushed out a breath and turned to Carter who was giving me a superior look over the rim of his champagne flute. Next to him stood Michelle, champagne glass in her hand. She and Patience greeted one another, and left to assist my mother in taking the children to the other part of the house where they would be overseen by the nanny. My eyes watched Patience for as long as I could, until they rounded a corner and she was no longer visible.

"You owe me a hundred bucks."

I turned to see Joshua now joining us and looking between our two other brothers. To my confusion both of those knuckleheads dug into their pockets and pulled one hundred dollar bills out, passing them to Josh. He chuckled as he pocketed the money.

"The hell is that about?"

"These two didn't believe me." He gestured between Carter and Tyler.

I waited for him to expound but nothing came. "Care to elaborate?"

Joshua cut his dark eyes their way before pivoting to me. "I told our dear brothers that the big guy had really done it. He'd gone ahead and fallen...hard."

I angled my head at him, still not catching on, and growing more frustrated by the moment. "Joshua, if you keep beating around the bush, I'm go–"

"All right," he chuckled, holding up his hands. "Calm down. After that eventful day in your office, I mentioned to our brothers that your wife really was the one, and that you may not have realized it then but you were definitely in love. They didn't believe me. Bet me a hundred dollars. Clearly, that little display a moment ago," he nodded in the direction the women and children had gone, "proved them wrong. Ergo, I'm two hundred bucks richer. End of story."

I looked from Joshua to the other two nitwits who just wore ridiculous grins.

"Mind your damn business, idiots," I growled, then brushed past Carter and Tyler toward the living room. My father, along with a few of his former colleagues and their wives, were in attendance. I shook off my previous annoyance and put on my game face to discuss business for the next hour or so before dinner was to start.

I rubbed elbows with a number of colleagues in the energy business. One had flown in from overseas to conduct business in Williamsport, specifically with Townsend Industries. We talked shop for a while, when an image across the room caught my eye. I watched as Patience walked over to Michelle, who appeared to be holding her same champagne flute. Patience whispered something in her ear and pulled back, handing Michelle another flute, while taking the one Michelle held and placing it on the dish of a passing waiter. Michelle appeared grateful, taking a sip of her new drink. The two women continued talking for some time. Unfortunately, my line of sight was cut off when my eldest brother stepped into it.

Carter was only an inch taller than me at six-three, so I didn't need to look up to see those smirking blue eyes peering at me.

"Need help with something?" I questioned, my tone clipped.

"They're lovely, aren't they?" His smile widening, he came to stand by my side so I could see our wives again. "It's great they get along so well."

I grunted in agreement.

"Of course, you owe me for the next time I want to spend the entire day screwing my wife. You're going to have to take the kid for a while. It's only fair."

I turned my head, glaring at Carter.

He shrugged. "I'm just saying."

I dismissed him with a look but I grew even more irritated at the deep chuckle he gave off. However, that aggravation was nothing compared to the heat of jealousy that overtook my senses when one of the guests approached Michelle and Patience. He was a popular attorney, who was in the beginning stages of running for district attorney. I glared at him as he shook Patience's hand but his hold lingered. Even from my vantage point, I watched his eyes narrow, as he took her in.

My feet were moving before I fully registered where I was going. I heard someone call my name behind me but I was too intent on the sight before me.

"Aaron," Patience smiled. "This is…" She paused when she saw the cold look in my eyes.

My gaze fell from her to the arm this man had now tucked behind my wife's back, as if he had every right to touch what was mine.

"Justin Arroyo," the man greeted. I'm certain there was a smile on his face but I was still staring at his arm. "Aaron, I've heard so much about you. My people have been trying to get a meeting with you."

"I'm sure they have."

His eyes widened, possibly due to my unfriendly tone.

"Yes," he pushed on, "I am running for district attorney and as you know–"

"That's great, but could you do me a favor?" I lifted my gaze to meet his head-on, tilting my head.

He looked to Patience and my hand tightened into a fist. I stepped closer.

"What would that be?"

"Take your fucking hand off my wife before I cut it off and feed it to you one finger at a time," I seethed through gritted teeth.

His hand snapped to the side at the same time two female gasps sounded.

"Aaron."

Even my wife's admonishment wasn't enough to ebb my anger.

"I-I–" Arroyo looked to Patience again.

"Don't fucking look at her." I edged closer to him, towering over him by at least four inches. "One mistake I can get past. The smartest men learn from their mistakes and don't do it again. I'm sure we won't be needing to have this discussion again. Am I right, Mr. Arroyo?"

"Y-y, well, uh–"

"Say *yes*."

"Yes," he stated hesitantly.

"You can leave now."

I watched as he paused, trying to figure out what'd just happened. He took a step back and then another, finally turning and walking away until he was on the other side of the room.

"Aaron, what the hell was that?" Patience whispered harshly.

"He was touching you."

She sighed, looking both frustrated and embarrassed. "He was just being friendly. He's going into politics, that's what they do."

"He can do it without his hands." I took her by the chin, cutting off any further protests with a kiss to her lips.

She still looked chagrined when I pulled back but no further protests ensued. Just a shake of her head and a roll of her eyes. Both of which, made me want to carry her into any one of the ten bedrooms in this mansion and not let her up for air. I pulled back only due to the memory of how sore she'd been earlier, though she'd tried to hide it.

Her ass isn't sore though, I thought. I silently agreed to give that thought some further entertainment later, once we were alone again.

"You're so...so," she fought to find the right word.

"I know." I grinned, tapping her cheek and walking away before I really did take her again. My cock was already stirring in my pants at the idea alone. I needed to get this night over with.

* * *

Patience

"I never would've believed it."

I glanced over, seeing a disbelieving Michelle shaking her head. "Believed what?"

"Deborah said..." She trailed off.

"Deborah said what?" I asked, referencing our mother-in-law.

"Nothing, just something she said in regards to Aaron. I just never really thought he'd ever...and he's worse than Carter. *Sheesh*," she exclaimed before taking a sip of the sparkling cider I'd given her.

"He's not that bad," I defended.

Michelle's honey-toned eyes bulged. "Not that bad? Did you not hear him threaten to cut that man's hand off and feed it to him?"

I swallowed a sip of my champagne, swallowing and nodding. "He didn't mean it," I stated weakly.

"I'm pretty sure he did."

I knew he meant it. That was the scary part. I knew he meant every word he said and it turned me on. I was sore as hell from the day before but still couldn't deny my body already getting warm and the flutters in my stomach at his possessiveness. I abruptly turned when I saw the shock on Michelle's face as she stared at me.

"You're enjoying it as much as he is. You two are peas in a pod."

I lowered my lashes, smirking. "Don't act like you don't get off on it when Carter's all jealous and badass. I've seen the looks between you two *and* let's not forget that little bun in the oven," I whispered the last part near her ear.

Michelle giggled. "Carter's not as bad as your husband."

"He's not too far off, either," I retorted.

Michelle shrugged and gave me a sideways glance.

Thankfully, a few minutes later, Deborah and Robert Townsend were ushering all the guests into the dining area. We sat down to a lovely four course meal that consisted of a mixed green salad, seafood gumbo, a choice of crawfish étouffée or filet mignon as the entrée, and white chocolate bread pudding with a brandy sauce for dessert. By the time I'd finished my entree I was stuffed. There was no room for dessert. I sat back and observed the table around us. Michelle sat to my left, while Aaron sat at my right, closest to his father who sat at the head of the table. Though his attention was on the conversation he held with his father and two other man, his left hand rested firmly on my right thigh. It'd been there since we'd sat down to eat.

I watched his beautiful profile and was reminded of that very first dinner where we'd met. I was so young and hadn't realized what was happening back then. I just knew that I was finally understanding a little bit of what I'd read about in those Danielle Steele novels I borrowed from the library when Ms. Ryan wasn't paying attention. A smile crested over my face, at the same time I caught Aaron's eye. Even the perma-scowl he wore turned me on. My nipples hardened and I thought to loosen the scarf I wore around my neck to cover my breasts, but then I remembered the marks on my neck. They would be exposed. He'd done it on purpose I was sure, staking his claim to the world. Marking his territory, as if the huge diamond and wedding band I wore weren't enough.

My hand covered his on my thigh and his hold tightened. I sat up to get closer to his ear.

"We should leave soon," I whispered seductively, biting my lower lip.

He gave a small shake of his head. "You're too sore."

I moved close to his ear again. "But my mouth isn't." I pulled back in time to see his eyes darken in that special way that always caused a flood in my panties.

"Ten minutes," he growled, his face just inches from mine.

I held in my giggle and turned my head across the table to see Joshua staring between us. He smirked and winked when his eyes landed on me, then turned his attention to the man sitting next to him.

Somehow, despite everyone still being engrossed in their dinner discussions, Aaron was practically pushing me out of the door, less than ten minutes later. He'd also had his mother agree on keeping the children an extra night, and drop them off at school the following morning. I'm sure it wasn't a hard sell. I barely had time to say my good-byes to Michelle, let alone anyone else. By the time the driver closed the door to the town car, Aaron was all over me.

CHAPTER 24

Patience

We stumbled through our bedroom door, Aaron's arm tightly banded around my waist. His teeth ran down my neck, the scarf I'd worn long ago discarded somewhere between the car and the bottom of the stairs. I shivered when he bit my sensitized skin and then sucked it into his mouth, easing the sting. He repeated that move over and over again as his hand went to the back zipper of my dress, pulling it down. I was grateful he hadn't yanked it off, tearing it, but I spoke too soon. Once the zipper was completely undone he tore at the sides of the dress in a hurry to completely remove it from my body.

"Don't rip it!" I admonished.

"I'll buy you another one," he growled just before I heard the tearing of fabric.

I wasn't given time to reprimand him again when I was spun around and the lace panties I wore were also ripped to shreds. A strong hand at my back forced me to bend over at the waist. His hands covered my wrists.

"Hands on the bed," he ordered. His hands went to the rounded globes of my ass, squeezing and pulling them apart.

I threw my head back, moaning loudly when I felt his hot tongue outline my tight hole. He kicked my legs farther apart, exposing even more of me to him in this vulnerable position. His tongue moved lower, until his entire mouth covered my sex. He ate at my cat like a man starving. He moaned into my pussy, the sounds sending little tingles through my core. My legs began trembling, and my arm muscles strained to hold me up. My toes curled into the carpeted floor and I lifted my head, belting out my husband's name as I came, coating his face with my essence.

I fought to regain control of my breathing. I turned just in time to see Aaron, still fully dressed, undoing his belt buckle. My hands went to his, pushing them aside. I'd said my mouth wasn't sore and I'd meant it. I wanted to deliver the same pleasure he'd just given me. I reached inside of his pants and wrapped my hand around his burgeoning erection. My fingers couldn't even wrap around it in its entirety. I pushed his pants to the floor with my other hand and sank to my knees in front of him. I kept my eyes on him because that was how he liked it. He loved watching me pleasure him and he wanted me to see it. I remembered since the first time he'd shown me. He'd been the only man I performed this act on.

I used my tongue to run a ring around the tip and then down the underside of his dick. I tasted the tangy, sweet drop of precum that emerged from the tip, swallowing it. Aaron's frown deepened. I smiled at his growing impatience. One hand went to the base of his cock while the other went to my throat. He held it to my lips.

"Open."

My mouth fell open and he wasted no time pushing in. I let my teeth lightly graze the top of him and I felt a zing of satisfaction at the hiss that came from his throat. I pushed his hand from the base of his erection, wanting it all to myself. I bobbed my head up and down, working to take more and more of him. He moved his hands from my throat and cock to my face, both of them now cupping my cheeks. His hips began pushing in and out, as he held my head in place. Per usual, Aaron took over, fucking my face.

"Take all of me," he growled when I gagged.

My vision began to blur from the tears that were beginning to emerge. I moved my hands to his hips, attempting to slow his pace down.

"Move your fucking hands," he ordered.

I dropped my hands to my sides, and relaxed my jaw, allowing him more space. I felt the tip of his cock hit the back of my throat. I also felt my own wetness dripping down my inner thighs. I continued to lick and suck where I could as Aaron pounded my throat.

"Hollow your cheeks," he grunted, face and neck straining. He was on the verge of coming. "You're going to swallow every bit of it."

That'd been a foregone conclusion, but I nodded my head in agreement anyway. Well, as well as I could with him still fucking the hell out of my face. I felt it when his cock swelled even more, and a split second later my tongue was coated with his hot, sticky semen. I swallowed what I could. He finally pulled out of my mouth, allowing me the space to swallow, just as another spurt of come squirted from him. I held my mouth open to catch every last drop, just as he'd directed.

I was exhausted by the time he finished coming, my jaw ached, but Aaron was like the damn Energizer Bunny. He lifted me from the floor and carried us to the leather chair that sat in the corner of the room.

I gasped and called his name, when I felt him insert a finger into my anus.

"Your pussy is too sore but your ass is mine."

Moaning at his salacious words, I glanced over my shoulder to see him with the same tube of lube he'd used the day before. I straddled my legs over either side of his, bending over to let him massage the lube in. Butterflies fluttered in my belly at the nervousness and fear that began to rise up. A butt plug was one thing, but Aaron's cock was another. No, it wasn't the first time we'd had intercourse this way, but it'd been a long time.

"A-Aaron," I stuttered.

"I won't hurt you … yet," he growled.

I closed my eyes as another flood of wetness seeped from my core. I remembered Michelle's words from earlier. I was just as bad as

Aaron. Even the thought of pain felt good as long as it came from him. I must've been some kind of masochist.

I braced my hands on either side of the chair, when Aaron lifted me by the hips and placed his cock at the entrance of my backside.

"Mmmm," I moaned as he breached me, stretching me to fit him.

"Don't tense up," he cooed in my ear.

I grabbed his hand at my waist, needing him to pause.

"Move your hand."

I continued to hold it, suddenly unsure that I wanted to do this.

"Move your hand," he ordered again, tightening his hold on me.

I did as he directed and again he slid farther into my ass. The burning sensation caused me to wince. He pushed until he was all the way in. He didn't move at first, letting me adjust to being stuffed in this way. His large hands around my waist traveled up to cup both of my breasts. I squirmed and moaned when he pinched my nipples, plucking them. I squeezed my eyes shut as the burning in my ass gave way to a deeper sensation in my core. I wiggled my hips.

"You-you have to move, Aaron," I pleaded, my body seeking more of this growing feeling.

His hands went to my hips again, raising me along his rod, and pulling me down again. His hips rose to meet me, pounding against my hips.

"Open your eyes!" he yelled.

I did and realized the mirror that lined our bathroom door gave us the perfect view of our lovemaking. I'm sure that's why he'd set the chair up there in the first place. I rose and fell on his cock, breasts bouncing as he made me his in every way imaginable.

"Touch yourself. Let me see it."

I widened my legs and moved my hand to my clit and began massaging it. Aaron's eyes zeroed in on my hand, watching me pleasure myself as he continued to take what was his from the back. Within a few minutes a tightness began building in my toes, making it's way up my body.

"I'm about to come!" I yelled, breathless.

Aaron's response was to grunt and pick up the pace. He smacked my hand away from my pussy and continued the job himself, pressing firmly against my clit, massaging it. My hips jumped at the increased impact and I came again, yelling his name. Soon after my climax, Aaron pushed my torso against his body, fusing our bodies together. He leaned over my neck, biting down and growling as he came inside of me. I held onto his arm and wrapped my other arm around the back of his head, running my fingers through his hair to soothe him as he orgasmed.

He held me tightly for a long while after he finished coming. I felt like he was forcing all the air from my lungs the way he held me so close.

"You're mine," he repeated over and over into the crook of my neck.

"I know," I agreed.

"Forever."

I swallowed. "Forever," I whispered.

Only my agreement seemed to calm him enough that he loosened his hold on me. Loosened but didn't let me go entirely. Not even when he pulled back, lifting my hips so that his cock fully expelled from my body on a loud "pop." He kept his hands at my waist, directing me to the bathroom and setting me down on the toilet. He went to turn on the shower for us to clean up before going to bed. I drifted off to sleep that night, completely satiated, wrapped in Aaron's arms.

* * *

A<small>ARON</small>

Taking another sip of the aged bourbon, I let the burn on its way down soothe my nerves. My eyes narrowed as I heard footsteps moving toward my office. I wasn't alarmed. Only a handful of people in the world had the access to get up to the office this late in the evening. Therefore, I wasn't surprised when a few seconds later, my office door was pushed open and standing on the other end was my younger brother, Joshua.

His eyes scanned my face before narrowing when they landed on the glass on my desk. He sighed, stepping inside of my office and shutting the door behind him. Moving to my desk, he sat down across from me.

"The only other time I've seen you drink was about six years ago..." He paused, waiting for me to saying something.

I remained silent, opting to take another sip from my glass.

Joshua nodded. "Yeah, you were tight lipped then, too. But now that I think about it, it was right around the time all that shit was going down with that Japanese company. You and Alicia were freshly broken up. One could've assumed it was the break up with her that drove you to drink, but we both know you didn't give a shit about your fiancée." He rested his chin on his fingertips, peering at me with his dark, brown eyes.

"You have something to say, say it," I stated dryly.

"Kyle and Kennedy are five, add nine months for pregnancy and that's almost six years."

I rolled my eyes. Joshua loved beating around the fucking bush. He knew as well as I did the reason I touched alcohol that night six years ago was the same reason I was drinking yet again that night. One woman. Patience.

"It must be bad. You're drinking a fourteen-thousand dollar brand of bourbon." He looked toward the twenty-five year old Rip Van Winkle bottle.

"I told my wife I love her," I confessed.

Josh raised an eyebrow.

"She didn't say it back." I sighed, and ran a hand through my hair, feeling foolish. I was never this goddamn insecure.

I stood, peering at Joshua at the same time he let out a low whistle.

He shrugged. "What'd you expect?"

I shook my head and moved to the window. He was right but I wasn't in the mood to admit it out loud. What had I expected? For her to open her heart to me again after it was crushed the first time? Yes. Selfishly, that's exactly what I'd expected.

"She's the puzzle piece I never knew was missing until it arrived," I stated, staring out of the window, my back to Joshua. "She calms me and makes me feel invincible, all at the same time. Do you have any idea what that's like?" It was a rhetorical question. I didn't expect my brother to answer. He surprised me when he returned with...

"Yeah, I might have an idea of what that's like."

I turned, gaze narrowed, and stared at him. His brows were knitted, eyes staring at the floor in front of him, a frown marring his features. I'd seen that look in the mirror many a night after Patience and I separated, and in the intervening years. It was the look of a man missing his other half. My heartstrings tugged.

Joshua lifted his head, noticing me staring at him. He schooled his face just before rising from his chair.

"But you have her here, now. You're married and you two have two beautiful children...don't fuck it up by rushing her," he warned, his voice deepening.

I actually felt the left side of my face kick up into a semi-grin. By all accounts, Joshua may appear to be rather lighthearted and easy going, but that's because most people don't get to see this side of Joshua. Save for the boardroom, he rarely showed his ruthless side to outsiders. But he is a Townsend through and through. We all have our less-than-innocent streak. Joshua was no different.

"Don't tell me how to handle my fucking wife," I growled for good measure. Dark side or not, Joshua could go fuck himself if he thought he could tell me how to handle Patience.

A smirk creased the hard lines of his face. "Just a little friendly advice." By then he'd moved past the desk, to pat me on the shoulder.

"Fuck off," I grunted.

Josh chuckled. "I'll just take this off your hands."

I peered over my shoulder to see him reaching for the bottle of bourbon. I grunted. *He can fucking take it.* "Tell the boys down at the club you fight at to enjoy it."

"You kidding? Those assholes wouldn't enjoy good bourbon if it bit them in the ass. I'll keep this for me."

I lifted my shoulder in a shrug before turning back to the window. I heard my office door open and close as Joshua departed. Sighing, I turned back to my desk to finish up the work I was supposed to be completing. However, my thoughts kept drifting back to my wife. I'd told her repeatedly that I'd loved her. And though her eyes lit up and she bit her bottom lip as she spasmed around my cock, from my words alone, it still clawed at me that she hadn't said the words back. Deep down I knew why. She was afraid. She had a right to be considering what happened after the first time she'd said those words to me. I told myself I wouldn't push. I'd give her time. Just not too long. I wanted…no, *needed* all of her. Body, mind, and soul. I was that selfish.

* * *

PATIENCE

For the next week I was reduced to wearing scarves or using makeup to cover the marks left by Aaron on my neck. I was amazed at how his passion showed up on my body.

I woke up the following Tuesday morning to an empty bed. That wasn't unusual, seeing as how Aaron was such an early riser. He and Kyle were usually down in the den working out and then going over Kyle's readings and studies for the day. Every now and again I would peek in on the two. It warmed me all over to see how gentle and loving Aaron was with Kyle. Our son blossomed under his father's care. The boy who hated to even say his ABC's, wouldn't hesitate to try to read a word out loud or recite new words he'd learned. Unfortunately, Kyle was still more shy around Kennedy and I when it came to reading but he was coming around and so much more quickly than I'd thought was possible.

When I got up to go see if Kennedy was awake and start breakfast, I found Kyle looking forlorn in the hallway.

"Hey, buddy. Where's Daddy?" I asked, brushing a stray curl out of his face.

Kyle's little shoulders rose and fell. "I don't know."

I gave him an odd look. I guessed Aaron must've had to leave early for work that day instead.

"Well, how about you come help Mommy cook breakfast?"

"Okay," he agreed, but his usual enthusiasm wasn't there.

On our way down, I tried to explain to Kyle that his father had a big, important job and sometimes that meant he wasn't going to have as much time to spend with him as he'd like. I think he understood, but the sad look in his hazel eyes told me he still hated it. I bit back my own anger at Aaron. The least he could've done was told Kyle he wouldn't be able to work together that morning.

I fixed a breakfast of pancakes, sausage, and fruit before telling Kyle to go upstairs and wake his sister. A few minutes later the pair were barreling into the kitchen ready to eat. It was the first time in a long time that it was just the three of us for breakfast. Though I'd always loved the days when the three of us would eat breakfast together, without Aaron there, something felt like it was missing.

The children ate and then I sent them upstairs to brush their teeth and get dressed while I took a quick shower and prepared myself for work. We were having preschoolers from Excelor Academy come over for story-time that day. I loved reading to children that young. Though Kyle and Kennedy were still young, it made me yearn for the days when they were babies or toddlers. They were so much more independent now than they had been just a few years prior. It felt like forever ago. I pressed my hand to my belly, remembering Aaron's words the almost week and a half prior. I wanted more children as well.

I stepped into the doors of the library, shaking my head to ward off those thoughts. I was angry at Aaron for standing Kyle up that morning. I didn't need to think about bringing any more children into the picture until he understood that he couldn't drop our children whenever work got busy.

"Morning, Patience." Moira smiled as I stuffed my shoulder bag behind the front counter.

"Morning. What're you reading?" I inquired, stepping closer to look down at the book she was thumbing through.

"It's a book on Mandarin. One of our members ordered it from the main library."

"That's interesting." I continued to look at the integral shapes and symbols that formed words in Mandarin.

"Look, there's your name," Moira laughed, pointing to one of the symbols.

My eyebrows dipped as I stared at the symbol. "That's the Mandarin word for Patience," I stated disbelievingly.

"It is. Beautiful, isn't it?"

I swallowed, nodding my head. It was also familiar. I'd seen that symbol everyday since Aaron had been back in my life.

"Look. *The Mandarin symbol for patience is made up of two separate symbols, one of which means the blade of a knife, and the other means heart. This symbolizes how difficult it is to practice patience...*" Moira read the meaning behind the symbols. "They've got that right," she mumbled. "Patience is hard as hell to practice sometimes, especially with some of the patrons that come in here." She giggled.

I swallowed down the lump in my throat and threw a smirk her way. My mind was far past thinking about any of the library's patrons. But I pushed away those thoughts. Thankfully, Moira soon closed the book and moved on to discussing our schedule for the day and what needed to get done. I retrieved the cart that held the returns and began organizing them to place back on the shelves. The morning went rather quickly, and ended with the visit from the preschoolers.

That afternoon a group of teens from one of the local public schools piled in after having a half day, many of whom needed to conduct research for a project. I was surprised at this day and age many teens even still used the library for research, but then I was informed that the teachers had required at least two books for this particular project. That reminded me to bring up an idea I'd been thinking of to Moira.

I thought it'd be a good idea for the library to host a tech and research series, open to the public but geared to many of the underserved pre-teens in the city. I told her of a similar series I'd been a part of while living in Oakland, where the tech gap continued to grow between the underserved and the more privileged students. She agreed to look more into it if I presented her with a put-together proposal. I planned on putting one together over the next few evenings.

I left work that day feeling accomplished, and as if I was doing some good for the community. Helping people, especially young children, discover a love of reading was my passion. It weighed on me incredibly heavy when I couldn't do the same for my own son. But seeing his growth under his father's tutelage quickly pushed those feelings aside. The reminder of that thought, sparked my anger again at Aaron. I'd sent him numerous texts throughout the day, and called at least twice but to no avail. Usually, he responded within a few minutes of a text. I knew he was okay, lest I would've heard from one of his security, or Joshua who worked with him daily. I figured I'd just take it up with him later that evening after the children were asleep.

CHAPTER 25

Patience

"Kyle and Kennedy, you two go wash your hands for dinner," I stated, standing at the doorway of the children's playroom. "Hey, you two, you hear me?" I questioned with a little more force in my voice when neither one of them moved from the children's table that sat in the center of the room.

I walked over to the table, and wasn't surprised to find Kennedy with her head in a book. She, like myself, could become so completely absorbed in a book that the people around us disappeared.

"Ken," I brushed a hand over her shoulder, "go wash your hands for dinner," I said again, pulling the book from her hands.

"Kyle, you–" I stopped when I realized that he was just as intent on what he'd been doing at the table as Kennedy had been. However, instead of reading, he was actually writing. "What are you making?" I questioned, stooping low next to Kyle.

He looked up at me with the biggest smile on his face. "I'm making Daddy a card for his birthday!" His hazel eyes shone bright with excitement, the type that only occurs when you get to be the one to do something special for your real life superhero.

I wrinkled my brows. "Kyle, it's not..." I trailed off, trying to remember today's date in my head.

"November thirteenth," Kyle and I said together.

I squeezed my eyes tightly, slapping my hand against my forehead. "I'm an idiot!" I gritted out.

"Don't say that, Mommy! It's not nice."

I blinked my eyes open to see a frowning Kennedy standing over me.

I grabbed her hand. "I'm sorry, baby. You're right. I shouldn't have called myself that. Mommy just made a mistake."

"I make mistakes during my studies, too, but Daddy says everyone makes mistakes and that as long as I learn from them, it's okay," Kyle informed me.

I tweaked his nose. "Your daddy's a smart man."

Kyle nodded in agreement. "That's why I'm making him the bestest birthday card ever! You like it, Mommy?" He held up the colorful card he'd designed by himself. My heart melted at the sight of the first card my son had ever made. He'd hated writing anything that wasn't completely pictures.

I went to stand, but something made me stop. "Kyle, how did you know November thirteenth was Daddy's birthday?" I knew Aaron hadn't told him.

Kyle shrugged with one shoulder. "A lady told me," he answered, casually.

"What lady? Your teacher?"

He shook his head. "No. She's invisible. Only I can see her."

"Ky–"

"Mooommy, I'm hungry!" Kennedy began whining before I could question her brother any further. I stood, still staring at Kyle finishing up his birthday card.

"Okay, sweetie, give me a minute," I told Kennedy, who was tugging my hand.

I went to my room to grab my cell phone. I needed to leave the house, but also had to find a sitter for the children. Carter and Michelle were at her mother's for the evening. Aaron's parents were out of town, as was Joshua. That left me with only one person left to call.

"Hey, Ty."

"Patience? What's up?" my youngest brother-in-law asked.

"Listen, I need you to babysit for a few hours."

"Woohoo!" I heard his clap through the phone. "'Bout time that brother of mine got off his high horse about me watching the kids."

"Aaron's not exactly here right now," I explained, while bringing the children's plates to the table.

"Where is he?"

"Out."

"Out?"

"It's November thirteenth."

"Shit!" he cursed. "No wonder Father took Mother on that unexpected trip. She always smothers him on his birthday."

I bit my lower lip. "Can you be here in fifteen minutes?"

"I'll be there in ten," he agreed.

I hung up and impatiently waited for Tyler to arrive. Once he did, I grabbed my bag, the card Kyle made, gave the children each a kiss, and was out the door. I started for my Honda CR-V that I'd had shipped from Oakland—the car I rarely got to drive these days—but was stopped.

"I'm sorry, ma'am, I can't let you do that."

I turned to see Daniel staring down at me. "Do what?"

"I'm under strict instructions from Mr. Townsend to take you anywhere you want to go."

I sighed. "Daniel, this is my car. I don't need you to—"

He shook his head. "I'm sorry. Boss' orders."

"Fine," I conceded, not wanting to waste any more time arguing. I still couldn't believe I'd spent the entire day angry at Aaron, forgetting that this was the one day of the year he needed the *most* support. Even though, he might not realize it. He always was isolated on his birthday. Well, he wasn't about to do that shit anymore. Like it or not, he had a family now. One that wouldn't let him run away from his past.

* * *

It took twenty minutes to get from the house to Townsend Industries. I knew this was where he'd be, working himself to the bone to push out any and all memories. I had Daniel drop me off at the front entrance of the building. Unfortunately, it was close to eight o'clock and the front of the building was locked. I opted to walk to the end of the block where I could enter the building from the garage.

As I rounded the building and made my way into the concrete garage, I saw that most of the spaces were empty. Everyone had obviously gone home for the evening, and the few cars that remained belonged to owners of nearby condos. I walked to the far end of the garage where the elevator stood; my heels against the cement were the only sound that could be heard. Suddenly, my hear rate quickened and an ugly, familiar feeling skittered down my spine. I clutched the bag I carried over my shoulder tighter to my side, and looked around. Again, all I saw were a few cars but nothing out of the ordinary. But that nagging feeling of being watched returned. The same eerie sensation I'd had in that bathroom stall in the park a month earlier returned.

I stopped walking, doing a full three-sixty turn to observe my surroundings. "Hello?" I called out.

"Mrs. Townsend?"

"Ahh!" I screamed. Before I could fumble for my keys that held my pepper spray on the chain, I realized who had called my name. "James!" I breathed, holding my hand to my chest, trying to catch my breath.

"I'm sorry, ma'am. Didn't mean to frighten you. I was doing my rounds," the security guard explained.

"No, don't be sorry. I'm here to see my husband."

James nodded and walked with me to the elevator, punching in the code that took me directly to the floor of Aaron's office. Once the doors closed, I inhaled deeply, shaking off that creepy feeling, and forced myself to remember I was safe. The day wasn't about me. I needed to focus on Aaron.

When the elevator doors opened, I stepped out into the empty lobby. The lights were low but I could see light coming from farther down the hall where Aaron's office was located. I pushed through the glass doors and walked steadily in the direction of the light. His door was partially ajar, and I pushed my way in.

His head turned in my direction and my heart dropped to my knees. His eyes were dark, but not like when we were intimate, or when he was angry. They were darkened by the memories he'd been trying to fight off.

I chose to leave the lights low. His scowl deepened the closer I moved to his desk. I placed my bag next to his desk on the floor and moved files and papers aside. I pushed up on my arms, planting my bottom on his desk, next to him in his office chair. He sat back, staring at me, wordlessly. Leaning forward, I reached out and ran my fingers through his dark, silky hair.

"Poor you," I cooed, "you've been fighting demons all day."

* * *

Aaron

My eyes drifted shut and for the first time that day the memories hadn't come rushing back. All I felt at that instant was my wife's hand stroking my hair. I had indeed been fighting demons all day. It was what I did on my birthday. I fought them, alone. Pushing through and using work as a distraction.

"I was so pissed at you this morning. Not for leaving me hanging but for Kyle."

My eyes sprang open at the mention of Kyle's name. I knew I was a coward for leaving so early that morning but I had to. I was in no shape to be around my family. A part of me wanted to tell Patience to go back home, to insist on it, but with her hand continuing to stroke my hair, relieving the ache in my soul with each pass, I couldn't.

"You don't have to do this alone, you know."

Finally, I reached for her wrist, halting her actions. "I do. I won't dump my bullshit on my family."

She shook her head. "It's not dumping for a husband to confide in his wife."

I gritted my teeth, anger suddenly rising in my chest. "You didn't want to be my wife, remember?"

She pulled her wrist free of my hold, eyes wide, mouth opened.

"You said it yourself. I forced you into this marriage. No need to pretend like you wanted it." I casually reached for the glass of seltzer water I'd been drinking. "Go home, Patience."

She turned her head away from me, staring out at the window. "I know what you're trying to do." She turned back to me. "Same thing you did back then. Push me away when we get too close."

My jaw tightened.

She eased off my desk and my gaze lingered on the six inch heels she wore that made her legs look phenomenal, even though they were covered by dark stockings. I would've preferred them bare. Slowly she removed the long jacket she wore, exposing the form fitting, white dress that stopped inches above her knees. Though the dress had long sleeves, the black lace detailing showed off the tops of her shoulders and arms.

"I know it's well past Labor Day, so I'm breaking the *no wearing white* rule, but I figured I could make an exception for my husband on his birthday."

My stomach muscles tightened.

She wiggled her hips a little, pulling the sides of the dress a little lower. "After all, it is his favorite color on me."

She was right. Aside from seeing her naked, I loved seeing her walnut skin covered in white fabric. The contradiction in color turned me on.

Patience moved closer, removing the glass from my hand and adjusting my arm to make room for her body as she sat in my lap. The irony is that as soon as I felt her weight against my body, the heaviness I'd been carrying all day began to lift.

She placed a quick kiss to my lips but pulled away too quickly for my liking. I was about to pull her back to my arms when she handed me something.

"This is for you."

I looked down to see a card. Obviously made by a child.

The left side of my mouth curled upwards. "Kennedy is such a sweet child." She was always leaving her mother and I letters or bringing them home from school thanking us and telling us how much she loved us.

"She is, but this isn't from Kennedy. It's from Kyle."

My eyes widened and Patience looked at me again, urging me to take the card. I did and read the outside.

"Happy Birthday, Daddy," I read out loud. I flipped the card open and grinned at the drawings of our entire family. "I love you very much," I finished reading.

"He transposed the I and the R in birthday, and the O and the V in love, but he's five." She shrugged. "And he wrote it all by himself."

I swallowed, still staring at the card.

"He wouldn't have done that without his hero."

I peered up at my wife.

"You're his hero, Aaron...and mine, and Kennedy's for that matter." She leaned in to cup my face. "You don't get to go through this day or any other day alone. I don't care how painful it is, how upsetting it is, or how vulnerable it makes you feel. You don't do it alone. Do you understand me?" She shook my face for good measure.

I hesitated and eventually sighed before nodding. "I do."

"Good."

Laying my head against her chest, I listened to the sound of her heartbeat. I drew strength from it. I closed my eyes when she began stroking my hair again.

"Tell me about it."

My hands tightened around her waist. "I've already told you."

"You told me there was an accident and you were seriously injured, your parents killed, and that it was your birthday. But we both know there's more to it than that. Tell me."

I pinched the bridge of my nose, hating the feelings of helplessness that washed over me. This was the very reason I avoided my family on this day. But Patience wasn't my mother, father, or my brothers.

They'd been there during that time. She hadn't. She deserved to know the full story…as much of it as I was willing to give, at least.

"My eighth birthday …" I began.

* * *

THEN …

"Happy Birthday, Aaron!" Aunt Deborah cheered, as she opened the door for the three of us.

A smile sprouted on my face and I went to respond to my aunt, but my father's greeting behind me, had me clamping down on my tongue.

"Deborah," he responded in the way that made me uneasy. "Where is Robert?" he questioned, sounding mean to my young ears.

My aunt blinked. "He's inside, of course. Come in, Jason, Jesse," she welcomed my mother, father, and myself, stepping aside and widening the door of Townsend Manor.

My father stepped past my mother, and I looked around. "I see you've redecorated."

"Yes, Robert and I decided it was time for a little bit of a change. The children are getting older," my aunt stated, smiling down at me. "We wanted a more child friendly environment. Aaron, when you come over to play with your cousins, you'll all have an entertainment room to yourself, and we've fixed up a bedroom, just for you."

My smile was halted by my father's next words. "You've not only changed my family's home, you think I can't take care of my son well enough so you have to give him his own room?"

I lowered my eyes to the floor. I'd become used to such scenes, growing up with my father.

"Jason, I'm sure Deborah didn't me–" My mother's explanation fell dead on her lips when my father gave her the deadly glare he always gave when she dared speak up in defiance of him.

I swallowed, knowing what that look meant.

Thankfully, my cousins, Carter and Joshua, came running down the stairs, yelling my name. Carter did a jump off the bottom stair, landing in front of me with his hand raised. We did our special handshake, that was only shared between us two.

"Happy Birthday, man!" he greeted.

"Thanks, man. I got that new game we've been wanting. We'll have to play it sometime," I told him, but looked back over my shoulder when my father cleared his throat.

"You won't be bringing anything over here."

"Jason," My uncle called from the top of the stairs.

I glanced up to see my Uncle Robert, holding baby Tyler in his arms as he moved down the stairs. Carter and I were only a few months apart. He'd turned eight before me. Joshua was younger, at only three, and Tyler was just barely six months.

"Robert." My father nodded, at his older brother.

"Happy Birthday, sport."

"Don't call him that. Aaron hates sports. He's nobody's jock, unlike your children. He will be running Townsend Industries someday," my father stated with his chin lifted.

Aunt Deborah quickly stepped in, directing us to the dining area where my birthday dinner was being held. Unfortunately, it was uncomfortable from the beginning. None of my birthdays were fun events…none of my days were as long as my father was around. He was always so mean to my Aunt and Uncle, when they were always so nice to me. I never understood it. I hated that as much as I hated the way he treated my mother and I behind closed doors.

Thankfully, the adults let my cousins and I leave the table after dinner so we could play a little bit before we cut my birthday cake. Carter and I raced up the stairs to the new entertainment room.

"Whoa!" I breathed out as soon as he pushed the door open. The room was huge with a movie theater screen along the front wall, a video game console that played any type of game we wanted, and a number of toy chests throughout the room.

"Here, dude. I'll let you be Goku since it's your birthday," Carter stated, handing me one of the controllers.

"Thanks, man."

We played for a while, both of us getting our turns at winning round after round.

"Aw, man!" Carter shouted, shoving me when he lost the last round. It was meant to be playful but it hurt like hell.

"Ouch!" I squealed, my hand going to my side.

Carter looked at me in confusion. "What's wrong?"

"Nothing," I lied.

"It was just a playful push. It didn't hurt that much," he explained, his eyes looking at the hand that still rested against my rib.

"It's no big deal, man."

But Carter was smart. "Lemme see." He pushed my hand away, lifting my shirt, revealing the large purple and yellow bruise that was a few days old.

"What's this?"

"Nothing, I fell at school."

Carter didn't bother waiting for me to explain. He was already running out of the room yelling for his mom and dad. I chased after him, calling his name, telling him to leave it alone. I didn't need anymore trouble, but he refused to listen.

"Son, what's the matter?" Uncle Robert emerged from the living room, looking concerned.

"Look!" Carter shouted, grabbing my arm and lifting my shirt to reveal the bruise to all four adults and my younger cousins. Everyone now stood in the foyer.

My aunt gasped and out of the corner of my eye I saw my mother drop her head.

I snatched my arm out of Carter's grip, quickly lowering my shirt to cover the bruise, but it was too late.

"You son of a bitch!" Uncle Robert shouted, grabbing my father by his shirt.

Chaos broke out as both men began shouting at one another.

"I should've never trusted you!" Robert yelled. "You said it was one time. You'd lost your temper one time. That it'd never happen again!"

Tears sprang to my eyes as I begged and pleaded for my uncle and father to stop fighting.

"And you!" Uncle Robert rounded on my mother. "What kind of mother lets that happen to her son?"

"Robert, stop it!" Aunt Deborah admonished, but he was relentless.

"I'm calling the police!"

"No!" my mother shouted. "Deborah, do something. He didn't mean it," she pleaded, lying to cover for my father yet again.

Tears were streaming down my face and my throat hurt from yelling at them both to stop.

"I'm calling the judge in the morning!" Robert insisted. "He will be removed from your custody immediately. Jesse, you want to be used as a punching bag, that's on you, but I will not allow my nephew to be treated this way by that…that buffoon!"

"Buffoon?" my father shrieked, going after Uncle Robert again.

I watched as my father missed and nearly landed on his face, stumbling into the railing of the staircase instead. He'd been drinking even before we arrived at my Aunt and Uncle's.

"I always knew you'd end up a failure, but to take your shortcomings out on a defenseless child is sick!" Uncle Robert continued.

"Jason, let's just go," my mother insisted, grabbing my father's arm.

"You can go, but you're not taking Aaron with you! Deborah, take the children upstairs," he ordered.

"You're not taking my goddamn kid!" My father pulled me, none too gently, from my Aunt Deborah's hand, pushing both my mother and I toward the front door.

"You son of a bi–Bring him back." Uncle Robert started for us but Aunt Deborah grabbed him.

"Robert, don't. We'll only make matters worse tonight."

"Listen to your wife, Robert!" my father taunted.

"We will be calling that judge in the morning," my aunt continued, giving my father the same look my uncle was giving him. Her eyes moved to me and I saw the water that filled her blue eyes. "Aaron, we will be there tomorrow to come get you," she promised.

I swallowed the sadness, fear, and confusion down. I would've loved nothing more to go live with my aunt and uncle but I couldn't leave my mother. I looked to Carter who stood at the middle of the staircase, continuing to watch everything. My eyes narrowed. I hated him for this. It was all his damn fault. He should've just listened to me and left it alone!

"You two aren't taking my son!" my father shouted one last time, as he pushed my mother and I out the door, slamming it shut behind him. He hustled us to his Lexus, forcing my mother inside the passenger seat by her head, and then pushing me in the back. He peeled out of the driveway and sped up even more once we got to the main road.

"Jason, slow down!"

I flinched at the sound of cracking bones as my father punched my mother directly in her face.

"Don't you ever fucking tell me what to do, bitch!" He punched her again. "How could you just stand there and let him berate me like that!"

He swerved, nearly hitting an oncoming car. He grabbed the steering wheel with both hands.

"They're not taking my fucking son! Violent? I got his violence. You saw how he charged me. I'll tell any fucking judge what happened. He's lucky his kids don't get fucking taken away!" my father continued ranting.

I dug my fingers into the leather seats, holding on for dear life every time he took a turn. Cars were honking at us left and right as he raced past them.

"Jason, you're going to get us killed!" my mother yelled. "Please, just, slow down." She cried and begged.

"Please, Dad!" I yelled, speaking up for the first time. My heart pounded in my chest when I heard the loud sounds of another car horn.

"Fuck that! He wants to take my kid? Over my dead body! I'll take us all out!"

* * *

"Those were the last words he ever spoke. Everything went black after that. The next thing I remember was waking up in a hospital bed, Aunt Deborah and Uncle Robert by my side."

That last part wasn't the complete truth. I remembered more after that. It was the more that'd continued to leave me bitter and angry at the world around me. It was the rest of what happened that night that taught me, not only was my father a monster, but there were more people out there nearly as bad as him.

"Baby," Patience whispered, pulling me into her. She cried. I could feel her tears as they coated my neck. When she pulled back, she quickly wiped her eyes before cupping my face.

"Is that why you're closer to Joshua than Carter even though you two are closer in age?"

Furrowing my brows, I stared up at her. "I guess. We were never really close after that, even though he tried. I was too angry for years. Then he went away to join the military. We grew apart even more."

"Until now."

I cocked my head to the side.

"We live right next to him. I know how loyal you are to him, to all your family. You both are married fathers now. Maybe you two can grow closer."

I shrugged and blew out a breath. "Maybe," I murmured.

The room grew silent for a few heartbeats.

"He was a sick man," Patience stated just above a whisper. "Your father," she said for clarity.

"I know."

She shook her head. "No. You don't know. He was sick. So sick, he couldn't put his own jealousy and bitterness aside for his family. You're nothing like him."

I swallowed, my jaw tightening.

She cupped my face. "Look at me."

I let my eyes linger at the corner of the room for a minute before finally pinning her with my gaze.

"I know why you left so early and stayed away all day. You wanted to protect us from you. From these feelings. But you're not Jason

Townsend. He's dead and he can't hurt you anymore, *if* you don't let him."

"H–" I hesitated, pushing out a breath, unfamiliar with the feeling of asking for help. "How do I stop letting him?"

She lowered her head, pressing her lips to mine before moving back. "You build new memories, better memories with us. Come home with me." Her voice was so soft, so full of want and love.

I stood, placing her on my desk, and stepping into between her parted thighs. "I'll go, but I need you first." Reaching my hand under her dress, I tugged at the panties and stockings.

"You can have me," she responded, her voice breathless. Just the way I liked it.

A while later we entered our house. I expected the children to be asleep, as either Michelle or Carter waited for us to arrive home. Instead, I entered my home to find my youngest brother with his bare feet kicked up on top of the glass coffee table that sat in our living room while Kennedy sat on one side of him painting the nails of his left hand and Kyle sat to the right, playing on his tablet.

"Daddy!" Kennedy, exclaimed, seeing me first.

I tore my angry gaze away from my shithead brother to my baby girl, scooping her up in my arms as she ran to me.

"Dad!" Kyle stated, tossing his tablet down and following his sister.

"It's after nine o'clock. You two should be in bed." I glared over their shoulders to Tyler who was just now rising from the couch.

"We were having way too much fun to go to bed, right, kids?" he moved closer to us, asking the twins.

"Yeah! Uncle Ty let me paint his nails when I told him you never let me do yours," Kennedy stated, giving me the biggest puppy dog eyes.

My heart lurched against my ribcage. She'd inherited the same sepia eyes from her mother, and I was a sucker for both. I turned to Patience who stood at my right, smirking at me. These women would be the death of me…and the rebirth.

"Thanks for watching them, Ty," Patience began, giving my brother a hug.

I grunted at the physical contact. Ty winked at me over her shoulder. I swear if I hadn't been holding my daughter in my arms I would've punched the hell out of him.

"Well, it's been a good night, kiddos. But Uncle Ty has to be at the field early tomorrow morning." He gave the children a kiss each but I pulled Patience away from him with one arm when he went in for another hug.

"Dad, did you get my card?" Kyle questioned.

I stooped low, still holding Kennedy who was now drifting off to sleep on my shoulder.

"I sure did. I'm going to display it on my desk at the office, right next to the picture I have of the three of you."

His face beamed with pride.

"Come on, buddy, it's time for bed." I took him by the hand and gestured with my head for Patience to walk ahead while I followed her up the stairs. "Hey," I called when she went to open the room to Kyle's door. I gestured again to our bedroom, leading her in.

She gave me a confused look.

"I want them with us tonight."

Her eyebrows rose. "With the way this one sleeps?" she questioned, rubbing Kennedy's back.

"I sleep with you every night and live to tell about it."

"Haha, you're so funny."

"I'm not joking. I wake up with a knee or foot in my rib almost every morning."

She rolled her eyes, turning to the bed. "Whatever, Aaron," she whispered.

We placed both children, who at least had been put in their pajamas by their Uncle Ty, into the bed. Patience changed into a pair of long flannel pajama bottoms, similar to the ones I often wore, and a sleeveless T-shirt. I put on a pair of my own flannels before doing my nightly routine. Right before crawling into bed, I went to Kennedy's room to grab a book from one of her shelves.

"Can't have bedtime without story time," I told Patience.

She grinned and crawled into bed. Kyle moved to lay his head on her belly. She began stroking his hair the same way she often did mine. Kennedy crawled up and laid on my stomach, as I began reading *Last Stop on Market Street* to the children. By the time I read the final words, their light snores could be heard. Laying my head back against the pillow, I stared down at the two creations the woman I love and I made together.

"Tell me about your pregnancy."

Patience lifted her head. Our eyes met.

"Were you sick a lot? Like Michelle?"

Her eyes widened. "You know?"

"I saw you exchange her champagne for sparkling cider the other week at Mother and Father's. Carter mentioned her not feeling too well that night."

She laid her head back down, still stroking Kyle's hair, smiling. "I was very sick the first trimester. Once, I had to go to the hospital for fluids because I was so dehydrated. That's when I found out they were twins. I wanted to wait until they were born to find out their genders but the ultrasound tech messed up and told me."

"Do you have pictures? Of being pregnant?"

"I didn't take many. It wasn't exactly the happiest time for me. But I have a few." She lifted slowly, being mindful of Kyle, to turn to the nightstand and open the top drawer. She pulled out a small photo binder.

My breath caught as soon as she opened it. The first picture was of her, six months pregnant.

"My friend, Judy, took this picture a few months after we started working at the library together."

"Judy. You were at The Cage with her," I stated, still staring at the picture but I felt her eyes on me.

"You remember her from that night?"

I looked from the picture to Patience. "I remember everything."

Her lashes lowered but she remained silent, flipping to the next picture. My heart muscles squeezed yet again at the sight of the newborns nestled side-by-side in an incubator.

"I was about thirty-five weeks when they were born. Kennedy was fussy and wasn't responding well to the medicine they were giving her to develop her lungs. They put them together and it helped. She calmed down next to her big brother."

She continued to flip the pages and aside from my having to dodge one of Kennedy's flailing limbs every so often, I listened intently. I enjoyed listening to story after story about the twins. The way Patience's face lit up as she talked about them as babies and toddlers drew me in. I looked down and found myself stroking Kennedy's hair. That seemed to relax her restlessness a little. A lump formed in my throat when I stared at them both. I regretted every moment I'd lost with them, but the gratefulness of them coming back to me was immense. It nearly overshadowed the constant cynicism I held for the world around me. Almost.

CHAPTER 26

Patience

I stepped off the elevator and proceeded toward the glass door that led to my husband's outer office. As soon as I pushed through the door I heard his deep, booming voice from his office, down the hall. He was ripping into someone for some infraction on their part.

"For their sake, I hope he's on the phone," I said to Mark as I approached his desk.

He gave a derisive snort. "Conference call," he responded.

"Ouch."

He nodded. "Yup. He's reaming out a whole upper management team. They deserve it though. Screwed up royally."

"I'll bet." Shaking my head, I leaned over Mark's desk. "I'll admit I'm a bit of a masochist, but I don't know how you do it."

Mark chuckled. He and I had grown a friendly rapport over the last few months. The fact that he outwardly never judged me for exploding on Aaron that day months ago, earned him a few points with me. Not that he needed my approval.

Mark leaned in. "Want to know the truth?"

I nodded.

"Mr. Townsend's tough as hell, admittedly, but he's just as tough on me as he is on everyone else." He looked down, holding his arms out. "Most people look at me and all they see is the chair. I've had former bosses not give me certain tasks because they figured I couldn't handle them. They never said anything outright, of course. That'd be illegal. And I would receive good annual reviews but when it came time for promotion?" He stopped and shook his head. "Mr. Townsend isn't like that. I get the grunt work like everyone else. He has no problem keeping me in the office late if needed. Sounds like a drag, but after so many years of being made to feel inferior because of my chair, it's a breath of fresh air… either that or I'm a masochist, too."

We both laughed.

Aaron must've heard our laughter over his barking because he stepped out into the hallway, his eyes zooming in on me. His scowl grew.

"Uh oh," Mark commented.

I smirked, moving past Mark down the hall.

"Yes, I heard you the first time you made that sorry excuse." Aaron continued, talking to whomever was on the phone. I noticed the earpiece in his ear. His eyes were glued to me, however. I reached him, pressing my hand against his abdomen. I felt his stomach muscles clench. Though his frown remained, I could see his eyes brighten. I turned my head upwards, beckoning a kiss. He didn't disappoint, plastering his lips to mine, and squeezing my hip. He moved away, granting me space to enter his office, before shutting the door behind us.

I circled his desk, going to sit behind it, in his chair. He raised an eyebrow my way and I gave him a wink.

"Yeah, Steve, that's the plan. How about you put it into action…" he continued on the conference call. I watched him pace, one hand in his pocket as he responded to whomever was speaking at the other end of the phone. I licked my lips at the image he made in his dark blue three piece tailored suit, and shiny, brown shoes. I'd been feeling extremely tired the past two days but just watching him revived me with new energy.

When he hung up, he glanced over at me. "Comfortable?"

I smiled, leaning back farther in his desk chair, crossing my legs.

"We're going to be late," I answered.

"The plane leaves when I tell it to."

I rolled my eyes. He was so cocky and full of himself. God help me, that was just one of the things I loved about him.

By the time I refocused my vision, he was standing over me. "You slept in this morning."

I shrugged. "*Somebody* kept me up late."

An actual smile touched his lips and my heart skipped a full beat. He bent down, cupping his hands around my upper arms, pulling me up to stand.

"That same *somebody's* keeping you up late tonight as well." He pressed a kiss to my neck.

I shuddered. "That's because we have an opening to attend." We were flying out to San Francisco for an energy convention Townsend Industries was hosting, and an art gallery opening that evening.

"You'll definitely be up later than that. What were you and Mark laughing about?" he questioned, abruptly switching topics.

I knew the question was coming and yet he still managed to surprise me with it. I grinned, pulling back to cup his face.

"Masochism," I answered.

He frowned, confused.

I pressed a quick peck to his lips before stepping out of his hold. "Come on. I know you think the world waits on you, but it's impolite to keep others waiting for too long." I tugged his hand. He barely budged and instead pulled me to him.

"Others *do* wait on me." He squeezed my hand, his other arm curling around my waist, to cup my ass.

"No." I forced myself to push away from his hold.

He sighed. "Fine. I'll save it for the plane. Let's go," he ordered, pulling me to the door. After Aaron paused to give more orders to Mark for the next two days while he would be gone, we were finally on our way down the elevator to the awaiting car. My hand rested in Aaron's and I leaned against his shoulder, yawning.

"Still tired?"

I shook my head. "No, I'm fine." I didn't have to look up at him to know he was peering down at me through skeptical eyes. "I'm glad Ms. Sheryl was able to come out and stay with the children over the next few days. They missed her a lot. You should've seen the way they ran to her this morning when she arrived." Ms. Sheryl had flown from her new home city of Houston to spend time with and babysit the children while we were out of town.

Aaron nodded as he held the car door open for me. It was a thirty minute drive to the private airport where we were leaving from. On the way, I actually fell asleep, waking only when Aaron shook me by the shoulder.

"Don't think you're sleeping this entire flight," he warned.

"Wouldn't dream of it." I giggled when he caught my lower lip in between his teeth. I pressed away from him, to head up the stairs to the private jet. Sure enough, my husband barely gave the pilot time to turn off seatbelt light before he was helping me out of my chair and directing us toward the private main bedroom. It was the most delightful plane ride I'd ever taken.

* * *

"Stunning."

I shivered as Aaron's compliment touched my ears. I looked up in the mirror to catch him admiring the long, royal blue dress I wore. My long locs were pulled back in a tight top bun, and a pair of diamond earrings that Aaron had just given me hung from my ears. I turned, peering at him from head to toe. He wore a tailored tuxedo, which highlighted his masculine physique to perfection.

"Ready?" he asked.

I nodded and curled my hand around his offered arm. "Tell me again who will be there tonight," I said as we moved to the elevator.

"Why? Thinking of running away with an artist?"

I looked up, smirking. "I think you just made a joke," I said around my laughter.

"I have a sense of humor. When I want to."

"Which isn't very often."

He lifted and dropped his shoulder. "Not much in the world to laugh about."

I rolled my eyes. "And Mr. Cynicism is back."

"You love me anyway."

My belly tightened. My mouth opened but the words refused to come out. I still hadn't been able to say those three words back to him. Every night and morning he told me he loved me since that first time, and every time I remained silent, biting my bottom lip like I was then.

"You're going to rub your lipstick off," he stated, frowning—the disappointment evident in his voice.

Before I was able to come up with a response, the elevator doors opened and classical music from our luxury hotel's ballroom floated to my ears.

"Aaron, we've been awaiting your arrival," a man's voice said as soon as we stepped off.

I glanced up and was greeted with a smiling older man who seemed familiar. I narrowed my eyes. "Michael Cavalleri," I stated just above a whisper. He'd been the attorney Aaron used to send me the custody forms.

"I see you still haven't forgiven me." He appeared chagrined. "I was just doing what my client paid me to do."

I rolled my eyes and looked up at Aaron who gave me a nonchalant expression. I wasn't expecting an apology from him either. I knew my husband. He did what he believed he had to, to keep his family, and out of his own twisted version of love. A love I returned and felt deeply. I just couldn't say it out loud.

"Don't worry, Mr. Cavalleri. I'm not expecting any apologies any time soon."

"Aaron, Neil's already arrived."

Aaron nodded, using his free hand to cover mine that rested on his right arm. After a few more moments of conversation with the attorney, Aaron and I stepped inside the art gallery.

"Neil McKenna, right?" I questioned.

"Yes," Aaron answered.

"He's the owner of the gallery?"

"No. But he is one of the main investors."

"And his family owns McKenna rehab clinics?"

"Yes. His father started them and he has taken the facilities national."

I remembered reading an article about the success of McKenna's expansion of the drug and alcohol clinics. His father had been a famed psychiatrist who railed against more traditional forms of drug and alcohol treatment. That was, until his own son fell victim to addiction and spent years in and out of his own facilities.

"He re-introduced the twelve step process as the main means of treating addiction in his clinics. I read it last year in the *Times*. It was a great article."

"A little bombastic for my taste, but I suppose the writer did highlight the important parts."

Aaron and I turned to the voice behind us, and I was greeted with the most charming grin I'd ever seen. I admired the tall, slender man with golden eyes and a high bun that held his honey blond locks. The bun was almost a complete contrast to the elegant tuxedo that neatly draped his runner's physique. If I wasn't standing on the arm of the most gorgeous man in the room, I might've thought this guy was it.

"Aaron, you never told me you had such a beautiful wife...or that you even got married for that matter. Shame, my invitation got lost in the mail." His eyes held a bit of mischief and wickedness when he turned them on me.

Aaron's hold on my hand tightened ever so slightly and he grunted. "The people that mattered were there."

I sighed, slapping my husband's arm lightly. "Don't be rude," I chided. "Mr. McKenna, we would've loved to have had you in attendance but there wasn't enough time to accommodate everyone's schedule."

Neil's smile grew. "She's good, Townsend." He turned his eyes back to Aaron. "You should hire her to do all your public speaking for you." Those golden eyes returned to me. "And much better to look at."

Such a charmer, this guy.

"Pleased to meet you." He held out his hand for mine.

"Don't touch my wife. And she's not for hire," Aaron interrupted. "Don't think this tuxedo will get in the way of me kicking your ass, McKenna." In spite of his words, I heard the light note in Aaron's voice. Aaron didn't make idle threats but he was kidding when it came to Neil McKenna.

"Good to see you, too," Neil said to Aaron, who grabbed his hand, shaking it firmly. "How's Carter doing?"

I squinted at the question regarding my oldest brother-in-law, as if there was a story there. I turned to Aaron who gave me a *we'll discuss it later* look. The three of us talked some more before Aaron and I made our way to another couple who wanted to discuss business with Aaron. On and on it went like that over the next hour or more. I finally glanced up and saw a man who was speaking with Neil at the opposite end of the room. Though the conversation between Neil and the man appeared to be friendly, the man's face was set in a scowl nearly akin to the one my husband wore on a daily basis. The scowl and the eye patch he wore over his left eye didn't detract from how handsome he was.

I turned back to Aaron, who was finishing up his conversation with a local investor, who—like most who we'd talked with—was trying to get Townsend Industries to invest in one thing or another.

"What was that about?" I asked when we walked away.

"Another hedge fund wants the Townsend name," he sighed.

I turned to stand in front of him, placing my hand to his chest. I glanced up into his hazel eyes that put on such a good front for the world…no, not a front. He was the strong, intelligent, savvy, and cunning businessman he portrayed himself to be, but he was so much more. "I see how this can get tiring after a while. Everyone asking you for something."

"It's nothing," he responded, curling his hand around mine. "I do it because I'm excellent at it and I love it. But not more than I love you and our children. The real question is, do I have your love in return?"

"A-Aaron," I stuttered but couldn't continue. He had more than my love. He had my entire soul.

"Are we interrupting?"

I turned, stunned by the man I saw across the room, now standing a half a foot away from us, as he stood next to Neil.

"You are," Aaron growled.

I looked between Aaron and the man.

"Ian just wanted to say hello," Neil interjected while Aaron and Ian had a stare off.

"Mrs. Townsend—" Neil began.

"Patience. Please call me Patience."

He nodded. "Patience, this is Ian Zerlinger."

I may not have recognized him at first sight but I definitely knew the name. Zerlinger Beer was one of the top leaders in the wine and spirits industry.

"Mr. Zerlinger, pleased to meet you."

He turned his dark, brooding eye on me and the edges wrinkled as he lifted his mouth in what could be construed as a smile. As if he needed more practice doing it. "My pleasure," he greeted, nodding but not extending his hand. "You are more charming than your husband."

"She's better than me at a lot of things. Kicking someone's ass isn't one of them," Aaron commented warningly, pulling me back into his arms and farther away from the two men.

Ian nodded, looking back to Aaron.

"We're leaving," Aaron informed them.

I was surprised but didn't say anything.

"We'll take up this conversation tomorrow," Ian affirmed.

Aaron grunted, placed his hand at my lower back, and after making our good-byes to the two men, along with a few others, he led us out of the gallery to the awaiting car. I could tell he was pissed and I knew it had nothing to do with anyone but me. He was eerily silent as we drove off from the gallery.

"Aaron–"

"You know I'd give you anything you wanted, right?"

I furrowed my brows. "What?"

"I don't know how to be gentle but I've tried. For you. For Kyle. For Kennedy."

I took his hand, tugging it until he looked from the window to me. "I know that. Where is this coming from?"

"You won't say it. I see it in your eyes, the way you look at me, the way you look *for* me even in your sleep. But you won't say it."

I pushed out a harsh breath. "Why? Why do I need to say it?" I commented, exasperated.

"Why the fuck won't you say it, is the real question!" he roared.

I attempted to move back to the other side of the seat but he pulled me closer.

"Why won't you tell me you love me?"

My eyes watered and I tried to look out the window instead of at him, but his hand caught my face, preventing me from turning.

"You know why," I whispered.

His face tightened angrily. "Because of what happened the last time you said those words," he stated, as if it was no big deal.

But it was to me. I pulled his hand from my face and turned away, closing my eyes as the memory of the first time I told him I loved him washed over me.

* * *

Then

"Why're you walking so fast?" I asked Aaron, laughing. I yanked my hand away from his hold. "Slow down. It's my graduation day. The last one I'll ever get. I don't want to rush through it."

He stopped and turned to me, frowning. That only made my smile grow. I could tell by then his different frowns. This was his concerned frown.

"It's raining, heavily."

"I know, right?" I stepped from under the umbrella he held over us, fully immersing myself in the rain.

"What the hell are you doing?" he growled, grabbing my arm, pulling me to him.

"Getting wet," I giggled. We had just come from my graduation. One my father had attended but left soon after. Even his absence hadn't dampened my mood, once I realized Aaron had kept his promise and showed up. Instead of going out with friends to celebrate as I had originally planned, I chose to spend the rest of the day and night with him. "What are you rushing for anyway?"

"We need to get to the bookstore."

It was my turn to frown. "For what?"

"I need to pick up something." He took my hand again, pulling me under the umbrella but it was too late. "You're soaked." He eyed the sleeveless white spring dress I'd worn for the occasion. My nipples hardened when his gaze lingered at my breasts. My body's automatic responses continued to fascinate me. It was less than two months since our first time together but in that timeframe he'd shown me pleasure beyond even my wildest imaginings.

"Will you make me strip?" I asked, breathless.

His nostrils flared, his hand tightened around mine. "Let's go," he responded, pulling me behind him into the bookstore.

"Hi Sam," I waved to the clerk as we entered.

Sam looked up, smiling wide, but it faltered a bit when his eyes fell on Aaron. "H-hi Patience. Congratulations…on graduating today."

"Thank you."

"Do you have it?" Aaron interjected.

"Y-yeah." Sam moved from the counter, to the shelf behind him, picking up a gift bag.

"My assistant took care of payment."

"Yes, Mr. Townsend. Payment's been taken care of. You're all set."

Aaron nodded and took me by the hand again, picking up the gift in his other hand.

I was so excited to see what Aaron had in the bag that I forgot all about Sam until he said, "Bye, Patience."

I turned and waved over my shoulder.

"What's in the bag?" I asked as soon as we made it out of the bookstore.

He didn't answer, instead moving to the car that was now directly in front of the store, pulling the door open. I didn't even bother to ask how the driver knew where we were, or had gotten there so quickly. We'd taken the subway from my graduation to get to the bookstore.

Once inside, Aaron told the driver to drive around a while, one of my favorite things to do with him. He pressed the button to roll up the partition before handing me the bag.

I took it, opening it up, and gasped when I pulled out a first edition copy of my favorite book ever, *I Know Why the Caged Bird Sings* by Maya Angelou. My eyes watered when I opened the book and saw that it was an autographed copy, addressed especially to me. She'd congratulated me on my graduation and thanked me for appreciating her writing.

"Aaron," I whispered. "How did you…" I trailed off. It was a silly question. He could do whatever he wanted. He had connections I'd never know about. But the fact that he took the time…

"I was late because I'd been making calls all night to ensure the book arrived on time. I had to reschedule a meeting for this morning, and–" His explanation was cut off by my lips on his.

My arms circled his neck tightly and I felt him lift me into his lap —soaked dress and all.

"I love you." I finally said the words that I'd been holding back for weeks. I swallowed when I felt him harden beneath me.

His hand went to my thigh, squeezing. "Say it again." He ran his teeth down the column of my neck.

"I love you," I stated, shuddering.

His hands parted my thighs and moved up to the seam of my panties. He began massaging me through the silk of the garment I wore just for him. He ordered me to say it over and over again, while he used his hand to wring an orgasm from me. By the time we made it back to my apartment, I was soaked, but this time it had nothing to do with the rain. We spent the rest of the night in bed, my voice growing hoarse due to the number of times he had me shouting these three words repeatedly.

It was the perfect night, so naturally, everything went to hell the next morning.

* * *

I WOKE UP, startled, by the banging on my front door. I blinked, looking around, groggy from the previous night. Aaron seemed just as surprised as I was.

"I know you're in there with that whore, Aaron!"

His eyes widened and his mouth turned downward immediately. "Stay here!" He pointed at me, putting his pants and a T-shirt he kept at my place on.

"What's going on, Aaron?" I sat up, covering myself with my blanket.

"Don't move from this bed," was all he said before heading out the bedroom door, shutting it behind him.

I continued to hear a woman's voice yelling and banging at the front door. It stopped and I could hear Aaron's voice though he spoke in more hushed tones. The woman sounded irate and she kept referencing someone as a whore. Finally, my curiosity got the best of me and I grabbed the button-up shirt Aaron wore the day before, using it to cover myself. I exited my bedroom and proceeded down the hall to find Aaron glaring at a woman. All I could see was the bottom half of her, as Aaron held his arm up, shielding her from looking inside.

"Who's this?" I asked, startling the both of them from their heated conversation.

"This is her?" she shrieked, pushing Aaron out of the way and stepping inside of my apartment. "How cute. She's even wearing your shirt. Whore!" she yelled in my direction.

"Excuse you? I don't know who the hell you think you're talking to, but it sure as hell isn't me!"

"Who else would I be talking to, bitch? You're the whore sleeping with my fiancé!"

Her hurled words slapped me across the face.

"Don't try to play Miss Innocent, bitch! You knew what you were doing!"

"Alicia, that's enough!" Aaron roared, yanking her by the arm away from me, toward the door.

"Aaron, what is she talking about? Aaron!" I yelled when he didn't answer me at first.

"Now she's playing the hurt act." Alicia began clapping condescendingly. "Bravo, sister! And the Academy Award goes to–"

"I said that's e-fucking-nough!" Aaron shouted, punching the wall next to where she stood.

His outburst silenced her immediately, but my head still swirled. A fiancée? That couldn't be right.

"Go home. We'll talk about this later."

"Home?" Alicia and I shouted at the same time. He shared a home with this woman?

"I just came from home and your father calling incessantly when he couldn't get in contact with you all night." She turned her eyes on me. "Now I know why."

"Why was my father calling you?"

"Because the Japan deal is going south and you're nowhere to be found."

My eyes volleyed between the two. I had a million questions but was rendered speechless. I was zoning in and out but I heard Alicia say something about a Japanese client pulling out because they deemed another service superior to Townsend's. His father had been trying to contact him all night.

"Your plane leaves for Tokyo in three hours."

"Fuck!" Aaron grunted. "Leave."

"Aaron, what ab–"

"I said leave. Don't ever fucking come back here again." He pushed her out the door, slamming it in her face.

I peered up to see him rushing past me to the bedroom. I was jolted into action, finally pissed enough to speak.

"What the hell was that?" I demanded, bursting into my bedroom to see Aaron gathering his clothing. "Aaron, look at me, dammit!"

He stopped, doing as I'd asked. "I'm sorry."

"Sorry for what? For having a fucking fiancée?"

He jaw clamped shut. "It's not like–"

"Not like what?"

"I don't have time."

"Don't have time to discuss you have a whole other life? Of course not," I scoffed.

"Don't be so dramatic."

My eyes bulged. "Are you insane?" I screeched. "*I'm* being dramatic? After your fiancée shows up at my door at six o'clock in the morning after we spent the entire night making love. A fiancée I had no idea even existed?"

His eyes closed briefly. "What do you want me to say?"

"Something!" I briefly closed my eyes, then opened them to meet his gaze. "Is she really your fiancée?"

"Yes," he answered flatly.

My knees went weak and I had to hold onto the dresser to keep myself upright. "D-do you love her?" Why that question even mattered, I didn't know but it did.

His lips tightened. "There are far more important reasons to marry someone than love." He tossed the last word as if it were garbage.

I swallowed, finally seeing, for the first time, the hardened, scowling, cold-hearted son of a bitch everyone else saw when they looked at him.

"You really believe that?"

"Doesn't matter what I believe. Look, I have to go." He started for the door with a suitcase in one hand. He'd left that same suitcase here one night after coming straight to my place after returning from an overnight business trip. He'd torn my clothes off as soon as I opened the door, barely giving me time to close it behind him.

"Aaron." I reached for his arm just before he exited the bedroom. "Wait…" I didn't know what to say. I was pissed but also felt like my entire heart was walking out of the door.

"Patience." His voice was soft, almost the same way he'd called my name the night before when he came inside of me, not for the first time. But then he turned and his face was the typical mask he wore for the world. "You're being too sensitive. What we had is done." He pulled his arm from me and walked away without a backward glance.

I flinched when I heard my apartment door slam shut.

CHAPTER 27

Patience

"Why, Aaron?" I stared at Aaron as we stood in the middle of our hotel suite, the bitter taste of that last day still on my taste buds.

"Alicia was business," he admitted. "Her father's company was beneficial to Townsend Industries at the time. He made a deal with us in exchange for protection."

I frowned. "Protection?"

Aaron nodded. "His family crossed some very powerful people. The Townsends were able to come to an agreement with said family, and in exchange, I was to marry John's daughter, Alicia. I would've gone through with it, but after you..." He blew out a breath and pushed his hand through his hair. "I never loved her."

I snorted as he answered the question I'd asked him six years earlier. I already knew that. I probably knew that the same day she showed up at my apartment, but I'd been too concerned with the breaking of my own heart to see what was in front of me.

"I know."

His eyes widened, surprised.

"You're not the only one who watches. I see you, too. The way your eyes light up around me and the kids. The parts of your history you've shared with me that no one else knows about you. Even your jealousy. I knew you never had that type of bond with anyone else. Even your tattoo." I pointed at his chest.

For a man who wasn't easily surprised, he was shocked again for the second time.

"I read it...in a book." I grinned. Our eyes connected, and I knew he remembered our first time together when I'd made the same statement. "When did you get my name tattooed on you?"

"Six months after. I went back to your apartment to find you'd moved, no forwarding address."

I nodded, wiping a tear away.

"I'm scared," I whispered.

He moved closer. "Of what?"

"You'll push me away again." I sighed. "I know you, Aaron. Alicia showing up at my apartment surprised you, but you used it. You used it because we were getting too close and *you* got scared." I gave a humorless laugh. "Stupid as it might be, I could've forgiven you for Alicia. I loved you beyond reason. But you used her showing up and your work to push me away. I-I can't go through that again."

He cupped my face. "I won't...I can't put you through that again. You, Kyle, and Kennedy are my reason for living. I almost lost you once. I don't make the same mistakes twice."

I lowered my head, shaking it. He'd never lost me. Not even close. Dumb as it may be, my heart was always right there with him. Waiting for him. My head rose, when he lifted my left hand, placing it over his heart, the same location where he'd had my name tattooed. I swallowed, my vision blurring a little from the tears. He stepped closer, pressing my back into the wall behind me.

"Say it." His voice was low, laced with steel.

My entire body began to vibrate with need.

His hand tightened around mine and he pressed closer. "Say it."

My nipples hardened, and moisture saturated my panties. "I love you," I whispered. Aaron wouldn't stand for that wimpy decree. My head lifted to meet his gaze, his hand under my chin.

"Louder," he growled, lips nearly touching mine.

"I love you!" I shouted with all the anger, fear, and love I held in my body, filling those three words. Because this man drove me crazy!

A sound began deep at the back of his throat. His lips were on mine in a nanosecond, demanding I open for him. The hand that had been under my chin moved to my throat, his thumb lining the column of my neck, possessively. My pussy ached with need. I needed him inside of me so badly, I hurt for it. Aaron obviously felt the same way, once again, ruining another item of my clothing, by tearing at it to free it from my body. The poor chiffon material never stood a chance against Aaron's big hand pulling and manipulating it away from my skin. Before I knew it, I stood before him completely nude. He stepped back, removing the jacket of his tuxedo, but keeping his eyes trained on me.

"Touch yourself," he instructed.

I worried my bottom lip.

"Now!" he growled.

My hands shot up to my painful nipples, pinching and plucking at them, while my head lolled back against the wall as the sensations moved through my body. Raising my head, I saw he was now stripped down to his briefs, a silk scarf in his hand. My belly jumped in anticipation.

"Turn around."

I hesitated but when he angled his head at me, I did his bidding.

"Close your eyes."

I shivered due to his warm breath scraping the skin of my shoulder. As soon as my eyes were closed, he covered them with the silk scarf, tying it behind my head, securely. I pressed my hands against the wall, anticipating his next move. My breathing increased, and his large hands came up, cupping my breasts and massaging them none too gently. My head fell back again, this time against his muscled chest.

I whispered his name and his hand moved to my throat once more. I felt his bare cock press against my ass.

"Why did it take you so long to say three little words?" His voice was right next to my ear, angry.

I didn't say anything.

His hold around my neck tightened, not dangerously, but it definitely heightened the eroticism.

"Y-you know why," I answered just above a whisper this time. "Ouch!" I jumped when the first smack against my ass occurred.

"Say it again!" he ordered.

I shook my head. "No!"

"Dammit!" I yelled when two more smacks landed across my ass. My backside stung from the palm of his hands but my pussy grew wetter and wetter, seeping down the tops of my inner thighs.

"Say it again or you won't sit for a fucking month!" he growled, causing my nipples to harden even more, painfully so. More than the anger, I heard the need in his voice. He needed the words just as badly as I needed him.

"I love you," I responded to his need. "Ahhhh!" I yelled when he sank inside of me, from the back all the way to the hilt.

"Again!" he growled.

"You say it!" I yelled back at the same time he surged into me again, the smacking of our bodies together reverberating around the room.

"I love you," he affirmed, no hesitation.

I grew even wetter.

Aaron pulled me from the wall, and pushed me to what I believed was the hardwood desk that sat at the opposite end of the wall in the suite. My eyes were still covered by the scarf when he pressed my head against the cool wood, one hand covering my hip, positioning me just how he wanted me. He thrust in deeply and I yelled so loudly my voice began going hoarse. He was so deep in this position I felt like he was in my throat. I moved my hand behind me, pressing against his belly.

"Ow!" I yelled from smack I'd earned on my ass.

He trapped my hand, holding it against my back, surging into me so deeply he nearly lifted both my feet off the floor. The desk he had me pressed against shook. I heard items falling to the floor, but Aaron was dogged, driving in and out of me, possessing me as if he needed to make clear, once again, who I belonged to. As if I'd ever forgotten. My pussy walls clamped around his erection, begging for more and for mercy at the same time.

"Again!" He ordered, his hips digging into me again.

I yelled my love for him over and over. Just like the first night I'd done it. And just like that first night, my orgasm nearly crushed me. But what differed this time around, was Aaron yelled his love for me, as we came together. His life-creating semen surging into my womb and my muscles flexing and spasming around him, milking him for everything he had to give.

Our bodies were so spent after that orgasm, we nearly collapsed onto the floor. But Aaron caught us. Lifting me and carrying me over to the couch that sat a few feet away. He laid my body on top of his, untying the scarf. I blinked my eyes open before turning to see his gaze piercing me. My belly flip-flopped at the love that shone there. I moved up and pressed a kiss to his lips.

"I love you," I whispered, my throat strained from yelling.

"I know." His fingers lined my shoulder and collarbone, causing me to shiver. He continued to stare, watching me closely. "No one will be knocking on our door tomorrow morning. No surprises," he assured.

I smirked. "I know." Lowering my head, I kissed the scar that ran diagonally across his chest. I kissed it all the way down to his breast bone—where the tattoo of my name sat—then stuck out my tongue, licking the intricate artwork that was my name on his body. I smiled when I felt a chill run through him. His cock came alive pushing against my thigh. I pressed more kisses to his scar and licked the tattoo some more before easing down his belly, feeling with my lips as I went. Moving so that I was on my knees between his legs, I took his semi-hard erection into my hands.

I bent low, kissing the tip. Lifting my eyes, I met his hungry gaze. I ran my tongue along my lips of the come that gotten on them before swallowing it, and closing my eyes to savor it. When I opened them again his hazels were still trained on me.

I bent lower, so my lips hovered just an inch above his cock. "Mine," I growled.

His dick jumped in my hand.

I opened my mouth wide, letting my head sink onto his shaft.

Aaron's hand moved to the back of my head, tightening as I bobbed on his erection. Just moments prior I'd felt too exhausted to move, but hearing the moans from my husband's mouth and feeling his dick swell in my mouth, energized me anew. I slurped and swallowed, hollowing my cheeks, then moved lower, taking his balls into my mouth before returning to his cock. Within minutes his semen was flooding my mouth.

It took me a while to catch my breath as we both panted while I laid across his chest again. My eyes were heavy and I was in no position to move for the rest of the night. I believed Aaron felt the same, but not too long after, he was pulling me up, maneuvering my hips and body up his body, so that my pussy hovered over his face. Yet again, my voice was left hoarse and I shook as I called his name while he took me to paradise with his mouth.

CHAPTER 28

Patience

For the third day in a row, I woke up feeling queasy. I frowned at the horrible taste in my mouth. Thankfully, I was alone in our bedroom. It was just after seven a.m. I usually woke up earlier than that but lately it seemed as if the only thing I wanted to do was sleep. *And* my husband. Sleep and orgasms satisfied me the most.

I climbed out of bed feeling a little guilty for not being up earlier to spend more time with the children before school. I had to pick the children up early from school since it was their last day before the Christmas break, anyway. I decided to take them to the movies or one of the local indoor parks to have fun. I grinned, thinking maybe I could convince Aaron to take off work early to spend some fun time with just the four of us as well.

Unfortunately, those thoughts were cut off when a sudden need to vomit hit me in the middle of brushing my teeth. I rushed to the toilet, lifted the lid, and heaved but nothing came out. I don't know how long I stood there, dry heaving, but afterwards, I felt exhausted as I sank to the floor. I willed myself to get up and finish brushing my teeth. After a few more close calls, I finally felt okay enough to make it down the stairs and to the kitchen to start breakfast. I also made a mental note to stop at a convenience store once the children were dropped off. I was so glad to have that day off.

"Morning, Mommy!" Kennedy's cheery voice greeted me as soon as I rounded the corner toward the kitchen.

I smiled down at her, adoring the two little pigtail buns that sat at either side of her head. "Morning, sweetie." I pressed a kiss to her forehead.

Lifting my gaze, I saw Aaron standing at the stove, flipping what looked like a blueberry pancake.

"You're getting good at that," I stated, stepping into the kitchen.

He lifted an eyebrow, smirking. "Flipping pancakes? I've been doing it since I was a kid."

I shook my head. "Not the pancakes, though they do smell delicious." I swiped one from the stack he'd set aside on a plate. My appetite had suddenly reared its head. "That," I gestured toward Kennedy. "Kennedy's hair looks adorable."

Aaron frowned. "I don't do adorable."

Giggling, I pressed a kiss to his bare shoulder. "Yes, you do. But I promise I won't tell anyone."

He gave me a heated look, but instead of saying anything he lowered his head, beckoning a kiss. Obliging, I rose on my tiptoes to meet his lips.

"Go sit," he jutted his head to the table, "the men are serving the ladies today. Right, Kyle?" He yelled the last part.

I heard little, sneakered feet running down the hall before Kyle appeared at the entranceway of the kitchen. "Right!" he answered.

I was sure he hadn't even fully heard what his father just said, but Aaron could've said they were taking a trip to the moon and Kyle would've agreed. He was that hung up on Aaron's every word.

"If you say so," I replied, smacking Aaron across his sweatpants-covered ass. I giggled when he growled in my direction, his eyes making promises his mouth wouldn't utter in front of the little ones. I warded off a shiver by turning to Kennedy. "The men are serving us ladies today, Ken. We deserve it, right, baby girl?" I asked, holding out my hand.

"Right," she agreed, high-fiving me.

Minutes later we were all sitting around the kitchen table, eating breakfast. The children were excited for their early release and Kyle was already talking about one of the books he'd asked Santa to bring him. My son was excited for books! I blinked rapidly, turning to the head of the table to the man who'd made that turnaround possible. Aaron's eyes moved from Kyle's to mine, pride shining in them. I hadn't known I could feel anymore love for this man, but it grew exponentially every day. Since returning from our trip to San Francisco, two weeks prior, I'd told him every day that I loved him. The fear of those words was wearing off and despite how this marriage began, I knew this was where I belonged.

I came back to the present moment, Aaron's eyes on me again. I was certain he'd read everything that'd just passed through my mind. His hand squeezed around mine. I hadn't even realized he'd clasped it.

"Huh, Daddy?"

Kennedy's inquiry drew our attention back to her.

"I'm sorry, sweetheart. What was your question?"

God, my heart squeezed from how tender he was with her. It was the side most people would never get to see of Aaron, but we were blessed enough to.

"I said," Kennedy began, sounding exasperated, "will you come with us to buy Christmas decorations? We're decorating tonight, right, Mommy?" She looked to me.

I smiled. "Yes, sweetie."

"Yeah, Dad. Come, please!" Kyle interjected.

Aaron looked over the two contemplatively. "I will do my best to join you, but if not, I will definitely be here tonight to decorate."

The children cheered. They understood their daddy had an important job and that sometimes he had to work long hours. But Aaron was diligent about keeping his promises to them whenever he made them. He hadn't missed one parent-teacher conference or meeting. He read to the children whenever he was home to tuck them in bed, and aside from his birthday, he never missed a morning with Kyle to workout and work on his reading. I still couldn't believe how far my son had come in such a short period of time. When I said as much to Aaron, he just gave me a cocky grin and retorted with, "*Why not? He's a Townsend.*"

Thirty minutes later, we were all making our way out of the door. Aaron gave the children each a kiss before pulling me into his arms. "Are you all right?"

I frowned, a V dipping between my brows. "Yes, why?"

"You've been sleeping in lately. Are you coming down with something?"

I shook my head. "I'm fine." I may have come down with something all right, but I wanted to wait until I had it confirmed before I said anything to him. Lifting on my toes, I pressed a kiss to his lips. "I'm fine. I'm picking the children up around one. I'll give you a call then to see if you can come shopping with us."

He nodded and stepped back, holding the car door open for me. I climbed in with the children, who waved to their father as we pulled off.

I would've loved for all four of us to have driven together, but Townsend Industries was on the other side of town as the children's school. It would've doubled our trip and either the children or Aaron would've been late. But that morning I would've been okay with it. For some odd reason a sense of foreboding came over me as soon as we passed the sign at the edge of our gated Cedarwoods community.

I shook it off, and instead focused on dropping the children off, who were giddy with excitement due to the holiday season. Christmas had always been a big deal for us. I made sure of it. Now, with their father and extended family it was even more of a big deal. The entire family was coming over to our home to help decorate and prepare for the next few days. Christmas Day would be spent at Townsend Manor.

Once the children were at school, I had Daniel take me to a local convenience store to pick up the one thing I'd been waiting to get my hands on since I woke up that morning. I moved to the feminine aisle to where the pregnancy tests were. There were more tests available than the last time I done this over six years ago. I decided to purchase two different tests just to be on the safe side.

After making my purchase, I made my way out of the store. As soon as my foot hit the concrete of the sidewalk a sensation of fear blanketed my entire body. Immediately, my head swung from left to right, taking in my surroundings. And as per usual, there was nothing out of the ordinary that I could identify. There were plenty of people out and about. I turned and saw Daniel waiting by the town car at the sidewalk, holding it open for me. Instantly feeling safer, I smiled. Aaron had finally broken down and told me that Daniel wasn't just a driver but part of his specialized security team, which was why he'd been so insistent in my taking a driver everywhere.

"Where to, Mrs. Townsend?" Daniel asked as I got in the vehicle.

"Home." I smiled. I had tests to take.

*   *   *

This feeling was so different than the last time. I stood, my back leaning against the bathroom wall for support as I held the pregnancy tests in my hands. Both tests read the same results. I grinned as one hand moved down to my belly, holding it. I wondered how to play this out. Should I tell Aaron as soon as I saw him later that day? Or should I wait? Christmas was in a few days. I could wrap the tests up and give them as a gift. What better present for the man who had everything?

My smile grew at the thought of waking him up on Christmas morning with a stocking that held the positive pregnancy tests. In that moment, I decided that's what I'd do. I placed the tests on the porcelain sink as I went back into the bedroom. As soon as I made it over to the bed, my cell phone rang.

I gave a perplexed look at the name of the caller. "Moira, hey," I answered.

"Patience, thank God you answered." She sounded breathless.

"What's going on?"

"I need you."

I frowned. Moira never sounded this dramatic.

"We had to move the Secret Santa to today instead of tomorrow. The children from the school are on their way over and there are still gifts to be wrapped and the food isn't set up. Can you–"

"I'm on my way," I assured her.

"Thank you!" she exclaimed.

"You're welcome. I'll be there in twenty minutes."

It was just after nine o'clock. I had plenty of time to make it to the library to help set up and stay for a little while before I needed to pick up the children. We had to stop home anyway so the children could change and drop off their belongings. I mentally recounted everything I needed to get done as I moved around the bedroom, pulling on a pair of skinny blue jeans and a grey sweater to head over to the library. It was my day off, so I didn't think Moira would be too concerned with my choice of clothing.

Once again, I was piling in the car, directing Daniel to the library. Unfortunately, as soon as we left the gates of the secured community we lived in, that eerie feeling settled over me. I shook it free, reminding myself that I was safe with Daniel. Nothing could get to me. I held my hand over my abdomen and inhaled deeply. I was sure my nerves were due to the confirmation of my pregnancy. Considering what I'd gone through my last pregnancy, I was probably reliving those events. *I'll be fine*, I told myself.

"Shit!" I cursed, realizing then that I'd left the two pregnancy tests sitting on our bathroom sink. I told myself it would be fine, I'd be home long before Aaron would be. I'd still be able to pull off my surprise.

* * *

Two and a half hours later, I was spent. I forgot how tired pregnancy made me. Between wrapping gifts, setting up tables and chairs, and then celebrating the Secret Santa giveaway with the children from the local public school, I was beat. And I still had my own children to pick up in the next hour.

"I really appreciate you coming in on such short notice, Patience," Moira stated as the children sat around the tables, eating Christmas cookies and playing with their new toys.

"You're so welcome." I yawned. "Excuse me," I stated, shaking my head.

"Tired? I know how busy this time of year can get for moms."

I laughed. "A little, but it's all worth it. I'm going to run to the bathroom and then head out."

Moira nodded. "That's fine. We're just about done here. Thanks so much. I'll see you after the break." She pulled me into a hug.

"Enjoy your holidays. See you in next year," I joked. The library was closing for the week between Christmas and New Year.

Parting ways with Moira, I stepped out to tell Daniel I'd be right there, that I just needed to make a bathroom run. He nodded and waited by the car.

I went back inside and saw that there was a line of children waiting for the main bathroom. Luckily, I knew there was a second bathroom, closer to the back office, that most employees used. I headed toward the back of the library, weaving between bookshelves as I went. The bathroom was at the far end of a long hallway that led to a rarely used back entrance of the library. I paused just before pushing the door of the bathroom open, looking around. The hallway was empty. I could still hear the laughter and talking from the festivities that were happening out front. Brushing my hesitation away, I entered the bathroom to do my business. I moved quickly, not understanding my nervousness but not questioning it either. After washing my hands once I was finished, I pulled the bathroom door open.

My head swung in the direction of the back door for some reason; I didn't see anything there. However, as soon as I turned my head in the opposite direction a dark figure towered over me. I opened my mouth to scream but it was covered with a hand holding a cloth. I felt the back of my head being gripped, pushing it into the hand at the front of my face. I struggled and fought, using my nails to scratch at the man's face. Unfortunately, it was covered by a ski mask, but somehow I was able to break free from the man who obviously meant to do me harm. I gulped in air, but when I tried to run for the nearest exit, I was spun around by my shoulder and the next thing I saw was a large fist flying my way. The pain was blinding and I passed out almost immediately.

CHAPTER 29

Aaron

Something isn't right. It was a feeling more than a thought. A deep, gnawing feeling in my gut.

"Mr. Townsend, as we–" The man in my office stopped short when I stood from the conference table. I could feel eyes on me, wondering what was happening.

"Get out," I stated flatly, without preamble.

"Mr. Townsend, we're here to discus–"

"Get. Out." I looked to my younger brother. "Joshua."

He didn't ask questions. Didn't give me a confused look. Rising, he said, "Gentlemen, my brother is extremely busy. How about we reconvene in about thirty minutes?"

I didn't stick around to hear what they had to say. I moved to my desk, and just as I was about to take out my cell to call my wife, my office phone rang.

"What?" I barked into the phone, knowing it was Mark on the other end.

"Mrs. Connors, the principal from Excelor Academy is on the line."

"Put her through," I insisted. A heartbeat later there was a beep.

"Are the children all right?" I asked without greeting her first. My heart rate quickened.

"Mr. Townsend, the children are fine. They're here in my office."

My eyes shot to the clock that hung directly across from me, on my wall. It was close to one thirty. Patience was over thirty minutes late picking the children up. My mind went into overdrive. She was never late for the children. She knew their schedule better than she knew her own. She'd only be late for one reason.

"Do not let them out of your sight. Do *not* turn my children over to anyone. I will be there in ten minutes." I hung up the phone and looked to Joshua.

"I'm calling Brutus," he began, his hands already dialing. Brutus was the head of security for Townsend Industries and the family.

I pulled out my cell, hoping I'd see a missed call from Patience. She said she would be calling me. When I didn't see anything I pressed the button to call her phone directly. It went straight to voicemail. Next, I called Daniel. His phone rang and rang.

I was outside of my office door on my way to the elevators before even realizing it. Joshua was on my heels.

"Give me the phone," I ordered as soon as I recognized he was speaking with Brutus. We stepped on the elevator as Joshua placed the phone in my hand. "My wife is missing. My children were left at school. I'm on my way to pick them up now. We need an entire family lockdown!" I barked into the phone. I hung up the phone after telling Brutus we were to meet at my house in thirty minutes, once I picked up the children.

"We'll find her," Joshua stated, his hand on my shoulder, squeezing it reassuringly.

I remained silent because for the first time since I was a young child, fear gripped my entire body. My vocal chords were wrapped in it, and I couldn't talk due to the anxiety coursing through my veins.

I got to the car, and told my driver to floor it all the way to Excelor Academy. I dared him to even think about stopping for a red light. We made it across town in under ten minutes. I charged through the doors of the exclusive, private school, ready to tear apart anyone that stood between me and my children. I burst through the main office door.

"Daddy!"

"Daddy!"

Kennedy and Kyle ran to me screaming.

"Where's Mommy?" Kennedy's innocent sepia eyes looked up at me, demanding.

My heart squeezed because for the first time I didn't have an answer. I'd called over and over again on my way to the school, still only receiving her voicemail. Brutus was already on the task of pinging her cell's location.

"Mommy's scared," Kyle said in a low voice.

I dropped down in front of him, taking him by the shoulders. "Do you know what happened to your mommy? Where she is?" I tried to keep the fear out of my voice. My heart plummeted when Kyle shook his head.

"I just know she's scared," he whispered.

I heard a sniffle and looked to Kennedy, whose eyes were watery.

"We're going to find her." I stood and carried both my children, Joshua walking alongside us as we followed my security to our awaiting vehicle.

* * *

"This son of a bitch is going to wish he never fucked with us." Carter growled, coming up beside me. Carter, myself, Joshua, my father, and three men from our security, including Brutus, were all in my office. My mother, Michelle, and all the children were upstairs on the main floor. Tyler was across the country preparing for an away game. The security he was traveling with had been notified of the situation and he was soon to board a private flight back home.

Meeting Carter's eyes, I nodded, agreeing with his previous statement. I squeezed my hands in fists, that helpless feeling overcoming me. By the time we'd arrived home, Brutus had traced Patience's cell phone to the library where she worked. He and his security staff had went to the library, finding an unconscious Daniel in the front seat of his vehicle and Patience's phone laying near the library's back entrance. It'd been smashed, as if someone had stepped on it. There was a camera in the library's back hallway but Brutus' firm had to work to hack in to the library's mainframe to get the video. Even that would save time over getting a police warrant, however.

"What the fuck do we know so far?" I demanded, going to Brutus.

Everyone circled my desk. Thankfully, none of my family had even tried to utter the words *calm down* to me. In my state, I'm not sure exactly how I would've reacted but it wouldn't have been too friendly, I know that for sure.

"Daniel's at the hospital. Still hasn't woken up, but the blood sample we took from him shows he was injected with some type of anesthesia."

I shook my head. "I don't give a *fuck* about Daniel. Where the hell is my wife?" I demanded, pounding my desk, staring at Brutus.

He didn't flinch. "We're close to getting the footage from the library's camera. Moira's already told you Patience was there because she called her in. You believe she wasn't involved in this?" His green eyes narrowed on me.

I'd had Moira brought to the house upon learning that Patience was last seen at the library. When Brutus spoke with her at the library, she'd said she called Patience in to help with a party because they were short staffed. I demanded he bring her to me, so I could look her in the eye to gauge whether she was telling the truth.

She was.

The background check I'd run on her and all the library staff months ago had come back clean. But the concern and the fear in her eyes told me if she had known something she would've spilled it. She'd said Patience had prepared to leave the library around twelve-thirty to make it to the children's school and pick them up on time. Which was why she wasn't concerned when she hadn't seen Patience at the end of the party.

I ran a hand through my hair. "She's telling the truth," I answered Brutus. "She was attacked." I stood up, staring Brutus in the eye. I felt the eyes of my brothers and my father land on me. I'd already informed Brutus of what happened to Patience while she was pregnant, back in Oakland. "I want the full police report. Any and all information." I knew that was somehow connected to her disappearance. I could feel it.

"What do you mean she was attacked?" My father approached my desk, his brown eyes hard.

I glanced around at Carter and Joshua, both of whom had a cold look in their eyes.

"A few months after she moved to Oakland...she was eight months pregnant."

"Fuck!"

"Shit!"

Joshua and Carter cursed in unison. The hard edge in my father's eyes increased as I recounted the story that she'd told me. I'd had our security increased and been trying for weeks to get the police records on the attack.

"Police say a guy named Ramirez was the culprit. He was arrested for a number of other break-ins and rapes in the city at the time," Brutus informed us.

"It wasn't him." I shook my head.

"How do you know?' Carter stepped up, asking.

"Patience…" I paused, blowing out a breath, my heart squeezing in my chest as the vision of the terror in her eyes as she recounted the night of the attack, to me. "She tried to convince herself the police were right, but it rang hollow when she said it out loud. The fear in her eyes–" I had to stop talking again when a wave of anger rolled through my body, nearly choking me. "She didn't believe it was Ramirez. We need those damn records now!"

"Office is sending them over. Just got word," Brutus answered swiftly. Within a second his phone was buzzing, informing him that the records had been sent to his email.

I brought his email up on the flatscreen that hung across from my desk on the wall. The first document in the file showed an image of Rafael Ramirez. He was thirty-two years old, making him around twenty-six at the time of the attack. I shook my head. I knew it wasn't him. Something in me was telling me this wasn't the guy.

"He was never charged with the attack on Patience. Police say it's because there wasn't enough evidence in her case. She never got a look at the guy, there were no fingerprints, and the only DNA found at the scene was hers."

My hands fisted at my sides as Brutus continued. *DNA*. Her blood at the scene. That's what the police found.

"But he also had an alibi for that night. He claimed he was at a bar with friends the night of the attack. Two friends corroborated his story, along with the bartender. Police said because the bartender was also his cousin he'd lie for Ramirez."

"It wasn't him," I stated firmly. We didn't need to be looking at this piece of shit anymore. "Get him off my screen," I demanded. "What else was at the scene?"

Brutus clicked on the other files he was sent until images of the crime scene appeared. A hush filled the room as we stared at the crumpled blankets and sheets on a queen-sized bed. Air flew from my lungs when I recognized the same floral sheets I'd spent many a night with Patience in, in her bedroom in her Williamsport apartment. The sheets were also stained with blood. There were also drops of blood evident on the hardwood floor. It was obvious there'd been a fight in that room. Patience had fought not only for her life, but for those of our unborn children.

"Take that down!" I heard Carter bark to Brutus before moving to stand in front of me, blocking my line of sight.

My eyes moved to meet his, then my father's who stood to his left, and finally landing on Joshua's darkened gaze, to Carter's right. "I'm. Going. To. Fucking. Kill. Him," I seethed through gritted teeth.

Carter nodded. "I know. We'll be there to help. But we need to get her back first."

"She's a fighter," Josh said. He nodded to the now blank screen that'd previously held those images that had me seeing red. "She fought to stay alive. She'll do the same this time around. She knows you'll find her," he reassured.

His words didn't soften anything inside of me. I knew my wife was a fighter. She had to be to fall for me. But she shouldn't have to fight. It was my job to keep her safe, and I'd failed. Again.

That harsh reality settled a coldness over me that I'd only felt one other time, and that was upon hearing about the first attack after her nightmare.

"I failed her. Twice." The admission nearly killed me.

"Son, no–"

I shook my head, cutting my father's words off.

"Listen, son, you couldn't have known. This isn't–"

"Tell me you'd be saying the same thing if this were Mother," I charged, for the first time raising my voice to my father.

The words caught on his lips. He clamped his mouth shut, nodding. His jaw ticked for a moment before he moved closer, cupping the side of my face. "You're absolutely right. I'd kill the son of a bitch who'd even think to put his hands on your mother. I expect no less from any of my sons when it comes to protecting their families. But self-pity isn't going to work in your favor right now. Now is the time to concentrate on finding your wife and bringing her back home to her family." He released me, stepping back.

We stared at one another for a few more moments. He was right. I'd have plenty of time later to lick my own wounds. My wife needed me.

"We've got video!" Brutus shouted.

All four of us turned to Brutus, who was already hitting his laptop to bring up what I realized was the video from the library's back entrance. We assumed that's where she'd been taken from since it's where her phone was found.

The video was a little blurry but I knew my wife as soon as she entered into the camera's line of sight. Her back was to the camera as she moved down the hall, entering the bathroom. My fists tightened and my breath stalled as a dark figure moved down the hall, slowly. The person wore dark clothing and a ski mask over their head, but by the build and size I could tell it was a male. He was approximately six-foot and lanky. A trickle of familiarity ran down my spine, but even running through my mind's rolodex of possible suspects I couldn't place him.

The room went silent as we all watched the video footage. My jaw tightened and my heartbeat went erratic when I saw the door open. Her head was turned in the direction of the back entrance. She couldn't see the man to her left, just a few inches from her. By the time she turned her head it was too late. He covered her nose and mouth with his hand. It looked like he held something in it. Patience struggled, flailing her arms, striking him in the ribs, disorienting him enough that she broke free. The tiny hope I had upon seeing her break free was quickly stamped out when I watched him grab her by the shoulder, spin her around, and land a punch to her face that rendered her unconscious. She fell into his arms, and the perp stooped low, hoisting her body over his shoulder and carrying her out.

"Argh!" I yelled, flipping the coffee table that sat in the middle of my office. Glass cracked and flew everywhere.

"Bro! You've got to calm down!" Carter shouted, grabbing my arm.

"Fuck you!" I yelled back. "Don't fucking touch me!" I seethed, pulling out of his hold. I growled and grunted as I hoisted a chair in the air, tossing it at the screen. I barely heard the loud crashing of the huge flatscreen as it fell from the wall. My own rage clogged my ears. I couldn't see anything in front of me. That image of my wife being assaulted replayed over and over again in my head. The feeling of seeing the fear in her eyes when she first told me of the attack didn't even compare to this. Then, it was bad enough that it was a memory. Now, I watched it play out right before my eyes. I couldn't stand still.

"Aaron!" I hear my father shout after me as I stormed out of the office. I had no idea where I was going but I needed some space. My legs carried me up the stairs to the main floor. Down the hall, I heard the children talking with my mother and Michelle. I moved in the opposite direction, going up the stairs to the second floor. I made my way into the bedroom and I was immediately hit by the half-unkempt bed. My side was made, just as I'd left it this morning. Patience' side was unmade, as what happened most mornings. I moved closer, letting my hand touch the silk negligee she'd worn the night before. I lifted it to my nose. It still held her scent. My heart lurched and I tossed the negligee back onto the bed, disgusted with myself. My wife needed me and I couldn't let go of my anger long enough to see anything clearly. I knew whoever had taken her had crossed our paths sometime before. My brain was too fuzzy with rage to figure out how or when.

I moved into the bathroom, thinking a splash of cold water on my face would clear my head. I stopped short when I saw two sticks sitting on the countertop. My knees weakened when I noticed two lines on one stick and a positive sign on the other. A sound I'd never heard before ripped from my lips and I bent over at the waist, holding onto the edge of the sink to keep myself from falling. I looked at the pregnancy tests again to make sure I was not seeing things.

After staring at the tests for some time, I did my best to normalize my breathing, standing upright. I backed out of the bathroom, turning from the entrance, and stopped when I noticed Joshua standing at the bedroom door.

"I came to check on you. Brutus says they may have a lead."

My mouth remained clamped shut but my eyebrow rose, silently telling Josh to continue.

"When he pushed the back door of the library open, we were able to see he already had a car parked next to the exit. Looks like a dark-colored sedan of some sort. There's no camera back there, but his people are working on enhancing the footage to get the make and model of the car and possibly the license plate. We might be able to get a partial."

My jaw tightened as I nodded. "The fuck kind of place doesn't have cameras outside their building?" I growled.

"It's a small library. Not the main branch. There've been budget cuts in the city..." Josh's voice trailed off when I glared at him. He knew as well as I did, I didn't want to hear that bullshit. "What's that?" He gestured toward my hand.

My grip tightened on the pregnancy tests that I still held.

"She's pregnant," I stated in a low voice.

Joshua's eyes widened as I held out the tests to him. He moved closer, eyes taking in the tests. That glare in his green-golden eyes returned tenfold. He clasped my shoulder. "We'll get her back. Or die trying," he affirmed.

I swallowed and nodded.

"We need to go back downstairs."

"In a minute," I told Joshua.

He gave me a look, but then spun on his heels and left for the stairway.

Turning from the bedroom door, I moved to the glass doors leading to the bedroom's balcony. I stepped out into the cold air. It was early winter but the weather was in the low thirties. My fingers curled around the frigid metal railings as I gazed up at the darkening sky. It was close to five and the street lights were already coming on. I lamented that Patience and I hadn't spent nearly enough time out on this balcony. She loved all types of weather. Closing my eyes, I inhaled, letting the cold air burn my lungs on the way down.

"Emma," I said out loud, "I need you. I need your help." I sighed, doing the thing I'd vowed I'd never do but feeling like I had no other alternative.

"I'm here."

My eyes opened and I turned to see her, long, brown hair still falling around the shoulders of her long, white nightgown. She floated closer.

"What do you need, Aaron?" She knew but she needed me to say it.

"Help me find my wife. Please," I begged.

She nodded. "To find your wife we need to broaden your perspective."

I frowned, lowering my brows. Emma didn't say anything further. She moved closer, pressing her hand to my forehead. Again, everything went black.

CHAPTER 30

Aaron

I blinked my eyes open to find myself standing on a darkened road, woods on either side as cars sped by.

"Where the hell are we?" I asked, glancing around, and turned to Emma anxiously. "Is she here?"

She lifted her gaze to me. "No. You are." She nodded for me to look over my left shoulder.

I pivoted my gaze and my heart nearly stopped. "What the fuck?" I growled, staring at the three bodies that laid at the side of the road, a banged up and crumpled cream-colored Lexus farther down the embankment.

"Heeelp!" the woman's weak voice called. *My mother.* "A-Aaron," she croaked out, calling my eight-year-old self.

I had no idea how I'd moved so close, but the next thing I knew, I was standing right over the bodies of my father, my mother, and myself, just moments after that fatal crash. It wasn't a car accident because my father had purposely driven us off the road. He'd tried to kill us all.

"He died on impact. Tossed from the car after the first flip," Emma stated, standing next to me.

I glanced over at my father's lifeless body. He had massive head wounds, his legs contorted in an unnatural way. I looked up as I heard a car speed past the scene.

"Help!" my mother wailed, trying to raise her hand to get the car's attention.

Anger filled my chest.

"They left us to die," I growled. "Why the fuck have you brought me here? I need to find my wife!" I insisted.

"I am helping you. Your anger clouds your vision, Aaron. You need to learn to see people for who they really are," Emma countered, patiently.

"I see them for who they are. Look at that…" I pointed angrily at another passing vehicle. "They all just fucking sped past us, leaving us to die. They could see the scene even from the road." The mangled vehicle should've been evident to the passing drivers that someone need their help.

"Emma! Emma! Save him!"

I turned, hearing my mother call for Emma. I frowned, as I watched Emma move from my mother's side to mine.

"Heeelp," my eight-year-old self croaked out, laying there in a pool of my own blood.

My heart squeezed in my adult-sized chest as I watched my younger self suffer. Just as I remembered that night, Emma moved to stand over me. She lowered to her knees next to my side.

"Heelp. It hurts." I sounded so weak.

"Shhh, little one," Emma consoled, moving her hand to cover my chest.

I remembered that moment. It'd played out in my mind repeatedly, throughout the years. I'd tried to tell myself I'd imagined it. I'd been laying on the ground unable to move due to the massive pain in my chest and stomach. I'd been ejected from the car's backseat, through the windshield. I suffered minimal damage to my head, cuts and bruises, but had been impaled by large shards of glass on my chest and abdomen. Emma's hand covered my chest and the searing pain I'd been in immediately ceased, and I felt covered by a warm glow.

I watched it all play out right in front of me, some twenty-eight years later. Emma leaned down to whisper in my ear that everything was going to be all right. I glanced up, watching yet another car pass. My mother had stopped yelling for help then. All I heard were her soft, tortured moans of agony.

"You knew my mother," I stated low.

Present-day Emma walked up beside me. "And she knew me, very well. I was with her from the time she was a child as well. She begged me to keep you safe until help arrived."

I snorted. "Help. All the cars that passed. Not one of them stopped. Selfish bastards."

Emma shook her head. "This moment right here is what has made you the most cynical. Not even your father could've done the damage this one moment did."

"No," I shook my head. "That moment just finished what my father started. He taught me he was an asshole. They," I jutted my head at another passing vehicle, "taught me that most people are assholes."

"Oh, Aaron."

"How is this helping me find my fucking wife?!" I yelled.

"Look at them, Aaron!" Emma shouted for the first time ever.

I would've been surprised if I hadn't been so angry.

"Those people. Look at them!" she insisted, moving closer to me, touching my forehead.

We were suddenly inside of the backseat of a car. I looked down to my left to see a little boy who couldn't have been more than three years old. His dark brown eyes were wide with fright.

"James! Those people look hurt!" a voice from the passenger seat beckoned.

I turned to see a dark-skinned woman, with a panicked expression, saying to the man in the driver's seat. "James! Did you hear me. Ow!" she howled when the man abruptly punched her in the ribs. She curled over, holding her side in pain.

"The fuck you want me to do, huh? I got all this shit in the car. You're high as hell. You want me to call the police?" he yelled, then shook his head. "Nah, those people will be all right," he stated. The car accelerated as he pressed his foot to the gas, leaving my dying family in the distance.

"And the next one," Emma stated, touching my forehead once more.

Again, we were thrust into the backseat of an older model car.

"Breathe, baby, breathe," the male driver in the seat encouraged.

"Ahhh! John, it hurts!" A woman shrilled.

I bent at the waist to see into the front seat. Immediately, I noticed the swollen belly of the blonde-haired woman. She held her stomach and breathed through another contraction. Her loud breathing eventually turned into a moan, which turned into another shrill yell.

A sight outside the window caught my eye, and from that vantage point, I saw my father's mangled vehicle, our bodies at the side of the road. I looked to the man driving the car to see his focus was on the woman next to him.

"He never even saw you," Emma stated as we passed. She touched my forehead again and we were back on the road.

"What's that supposed to prove?"

"Perspective. It changes when you get up close."

I remained silent.

"Sometimes people can't see your pain because they're too busy dealing with their own. Those people who passed you that night had their fill of their own pain, in one way or another. They couldn't see yours. But, Anita, the one who was with James, she was able to look past hers for a little while. When they arrived home, she snuck off to a local pay phone and called the police, reporting the accident. It could've been the next day you were found. That road was so seldom traveled."

"What does this have to do with Patience?" I asked, growing impatient.

"Perspective, Aaron. Widen your perspective." She touched my forehead again.

That horrible scene of my childhood faded to black.

* * *

I BLINKED MY EYES OPEN, and we were back in the past again, but not of me as a child. This time, we're in the middle of the street and I see myself hold the door open for Patience, that first night at Buena Sera. My chest tightened as I watched the scene play out before me. Patience and I walking down the sidewalk toward the bookstore. I moved to get closer, to watch us, but I was stopped by a hand on my arm.

"No, watch from here. There's something you need to see." Emma commented.

I stilled, looking from her to the scene. We waited a few minutes, until Patience and I emerged from the bookstore.

"Keep watching," Emma stated.

I turned to watch us walk down the street.

"No. Not there." Emma turned me back to the bookstore. "There."

Lifting my gaze, I froze. The nerdy, bookstore clerk peered out of the glass window. I inched closer, needing to get a better look for some reason. But before I got too close, he moved from the window, to the door, peering out, watching Patience and I. He stepped out from the doorway, glancing over his shoulder before following us, leaving the bookstore unattended. We entered the ice cream shop not too far from the bookstore and he stood there, watching through the window.

"He followed you that night," Emma whispered. "To her apartment…" She trailed off, but her hand touched my forehead again.

In an instant we were fast forwarded to later that evening, to the front of Patience's building. I followed Patience inside, and a few moments later, the same bookstore clerk was there. He stood outside of the building. I could only see his profile from my vantage but he appeared to be pissed. His fists tightened at his waist and he stomped his feet, eventually yelling, scaring a few passersby, but he was obviously too far gone to even notice. He just kept standing there, as if he could see something.

"How long did he wait there?"

"All night," Emma answered without hesitation.

I swallowed. "He was in love with her."

"Obsessed," she countered.

"That was almost seven years ago."

Emma finally turned to me. "Obsession rarely goes away."

My stomach muscles clenched. "It's him."

Emma nodded.

"Show me more," I demanded.

Emma obliged, showing me scene after scene of this fucking maniac waiting outside of Patience's apartment. We flashed to her graduation day, when we'd gone in to pick up the gift I had ordered. At the time I hadn't caught it, too enamored with Patience to see it, but from my new vantage point I watched as the bookstore clerk threw daggers my way. But when Patience wrapped her arms around me, kissing me in front of him, his rage-filled eyes turned in her direction.

The next scene was from inside of the bookstore again, only Patience was alone, a solemn expression on her face. Somehow I knew it was because of me.

"Hey, Patience. It's been a little while," he intoned.

She gave him something that was supposed to be a smile but it was just a movement of her lips.

"Picking up."

Patience nodded, taking the book and quietly paying for it.

"I'll see you soon," he stated, hopeful.

Patience shook her head. "I'm moving tomorrow."

He went pale as a ghost. "Wh-where?"

"Oakland. Thanks for your help, Sam. Take care." She exited the bookstore and again, he peered out of the window, watching her every step.

"Final scene," Emma informed.

Suddenly, we were in front of another brick apartment building. I didn't recognize it at first; I knew it wasn't in Williamsport. I looked around and stopped short when a male figure wearing all black passed by us. I caught a glimpse of his face just before he lowered his ski mask. It was him. The night he attacked Patience.

"Seeing her pregnant sent him over the edge."

My jaw firmed as I watched him patiently wait outside of the front door until someone exited, allowing him to slip in, unnoticed.

"I want to see it," I told Emma.

She shook her head.

"Emma!" I growled, needing to see the next scene.

"No, Aaron. Seeing him attack her won't do any good now. You need to get back to help her. Now." Before I could protest, Emma touched my forehead and I was back out on my bedroom balcony. I wasted no time. I turned from the balcony, moving quickly through the bedroom doors and down the stairs until I reached my office.

"I know who has her," I blurted out, bursting through the office.

All eyes were on me.

"Who?" Joshua, Carter, and my father shouted in unison.

CHAPTER 31

Patience

I can feel the entire left side of my face throbbing in pain, well before I open my eyes. It's as if that side of my face has grown it's own heartbeat and each time it pumps, pain lances through my head and down the entire length of my body. I struggle to open my eyes. My right eye eventually opens all the way, but the left is swollen, allowing it to open only a slit. My sight is blurry and I fight to clear my mind. I can't remember what happened, why my face is in so much pain.

"You're awake," a male voice sounds, but not the right male voice.

Aaron's voice, though always laced with a harsh roughness, always sends a sense of comfort over me. This voice does the opposite. My senses go into high alert. The hairs on the back of my neck stand on end.

"Wh-where am I?" I fight to sit up, but the pain causes me to reach up for my head. My hands are caught, unable to reach. That's when another source of pain grips my wrists. Peering down, I discover they are tightly bound with rope. I see red marks and cracking. The rope is tearing at the flesh of my wrists.

"What?" I manage to squeak out.

"You like rope, don't you?" A man emerges from behind me. I realize I'm sitting on a mattress in the middle of an empty room, my hands bound to the rope, tied around a floor-to-ceiling pole in the room. "He used rope in that *disgusting* club you went to!" the man seethes.

"What? Ah!" I yell when the man smacks me across the face so hard my neck snaps to the right.

My eyes water from the pain.

"Don't lie to me, Patience! You know what I'm talking about. That club in Chicago. I was there. I saw you go in the club with your little whore friend! You didn't leave until the next morning in a car that *he* ordered for you!"

I blinked, wondering how this man...this stranger knew so much of my life. I'd never told anyone what happened that night at The Cage.

The man stepped forward, towering over me. I peered up at him, blinking to clear my vision. He was tall, with mousy brown hair. He wore all black, but I could make out his lanky build. He seemed familiar but I couldn't place his face. Then I remembered.. *all black.* Just like the man...

"It was you," I whispered. "You attacked me."

"I didn't attack you! I was trying to *save* you," he uttered, almost as if he wanted...no, needed me to believe him. "It wasn't right!" he yelled, pulling me up to stand by my forearms.

I felt sick when he pressed his body against mine.

"You having his babies. They're supposed to be mine!" he screamed in my face.

Babies. *Oh God.* I was pregnant. My hands moved to instinctively cover my belly, protecting my unborn child yet again from this monster, but I stopped. I couldn't let him know I was with child. I just knew that would send him over the edge.

"I-I'm sorry. I-I didn't know you cared," I whispered, nearly choking on the lie. I knew aggression wouldn't work with him. He'd already gotten violent more than once when I returned his aggression with my own. Maybe soft-talking would prolong my life until help arrived. I knew my husband would tear this city apart to find me. That I had little doubt about.

"I cared," the man stated in a voice that was much more tender. He nodded, moving closer and cupping my face. "We're supposed to be together. Ever since I saw you that first time you came into the bookstore, I knew," he breathed out, cupping my face tighter and moving his lips toward mine.

I tried to pull away but his grip tightened.

His lips on mine caused bile to rise in my throat. I sealed my lips shut but gasped in disgust when he licked my lips. He seized on the opportunity, his tongue darting into my mouth. I tried to tell myself to play along but I couldn't. Repulsed, I clamped down on his tongue with my teeth.

"Ow! You bitch!" he yelled before punching me again.

The pain in my face increased right before I doubled over from another punch of his, this time to my stomach. Bending over at the waist, I fell back to the mattress and curled up in a ball to protect my stomach as much as I could.

"This is the thanks I get for loving you all these years!" he shouted.

All these years?

"I watched you with him. Night after night. Taking him to your apartment like a common whore!" he yelled as he paced back and forth.

Whore. He'd shouted that word over and over again the night of the attack. But Aaron had never been with me in Oakland. He'd mentioned a bookstore. I closed my eyes as he continued to rant on and on about Aaron coming to my apartment, how he'd wait outside of my building all night, how I teased him at the bookstore.

Bookstore.

I gasped. "Sam?" I said out loud.

"Why did you choose him over me?" He moved to me, then stooped low on the floor next to me.

I peered up at him from my huddled position on the mattress, blinking rapidly. It was Sam.

"I-I didn't know you were interested." That was a partial lie. I kind of had an inkling Sam had a crush on me, all those years ago, but I never gave it much thought. Then when Aaron came into the picture, I couldn't see anyone but him. Truthfully, that's how it'd always been. Aaron had been it for me since I was fourteen years old, after our first encounter.

"I wanted you. Waited for you. Moved to California for you! I even killed for you!"

My one eye bulged at his last statement.

He stared at me, wide-eyed, as if I was supposed to be impressed. "Yeah," he continued, nodding his head, excited. Rising, he moved over to a desk that stood a few feet from the mattress. I had barely noticed that something was on the desk, before a laptop, a black cloth draped over it. "See?" Sam stated, pulling the black sheet from the desk.

I bent over, covering my mouth with my hands, gagging.

"Look at him!" Sam yelled, moving closer to me.

I shook my head. "No!"

"Look!" he demanded again, this time grabbing my head and forcing me to stare at the jar that contained a head sitting on the table.

"Say hello to Vince," Sam giggled like the lunatic he was.

"Oh God!" I groaned. "You didn't," I whispered.

"I did. I wasn't about to let another fucker steal you from me! That late night he left your place, I followed him home, shot him up with the same stuff I shot your driver up with today, and dragged his body to my trunk. You ever heard a man scream as you gut him?"

A sob broke free from my lips. Sam was truly sick. I had wondered what happened to Vince after our first night together. I'd thought that he'd gotten what he wanted and moved on.

"He couldn't have you!" Sam gritted out. "I had to leave California soon after. My parents forced me back home," Sam stated glumly. He moved around to face me again. His eyes widened in excitement, as if he were a child who was just told they were going to the state fair. He was truly unhinged. "But as soon as I could, I came looking for you again. I went back to Oakland, followed you to Chicago," he spat out. "And soon after you moved back to Williamsport to be with him." His eyes hardened as he glared at me accusingly. "But I knew...It was for me. You were brought back here for me. See, the first time I was stupid." He shook his head. "I wanted those babies inside of you dead!" he hissed. "Walking around pregnant, proof to the world of the type of whore you were. So many times, I wanted to kill those little bastard seeds."

I gasped, horrified and angered at how he referred to my children.

"I messed up the first time, but thought I could use them. That didn't work. Anyway, now is our time. Maybe I should kill them just so he no longer has any connection to you."

"You psycho!" I kicked out, catching him in his thigh. "Don't fucking touch my children!" I screamed and yanked at the ropes, trying to free myself. *So help me God, when I get free I am going to kill him with my bare hands!*

"Oh!" He laughed maniacally. "There's that passion I love in you. Don't worry," he stated, pulling my face to his and kissing my forehead, "we will make our own children, once I'm done with them."

He stood, moving to the desk and throwing on a dark ski mask. After grabbing the set of keys that sat on his desk, he started for the wooden door at the far end of the room.

"Where're you going?" I yelled.

He kept moving, ignoring me.

"Don't you touch my children! Aaron will rip you apart, you son of a bitch!" I tugged and yanked at the ropes, doing nothing more than causing more damage to my wrists. But I didn't feel the pain, my concern was for my family.

Sam stopped short, turning to me. "Not if I get to him first," he warned.

Pure terror moved through my body. The look in his eye could only be described as stark raving mad. After he slammed the door shut, my knees went so weak that my body fell limply back to the floor.

I had no idea what to do.

* * *

Aaron

"What the..." Carter breathed out, standing a few feet from me as we looked around the empty room. All around us, posted on the walls were pictures of Patience, going back years.

"He built a shrine to her," Brutus stated out loud what was evident to our eyes.

We were standing in the middle of the former bookstore. The same one Patience used to frequent while she was in graduate school. The same one I'd taken her to that first night after dinner at Buona Sera. The same one where an obvious obsession was born.

Thanks to Emma's visions, I was able to tell Brutus that Sam was responsible for Patience's kidnapping. I gave him the details that I knew. His name was Sam, he'd worked as a clerk at the vintage bookstore six years earlier. Though the store was now closed, Brutus was able to use the information to get all of Sam's information. His full name was Samuel Granger. Born and raised right here in Williamsport. His grandfather had opened the bookstore some thirty years prior and passed it down to Samuel on his eighteenth birthday.

I looked around at the empty space, the walls littered in images of my wife. There were pictures of her from years earlier. I was in some of them, though my face had been crossed or cut out. The son of a bitch had replaced my face with his in the pictures of she and I together. A cold chill passed through my chest when I turned to see more pictures, more recent images of Patience as she went into the work at the library. Pictures of her inside of the library working. But my entire heart damn near stopped beating when I discovered the pictures of Patience and the children playing in the Williamsport City Park.

"I'll kill this motherfucker myself," Carter growled beside me.

Following his gaze, I saw him staring at one of the photos that had Patience standing next to Michelle as they walked with the children into a store. It was the day they'd gone shopping for Halloween costumes. He'd been there. Watching my family. My entire body began to vibrate with an anger I'd never felt before.

"No," I shook my head, fists clenched at my sides, "he's all mine."

Brutus emerged from behind Carter and I. "He's not here,"

I wanted to rip his head off for stating the fucking obvious. I turned angry eyes on him and even at six-foot-six, outweighing me by eighty pounds, he took a step back. I was sure there was a crazed gleam in my gaze.

"We've got more information, however," Brutus stated slowly, as if measuring his words to not set off a ticking time bomb.

Me. I was that time bomb.

"Health records. Samuel Granger was admitted to the Williamsport Behavioral Health Facility."

"For what?" I questioned.

"He was a troubled kid. Apparently, he was adopted at the age of three. Before then he was born to a drug-addicted mother. His adoptive parents, Bobbie and Charlene Granger, did their best but he had a difficult time connecting. He was only calm when it came to reading. A loner throughout his school years. He was put on meds for depression but tried to kill himself his junior year by hanging. His mother came home early from work and found him just in time. There was a girl at school he'd become infatuated with and when she rejected him he tried suicide. He was admitted for three months to the psych ward. After that he withdrew from school, rarely leaving the house except to visit his grandfather's bookstore.

"His grandfather gave him the job, hoping it would help stabilize him. His parents continued to seek help for him due to numerous violent outbursts he had with them. But they were given meds and told to work it out in therapy. Sam refused therapy after turning eighteen. His grandfather died, leaving him as the beneficiary of the store. From the looks of it, his parents mostly ran the business, leaving Sam to be the clerk and spend his days here helping customers and reading. This is obviously where he came across Patience. As you can see," Brutus waved a hand around the room, "he grew obsessed. His parents eventually realized it when they found a shrine in his closet that he'd built to her. They tried for almost a year to have him committed. By then he'd moved to California."

"He followed her," I growled.

Brutus nodded. "A judge finally found him incompetent and he was again put into the facility for almost a year. Somehow he was able to convince the doctors that he was stable enough to be discharged. He moved back in with his parents."

"Why the fuck didn't they warn Patience?"

Brutus shrugged. "Maybe they thought they could handle it. They likely didn't know he attacked her or even why he'd moved to California."

"Where the fuck are they now?" I'd hold them accountable for this situation just as much as I would their crazy, fucked up son.

"Dead. Six months after he was discharged they died in a car accident. Father was driving and had a blood alcohol content well over the legal limit. But..."

"What?" My eyebrow peaked.

"Neighbors say he didn't drink. By all accounts Bobbie Granger never touched alcohol, hating the way it made him feel out of control."

"He murdered his own parents," I surmised.

"Looks like it but it's never been proven. Not long after their death is when he shut down the bookstore and went to California again, only to move back to Williamsport. His behavior became more erratic and aggressive once she was back."

Another chill ran through my body. I was the catalyst for his aggression. Seeing her with me and our children. And now she was pregnant and alone with that psychotic fuck and I had no idea where.

"He's not here, so where the hell is he?"

"We're digging up financial and real estate records. He purchased two plane tickets to the Bahamas just five days ago."

I narrowed my eyes. "He'll never make that flight."

"Fucking right he won't," Joshua growled, sounding as pissed as I was.

I could've done all of this on my own, but I was glad I had my entire family with me in that moment.

"Who's that?" I questioned, when Brutus' phone rang.

"Office. They've got something..." He trailed off, answering his phone.

I watched, feeling helpless as he told whoever it was on the other end to send the information.

"He has a house. A cottage about twenty minutes outside of the city. Was owned by his grandfather. Rarely used. Sending GPS coordinates to all your phones now."

Brutus' words were in the background as I made a beeline for the door. I burst through the door of the closed down bookstore, and jumped in behind the wheel of my Tesla Roadster.

I was pulling up the coordinates of that madman's house as Joshua jumped in the passenger seat.

"Carter and Brutus' guys are following," he stated as I pulled off.

I didn't need anyone else for this but I guessed I was glad they were all there.

"Shit, I forgot how fucking crazy you drive," Joshua commented.

I grunted as I rounded the corner, driving through a red light. In my head, I dared any shit cop to try and stop me. I was going to get my woman back and then bury the bastard that'd tried to take her from me.

CHAPTER 32

Patience

"Dammit!" I groaned at the growing rope burn on my wrists. I'd been trying feverishly, ever since Sam left to free myself. A small thread of the rope had frayed after rubbing them continuously along the rusty metal pipe I was tied to. It felt like hours upon hours I'd been trying to untie myself, with very little headway.

My throat was hoarse from yelling, trying to alert anybody that could be nearby, but to no avail. I had no idea where I was. The one window in the room was covered by dark drapes. Just then I had an idea. I remembered that I had a couple of bobbie pins in my hair, that I'd used to pin up my locs that morning. I bent down, lowering my head to my hands, and fiddled for a bit, searching for the pins. I was able to reach about two of them. I stuck the tips in my mouth, working to pry off the rounded, rubber edges to get to the sharp pointed metal tip.

Spitting the rubber balls out, I twisted the pins around and worked to use the now sharp edges of the bobbie pins to cut through the rope. It was slow progress, but still moved quicker than rubbing back and forth against the metal pole. I pushed past the pain still throbbing in my head and my wrists. I could give into it when I was safe. I needed to concentrate on the task at hand. I breathed and continued to work my fingers, trying to free myself.

"We gotta go!"

I jumped when Sam bust through the door, yelling. He had an even more crazed look in his eye than when he'd left. He moved in my direction with purpose. I backed up against the pole, not knowing what to expect. Of course, I didn't manage to get very far, still being tied up and all.

"Don't touch me!" I kicked at Sam, landing my heel against his shin.

"Ah, shit!" he screeched. "The fuck is your problem?!" He grabbed my face painfully. "I'm doing this for us!" he hissed, his spittle landing on my nose and mouth. "They found out it's me. They know my apartment. We've gotta go." Sam was frantic. He went for my wrists, untying me from the pole, but my hands were still bound to one another.

My first instinct was to make a dash but something told me not to just yet. Instead of trying to break free, I tightened my fingers around the bobbie pins, to prevent him from seeing them in my hands.

"We've gotta go out back. My truck is about two miles down the road." He was more talking to himself than to me at that point. His dark eyes were glossy and I just knew there was absolutely no point in trying to reason with him. He was too far gone.

"Let's go!" he urged, angrily, tugging on the rope, pulling me behind him. The more he pulled the tighter the ropes became around my wrist, causing more pain. I began fearing blood loss to my hands with every squeeze.

We stumbled out of the back entrance of what I'd then come to realize was a cottage of some sort. I blinked as we exited the building into the cold winter air. I wore only the sweater, jeans, and a pair of ballet flats that I'd worn to the library earlier.

"Thinks he can take you from me. You're mine!" Sam yelled, tugging again at the ropes, dragging me closer to him.

I stumbled as we made our way through the densely wooded area, falling to my knees.

"Come on!" he growled, impatiently, lifting me up underneath my arm.

I glanced over my right shoulder to see we were about two yards from the cottage. I thought back on what Sam had said when he first entered. The "they" he mentioned had to be Aaron and his security. It had to be. I knew he would be doing his damndest to find me. Everything in my body told me he was. It was as if I could feel his anger and his terror. I swallowed, reminding myself to remain strong for him, Kyle, and Kennedy. I had to keep alive long enough for him to get to me.

"Ahh!" I yelled, tripping and falling again over a large rock that I hadn't seen in the darkened woods.

"Get up...Ahhh!" Sam yelled, when I sprang up and drove the bobbie pins directly into the side of his face. I cursed myself. I'd been aiming for his eye but missed. Still, his shock and pain from the two pins now sticking out of his face caused him to lose the grip he had on the rope. I didn't think twice. I took off in the opposite direction we'd come from. Unfortunately, I had no idea where I was going, and what I thought was the direction back to the cabin, turned out to be wrong. Not only that, but I could hear Sam hot on my heels.

I ducked behind trees, doing my best not to make too much noise by stepping on branches or twigs. But no matter how careful I was it seemed I was rattling the entire damn forest with the silence that surrounded us. I was feeling weak and woozy. It occurred to me that I hadn't eaten all day. The only thing keeping me on my feet was my adrenaline. That and the desire to protect my unborn baby. I pressed my hand to my abdomen, hoping that the baby growing inside would be okay. Then I remembered Kyle and Kennedy. I had to fight for all three of them. I had to keep going.

"Your daddy is coming," I whispered to the little one inside of my womb. I pressed forward, moving behind another tree and then stilling myself to listen for Sam.

"Patience, we don't have time for this!" he hissed, losing it.

I could hear the crazy in his voice. He was so on edge.

"We're taking a trip to the Bahamas!" He continued to talk out loud as if that would make me go to him. "You love the beach. You told me so!"

I shook my head, not remembering ever telling him such. Though, it could've been possible in one of the conversations we had in passing at the bookstore. Obviously, those talks meant more to him than they ever did me.

"We're going to get married and you'll forget all ab–" He stopped short at the same time my ears perked up.

In the distance I could make out faint lights and the sounds of screeching tires as the cars stopped short. My heartbeat picked up. Seconds later, I heard a sound that nearly caused my knees to buckle.

"Patience!" It was Aaron's voice calling for me.

I went to open my mouth to respond but stopped, not wanting to give my location away to the madman pursuing me. I held my breath, trying to decide what to do. *Do I yell and give Sam the chance of reaching me before Aaron? Or do I scream and run like my hair is on fire and hope to God Aaron gets to me first?*

Noise too close for my comfort behind me had me almost leaping out of my skin.

"I will find you!" Sam seethed.

Fuck it, I thought. He was too close and I was surely going to get caught if I just stood there. I grabbed a rock that was on the ground, stood up, and turned behind me. I could barely make out his movements but I aimed the rock for his head and threw as hard as I could with my still-bound hands.

"*Ow!* Fuck!" he groaned, and I knew I'd hit my target.

As soon as the rock was free from my hands I took off in the direction of the headlights.

"Aaron! Aaaron!" I yelled as hard and as loud as I could. Running was difficult with my hands bound in front of me, but heavy footsteps behind me forced me to pick up my pace. I heard loud footsteps, backtracking out of the cottage down into the brush of the forest. "I'm here!" I pushed past the fear to yell.

The cottage came into sight and I saw four large figures barreling in my direction. Even in the darkness of the evening light, and the fact that they were wearing all black, didn't stop my body from knowing exactly which one was my man. I moved past two of the male figures and collapsed into the arms of my husband's.

"I'm here. I got you," he crooned, his strong arms tightening around my body. I began to shiver uncontrollably. Burying my face into Aaron's chest, I tried to control my breathing, even amongst the yelling and running going on all around us.

"Get the fuck off of me! I'll kill you all! Don't touch her!"

That crazed voice had me burying my head deeper into Aaron's chest. I couldn't look back, didn't want to even see his face again.

"She's mine!"

"I'll fucking ki–" Aaron released me and began to charge Sam.

"Not here, bro." Joshua and Carter stopped Aaron, leaving the man I knew as Brutus and another one of his security guards holding Sam.

Joshua and Carter both had trouble holding Aaron back. He managed to free himself from them, taking a swing at Sam, landing a fist to the side of his face. He went for another one but his brother's were there again.

"Aaron, not now," Carter tried to reason.

"Get the hell off me!" Aaron yelled.

"Aaron, I swear on my life, you'll get the chance to handle this piece of shit. You have my word. But right now Patience needs you," Joshua stated in a stern voice. He moved closer to say something low in Aaron's ear. I couldn't hear what he said but after a few heartbeats, Aaron took a step back and moved to me, scooping me up in his arms and carrying me to the front of the cottage.

More security greeted us, holding the door of a large, black SUV with tinted windows open. After placing me in the back, Aaron climbed in, pulling me into his lap. I leaned against his shoulder as he frantically freed my wrists from the restraints.

"Hsss!" I hissed then the rope rubbed against my skin for the last time, revealing the cuts and bruises left behind. I flinched when Aaron's big hand lifted to my face.

"It's okay," he cooed, using the softest voice I'd ever heard from him. "You're safe." He pushed my locs away from my face and through my one eye I made out the ticking in his jaw as his eyes skimmed over the bruising on my face.

"I-I'm okay," I lied, trying to reassure him. I wasn't okay, though, and he knew it. I was petrified.

"I got you," he crooned.

I lifted my head as the car started moving. "The kids," I said, suddenly. "H-he said he would hurt them. Are they…are they…" I couldn't even say it.

"They're home. Safe."

"Are you sure?" I asked with force.

Aaron didn't respond. Instead, he shifted, digging his phone out of his pocket. He pressed a number and waited. "Mother, put the kids on. Patience wants to speak with them." He handed me the phone.

"Hi, Mommy!" Kennedy's voice yelled.

"Mommy!" I heard Kyle's voice in the background.

The vision in my one good eye blurred as tears filled it.

"H-hi, my loves," I croaked out.

"Mommy, you were scared. I told Daddy," Kyle's concerned voice pushed through the line.

"Mommy's okay. I'm not scared anymore."

"We'll be home soon," Aaron stated, taking the phone again.

I watched as he hung up.

"They're safe. And so are you," he reassured, cupping my face. His hand moved down my body to my stomach. "And the baby," he stated, his voice lowered.

I didn't even have time to register how he knew about the baby. I was physically and mentally drained. I needed his warmth. I moved impossibly closer, lowering my head to his shoulder. When his arms around me tightened, the few tears that had already begun to trickle, evolved into a geyser. I released all my pent-up emotion on his shoulder, dampening the dark shirt he wore. He held me through it all.

* * *

Aaron

"Mr. Townsend, we need to examine her."

I watched as the doctor's hand yet again made a move for my wife, who remained on my lap, her head buried in my shoulder.

"I'll kill everything you love if you try to touch her again," I informed him through gritted teeth.

The doctor's eyes widened and he instantly took three steps back. Behind him, I could hear the sighs coming from my father, Carter, and Joshua. We were in one of the guest bedrooms at Townsend Manor. We'd brought Patience here instead of home to have her checked out and examined by our on-call medical team, but I couldn't find it in me to give the doctors enough space to let her be touched by anyone but me. She hadn't released me since she began crying in the car. Save for a few hiccups, she was completely silent.

I knew I was being unreasonable. She needed medical attention. For the bruising on her face and rope burns on her wrists. For the baby. I knew it, but I couldn't let her go. Seeing another man's hands on her—even if that was a doctor we hired to care for her. I myself just couldn't bear it. I pulled her into me even more.

"Aaron," my father began.

I shook my head, silently telling him not to bother. I wasn't budging. I'd hold her for as long as she needed me to. Then the doctor could do his damn job.

My father wouldn't relent. He knelt beside the bed we rested on. "Aaron, she's safe. No one in this room is going to do anything to harm your wife."

I ground my back teeth. Rationally, I knew this already.

"But she needs medical attention. Your job is to protect her, even if that means letting her go…just for a little while."

My hand moved to her belly where I hoped our unborn child still grew.

"H-he's right," Patience whispered in my ear, seemingly coming out of the almost catatonic state she'd been in.

I tightened my grip.

"Aaron, the baby," she whispered.

I hesitated but eventually pushed out a full breath and reluctantly loosened my grip from around her. Slowly, she sat up, pushing her hair behind her ear.

Another surge of anger moved through me at the sight of her swollen face. She moved off my lap to the side of the bed.

The doctor moved closer, albeit hesitantly. My father stepped back, giving him more room.

"Is there anything, health wise, I should know?" the doctor asked, attempting to be sensitive.

Patience stalled, her gaze bouncing around the room, embarrassed. That look tore at my soul. I was going to rip that son of a bitch's limbs off and beat him with them.

"I-I wasn't raped," she uttered. "He hit me in my stomach…I'm pregnant," she confessed.

Out of the side of my gaze I could see my father and Carter's heads raise. Joshua already knew since I'd revealed it earlier.

"Do you know how far along?" the doctor questioned.

She shook her head. "I just found out today." Her voice cracked but she cleared her throat.

I sealed my eyes shut and inhaled, summoning every bit of strength I could. Opening them, I listened as Patience answered the doctor's' questions. I had to restrain myself when his hands went to touch her. I repeated over and over that he was helping her as I watched him clean out her wounds and carefully bandage her wrists. He carried a portable ultrasound as part of his service so he brought it out to use.

"The baby's heart doesn't begin to beat until around six weeks. So, it's unlikely we'll hear that today because you're so early on." He paused, tossing a weary glance my way. "Uh, typically prior to eight weeks it's best to do a transvaginal ultrasound." He continued to stare, uneasily at me.

"What's that?" My voice was hard.

"An internal ultrasound," Patience answered in a small voice.

"Internal?" I stopped, immediately shaking my head. No fucking way he was about to spread my wife's legs.

"I-I can attempt a transabdominal ultrasound," he rushed on. "That may let us get a good image of how the baby's doing." He locked to me then back to Patience. "I'll need you to lift your shirt."

I growled low in my throat.

"As part of the exam," he rushed out, staring at me.

"I-it's okay," Patience insisted, grabbing my hand.

I pushed out a harsh breath and looked to my brothers and father, waving my head to the door. They instantly understood and left the room, giving us our privacy. I nodded at the doctor, telling him he could proceed with the exam. Patience squeezed my hand as he lathered her stomach in that ointment they use. A minute later we were both staring at a grainy black and white screen, a visible black circle with what looked like nothing more than a lump at the center. And then another lump appeared. I had no idea what the hell I was looking at, but the gasp that came from Patience's mouth had me on high alert.

"What's wrong?" I demanded of the doctor.

His bushy, greying eyebrows were raised. "It looks like twins." He stood up straight. "You already have twins, right?"

Patience nodded. "A boy and a girl..."

He nodded as my eyes volleyed between the two of them. *What the hell's going on?*

"They were fraternal. Looks like these twins are identical."

"Twins," I stated, hardly unable to believe it.

"Are they all right?" Patience asked, fear lacing her voice.

"They look healthy so far. No heartbeat but from the size you look to be about four weeks. I recommend making an appointment with your OB as soon as possible. I'm going to leave some of this ointment for your wrists..." he continued.

I listened intently as he told us that he didn't believe she had any broken bones in her face or ribs. Just some severe bruising that would take a few days to go down and weeks to heal. He showed me how to properly dress the bandages on her wrists and recommended after a couple of days to leave the bandages off entirely for better healing.

After about thirty minutes, he was leaving with assurances that he'd back the following day.

My father, followed by Joshua and Carter, entered the room.

"We're going to be uncles again, huh?" Josh questioned, a small smile at his lips.

Patience returned his smile with a small one of her own. "Twice over."

All three faces widened in shock.

"Twins," I affirmed, pulling my wife into me.

"You really know how to knock it out of the park, don't you?" Carter teased. "You keep this up and you'll be stuck with this guy forever," he said to Patience.

I narrowed my gaze on him, but felt her look up at me. "That doesn't sound so bad."

Her words pulled me back, staring down into her face. My heart squeezed at the fact that I could only see one of those sepia orbs I loved so much.

"We should bring the kids over–" my father began.

"No." Patience shook her head, surprising all four of us. "I don't want them to see me like this."

Pain seared me.

"They'll be frightened."

"Are you sure?" I questioned.

She nodded. "Tomorrow."

My father agreed to stay at our house with my mother and the children for the night, while Patience remained with me at Townsend Manor.

"You sure about this?" I questioned again as the three exited the room, closing the door behind them.

She nodded. "Yeah. I know they're safe at home." She buried her face into my chest again.

"How did you find me?" she finally asked after a few minutes of silence.

I went to tell her it was Brutus and his team that helped track Sam down, but what came out was the truth. "I had help…supernatural help."

She sat up, giving me an odd look.

I wanted to tell her she needed to rest but I couldn't. Per doctor's orders, she couldn't go to sleep for another eight to ten hours due to fear of a possible concussion from the blow she'd received earlier.

"Explain."

I sat up, facing her. "Her name's Emma," I began. And as soon as I did, a smiling Emma appeared at the corner of the room. I told her all about how my first memory Emma occurred when I was just a baby, and yes I remembered that far back. I shared with her secrets I'd never told anyone. Like, how my father found me in my room talking to Emma when I was barely four years old and beat me so badly I had bruises for days afterwards. I told her how he beat me because he said I wasn't going to turn into a freak like my mother. When she asked who this Emma was, I told her the truth on that as well. Emma was a distant ancestor of mine. My grandmother's great-grandmother, on my mother's side. Many in my mother's family had these supernatural visions. They could be traced back as some of the original victims of the witch-hunts in North America.

"How did she help you find me?" Patience asked, intrigued.

She didn't look at me as if I was completely out of my mind.

"She helped me broaden my perspective," I answered, looking toward a smiling Emma. I glanced back at Patience. "She showed me parts of the past. Sam had been following you for years. Your relationship with me set him off, then and now. This sounds crazy as hell," I grunted, running my hand through my hair. I knew Patience had to be thinking I was insane to be admitting to seeing ghosts or spirits, or whatever the hell Emma claimed she was.

"Yeah," Patience stated, nodding, half of her mouth turned upwards. "But…it kind of makes sense. I mean, you have this larger than life energy about you. Even when you scare the hell out of people, they still gravitate to you."

I paused, reflecting on her words for a while.

"This type of gift runs in your family?" she asked.

I gave a one shoulder shrug. "Apparently. On my mother's side."

"Kyle," she stated.

"What?"

She lifted her head. "Kyle, he's so intuitive. Sometimes he sees and knows things no one's ever mentioned to him. Like, your birthday. He said a woman told him the date. Is he ... like you?"

I looked toward Emma who nodded.

"Is she here now?" Patience asked, turning to glance over her shoulder.

"She is."

"Tell her I said thank you."

"She says you don't owe her any thanks," I repeated Emma's words.

"And Kyle? Has she visited Kyle."

"On occasion," I answer, again repeating Emma's response.

"I guess it's why kids and animals are so drawn to me. They can see things others can't."

"They see your goodness," Patience and Emma say at the same time.

"It's not fairies, as the children like to call them," Emma continued. "The light they see is the inner soul. The one you believed you didn't have. Your father tried to tamp out your light. Even you, yourself were afraid of it. But no matter how hard you tried, it's still there, visible to those whose eyes are open to it. Like children, and your wife."

I swallowed and turned back to Patience who was staring at me.

Her hand cupped my face. "You're a good man, Aaron."

The woman who I didn't think could bury herself in my heart any further just found six more feet to dig herself in my soul. I wasn't convinced she was one hundred percent accurate on my being a good man, but I didn't give a shit either. I was hers and she was mine. I spent the rest of the night telling her all about the night of my accident, and how the bitterness I gained that night, impeded my trust of others afterwards. And how Emma showed my dismissal and distrust of others could also blind me to what was really going on around me, including having possibly seen Sam's obsession before it ever got to this point.

"You can't blame yourself for his craziness," Patience conscled.

I refrained from blurting out that she was wrong. I could and did blame myself for not protecting my family. Instead, I kissed the palm of her hand that stroked my cheek and made a promise.

"He will get what he deserves," I vowed.

CHAPTER 33

Three weeks later...
Aaron

I stood over my sleeping wife's form, looking down on her. Admiring her. The bruises on her face had healed and most were gone from around her wrists. The emotional marks still lingered, however. Just a few hours earlier, she'd awaken from another terrible nightmare. I leaned down and pressed my lips to her forehead.

I was caught off guard when her eyes opened, staring at me. She remained silent for a while, instead taking in my all-black ensemble. She stared at me from head to toe before speaking.

"You're going now?"

I narrowed my eyes. I hadn't told her where I was going but she didn't seem surprised to see me dressed to leave so early on a weekend morning. She moved, sitting up on her knees, her hands going to my shoulders.

"I know where you're going." Her hands moved up, cupping my face. "After this..." she trailed off, her gaze going over my shoulder before moving back to me. "He gets no more of our energy. After this, it's done," she said with finality.

My heart swelled at the conviction in her voice and I pulled her to me, crushing her lips to mine. I moved back before I could get too absorbed in the kiss. I pressed a kiss to her forehead, and then leaned down to kiss her slightly rounded belly. Her pregnancy wasn't obvious to others just yet, but I had every centimeter of her body memorized. I could see even the most minute changes.

I pulled back and went to the bedroom door, taking one last look at my wife. The fear and anger at the thought that she'd almost been taken away from me permanently, pushed me out the door.

I opted to drive my own vehicle this time, not wanting a driver to know where I was going. Plus, I had security beefed up around our home and community. No need in taking security off my family for this trip. Within minutes, I was speeding down the road in my Tesla, hands tightly gripping the steering wheel, my body rigid with anxiety. I'd waited three weeks too long for this day. The son of a bitch who tried to take my whole world from me was not going to survive until the end of the day.

* * *

"We've been waiting on you," Joshua stated as I stepped into the darkened, concrete room. I took in the gleam in my brother's eye. He loved this type of shit. Joshua has his dark side just like the rest of us Townsends. It was an added bonus for him that I was about to take out the scumbag that stalked and attacked my wife.

I took in his all black ensemble before looking around the room, spotting my two other brothers, arms folded over their chests, staring ahead at the center of the room. Tyler's green eyes turned on me, narrowing before he turned back to the middle of the room. He was still pissed that he wasn't there to help the rest of us locate Patience.

I pushed past Joshua, moving to the middle of the room where Sam was seated, hands tied behind his back in a wooden chair. There was an overhanging light, illuminating Sam and the space around him.

"Untie him," I barked out.

Joshua moved past me. From the corner of my eye I caught the glare of the knife in his hand. Sam lifted his face, color draining from his already pale face when he saw what Joshua was holding.

"No, no, no!"

"Shut the fuck up!" I yelled, frightening him even more. My entire body warmed in satisfaction at the look of fear on his face.

Joshua moved behind him, cutting the zip ties that'd bound his wrists.

"He's been fed properly, right?" I grunted, eyes locked on Sam but asking the other three men in the room.

"Fed, warm bed to sleep in, and kept comfortable the last three weeks, as per your request," Carter answered behind me.

"For the life of me, I don't know why you'd want this piece of shit kept comfortable," Tyler growled.

I moved closer to Sam, bending my knees and peering up at him. "I have my reasons." A sardonic smile creased my lips. "Isn't that right, Samuel?"

I heard grunting behind me but paid it no attention.

"Look at me!" I ordered.

Sam blinked a few times, his eyes peering down at me. They narrowed on me. He was growing angry. *Good.*

"My wife..." I paused, grinning even more when I watch his eyes glaze over at those two words. "*My* wife," I repeated, "thinks I'm a good man. She tells me almost every day." I shook my head. "She is my lifeline."

"You don't deserve her!" he yelled.

I nodded. "That, we can agree on." I cocked my head to the side. "She's wrong. I'm not a good man." I rose to my full height, standing over him. "A good man wouldn't do what I'm about to do to you." I took a step back. "Stand up."

"Fuck you!" he yelled.

A chuckle broke free of my lips. "I said, stand the fuck up!" I kicked the chair out from underneath him as I repeated my words.

"Unf!" He groaned when he fell on his ass. "She loves me!" he screamed from the floor.

"This fucking guy is whacked!" Tyler yelled behind me.

I bent low, moving in close to him. "You think so? Was she in love with you when she was riding my dick last night? How about when she gave birth to my children? Or now that she's pregnant with two more of my children? She still love you?" I taunted, knowing my words would finally send him over the edge.

"Grrr-ahh!" he growled, lunging at me. However, he yelled in agony when I stood, dodging his lunge, and pressed the heel of the steel-toe boots I wore to his face.

Blood poured out of his nose but the crazed gleam in his eyes revealed he was too far gone to care. Excellent. That was just where I wanted him.

"Fuck yo–" He couldn't get the full curse out before my right cross landed on his chin. Just as he was falling from my punch, I landed another kick to his kneecap. The second time, warmth infused my body when I heard the crunch of bones breaking. His yelp of pain also sent a shiver of elation through me.

Sam was beyond reason at that point, which was just where I wanted him. I could see the agony on his face but my words had set him off. He limped, charging me, screaming that Patience was his. I saw red and blacked out. I caught him with a quick jab and then a left hook to his right ribcage, causing him to buckle to the ground. For most that might've been enough, but this was the bastard that'd tried to kill my children while my wife was pregnant the first time, then attacked my woman again. The image of him punching her on that video replayed in my mind. The fear I still saw in her eyes most days over the past three weeks, wreaked havoc on my soul. No. This motherfucker could not live to see another day.

I pounded into his face and chest with everything I had. He flailed his arms and legs at first, as I straddled his body. Eventually, his arms fell to his side as he lost consciousness, but I continued the brutal hammering. Even once my arms grew heavy with exhaustion I stood, and broke one of the legs free of the wooden chair he'd been sitting in when I first entered. I used that leg to beat the rest of the life out of that deranged, son of a bitch, until there was nothing left.

By the time I was finished, my chest heaved, as my lungs struggled for air. I felt like I was coming to from fainting. I looked around, seeing the bloody mess that was once Sam laid out on the floor. His face was unrecognizable; blood and brain matter now coated the floor. My entire body was covered in blood but I knew none of it was mine. The room was completely silent.

I tossed the wooden chair leg aside, the sound reverberating against the concrete. It wasn't enough. I growled and kicked the lifeless body again and again. I wished I could bring him back to life just to do it all over again.

"That's enough!" I heard in my peripheral but I didn't stop.

I kicked and kicked again until three pairs of arms tugged at me.

"He's fucking dead!" Carter yelled.

"Bro, enough!" Joshua added.

"We need to dispose of the body," Tyler chimed in.

"Fuck him!" I growled.

"Let it go, bro," Joshua stated. "He's gone. He can't hurt her anymore."

His words finally mollified me. She was safe. My wife would no longer have to worry about that motherfucker ever again. Or anyone else, as long as I was concerned.

I held up my hands, silently telling my brothers I was fine. They could release me.

I turned from the body. The sight of it still angered me and I needed to regain my sanity to go back to my family.

"You need to clean up," Joshua came up behind me, stating. "New clothes are in the bathroom. Shower, get this shit off of you, give me your clothes and we'll burn it with the rest of this filth."

I nodded, heeding Joshua's words. I sauntered off in the direction he pointed, reaching the bathroom that was a total contradiction to the room I'd just come from. Whereas the large, empty, concrete space was dreary and dark, the bathroom looked as if it could've been a part of a luxury home or hotel. A full size shower, granite tiles on the floors and walls. There was even a huge bathtub for soaking. This was on one of Joshua's buildings.

I didn't dwell too much on my brother's affairs. After removing my clothing, I stepped in the shower, and let the hot water wash everything away. I wasn't about to let Sam or anyone else come between my wife and I any longer. Even if that someone was me. We'd been through too much. She was mine and there wasn't a damn thing anyone could do about it.

I'd promised her that once I returned home, that it was over. He was no longer a part of our lives and I meant it. Sam was dead. The only other time I'd see him again would be in hell. But before then, I had a wife and children who needed me. They'd get my full attention from there on out.

EPILOGUE

Patience

"Oww! It huuuurts!" I yelled and moaned from the hospital bed.

"I know, Patience. Just one more push!" the doctor insisted. I wanted to tell her to go fuck herself. I was exhausted after twelve hours of labor. The last thing I wanted to do was push out not one but *two* babies.

"Come on, baby. Just a little more," Aaron cooed from my side.

Despite the pain and exhaustion, the tenderness in his voice and the vice grip he had on my hand spurred me forward.

"I'm not having anymore of your twins!" I insisted and then inhaled deeply, readying myself for the next push.

"If you say so." He pressed a kiss to my forehead.

"Push, Patience. One…two…" The doctor continued counting as I pushed, bearing down with everything I could. "The head's out. One more…come on."

Seconds later, loud wailing pierced the air as our baby boy was born. I barely had time to welcome him with a kiss to his little reddened face before his identical twin made it clear he was ready to make his entrance into the world as well.

Aaron quickly passed the baby to one of the nurses, and grabbed my hand again, his free hand massaging my shoulder as he and the doctor encouraged me to push. I put everything out of my mind and just listened to the sound of Aaron's voice. It was the beacon of light through the pain.

Eight minutes after his brother was born, our third son entered the world. His cries were even louder than his twin's. It wasn't lost on me that both babies' crying ceased as soon as they were placed into their father's arms. I knew then our two boys had fallen as hopelessly in love with their father as their mama had. My only regret in that moment was that Kyle and Kennedy couldn't be in the room.

It took a while to clean me up as I'd had some tearing during the birth and needed to be stitched up. Afterwards, both babies were placed on my breasts so they could begin latching. Andreas, the oldest, latched immediately, while his younger brother, Theirs, struggled a little but eventually caught on.

I noticed how aggressively both twins began sucking, taking in all the colostrum they could. I glanced up to a frowning Aaron.

"What's that look?" I grinned, already knowing what he was thinking.

"They're sucking on what belongs to me." His frown deepened.

I didn't even bother looking up toward the nurse who gasped at his words.

"Jealous of your own sons?"

His shining eyes rose to meet mine. "Maybe a little." He bent down, pressing a kiss to my lips before sitting down at the side of the bed. His large hand went to stroke one baby then to the next one.

"I'm sorry I missed this the first time around."

"You're here now."

He nodded. "And I'll be here for our next two...or three births."

"Three?" I gave him a glare. "You said you wanted three more kids. We just had two. How does that equate to two or *three* more births??"

The left side of his face kicked up. "I lied."

Shaking my head, I mumbled an expletive under my breath. "I'm not having any more."

Aaron leaned over and kissed my lips before kissing the tops of the babies' heads. "I bet I can get you to change your mind." He had the audacity to fucking wink at me.

I went to give him my retort but his next words blew me away.

"Marry me."

I wrinkled my forehead. "I just delivered two children, but you're the one who's delirious? We're already married."

The gleam in his eyes grew as he nodded. "Marry me again. This time on a white sand beach while the sun sets as we say our vows."

My eyes were blurry before he'd even finished this last sentence. "You remembered?" I whispered. I'd once told him during a late night conversation all those years ago that while I never imagined a big wedding, I had wanted one on the beach, at sunset.

"Every word you've ever said to me." He bent low, his face just inches from mine. "Marry me again." He removed a box from his pocket, opening it, showing off my diamond ring. The ring I hadn't worn in months due to the swelling from my pregnancy. Pulling it out, he turned the ring so I could read the inscription on the inside of the white gold band.

I smiled widely. "Aaron's Patience," I read the words.

"Forever. Even if these two haven't gotten the memo yet." He gestured to the two newborns in my arms who were nestled against my chest, still suckling away.

I giggled and then nodded, tears running down my cheeks. He cupped the back of my head, fusing our lips together.

I was his and he was mine. Always had been. Always will be.

***

Want to read more of the Townsend brothers? Check out Joshua's story next in Meant to Be. Click here to get your copy today.

Did you miss Carter's story? Check out how Carter and Michele met in Carter's Flame. Click here.

Looking for updates on future releases? I can be found around the web at the following locations:
Newsletter: Tiffany Patterson Writes Newsletter
FaceBook private group: Tiffany's Passions Between the Pages
Website: TiffanyPattersonWrites.com
FaceBook Page: Author Tiffany Patterson
Email: TiffanyPattersonWrites@gmail.com

More books by Tiffany Patterson

THE BLACK BURLES SERIES
BLACK PEARL

Black Dahlia
Black Butterfly
Forever Series
7 Degrees of Alpha (Collection)
Forever
Safe Space Series
Safe Space (Book 1)
Safe Space (Book 2)

RESCUE FOUR SERIES
ERIC'S INFERNO

Carter's Flame
Emanuel's Heat
Non-Series Titles
This is Where I Sleep
My Storm
Miles & Mistletoe (Holiday Novella)
Just Say the Word

THE TOWNSEND BROTHERS SERIES

MEANT TO BE

For Keeps
Until My Last Breath

Tiffany Patterson Website Exclusives
Locked Doors

Printed in Great Britain
by Amazon